RAVE REVIEWS FOR
BARRY HOFFMAN!

"Hoffman creates characters of uncommon psychological depth. He takes on controversial issues unflinchingly. He has created a new sub-genre of sociological horror."
—*Hellnotes*

"Barry Hoffman's characters come to life on the page and resonate long after the story is done."
—Poppy Z. Brite, author of *Lost Souls*

"Hoffman captures his characters' rage perfectly and creates a fascinating scenario. *Judas Eyes* comes highly recommended."
—*Rue Morgue*

"Barry Hoffman can really tell a story!"
—Charles de Lint, *Fantasy & Science Fiction*

"Hoffman's characterization transcends the simpleminded killing-machines who populate the genre."
—*Publishers Weekly*

MORE PRAISE FOR
BARRY HOFFMAN!

"Hoffman writes lean, mean prose—razor sharp and relentless."

—*Cemetery Dance*

"Quite a literary force to be reckoned with."

—*Locus*

"A new voice—and a telling one—in the horror genre."
—Richard Matheson, author of *I Am Legend*

"Quick-paced and richly textured. *Judas Eyes* disturbs without apology, and entertains without softening its approach."
—*Mystery Scene*

"*Judas Eyes* brings back, in a different and original key, several classic signs of horror narrative."

—*Inside Horror*

SO MUCH BLOOD

"You were first on the scene," Shara said. "Want to give me your impression?"

Now he looked at her quizzically.

"Look, Clay, I'm not here simply to look at a three-month-old crime scene," she said, deciding to level with him. "I want to worm my way inside the killer's head. For that, I need to know what you saw; not just the details of your report. I need your take on the killing."

He closed his eyes, as if reliving the scene, then looked at her, a bit ashen.

"The amount of blood was what hit me first," he said, in not much more than a whisper. "I thought she had slit his throat with a knife, but later found out she'd done it with a chain," he said, shaking his head. "Had to be a powerful woman to do *that* kind of damage with a chain."

Other *Leisure* books by Barry Hoffman:
BORN BAD
EYES OF PREY
HUNGRY EYES

BARRY HOFFMAN
Judas
Eyes

LEISURE BOOKS NEW YORK CITY

As always, to my children
Dara, David and Cheryl . . .
and to my newborn granddaughter
Tyler Renee Campbell

A LEISURE BOOK®

January 2002

Published by

Dorchester Publishing Co., Inc.
276 Fifth Avenue
New York, NY 10001

ISBN 0-8439-4956-2

The name "Leisure Books" and the stylized "L" with design are trademarks of Dorchester Publishing Co., Inc.

Printed in the United States of America.

Visit us on the web at www.dorchesterpub.com.

ACKNOWLEDGMENTS

Thanks to my partner in crime Buddy Martinez for the wonderful layout and design. Many thanks to Perry and Marsha Thompson for navigating me around Atlanta. Any errors in describing Atlanta are mine alone. Much appreciation to Jennifer Barnhart for proofing. Words cannot express my admiration for the wonderfully talented Harry O. Morris who provided another extraordinary cover. I shed a tear for Rick Postlethwaite who came up with the original title for this book, *Eyes to the Soul,* which we were unable to use. Thanks, Binz, for coming up with *Judas Eyes* in a pinch. Don D'Auria, editor of Leisure Books, once again provided invaluable insight. As always, thanks to the gifted Richard Christian Matheson for his suggestions and encouragement.

PROLOGUE

(NOVEMBER 1998)

Y ou could set your watch by Lamar Briggs.

Like clockwork, during the 8 a.m. to 4 p.m. shift he'd be at his desk promptly at eight, and out the door with his partner at precisely four. He had put in no overtime in the six months that had passed since The Nightwatcher case. All had been routine. *Too* routine, and he was in a rut. There had been homicides. In Philadelphia, violent death was a given. A pimp beats his whore with a little too much gusto. Drug deals gone awry. Domestic violence, all too common. A challenging case, though, like trying to catch the elusive Nightwatcher? That was too much to ask so soon after Lysette Ormandy had Briggs running in circles. Such cases were rare. One, maybe two a year, if he was lucky.

His shift over, the all-consuming paperwork finally complete, he was history at four.

Like clockwork, to decompress he'd have a drink with his partner, Nina Rios, at a local cop watering hole. It had become a tradition; a part of his day. He and Rios had butted heads when she'd first been assigned as his partner. He'd been more than a little resistant to having a woman as a partner, especially one whom he felt hadn't paid her dues to merit a promotion to homicide; one who'd been promoted to fill the vacancy of another woman leaving the department. Quotas had to be filled. To hell with seniority, experience or qualifications. A Puerto Rican, Rios filled *two* quotas.

Truth be told — though he wasn't about to admit it to her — now he wouldn't trade Rios for anyone else in the homicide squad. She had been rough around the edges when they had first been partnered, but she had also been a quick study and physically a match for most any man. Plus she scored points by not being intimidated by Briggs. Scored more points by taking the initiative and not deferring to Briggs, the more experienced detective. Scored points by her willingness to learn from his experience. Scored points by being a team player, rather than a rogue. Hell, she was reluctant to take credit when credit was due. He'd come to trust her and depend on her. It was the supreme compliment Briggs could offer to any partner.

They'd first hashed out their differences over drinks after work, early in The Nightwatcher investigation, and now shared a drink after work out of habit. Sometimes they didn't even talk, but let a comfortable silence engulf them.

At four-thirty, he was off.

Like clockwork, he was on his way home, where he belonged. To Vivian, his wife of nearly twenty years, and his fourteen-year-old daughter, Alexis. Briggs had been married to his job far too long. He had taken the job home with him and quite honestly had become a lousy husband and was not much better as a father. His marriage had been strained, to say the least, when over a year before his daughter had been brutally raped and beaten. It had been a turning point in his life. One of those defining moments where he had to come to grips with what he'd become and what was truly important to him.

For close to four months afterward, Alexis was little more than a rag doll. She couldn't speak, couldn't walk without assistance, and for the most part, stared vacantly into space. Knowing what he had almost lost, Briggs became the devoted father he should have been long before. He learned to leave his job at the office. He began to spend quality time with his daughter, reading to her, even when he wasn't sure she understood the words. He took her to therapy whenever his shift allowed, and learned to just be there and enjoy every moment.

His wife had seen the change in him, and they, too, had begun to bridge the chasm that separated them. How could he have been so blind? he now asked himself. Unlike others he knew — too many others — his job *wasn't* his life. Vivian and Alexis were the center of his universe. Without them he'd be a shell of a man. Ironic, he often thought, that it had taken such a tragedy to wake him to what was really important.

That afternoon, like clockwork, he headed home to his family after a drink with his partner.

Then his cell phone rang, and all he had created was shattered.

The watch stopped ticking. His life imploded.

ONE

"Briggs, remember me?" a voice not much above a whisper asked. "Told you I might have some information about that rapist," he continued, as if assuming Briggs needed a reminder.

Briggs remembered the first call he'd received at the station vividly. Almost the same words.

"I might have some information on the rapist who's been attacking those young girls. How can I reach you when you're off duty?"

Briggs *should* have passed the information on. It wasn't his case. There had been three vicious rapes of black girls aged ten to thirteen in seven weeks, but unlike Alexis, the girls hadn't been beaten. Thankfully, it wasn't *yet* a case for homicide.

Briggs explained as much to the caller, but the man had ignored him and again asked how he could get in touch with Briggs.

"Why me?" he'd asked the stranger.

"Your daughter," had been the answer, as if the two words explained it all. And they did, Briggs knew.

Briggs recalled how after Lysette Ormandy, The Nightwatcher, had turned herself in and had later been acquitted of killing of the lowlife who'd raped her, an attempt had been made on her life. Nina had reacted quicker than he and foiled the attempt, but Ormandy's lawyer had been fatally wounded. Two days later there were profiles of Nina and Briggs in the *Daily News*, with prominent mention of the rape of his daughter.

The caller had known he had found a sympathetic ear in Briggs. Despite his better judgment, Briggs had given the man his cell number, yet he had heard nothing in two weeks. A crank, he'd thought, but now the man was back.

"How far are you from the Markwood Playground?" the man asked.

He was on 20th and Walnut, heading towards the Schuylkill Expressway, literally no more than five minutes away. He told the man so.

"Get your ass over here if you want to prevent another rape. North of the playground. Behind the fence that separates the park from the railroad tracks." The phone went dead.

Briggs knew he *should* call for backup. At the very least he knew he *should* call his partner, whom he'd left just a few minutes earlier. But he had to do this on his own. For Alexis. For himself.

What the mystery caller had not known was that the rapist The Nightwatcher had killed was the same man who had attacked Alexis. Only Briggs' family, the detective who had connected the albino with his daughter's attack, and Lysette Ormandy knew this. Briggs had come to grips, or so he'd thought, with not having caught the rapist himself. Still, though he knew it irrational, in a corner of his mind he continued to blame himself for not being able to protect Alexis from the bastard. And for him there'd been no closure. An amateur had killed the scum, not the trained professional who had fruitlessly searched for him for months after the attack.

And while Alexis had shown what the doctors said was "remarkable" improvement in the past three months . . .

— *since she'd been going to the forest* —

. . . she was still a shell of herself. She could now communicate with sign language, her motor skills having markedly improved. She had also learned to read again. But she was still mute, with few exceptions, and even worse for Briggs, she was unable to display any emotion at all. Outwardly, she didn't laugh, didn't cry, didn't get angry, didn't pout. She could only express her emotions with her hands — sign language — and Briggs knew this frustrated her even more than the slow progress she'd made walking from the living room to the kitchen. If she wanted a soda, she would stubbornly refuse to allow her father to get one for her. It took her a good twenty minutes, but Alexis would shuffle into the kitchen and back again, her hands telling her father, "See, I can do it myself."

Briggs *shouldn't* have gone after the bastard alone, but he had to. Catch the fucker and maybe the dead albino would no longer haunt his dreams.

It had been overcast all day, though the rain that had been forecast had held off until he and Rios had finished their drinks. For the second week in November, it was unusually warm. It wasn't Indian Summer, but the thermometer had skirted sixty degrees each of the past two days. Now, with the rain, the temperature had fallen a good ten to fifteen degrees.

What had been a torrential downpour was now a steady drizzle, as Briggs turned right onto Spruce Street from Twenty-third. He parked his car next to a fence with overgrown weeds so thick it couldn't be seen and made his way on foot to where the caller had indicated the rapist had snatched his latest victim.

At first he couldn't see anything with the mist and approaching darkness. And all he could smell was dogshit. While the playground, further south, was a haven for youngsters, the northern portion of Schuylkill Park was home to gays and dogs, the latter of whose owners would unleash them to run in the sprawling fields. While someone's sexual orientation didn't bother Briggs, as long as they didn't make a pass at him or try to convert him, he knew there had been any number of complaints about gays openly displaying affection for one another so close to where children played.

The rain had sent any lovers scurrying, but there was no getting away from the smell of dogshit that assaulted his nose. If anything, the smell was stronger due to the rainfall. He was sorely tempted to keep an eye to the ground, so as not to step in any excrement, but instead he cast caution to the wind, the more pressing objective being to stop another child . . .

— *Alexis, his mind screamed* —

. . . from being scarred for life.

Seeing and hearing nothing, he wondered if he'd been lured into a trap by someone he'd put away, who was now lying in wait to exact revenge. His every instinct argued against forging ahead, yet he plowed on.

A movement beyond the fence, precisely where the caller had told him, caught Briggs' attention.

He was primed for this moment. Approaching forty, he had been overweight and out of shape before the attack on Alexis. Now, with his chiseled frame, he resembled basketball star Karl Malone. If he had to, Briggs felt he could run anyone to ground, the result of jogging daily and working out in a makeshift weightroom he'd constructed in his basement. He was determined that no one escape his grasp because he was out of shape. He owed it to Alexis.

His tar-black skin made him a hard target to spot as he quickly made his way towards the fence. A steady rain now fell. His scalp shaved, he had to constantly wipe away water that cascaded down his head, so as not to obscure his vision.

He was close enough to the fence now to see a figure on the ground struggling, and another straddling her, knife in hand. He inched closer still. The rain was hindering the man atop the girl. Briggs had to get closer before he made his move. He didn't want the fucker in a panic slashing the child with his knife. Yet the thought of him inside of her tore at his consciousness.

Six feet from the fence, he saw the man — short, squat, and as dark-skinned as Briggs — rise and drop his trousers.

Briggs responded impulsively. "Police!" he shouted. Before he could say anything else the man bolted like a frightened rabbit, slipping on the rain slicked stones by the railroad tracks. He held a knife in one hand, his unbuckled baggy pants that threatened to drop to his feet in the other.

Briggs wished the bastard had made a threatening move towards the girl. He would have fired and kept firing until his revolver was empty. Wished the fucker had pulled a gun. Briggs would have had ample justification to fire away in either case. But the little shit ran, and Briggs wasn't about the shoot him in the back.

Briggs deftly made his way over the fence, taking a quick look at the girl. She was now in a fetal position, sobbing, but otherwise she appeared unhurt . . .

— unhurt physically, but forever marred emotionally, he thought. Alexis had been physically battered. Worse, though, she had been an emotional wreck for months. And, scars remained. Unhurt, my ass, he chastised himself —

. . . and he ran after the fleeing figure, moving quickly but not recklessly so as not to slip on the stones. He quickly gained on the man, a good foot shorter than the six-foot-four Briggs. Plunging ahead in panic, the other man's Nikes, Adidas or Reeboks were of little use on the wet stones.

"Stop or I'll shoot," Briggs yelled, and when he didn't stop Briggs fired one shot in the air. Briggs shouted at the man one final time and was surprised, and a little disappointed, when the man complied.

As he turned to face Briggs, the man's eyes darted for a moment to a concrete bunker, possibly a long abandoned watchpost for a railroad worker. It offered no protection and Briggs saw the man knew it. He faced Briggs, knife in hand.

Come at me, Briggs' mind screamed, *so I can blow you away*. But ever the good cop, he had to do the right thing. He had to wait until attacked.

"Lose the knife, fucker," he said, more a snarl than a command. He lowered his gun, ever so slightly, giving the punk every opportunity to pounce . . . and die.

But the man — Briggs thought he was in his early-twenties —

smiled, dropped the knife and raised his hands. His pants fell to his ankles.

"Pick them up . . . *slowly*, you sick fuck," Briggs commanded, moving closer, but staying safely out of reach.

"I didn't do nothing to her," he said, picking up his pants and fastening his belt, his eyes glued on Briggs.

"Only because I got to you before you could." He was being baited, he knew. *Read him his rights and call for backup*, his mind scolded; but the adrenaline was still pumping, and he wanted the arrogance replaced by fear.

"Your mistake," the man said. "My girl and I were making out. No law against that."

"And the other three you raped?" Briggs asked. "Girlfriends, too?"

"I don't know what you're talking about, Pig. Nobody gonna finger me. You got squat."

Again, he flashed the smile. And Briggs knew it was true. He had squat. The other girls who had been attacked had said they couldn't identify their assailant. And this sack of shit was confident the girl he'd just assaulted would dummy up, as well. No, he wasn't just cocky or blowing smoke. He *knew* he was home free. Briggs no longer saw the dark-skinned rapist smiling at him, but instead saw the albino who had raped Alexis. And he wasn't smiling, he was leering at Briggs — mocking him — knowing Alexis was in no condition to testify against him.

Briggs holstered his gun, moved within arm's length of the albino, and began wailing away at the man's midsection and ribs. The rational part of his mind demanded he leave nothing more than broken ribs and black-and-blue marks. He could always claim he'd had to protect himself, and he would be believed. He wasn't rational, though. Giving full vent to his rage and frustration, he began pelting the now powder-white face and reddened eyes that stared back at him. He kept pounding long after the smile was gone and stopped only when the figure collapsed, unconscious.

Briggs awoke as if from a bad dream, staring down, not at the albino, but at the rapist he'd pursued. He felt for a pulse and breathed a sigh of relief when he found one.

Through the rain, which was now coming down in torrents and washing away the blood from the fallen figure's face, Briggs heard the plaintive sobbing of the child who'd been assaulted. Alone. Not knowing if her assailant would return. Possibly injured. Definitely in shock.

He dragged the unconscious man toward the fence and cuffed him. "You're not going anywhere, fucker," he said, and shivered as the rain pelted him.

He ran back to the girl, still in a fetal position, and cradled her in his arms.

"I'm not going to hurt you," he said soothingly, when she initially shrunk back from him. She finally focused on his face as he continued to speak to her, his voice calmly trying to reassure her.

"I won't let anybody hurt you, Alexis."

She held onto him tightly, sobs still wracking her body.

Briggs continued to hold his daughter, comforting her with a non-stop patter, knowing there was something else he should be doing, but nothing as important as consoling his daughter.

An explosion brought him back to reality. A gunshot, he knew, quickly followed by a second and a third. He looked towards the concrete bunker where he'd left the rapist and could dimly make out his figure. Saw another figure — crouched — running from the bunker beside the tracks south towards the Bell Atlantic Building that bordered the Schuylkill River, leading to the South Street Bridge.

He tried to get up, but the girl held onto him tightly.

"Don't leave me. He'll come back," she cried, and he heard the panic rising in her voice. "Please, don't leave me," she repeated, over and over again.

He rationalized to himself that the fleeing figure was long gone, and chase was fruitless. No way could he leave this child.

"I'll stay with you, honey. Now calm down, okay? I'm not going anywhere."

His mind finally clear, he took out his cell phone and made two calls — one for backup and an ambulance, and a second to his partner.

There was nothing more to be done other than console his daughter. He had saved her from the albino, but she needed him now more than ever.

TWO

SHARA

Going to sleep, Shara knew she would awaken within two hours. She'd never needed much sleep. She had always slept in fits and starts, whether as prey when she'd been haunted by her half-brother's hungry eyes, or predator when she'd decided to run no more. She would awaken refreshed whether she'd slept two hours or four. Being a light sleeper, a passing fire engine, stray cats having it out, or the discarded beer bottle thrown against a wall would instantly end her slumber.

None of those would rouse her tonight, though. It would be *the dream*; the one she'd had almost nightly for the past two months. At first it had been like a radio station from a distant city, there on the edge of her consciousness, but without power to sustain itself for long. It had intensified with each passing night, like an approaching hurricane. Now she lived it, smelled it, tasted it — was part of it. But unlike the dreams that had forced her to kill, the meaning of her current affliction eluded her.

Lying on her back, staring at the mirrors that covered the ceiling — as well as all the walls of her room — Shara waited for sleep to overtake her.

She found herself, as always, a voyeur in the back seat of a car, the coppery smell of blood almost making her gag. Looking up, she saw the woman, though as usual she couldn't quite get a fix on her face. Blood, smeared across the woman's face, obscured her features. They locked eyes for a split second before the woman opened the door and bolted for the woods.

Peering over onto the front seat, Shara saw the figure of a man, his pants unzipped, penis hanging out, blood oozing from a wound in his neck onto the front seat.

Then Shara found herself in pursuit of the woman in the woods. No, she corrected herself, she was chasing a woman *of* the woods. Gaunt, with long blond hair, the woman had the look of someone who kept in shape. Her feet barely touched the ground as she ran, deftly sidestepping every branch, bramble and bush in her path. Shara, meanwhile, nipped at her heels heedless of the very same branches, brambles and bushes that slashed at her like whips, drawing blood.

The woman she pursued was no longer clothed. Shara recalled that when the woman had exited the car she'd had on blood-soaked jeans and a pullover. Now, like shedding her outer skin, she was naked. Shara, too, was naked, though she could never recall whether she had ever been clothed.

The two ran almost in unison. When Shara tried to pick up the pace to catch the fleeing figure, the woman did likewise. When exhaustion slowed Shara down, her quarry eased up as well, as if to tease her.

As they ran deeper into the woods, Shara was certain she saw the figure of a wolf partially emerge from the woman's back, only to be yanked back within by an unseen hand. A growl of discontent pierced the stillness. Then the face and shoulders of an old man appeared. Before he could fully emerge and make the hunter the hunted, he too was summoned back. He bellowed in anger when he wasn't allowed to have his way.

They came to a stream which the woman crossed without hesitation. Shara followed suit, for the first time gaining on her. Her prey was nowhere near as swift in the water as on land. As the water reached Shara's breasts, she lunged, grasping the woman by the shoulder, and they both went down underwater. Beneath the surface, the woman stopped struggling and turned to face Shara. In the murky water Shara still couldn't make out her features, but as they broke the surface, Shara found herself looking at *herself* — not just someone who looked *like* her, but her mirror image.

The woman wrapped her arms around Shara and melded into her.

Shara awoke then, as she always did. The words "I am she. She is me," tumbled out of her mouth over and over.

Knowing what she would see — since she had now had the dream dozens of times — Shara lay on her back and looked at herself in the mirror overhead. She was sopping wet from head to toe, but not from sweat. She could smell the stream water, feel the dirt between her toes. There were scratches and bruises all over her body from the branches that, like living entities, had attacked her after the woman had managed to elude them. Her muscles ached from the chase, blood oozed from her wounds, and for a few fleeting seconds she felt the presence of that other woman within her.

From long experience she knew what would happen next. She felt her mirror image give up its grip, saw the cuts and bruises heal before her eyes, and soon all aches and pains had subsided. There wasn't a trace of blood from her wounds. Even the blood that had dripped on her sheets had vanished.

The first time she'd had the dream, Shara hadn't simply laid in bed. She'd bolted to the bathroom, nauseated and disoriented. The urge to vomit, though, had passed before she had made it to the toilet. She turned on the shower — also surrounded on all sides by mirrors — and saw that the cuts from the branches had vanished. Looking down at the water as it dripped from her body, though, she had seen faint traces of blood.

That first night she'd been exhausted and had gone back to sleep; two hours of dreamless bliss. When she'd awakened the dream was vividly etched in her memory. This hadn't surprised her. She often remembered her dreams, which for years had been nightmares, in great detail. This was especially helpful when she was on a case. No, she corrected herself, not a case, a *chase*. Hunting people was her job. The *chase* kept her demons at bay. While asleep her subconscious remained at work on the puzzle at hand. She would awaken with the dream fresh in her mind, often a revelation or new avenue of exploration having been discovered.

This dream, though, was related to no chase and its significance totally eluded her.

I am she. She is me.

"What the hell did that mean?" she'd said aloud, as she replayed the events. She also wondered if awaking and seeing herself heal had actually been a dream within a dream.

She put it out of her mind until the next night, when she was revisited by an instant replay of the night before. This time when she awoke, she decided to investigate the dream itself. With lipstick, she drew an X on the bathroom mirror. If it were a dream within a dream the X would be gone after her next catnap. It wasn't. When she awoke the X was just where she had drawn it.

The next night was the first she watched herself heal from her bed. Though the chase had been exhausting she hadn't gone back to sleep.

At other times she'd gotten up and watched herself heal in one of the mirrors that surrounded the room. She would get close so she could almost touch the mirror. For a fleeting moment she would see the figure within her flee. Then she would be alone with herself, as she had been for most of her life. The rest was like watching a movie in reverse. The gashes closed, bruises disappeared, as did the blood, and her hair and body would no longer be wet.

I am she and she is me.

The phrase resonated through her mind like a ping pong ball bouncing inside her head.

"How could she be me?" Shara said aloud to the figure in the mirror. While they were both on the scrawny side, the woman she'd pursued was medium height, while Shara was just over five feet tall. Her prey was fair-skinned, while she was tawny. She'd never known her father and her mother refused to speak of him. While her mother was Italian, others often thought she was Hispanic, even black — nothing like the woman she pursued. And her hair was brown with natural curls, when she let it grow. The companion of her dreams had long straight dirty-blond hair.

And while they both had ample breasts, somewhat out of proportion to their slight build, hers were adorned with six sets of tattoos — six sets of eyes; one pair for each of the six men she had hunted down and killed two years earlier. Five sexual predators who had slipped through the judicial system on technicalities and had continued their atrocities against women and children. The sixth had been her half-brother. He had been a sexual predator in his own right who had traumatized Shara when she was eleven. He had locked her in a cage and forced her to do unspeakable things to herself while he took pictures. The photos were mainly of her face and its different shades of terror. She had killed the first five men so when she killed her half-brother no one would suspect it was him she had been after all along. She hadn't killed since, though she'd never lost the hunger for the hunt.

The woman she'd chased in the woods had had a tattoo high on her inside thigh, close to her genitals. The tattoo was of a wolf, much like the one Shara had seen imprisoned in the woman's body.

I am she and she is me.

Whoever she was, she was getting closer. What had been dim and murky — shadows without substance — was now so clear Shara could hear the woman breathe, effortless as it was, when she ran through the strangely silent forest. She could smell the blood of the men this woman had killed. She could make out the sounds of her prey's feet as they gently touched the ground. Even the colors of the forest were more vibrant; almost blinding at times.

They were destined to meet, Shara knew, and she welcomed the opportunity. She didn't dwell on the dream while awake. It didn't consume her as it might others. She lived for the moment. When the time came, when dream and reality merged, so be it. There was no sense in trying to puzzle out the unfathomable, she'd thought, too. Still, every once in awhile, despite herself, she couldn't help but think of *her*.

I am she and she is me.

Her mirror image.

Her sister.

No, her *twin*.

Better yet, someone to end the loneliness that was her constant companion.

THREE

(DECEMBER 1998)

SHARA

Dressed in a conservative pants suit, today Shara was a member of Lamar Briggs' legal team. Highly adaptable, she could be anybody, which only added to her sense of having no identity whatsoever.

Those she dealt with in her new occupation had dubbed her The Chameleon. Though twenty-five, she could transform herself into a homeless woman of fifty, a dour cleaning lady, a hooker barely eighteen, or a straight-laced school teacher. It was far more than just clothes and makeup. She had the unique ability to *become* the character she chose. It was as if she could slip out of Shara and with her mannerisms, speech and the way she carried herself become someone else entirely. Truth be told, she sometimes scared herself. She sometimes wondered if she might get trapped within a character, with Shara lost forever.

Thoughts like those reminded Shara she still carried a lot of baggage. Killing her half-brother had released her from one hell. A year as a deputy in a sleepy town in Pennsylvania's Poconos had been part of her healing process. Predator and prey, hunter and hunted, she had been all.

She had even been a parasite, feeding on her friendship with

Deidre Caffrey, a well-intentioned reporter. She had betrayed Deidre at eleven, again when on the prowl for her half-brother and once more, for good measure, when with Deidre she had driven Lysette Ormandy, The Nightwatcher, to ground. Despite the best of intentions, whenever she had dealt with Deidre she had become a bottom-feeder. She had constantly betrayed this woman she wanted to befriend, without batting an eye. She had felt like a shit later, but it hadn't yet deterred her from abusing one of the few people she could have called a friend.

And, Deidre, no fool, had come perilously close to the end of her rope. Despite hopes to the contrary, she seemed to know Shara would continue to use and abuse her. She had suffered in silence, apparently hoping *next* time Shara would finally be true to her word. But Shara could sense even Deidre had begun to resent the constant duplicity.

Shara wondered why she intentionally deceived those whom she most valued. Time and again she had been determined to turn over a new leaf, only to revert to form when push came to shove. All she knew for certain was if she were someone else she wouldn't turn her back on herself. Acknowledging that had been depressing as hell.

When Lysette had gone into a coma after being framed for killing a young child — which finally discredited her Nightwatcher persona — Shara had taken over her job as assistant manager at an upscale strip club. She knew it was only temporary. Knew, too, it would not feed the needs that drove her. Shortly after Lysette came out of her coma and was back at work, Shara had become a bundle of nervous energy. She was restless and fidgety, tense and irritable. And she had turned to booze. A drink or two to steady her nerves soon became four, five or six — whatever it took — to get her through the day. She had substituted one narcotic for another, and alcohol was an addiction she didn't need. Along with this feeling of restlessness, the tattoos that dotted her breasts had begun to itch; just as they had before she'd begun stalking each of her six victims.

She had deluded herself into believing she wasn't a serial killer. She had convinced herself she had killed five animals in order to get to her half-brother. But somewhere along the line stalking had become a narcotic. And like an addict she had to feed her need. She had temporarily sated that need when she'd hunted down The

Nightwatcher. She'd also discovered it was the hunt, the chase, the capture she relished. She didn't need to kill to feel fulfilled. She knew it was the same for most serial killers. Killing was just a method of disposal; necessary to stay one step ahead of the authorities. But the kill didn't bring the thrill. Shara knew she was perilously close to crossing that fine line between predator and killer. The question was how to feed her growing need without crossing that line?

Deidre had suggested she return to the police force, but Shara had rejected it out of hand.

"I'm not good with authority, and it would be years before I rose to a position where I could be one of the hunters. *Too many years*."

And she had spurned Deidre's proposal that she become a private investigator.

"Spend eighty to ninety percent of my time on surveillance?" she'd said, shaking her head. "Catching men cheating on their wives, women cheating on their husbands — hell, women cheating on women! After all, it's the nineties. No, there's no sport in that."

And *sport* was what she needed.

How to feed the need? That had been the question gnawing at Shara as Lysette slowly worked her way back into her job. Shara knew she could stay at the club as long as she wanted. There was no need for a hasty decision. But, she also knew it was time to move on. But move on to what? She'd found her answer on *Oprah!*

Shara didn't watch as much TV now as when she'd been stalking, but she still taped her favorite shows: *Jerry Springer*, reruns of *M*A*S*H* she'd recently gotten hooked on, *One Life To Live*, *Action News*, a movie on HBO or Showtime. And, of course, there was *Oprah!*

Sipping a beer at two in the morning, after her shift at the club, she would fast forward her VCR through most of the day's shows. Transsexuals on *Jerry Springer* she could do without. *M*A*S*H* allowed her to laugh and cry at the same time, as usual. She sometimes wondered if her life was much different than Alan Alda's Hawkeye Pierce. He was slogging through quicksand, going nowhere fast, alcohol his succor. Kind of like looking in the mirror at someone she knew all too well, she thought. *One Life To Live* was mostly a rehash of recent events. To hell with that, she thought, and fast-forwarded to the end.

Then *Oprah!* came on with a show about bounty hunters. Why not? she thought. She'd give it a listen. And a new world opened to her. Months later, she still vividly recalled key phrases that would shape her future.

"Once you've hunted after a human, there's nothing better," one had said.

"Amen," Shara had responded to the man on the tube, lifting her beer in a toast. For Shara watching TV was still an interactive experience. She responded to what was said, not caring that she couldn't be heard.

" . . . any reasonable force."

" . . . no need to read him his rights. A fugitive, he has *no* rights."

"Career open to anyone."

"To anyone?" she asked the man on the screen. "Damn."

" . . . no license, no schooling necessary," he said, as if responding to her question.

"I lie to people for a living," a woman confided to Oprah.

"I lie to people," Shara answered, "because . . . because *it's my nature*."

They were speaking to her. No, *about* her. And it was music to her ears. She rewound the tape and studied the men and women as they spoke. Some were her age, others far older. There was even one retired couple well into their fifties who supplemented their pensions through bounty hunting. She saw life in the eyes of these men and women who shared their stories with Oprah. The hunt. The chase. The capture. All a narcotic for the soul.

She gave her notice at the club the next day. Oddly, Lysette seemed relieved. Am I losing her, too? Shara had wondered. She had confided in Lysette, had been there for Lysette in her time of need, but it seemed as if she and Lysette were drifting apart, much as she and Deidre had drifted apart. Shara gave it little thought, though. Opportunity awaited and she was intent upon seizing it.

She'd paid her dues over a two month period as an apprentice, in a manner of speaking, to a local bounty hunter. Over the next four months she had grudgingly gained the confidence and respect of bail-bondsmen, and with it steady work. The money mattered little. Able to feed her need, the hunt without killing was its own reward.

F OUR

SHARA

Shara was ushered into a closet-sized private room at Graterford Prison, where she had gone to meet Briggs. She knew this was highly unusual, but then Briggs was not your typical inmate. The guards of Graterford held him in high regard. He had shot a rapist in cold blood. That was something most of them had hopelessly fantasized about.

Shara recalled her surprise when she'd heard the District Attorney's office had objected to a request for bail. A Channel 6 Action News reporter had the most detailed story.

"Common Pleas Court Judge Olivia Sloane today denied bail to Philadelphia homicide detective Lamar Briggs, charged with the murder of Nelson 'Biggie' Shaw," one of the station's veteran reporters solemnly told viewers, with City Hall as a backdrop.

"Shaw, who is alleged to have raped three young South Philadelphia girls, was interrupted by Detective Briggs while attacking a fourth youth. Shaw was found handcuffed to a fence behind Markwood Playground. He had been viciously beaten and shot three times. Anonymous sources within the police department have told Action News the gun found beside Shaw was not Detective Briggs' service revolver, but what is commonly referred to as a throwaway piece — a second, usually untraceable, firearm many policemen carry.

"Detective Briggs, whose daughter was herself brutally raped two years ago, was not actively involved in the rape investigation. He has been suspended without pay with the intention to terminate his employment from the department.

"In a statement released by the District Attorney's office, Judge Sloane's decision was hailed. 'The people of this city will not tolerate vigilante justice. Like any other alleged murderer, Detective Briggs will await his day in court in prison.'"

Shara tuned out the rest.

Briggs had been separated from the general population for his own protection. He was a cop, after all. Even if Graterford didn't house anyone Briggs had personally sent away, there were certainly friends and relatives who would be more than willing to take him out. No way anyone from the top on down was going to face the music if a shiv ended up planted in Briggs' back.

And while prisoners and their wives and lawyers had to speak to one another on the phone with a glass partition separating them, Briggs received the privacy of a small room. The guard who escorted him in didn't even handcuff him to the metal table, the only furniture other than two folding chairs in the room. From the look he gave Briggs, if *this* prisoner wanted a conjugal visit, it was the least he could do for the man.

Shara knew Briggs, but not well. They had first met when she'd helped track down The Nightwatcher. Briggs, though, was unaware he was face-to-face with the killer he had unsuccessfully hunted for four months.

When Lysette had gone into her coma, Shara had received Briggs' permission to take his daughter down to the shore once a week, as Lysette had. Lysette had told Shara about the healing powers of the forest in Cape May, New Jersey, but Shara hadn't paid much attention. Supernatural drivel was not something in which Shara held much stock. Her first venture into the woods, then, was her first experience with the supernatural — or at least the unexplainable. It was the main reason she could so easily accept the dreams she now had, as well as their aftermath.

Alexis Briggs' healing forest, on first glance, was nothing more than dead trees. No, *more* than dead, Shara had thought. Not only were they devoid of leaves, but of bark as well. A petrified forest is what came to mind; a graveyard for dead trees.

Upon entering, the silence had engulfed both Shara and Alexis. One moment there had been the sounds of waves crashing on shore and seagulls overhead, then utter and complete silence. No matter what the temperature outside, once in the forest it was balmy, though without a trace of humidity. And once in the forest the mute Alexis was transformed. *Healed* was the only way Shara could describe it.

Alexis had explained the feeling to her once.

"It's like there are hundreds of repairman on break inside my head. As soon as I enter the forest, they get to work. They repair thousands — even millions — of electrical connections that were severed when I was attacked. It's all done in a rush and soon I can walk on my own, talk . . . be normal."

Not quite normal, Shara had thought, though she had said nothing. Alexis was able to talk, but her words were totally devoid of emotion. She couldn't verbally express joy or anger, surprise or frustration. Everything came out in a flat monotone, as if she were in shock. This lack of emotion had initially been unsettling. But Shara could read the emotion in the girl's eyes and she now hardly noticed the speech impediment. Later, after Alexis had learned sign language, she could also express her emotions with her hands.

Outside the forest, Alexis reverted to her mute self.

"The only problem is," she told Shara when she was in the forest, "when we leave it's like a tornado rips through my mind, and almost all the repairs are destroyed. I come out a little better each time, but it's like a snail scaling a mountain."

Once out of the woods, Alexis couldn't speak and needed Shara's help to walk to the car. It must be frustrating for her, Shara thought many times. Within the forest she was whole. Outside, she was totally dependent on others.

It was in the forest that Shara had also learned Alexis had psychic abilities.

"It has nothing to do with being here," Alexis had told her. "When

I was . . . attacked, parts of my mind were damaged, but . . . how can I explain it . . . another part of my brain was turned on. I can read your thoughts with just the slightest touch. Read your past."

She instantly knew Shara had been the killer her father had sought. Knew all the torment Shara had gone through before she had killed. Knew things Shara had always intended to keep to herself. Alexis couldn't control this power of hers, though, and Shara had learned to live with the fact she could keep no secrets from this girl.

It had been Alexis who had told Shara that her father hadn't killed Biggie Shaw. Knew it for a fact, not out of blind devotion to her father. Knew all that had happened that late-afternoon when Nelson "Biggie" Shaw had been shot.

"Can you describe the man who did the killing?" Shara had asked.

"I can only see what my father saw," she said and signed the frustration that she couldn't voice. "I'm not like a computer that can enhance an image. What he saw, I can see. Nothing more."

A month later Briggs sent a message through his wife that he wanted to see Shara.

Sitting across from him now, she saw a despondent, desperate man. A bull in a china shop, she'd heard his partner Nina Rios once describe him. Now he looked beaten, defeated, even a little pathetic.

For several moments they sat in silence, Briggs unable to make eye contact with her. She was reminded of herself when her half-brother had finally broken her, fourteen years earlier, locked inside a cage. For ten days she had refused to capitulate. He'd made her act out every sick fantasy that came to his mind, all the time clicking away with his camera. When she had finally caved in, wanting only to die, it had ironically been her salvation. No longer combative, he quickly tired of her and within a day she was freed.

Briggs was approaching *his* breaking point, Shara could sense. If he gave up, though, there would be no salvation. Only prison. And he'd leave a completely broken man.

He finally gathered himself and looked at Shara.

"How's Alexis holding up?" he asked her. "The truth. Don't protect me. Don't bullshit me."

It came out as a plaintive request, not a demand. His voice had softened, lost its gruff edge. Lost its life.

"Not particularly well," Shara answered. She wasn't about to spare his feelings with platitudes. She wasn't here for Briggs. She was here for Alexis. "She feels responsible for your being here—"

"But I didn't kill anyone," he interrupted.

"She knows. But she feels if she hadn't been raped you wouldn't have gone after Shaw alone. She feels responsible for the rage that made you lose control and beat Shaw. She's withdrawn more into herself, afraid you'll go to prison."

Briggs was silent for a moment, staring down at the table. When he spoke he made eye contact with Shara. "I don't see you as a bounty hunter."

The way he said it made it sound like her job repulsed him.

"Which is exactly why I'm successful," Shara said, ignoring his tone.

Briggs had gone silent, possibly digesting Shara's comment and wondering why her not looking like a bounty hunter made her good at the job. Just as possible, he was continuing to unravel with the threat of prison looming, in which case he would need to be prompted.

"So why am I here, Briggs?" Shara asked.

He blinked at her in surprise. He *had* been someplace else. Where, she couldn't imagine. Had no desire to find out. Her interest in Briggs revolved solely around Alexis.

"Why am I here?" she repeated, now that she had his attention.

"I want you to find out who killed Biggie Shaw," he said, finally making eye contact with her.

Shara knew Briggs loathed asking for help. To swallow his pride, as he was doing, was a big step for him. She didn't know if it was a step forward or backward, judging from his demeanor.

"That's what the police are for," she answered. She knew the police had completed their investigation. Nina Rios had told her, but for the moment she decided to play dumb. She wanted to draw him out. Awaken him, in a manner of speaking.

"They've got their killer. *Me*," he said, without raising his voice. "It's not that they don't believe my story. They think I may have been delusional, in shock or fucking insane when I shot the bastard."

The last he said with a bit of venom, which Shara took as a good sign.

"And I can uncover what they couldn't?" she asked, skeptically. "After all, I'm *just* a bounty hunter, not a *real* cop."

"If you sincerely believe me," he said, ignoring her last comment.

"What if the killer *can't* be found? What are your options?"

"He's *got* to be found," Briggs said, for the first time raising his voice, finally showing some sign of the fire that had burned within the detective who had caught most of those he pursued. "Any other option is unacceptable."

His eyes were now locked with Shara's.

"Humor me. Tell me what they are."

He waved his hand in disdain, but finally shrugged and relented. "I can go to trial and plead diminished capacity — temporary insanity. But my story contradicts that theory. Yes, I could have — *was* — temporarily insane when I beat the fucker. But to leave him unconscious, go to comfort the child he'd attacked, and *then* return to shoot him . . . My lawyers tell me that's premeditation."

He let out a sigh of exasperation before going on. Being on the other side of the judicial system had humbled Briggs. He was one of those who looked at the world in terms of black and white; right or wrong. He caught the perp and, as far as he was concerned, that was it. But there were different degrees of guilt, and those who killed in the heat of passion had to go through just what Briggs was going through now — faced with making an impossible choice.

"I could plead innocent," he went on, "and hope a jury believes me. But I didn't call for backup when I got the tip. I didn't even call my partner. I wanted to go after him, the prosecution will argue, so I could exact revenge for what happened to Alexis. And it's true."

"But you didn't kill him."

"He never gave me the opportunity. I would have killed him to protect the girl or in self-defense, but he ran. I *wanted* him to attack me, so killing him would have been justified."

"So what's left?"

"A plea bargain. Manslaughter — five to fifteen. I could be out in, say, three years," he said with resignation.

"It's a generous offer," Shara told him. "A walk in the park for someone like you. What's the DA afraid of?"

"Going to trial. I'm told I'm a sympathetic figure, and Biggie Shaw was scum. A trial would bring Alexis' rape out in the open. And even though he's dead my lawyers would try Shaw, suggesting that even if I *had* killed him I'd done a public service. Shaw's victims would have been called to testify and the dangers of living in the city would be magnified. *That* the DA definitely doesn't want. The city's becoming safer, so we're told. The Mayor wants to attract people from the suburbs back into the city at night. And there's always tourism. Children raped then taking the stand is bad for business."

"Why not take the plea?" Shara asked, though she knew.

"No. I *won't* be away from Alexis one more day than I have to. I didn't kill Shaw. You've got to believe me."

"I *believe* Alexis, and she says you didn't kill Shaw."

Briggs looked at her quizzically.

"Look, Briggs, I know you don't believe your daughter has psychic power, but she does. You were in shock when Rios arrived at the playground. She's one smart cookie. She wanted to give you time to gather your thoughts, so she made sure you were taken to the hospital for observation. Your wife and Alexis visited. Remember?"

Briggs nodded.

"One touch of your hand and Alexis saw what happened through your eyes. Knew what you had done. Knew you hadn't killed Shaw. *You* don't have to believe she has this . . . gift or ability, but I *know* she does. I *know* you're innocent. I'll find the killer. For Alexis. She needs you. Just understand who I'm doing this for."

"Your fee—"

Shara waved him away dismissively. "How do you measure friendship in dollars and cents, Briggs? Of all my friends — and I can count them on one hand — Alexis is the only one who would *never* abandon me. It's priceless."

"What about expenses? Without money you might cut corners. I want all bases covered, whatever the cost."

Oh, I'll cut corners, Shara thought, but not to save money. And not in the sense Briggs meant. She looked at Briggs and shrugged. "Your defense fund can pay my expenses. Your fellow officers and strangers alike have raised quite a warchest. It's probably best I be employed by your defense team, anyway, now that I think about it. It could be useful in my approach to some people."

Shara got up and knocked on the door. Before a guard came she looked at Briggs again. He didn't look hopeful. "I'll find the killer, Briggs. Hunting people is what I do best. Usually, I know who I'm hunting, but this is merely a variation on the theme. I'm not about to let Alexis down."

The door opened and she left. She knew she'd have to convince Briggs by her actions.

Nina Rios was outside. She had insisted on coming.

"Well?" Nina asked. "Will you help?"

It was the first week of December and a light rain was falling. A chill in the air and blustery winds made the rain feel like needles slashing at her face . . .

— like the branches from her dream —

It had been raining the better part of the week. Better than snow or ice, Shara thought. She was not a winter person. She didn't mind the cold, but always an aggressive driver, with ice or snow on the ground she felt she was an accident waiting to happen.

Shara ushered Nina to her car and turned on the heater; not too high, though. She detested heat as much — *maybe more* — than snow or ice. She hadn't told Briggs' partner there had never been a question of her taking the case. Nina knew nothing of what she and Alexis shared. Shara meant to keep it that way.

"So?" Nina asked again.

"He's got no one else to turn to. You've been warned off the case — he's aware of that. We came to a meeting of the minds."

"Can I do any canvassing? To hell with being told to steer clear. He's my partner."

"He's lucky to have you," Shara said, and meant it sincerely. Seemed like everyone had someone to lean on — everyone except her. It was a shame Briggs was so self-absorbed in his own problems that he failed to realize how lucky he really was. "And, no, you won't do any canvassing — nothing that will get you in hot water. Bad enough that Briggs knows his daughter blames herself for what he did. Imagine what it would do to him if you got kicked off the force trying to help him," she said.

"There must be—"

"I didn't say you couldn't be of help," Shara interrupted. "I could use some insight from the detectives who handled the investigation. Not just their official reports, but their impressions of those they interviewed. You told me your sergeant was sympathetic. Lay it in his lap. Tell him it's Briggs' only chance. And tell him Briggs won't last in prison. Being away from Alexis has already taken a toll on him. Prison for Briggs is a death sentence. Get me everything you can. I'll let you know if there's anything else you can do."

That night Shara was certain she'd dream about her hunt for Biggie Shaw's killer, but she woke up in less than two hours bloody and sore from another trek through the woods. She lay on her back watching herself heal.

"Stop toying with me," she said aloud as the figure within her departed. "Isn't it time we met? This is getting old real fast."

She thought she heard someone giggle, and shook her head. Someone fucking with her mind, she thought. Or maybe it had been her imagination.

She stayed up the rest of the night going over the file Nina Rios had brought her at 11 p.m. It was a way of making amends. She felt she'd cheated Briggs by not dreaming of *his* case. She'd work the night, if necessary, to worm her way into the world of Biggie Shaw. But where to start? Invariably once she puzzled that out, momentum carried her the rest of the way.

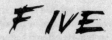

FIVE

(AUGUST 28, 1998)

MICA

Thinking about her client from the night before brought a smile to Mica's face. A well-heeled, influential CEO, he had a lavish apartment he used no more than two to three hours a week, where he would play out his fantasies with Mistress Maya.

If the public only knew, she thought, and laughed aloud. But men like Joseph were not politicians, nor public figures. They shunned the spotlight. Yet they were every bit as powerful — *many more so* — than those in the public eye whose every move could be scrutinized by a nosey journalist, prosecutor, or special counsel appointed to poke into affairs that were none of their concern.

She'd been at the apartment, only a faded and fraying housecoat covering her, before he arrived.

She quickly gauged his mood when he entered.

As was often the case, when he came in without even acknowledging her presence, she knew he wasn't yet ready to give himself to her. He was preoccupied with decisions either made or postponed until given further thought. He hadn't yet shrugged off the air of superiority that was his shield.

That was her job.

He babbled to her about some screw up at the office, as he made his way to the bar in the corner of the living room and poured himself a scotch. He offered her nothing. He definitely *wasn't* ready for her yet. He wore an Armani suit, the same he had worn all day, yet it looked like he'd just put it on. He was obsessive about his attire, she knew. Only the faint aroma of cigarette smoke told her he hadn't changed before coming over.

"Get out of those clothes and take a shower," she commanded.

He ignored her and brought the glass to his lips.

She knocked the glass from his hand, the liquid leaving a stain on his spotless white shirt.

His eyes were ablaze with anger.

The trill of his cell phone interrupted their foreplay. As he took it from the inside pocket of his suit coat she grabbed it from him and flung it against the wall. It wasn't the first such phone she'd destroyed.

"Bitch," he said, barely able to contain his rage.

"You're not ready for me, Joseph," she said, picked up her coat from a couch and walked to the door. As a part of their role-playing, once — and only once — he had let her leave. She hadn't returned. Hadn't responded to his phone calls for three days. Now, she knew, he would never take that chance again.

Suddenly he was on his knees, crawling to her on all fours, groveling, apologizing — his pleas barely decipherable.

She stood over him, the belt of her housecoat tied loosely so he could see her breasts. And on his knees he could easily look under the housecoat and see her snatch.

She played the role of his mother, who had been too busy for him. His mother had never been there for him when he was a child, but she was now.

He stole a look at her exposed breasts, knowing he would be punished if caught. He was no longer thinking about his job, his responsibilities or the pressures of his work that ate at him. He was now hers and they could begin . . .

*   *   *

Mica was in a foul mood, as she made her way on foot the last few blocks to Madeline Erskine's dungeon. Actually, she was going to Maddy's house; a spacious two-level townhouse built at the turn of the century, at Third and Argonne in midtown Atlanta. Madeline, the owner of a chain of travel agencies was Maddy to her friends. She insisted Mica call her Maddy, though Mica didn't much care for the woman.

Mica hadn't wanted to go to Maddy's exclusive gathering; one couldn't call it a party. She didn't *have* to go to good-old-Maddy's that night. She had more than enough clients of her own. Maddy, though, had called in a favor, so Mica couldn't very well reject the *invitation*.

A dominatrix by trade, Mica relied mainly on long-time clients. According to Maddy, five of the six people invited to her dungeon were out-of-towners; "very influential people," who had been promised a "special" evening they'd long remember. Mica would make the best of it, but it was a hot, sticky August evening and given the choice she would rather be in a cool bath in her loft.

Mica considered herself one of the fortunate ones. She'd run away from home at sixteen, and once arriving in Atlanta had quickly spent what little money she had been able to squirrel away. Fucked once against her will, if she had to get fucked now she would damn well get paid, she'd decided.

She'd turned down the advances of the first two who had approached her; flashbacks of her rape replaying itself — spooking her. She *didn't* want to be touched. *Didn't* want to give up control.

Then how the fuck are you going to make enough money for the roach-infested closet referred to as a hotel room? a voice in her mind had asked.

At first she *hadn't* let anyone touch her. She'd given two men blow jobs and one a handjob before calling it a night. She didn't fear disease, as the wolf within her had been protective. She had smelled each of the men before accepting his offer. Sniffed like the animal within her for signs of disease. Satisfied, she'd only given a little of herself for a bed and communal bathroom, with enough left over for a meal and some candy bars to tide her over.

Walking down Peachtree at Tenth, just past the Wyndham Hotel, she had seen a car slow, then pass, go around the block then slow down once again. This time it stopped, and she was offered a ride that changed her life.

The driver's name had been Colleen — she used no last name, like Cher or Madonna — and she had taken Mica in and molded her into a dominatrix. Since Colleen preferred the submissive role, Mica retained most of the control. Those times when Colleen had her own need for control she had friends who were more than willing to submit.

Colleen gave Mica a home, taught her a trade, even gave her a new identity. She became Terése, with a social security number, driver's license and credit cards; everything she needed to start a new life. She was Terése, though, only in the straight world. Terése owned a loft on Standish, just off Deering Road. Terése paid taxes. Terése kept mainly to herself. In time, Terése bought into Colleen's art gallery. To all but a few in the straight world she was but a name and a face.

Oddly, for her occupation, she had chosen a name similar to her real name — Madame Maya. In the confines of her loft, though, she was Mica Swann, if only to herself.

Mica wasn't the least bit ashamed of her occupation. Quite to the contrary, she performed a service and met a need, which was more than most could say. Her clients were men, and increasingly women, who were power brokers of Atlanta. During the day they worked in a pressure cooker, making decisions that could affect hundreds, sometimes thousands of lives. If an error in judgment was made they might try to shift responsibility, but ultimately knew they were the ones who were accountable. *The buck stopped with them.* Such people needed an outlet. Some turned to alcohol or drugs, others abused their wives or children, and still others had affairs, effectively destroying their marriages. Some, though, came to her.

They desperately needed to relinquish control; refrain from making *any* decisions no matter how inconsequential. They wanted to be told what to do and be punished if they did wrong. For a few hours all responsibility lay with Madame Maya. She gave them pleasure. She gave them pain. Most of all, she gave them peace of mind as they willingly became putty in her hands without any emotional commitment whatsoever. They weren't cheating on their spouses. She was a masseuse of the soul.

Television and movies portrayed those who partook in S/M as perverts, degenerates or deviants. Little did the public know that some of the pillars of Atlanta society submitted to Mica's will, and went home afterwards the better for it. Few of her clients divorced. Many actually told their lovers or spouses they were seeing her, though not by name. Few of her clients drank to excess or indulged in drugs. Sex with their significant other improved after a session with Madame Maya.

Balance. Equilibrium. Call it what you want, but that was what Mica offered. One could do worse for a living. Most did.

When she'd started she *had* to go to the clandestine gatherings to build her clientele. Some had availed of her services for as long as five years on a regular basis. Others just had the need for her on occasion. She'd unjustifiably gotten the reputation as a snob, because there were those who she refused to take on; wealthy and influential, but to Mica lacking.

"Who is she to pick and choose?" she heard others say.

"The nerve she's got to reject . . ."

"One cold fish."

"Without conscience."

"Coward. Wouldn't tell him *why* he wasn't good enough for her."

They didn't understand, and she refused to tell them. It should have eventually become apparent. The wolf within literally sniffed all potential clients. Some *were* lacking. Some were HIV positive. A few even *knew* they were, yet engaged in practices that could infect others. Some carried herpes or other sexually transmitted diseases. The wolf within weeded these out.

That was why she refused to charge the first time she met with anyone new. She was under no obligation if she didn't take their money.

The others should have suspected, for Mica didn't reject anyone based on looks or status. Mica cared nothing about a client's physical appearance. Some of her clients were obese, aged and infirm. Some of those she rejected were studs or particularly attractive women. *All* within a year manifested outward signs of their disease.

The wolf within, dormant for the most part, wouldn't allow her to fall victim to disease. Sometimes, when she felt unkind, she thought it might have been out of self-preservation. What would happen to the wolf if *she* succumbed to disease? Whatever the motive, she could pick the fair from the foul just by smelling.

She only gave up control one month during the year, when the wolf within her demanded. It seemed a fair trade. And then it was only to Jeremy, who besides Colleen, was her only close friend.

She first met Jeremy her second year in Atlanta. He was painting by the lake in Piedmont Park. She saw children with their sailboats, roller bladers, lovers walking or enjoying a picnic — even a few fisherman. She looked at Jeremy's painting and saw slashes of color.

"Is that a sailboat?" she had asked from behind him, pointing to a squiggle on the canvas.

He looked at her and must have read the mischievous smile on her face and responded in kind. "No, that's a child, silly girl. Here's his sailboat." He pointed at another smear that looked nothing like a boat.

"You make a living selling these?" she asked, genuinely curious. She hadn't yet bought into Colleen's gallery and knew little about art.

"Barely. This is all I own," he said, pointing to a knapsack and several frames draped with canvas. "And my paint and palette, of course. I sell what I paint for whatever I can get. Friends let me crash. I only need money for food, paint and canvas."

"Do you do nudes or just . . . that?" she asked, pointing to the lake.

"I specialize in nudes," he said, flashing a smile. "I give life to people — to the human form; the human spirit."

Mica gave him one hundred dollars for the incomplete seascape, then another five hundred. "Then come and paint me."

Jeremy stayed with her for several weeks and they became fast friends. He, too, had been a runaway; from the Midwest, was all he would say. They both had their secrets and neither had any desire to pry.

Jeremy's nudes were much like his seascapes at first glance. Mica looked at the first he painted of her and saw no human form. *No form at all.* But it did look markedly different from the other painting she had bought from him.

"That's how you see me?" she asked, a bit disconcerted.

"As you were then. As you are now, I see someone entirely different."

"Then paint me again," she said, giving him another five hundred dollars.

He shrugged and did as he was told. And again, she couldn't decipher herself amidst the array of colors. She did notice that he had used darker tones, and the pattern looked more animated than the first. She smiled, as she understood.

"They're both me. Different mood, different me."

Over the next few weeks she had him paint her nude a dozen times and he always came up with a new wrinkle. Lying naked, as he painted, they talked. She told him what she did for a living and he peppered her with questions.

"Why don't you make a pass at me?" she asked one day out of the blue. "Are you gay?"

"No. I'm most definitely *into* women — figuratively and literally," he said with a laugh.

"I'm not your type, then?"

"You're very much my type."

"Well, then, what gives?"

"You won't have me. Or, at least something within sends out a warning, 'Look but don't touch.'"

"The wolf within me. My protector," she said, knowing he wouldn't understand.

"Whatever," he said, apparently *not* comprehending. "I'll have you only when you want me."

Truth be told, she didn't want him then. Didn't want anyone. He was handsome enough, she thought. About her height at five-foot six-inches. Her build, too, though he didn't work out as she did. He was lean, but a bit soft. He had raven black hair that came to his shoulders; she, golden blond that made its way to the middle of her back. She couldn't tell his ancestry. He was dark, but if he had black blood in him it was mixed with a dozen other races. Some of his features were similar to those of the American Indians who lived in Atlanta. She, on the other hand, was pale, even with a tan.

Soon he had enough money for an apartment of his own; and later a loft. Mica, though, remained his benefactor. She had even hosted a show at the gallery for him. He'd sold two paintings and had commissions for several nudes.

"Married women fall all over me," he told her. "They tell their husbands I paint them clothed, and when they look at the painting there's nothing to suggest otherwise," he laughed.

"Do you have sex with them?" Mica asked.

"You know I do, so why ask? I told you, I have an unquenchable thirst for women."

"Maybe you'll have me one day," she said, toying with him.

"Not until you rid yourself of your guard dog."

"Guard *wolf*," Mica said.

"Whatever," he said, shaking his head in mock annoyance.

In February she called and told him to bring over four or five paintings he thought she'd like. When he arrived, she gave him ten thousand dollars.

"I don't need your charity anymore," he said sounding annoyed, then apologized. "I didn't mean it to come out that way. Because of you, I now make a decent living for myself."

"I'm buying your time, Jeremy. I want you to stay with me for the month. No painting. Just pleasuring me."

"I don't understand."

"You can't. I'll show you what I want. Next year — *every year* — you'll be mine for February.

The wolf within her was going into heat. For three weeks there would be foreplay. Only that last week would she allow him to have sex with her. Some might call it lovemaking, but for Mica it was pure sexual gratification.

When he was naked she saw hair covered his entire body. She wondered if he had some wolf within him. The only outward sign of her wolf within was her thick black pubic hair. Jeremy had been taken aback when he'd first painted her nude. He had asked if she bleached her hair blond, after seeing the thick dark thatch that covered her genitals. She had told him no without elaborating. Her pubic hair was an outward manifestation of the wolf within. It grew thicker yet in the winter, even more so when she went into heat.

While they didn't have sex the first few weeks, it didn't mean they didn't achieve orgasm. She would let him touch her; the *first* man since her rape. She'd sniffed him first and was satisfied he was disease free, and he'd sniffed her, as if it were part of some ritual. He had been up front about the affairs he'd had with other women, but he'd always used a condom, he told her.

Best was when he'd painted her with strawberry yogurt — from her forehead to her toes. He licked her clean, first those not considered erogenous zones; at least those areas Mica insisted were not *her* erogenous zones. She found herself excited, nevertheless. In heat, every touch excited her. She came and came often, well before he licked her breasts, behind her ears and thighs — *her* erogenous zones — that literally set her howling. He howled back, she thought, to please her. The wolf within was certainly pleased.

When his tongue entered her vagina, she tore at his back with her nails. She wanted him to enter her, but it wasn't yet time. Then it was her turn to lick him. A part of her wanted to reciprocate in kind; take it nice and slow, even tease a bit, but the wolf was far too selfish. Too impatient to lick him from stem to stern, with her nose, then her tongue, she nuzzled his groin, licked his testicles, then took him in her mouth. Now *he* howled, and she joined him.

The few times they went out during the month she was insufferable. She was aggressively possessive, instigating arguments with nis female friends and putting them in their place with her caustic tongue. It was a side of her he hadn't seen, not that it seemed to bother him.

Finally, the last week in February she was ready for him. As he lay in bed, she urinated on him, her signal that it was time. Again, he reciprocated. The warm urine splayed on her body drove her to ecstasy. She wanted no foreplay now. She wanted him to mount her, wanted him within her, wanted him *now*.

As if it were the first time he'd had sex, he nervously tore at a condom wrapper. She waited until he had put it on, then ripped it off.

"Aren't you worried I could carry—"

"Disease," she finished for him. "No, you're pure."

"What if you get pregnant?"

"I won't conceive. You could construct a calendar by my periods,

I'm so regular. But I haven't had one this month. There'll be no unwanted pregnancy. Now shut up and fuck me."

Over the next five days she gave herself to him as she would to no other. He was the dominant; she the submissive. And for all intents and purposes, she *was* a virgin. This was the first time she'd *let* a man enter her. That other — he'd forced himself on her. It certainly wasn't love-making. It hadn't even been sex. He had violated her. As far as she was concerned, Jeremy was her first. And her last.

After the fifth day she — more accurately her wolf within — was sated. Jeremy wouldn't touch her again for a year. Oddly, he didn't seem to mind. Over the next six years she was his in February. The rest of the year they were friends. They loved one another like sister and brother. He seemed to understand her need. He also knew that no emotional commitment came with it.

*   *   *

As Mica walked to Maddy's house, she was unaware she would never see Jeremy again.

SIX

SHARA

Where to start? Shara thought, glancing at notes she had written as she'd gone over the file Nina Rios had brought over.

She'd all but memorized what there was to know about Biggie Shaw, the life he'd led and the girls he had defiled.

Shara had bought a home four months earlier, soon after Jonas Caffrey, Deidre's father-in-law, had passed away. Deidre had said she could remain in Jonas' apartment as long as she wanted, but Shara wanted the privacy only a place of her own could provide. At some point Deidre would be going through Jonas' belongings and Shara didn't want her popping in unexpectedly. And she had needs that the cramped apartment wouldn't allow.

She had bought a two-story house on 5th between Spruce and Locust Streets, and soon began extensive renovations; starting with her room with its wall-to-wall and ceiling mirrors.

Her workroom housed over forty-thousand dollars in computer and surveillance equipment. She could hack without being traced, create false identities for herself without meddlesome middlemen, and illegally wiretap even the most extensive anti-wiretapping devices.

When it came to technology, she was intent on staying one step ahead of the competition, whatever the cost.

One wall had left been bare. Now, on the corkboard that covered it, she had placed two maps. On one, she'd stuck colored push pins where Biggie Shaw had attacked each of his victims. On another, pins where Shaw and the victims resided.

The rapes had occurred throughout various neighborhoods in South Philadelphia and Center City. Philly was a city of neighborhoods, each an entity unto itself. You could drive up 22nd Street from Moore to South Street and pass a sea of black faces. Yet, the drive could encompass the turf of three or more distinct black neighborhoods. And being black didn't mean you could venture from one neighborhood to another with impunity.

The first girl had been attacked as she left a library within the neighborhood she resided. The second victim had just left Liberty Place, a moderate-sized mall at 17th and Chestnut Street in Center City. The third, close to the Christian Street Y at 16th and Christian, back in South Philly, but *not* in the same neighborhood as the library. And Biggie Shaw had met his maker in a playground mostly frequented by whites. Some still referred to it as Taney Playground, named after a white gang that had plagued the area until the city finally reclaimed it. Four attacks in four separate locations having no connection with one another.

The four victims though, along with Shaw, all lived in the *same* neighborhood — just south of Washington Avenue down to Federal Street and from 17th to 23rd Street.

Biggie could have known his victims, Shara thought. The girls told the police they didn't know him, other than by sight. But one of the detectives had told Nina Rios none of the girls had been overly cooperative, even with Shaw dead and no court testimony necessary. They had chalked it up to general hostility towards the police. Shara didn't buy it, but let it rest for the moment.

She was more interested in Biggie Shaw himself. He was single and had been arrested twice with small amounts of crack cocaine on him. A user, not a dealer. Yet, even with a record and single, he'd been a foster parent at the time of his death.

Hacking into the Department of Human Services files, Shara saw he'd had three foster daughters, each for nine to thirteen months. No matter how overburdened and understaffed DHS was, that Shaw had been deemed qualified to become a foster parent felt wrong.

That was where Shara would start. It would lead her to Biggie's killer, she knew intuitively. It was an avenue the police hadn't explored, and with justification. Shaw, after all, was dead. Why look into *his* background?

Saying she was an investigator for the Lamar Briggs defense team, Shara made an appointment with the DHS caseworker responsible for the placement and safety of the three girls put in Shaw's care. Shara intentionally made it a lunch appointment, at a restaurant she selected — The Corned Beef Academy at 17th and Walnut. She wanted Danielle Jamieson out of her element and away from the prying eyes of her co-workers.

Danielle Jamieson was a tall dark-skinned black woman who carried herself with dignity; not haughty arrogance, but with pride. From afar she was attractive, even beautiful, though in her mid-forties she had passed her prime.

But the beauty was more an illusion. While not unattractive, Shara saw it was her carefully applied makeup, long straight black hair, impeccably-tailored clothing and regal bearing that gave the impression of beauty.

Up close, her lips were a bit too large for her narrow face, her eyes too far apart and her ears overly long, reminding Shara a bit of *Star Trek*'s Mr. Spock. Large decorative earrings kept one's eyes from focusing on the ears themselves.

Moreover, while she gave the impression of a killer body, that too was part illusory. She *did* have stunning long legs, accentuated by a skirt just a bit *too* short for someone her age. With eyes drawn to her legs, one didn't notice that for all intents and purposes Danielle Jamieson was flat-chested.

Danielle Jamieson spent a lot of time creating herself each morning, of that Shara was certain.

She initially eyed Shara with suspicion, as they made small talk over lunch. Shara devoured her rare roast beef sandwich, while her guest picked at her salad.

"What can I do for you, Miss Farris?" she finally asked with a hint of exasperation in her voice. "With my caseload, I can't indulge myself with two-hour lunches."

Shara decided to knock her down a peg real quick, without totally alienating the woman.

"Tell me how Nelson Shaw got to be a foster parent to three girls."

Shara could see the fear in the woman's eyes for just an instant. Neither the police nor the media had dug deeply enough to uncover Biggie Shaw's secret. He was dead, after all, and any focus on him was directed to the girls he had raped. Though momentarily disconcerted, Shara saw Jamieson recover quickly.

"There wasn't much demand for these girls. They were older — fourteen or fifteen — and not particularly attractive. And they had low IQs."

"Retarded?" Shara asked.

"No, but borderline learning disabled," Jamieson said, emphasizing the politically correct term.

"Not the pick of the litter," Shara finished for the caseworker, who looked at Shara with distaste. "And malleable," she added.

"In hindsight," Jamieson admitted, her eyes on her half-uneaten salad.

"How did he get the girls without a wife?"

"He *had* a wife," she shot back, then paused. "At least I *thought* he did. We're overburdened—"

"Look, I'm not here to lay blame at your feet. I just want the truth," Shara interrupted.

"He brought in a woman I *now* know was LaVerne Thomas as his wife," she said, her shoulders sagging. Again, her eyes avoided Shara.

"Did you check up on the girls; you know, go visit them at Shaw's house?"

"Yes!" she snapped. "I *do* my job, Miss Farris."

Shara wondered how well, but said nothing.

"Anything unusual?"

The caseworker paused for a moment, breathed in deeply, then answered. "His wife was never around when I'd pop in."

"He returned each girl within nine to thirteen months," Shara said changing the subject. "Why?"

"There would be a family emergency or he'd have to go out of town on business, along with his wife."

"Did he abuse them in any way?" Shara asked, not wanting to put words in the woman's mouth.

"At the time I'd have said no. To the contrary, there were no complaints of abuse of any kind. He bought them good clothes and jewelry, took them to concerts and sporting events. He made sure they went to school. He appeared to be an ideal foster parent."

She paused, making eye contact with Shara again.

"In hindsight, I now know he raped them. You've been beating around the bush, but that's why you're here. It's been gnawing at me since he was killed and it all came out in the papers. I'd failed these girls. In hindsight, it was obvious why he wanted them; what he did to them. But should I have known? Am I culpable? I don't mean legally, Miss Farris. But, did I unwittingly provide him with children to violate? Was it because I'd blinded myself because he appeared an ideal foster parent, and we have so few? Not one day goes by that I don't think of those girls. I ask God for guidance. For forgiveness. How could I have been so easily duped?" She began to sob softly.

Shara let her go on. Just like her beauty, her tough-as-nails attitude was a mask. Shara had considered the possibility Shaw might have paid the woman to bend the rules to satisfy his sexual appetite. But she could see Danielle Jamieson was beating herself up daily. No way she was an accomplice.

"Can you tell me where the girls are now?" Shara asked when she had composed herself.

"That's confidential," she said without much conviction.

"Look, Danielle," Shara said, intentionally using the woman's first name. "I'm not laying responsibility at your door, but depending on what I learn, the shit may well hit the fan. Your supervisors and co-workers will desert you like rats on a sinking ship. You make an easy scapegoat, a convenient sacrificial lamb. And you know it," Shara said, painting her future in colorful clichés, to make her point. "Help me and I'll do what I can to make sure the shit doesn't land on you."

Jamieson picked up a briefcase she'd brought with her, and from it extracted a folder which she gave to Shara.

"My job's my life. These children are *my* children. To think I allowed them to be . . . violated. I no longer care how swamped I am. I check, then double check every prospective foster parent. I work evenings and weekends on my own time. Penance, if you will. Something like this will never again occur on my watch. Help me keep my job. Please. Allow me to redeem myself. In the name of God, please," and again she began sobbing.

Shara gave the woman her pager number. "I won't bullshit you, and I make no promises. Were you culpable? you asked before. I don't know yet, but I won't throw you to the lions if you've been straight with me. And some free advice. Watch your back. And, it wouldn't hurt if you could dig up some dirt on your supervisors. Kinda fight fire with fire."

Danielle Jamieson shook her head. But Shara knew she'd think about it. A lot. Self-preservation might make her change her mind. At least Shara had planted the seed.

*   *   *

With the molestation of three minors confirmed in Shara's mind, she next went to see LaVerne Thomas, Biggie Shaw's "wife." Jamieson's file had her working at a restaurant at 20th and Tasker Street, in South Philly. A little homework showed the restaurant was owned by Biggie's three brothers.

Dressed as a bag lady, Shara saw a lot of traffic, but few stayed more than a few minutes. A front, probably for drugs, she decided. And, from what Shara could see of LaVerne, she was a user, as well. She went through a box of Kleenex like a bag of potato chips, and disappeared into the back half a dozen times, returning far more chipper than when she left.

When LaVerne locked up at 6 p.m. — two Biggie look-a-likes having left fifteen minutes earlier — Shara was in jeans and a leather coat.

LaVerne almost bumped into her as she turned from the door.

"Twenty dollars, if you give me a listen," Shara said, holding out a bill. "Guaranteed it's worth your while."

LaVerne took the twenty, said nothing, but followed Shara to her car around the corner.

LaVerne Thomas looked very much the worse for wear. Short as Shara and just as lean, she was dark-skinned like Biggie. She had dyed her hair blond, but already Shara could see the black roots. Her eyes were watery, her nose running and she reeked of body odor.

Shara got right to the point.

"I'm working for lawyers for Kimberly Watts, the last girl to live with Biggie. She's filing a suit against the city. There's a sizable reward for someone who could help corroborate her claim."

"What the bitch claiming?" LaVerne asked, wiping her nose with the cuff of a frayed coat.

Shara ignored her.

"You and Biggie seeing one another before he was offed?"

The woman laughed. "Biggie's my half-brother. Same father. Took the last name of our mothers."

"So you weren't man and wife," Shara said, casually.

"Fuck no—" LaVerne started, then stopped, as if she'd had a revelation.

"Then why did you claim to be when Biggie wanted to become a foster parent?"

LaVerne tried to get out of Shara's car.

"I said there's a reward," Shara said, as LaVerne fumbled for the door latch. "It can be substantial if you help," Shara added quickly and LaVerne looked at her, as if unsure what to do.

"If you don't help, well . . . I can always contact the police. You know, impersonating his wife to facilitate a crime."

"What crime?" she asked, and now she was scratching her head like she had lice.

"Why did he want the girls?"

"You know damn well. That bitch Kimberly Watts spelled it all out for you, right. He wanted a handy lay. Biggie was no fool, mind you. Family across the street had a foster kid and it gave him ideas. Even though there was plenty of pussy out there, Biggie liked them young. Liked to call himself a cherry popper," she said with a laugh, still scratching her head.

"You ever see him with one of the girls?" Shara said, holding out another twenty.

"Once," LaVerne said, plucking the bill from Shara's hand. "The first girl; I don't remember her name. I needed money for . . . for stuff, you know. I had a key to his place and he was getting it on with her. Weren't no big thing, though. He treated them good. And no one else would have them. They were dumb and all but the last butt ugly," she said, drawing out the last word. "Put a bag over they head so you wouldn't puke. Biggie didn't care though, long as they were young."

"Why did he return them?"

"For fresh pussy. He tired of them when they could fuck like any other woman. Biggie's dream was to pop every virgin's cherry, then teach them to satisfy a man. Then onto a fresh piece of meat, even younger. Now, when do I get my money?"

Shara gave the woman a card. It had the name of a phony law firm, but the number was real; one of those accident lawyers who pitched their wares on the tube during *M*A*S*H.*

"Soon as that creep that killed Biggie goes to jail the city's going to want to settle. Soon as you hear you call this number," Shara said tapping the card. "Now I just need a Polaroid of you."

"What the fuck for?"

"To prove to these schmucks I spoke to you. And, when you go to claim your money, they'll know you're who you claim."

*   *   *

The biggest difference between a cop and a bounty hunter was the short cuts you could take. Shara didn't have to see minors with their parents. She didn't have to tell anyone they were entitled to a lawyer, and if they asked for one, she was free to ignore their request. It allowed her to enter a world the police probably couldn't, even if they'd had the inclination.

Shara quickly tracked down the first two girls Biggie had taken under his wing, to confirm LaVerne Thomas' story. One of the girls had dropped out of school, had one baby in her lap and another on the way. No husband. On welfare. No prospects.

The other was in a group home. Every day at 4 p.m., she took half a dozen kids to a playground.

Shara used the same ploy with them she'd used with LaVerne Thomas. The two had nothing to hide. Most depressing for Shara, they didn't know they'd been victimized. When they talked about Biggie their eyes lit up. Clothes, jewelry, spending money . . . oh, and the sex was good.

"Taught me how to please a man," said the one who would soon be the mother of two at seventeen.

Didn't teach you about birth control, Shara wanted to say, but held her tongue.

Kimberly Watts, the last girl, was another story entirely. Shara watched Kimberly at a pizza parlor she'd gone to after school. She had once been beautiful, Shara thought. Still was with smooth chocolate-colored skin. Only when she turned her head did Shara see the scar on her right cheek. The scar itself, which ran from the girl's eye to her jaw-bone, wouldn't have marred her beauty except it hadn't been properly treated when she'd been injured. It was a good half-an-inch wide and the whole side of her face looked like it had been shot with Novacaine. Half her face functioned as it should. The scarred half could have sported a sign "Out Of Order."

She ate her pizza with a plastic knife and fork. She cut each piece methodically, and seemed to chew on it for an eternity. She was calm and controlled. *Too* calm. *Too* controlled.

Shara asked if she could join her, and Kimberly Watts simply shrugged, as if she didn't care one way or the other.

Shara went into her now well-rehearsed shtick about representing one of the girls in a civil action against the city.

As with the others, Kimberly needed little prompting. Clothes, jewelry, food — "good food, three times a day, plus snacks."

By now Biggie seemed to have it down to an art form. But then Kimberly's story took an unexpected turn. She hadn't been as malleable as the others.

"Biggie wanted me to touch him down there," she said, staring into her lap. "I didn't want to, but I did. He came into the shower with me. I *knew* it was wrong, but I let him. He'd been so good to me. Then he wanted to have sex."

She looked at Shara. "Sex when you're not married is a sin. I told him that and he laughed and . . . raped me."

Shara leaned closer to the girl. She was barely talking above a whisper, but unlike the others she *knew* what Biggie had done to her.

"I fought him, but he was too strong. After, I cried for hours. He was scared. Afraid I'd tell somebody. He said I'd led him on. Said I was a tease. Said it was all *my* fault. I even said I'd tell Miss Jamieson and he promised never to do it again. But he did," and she stopped and raised three fingers one at a time. "Three weeks later. And again, three weeks after that."

Shara didn't have to prompt her with questions. As she listened, all her questions were answered.

"After the third time," she said, again raising her fingers one at a time — the number etched in her memory — "I tried to call Miss Jamieson with him there. I wanted him to know I weren't scared of him. I *was* . . . scared, you know, but I didn't want to have sex with him no more."

Her left hand now began to shake as she went on, and Shara saw terror in her eyes, as if she were reliving what she was reciting.

"He took the phone from me and dragged me to bed. He raped me one more time, slapping me when I cried, which made me cry harder, which made him slap me more, which . . ." and now she was sobbing.

Shara said nothing, but reached out and held the girl's shaking hand, then waited as she composed herself.

"When he was done he grabbed me by the throat and told me if I said a word to *anyone* he'd kill me . . . *after* he and his brothers had turns raping me. He never touched me again. He started going out almost every night. I didn't know why, but as long as he be out the house he couldn't rape me, so I didn't care none."

She stopped talking and closed her eyes. Shara was going to ask a question, but she opened them, looked at Shara and went on.

"One night he came back and woke me up. Told me he raped this girl coming home from the library. Said it was *my* fault, 'cause I wouldn't do it with him. Told me she was better than me. Younger. And it be her first time. And . . . and, he told me she wouldn't dime on him. She knew who he was, but she wouldn't tell, just like I wouldn't. He told me about *all* them girls he raped. Knew how much it would hurt me. When he was killed I cried all night. Thanked the Lord for answering my prayers."

Now she fell silent.

"Why didn't you tell the police after he was killed?"

"A.C., Biggie's brother, was with me when the police came. He'd heard what Biggie had done to them other girls and told me to play dumb. Laughed when he said it. 'Tellin' a dummy to play dumb.'"

"Why not tell Miss Jamieson?"

Kimberly vigorously shook her head. "I'd be damaged goods and never find a foster home. I put it behind me. Now I'm with a good family. Gotta put it behind me. Gotta put it behind me," she repeated over and over.

Shara held the girl's hand, which had started shaking again, in her two hands, and let the girl cry herself out. It was all she could do not to cry herself.

"Will God forgive me?" she asked Shara, and no longer playing a role, Shara tried to comfort her.

"Listen to me, Kimberly. You did nothing wrong. There's nothing for God to forgive. Biggie forced you to have sex with him. Threatened you if you told. There's nothing to forgive," she repeated, as Kimberly gave her a weak smile. "Nothing to forgive," she said again, as if repeating it would make the girl believe her.

She took Kimberly's picture before she left and when she gave her the card with the name of the phony law firm, she took it back, crossed out the number and put down her pager instead.

"If you need anything or just want to talk to someone, call this number and I'll get back to you. You've been hurt enough already," she said, as much to herself as to Kimberly. No way she'd dupe this child.

Kimberly looked at Shara strangely, but took the card, and smiled weakly.

Much as Shara sympathized with Danielle Jamieson, *someone* was culpable for what had happened to the three girls Biggie Shaw had defiled. *Someone* should pay. The girls, especially Kimberly who had resisted Biggie, needed help. Sweeping it all under the carpet was now unacceptable to Shara. She would save Briggs' ass, but something had to be done to ease the torment Kimberly Watts had gone through.

With Biggie dead, though, Shara despaired that there was no one to be held accountable. She didn't like the thoughts she was having. She'd had them before and killed six men. Had Biggie been alive, she feared she would have killed him. It had been Deidre's worst fear when she didn't turn Shara over to the police. Shara had told her she no longer had the need to kill, but deep within she knew she could — *would*, if provoked . . . provoked by someone like Biggie Shaw. She scratched at her breasts through her shirt; the eyes had begun to itch.

Someone would pay, she said to herself. Somehow.

*   *   *

At home Shara pushed thoughts of vengeance aside by plotting her course. That the girls Biggie Shaw attacked knew and could identify him, yet hadn't was the key. The parents of one of the victims, Shara was certain, had set Shaw up and killed him when Briggs hadn't.

"Which one of you was it?" Shara said aloud, pacing in her work room.

"Not the one who lived with only her mother," Shara said aloud. Talking aloud, as she did to the television, seemed to help clarify her thoughts.

"No, not her." As with so many in the black community, the child had been born out of wedlock. The girl had never known her father. The woman had two other children; the youngest three years old. Neither of their fathers were around either.

She also discounted the next victim, who lived in a traditional nuclear family. No matter how great the anger of the father, he had someone to lean on. Moreover, his mother lived with them, adding additional stability.

"Everett Gaines," Shara said, "It's got to be you." Gaines was a single father, with one daughter, Ivy, Biggie Shaw's third victim. A clerk at the post office at 19th and Chestnut Streets, he had taken a week off from work after his daughter's attack. "Nothing odd in that," Shara said aloud, as she looked at the man's records of absences on her computer.

Ivy Gaines had been raped returning from the Christian Street Y, where she was on a girl's basketball team. Twelve years old, in sixth grade. When the police interviewed Everett Gaines, after Biggie Shaw's death, they had noted his daughter was still in shock. She'd been totally unresponsive to their questions, staring vacantly at the television. Again, nothing out of the ordinary in that, Shara thought.

But, Ivy's father had taken an additional two weeks of vacation time just prior to Biggie's death, returning to work the day *after* Shaw had been killed.

Back to her computer, Shara had no trouble hacking the root password on this, her umpteenth UNIX system to access Ivy's attendance record at school. It never ceased to amaze her how system administrators left the default passwords for the service accounts on their supposedly secure systems. Now tapping into the attendance records of Ivy's school Shara saw Ivy had returned to class when her father had returned to work after that first week. She hadn't been absent since, so Everett Gaines hadn't taken the additional time off to comfort his daughter. He'd been stalking Biggie. Had killed him when Briggs wouldn't.

"Gotcha," Shara said aloud, in triumph. "Now to break you."

She decided to visit the Gaineses to take a measure of the man and see how his daughter was progressing. Shara decided to be straight with Gaines. She was working for Briggs' defense team. She didn't expect hostility; actually, quite the opposite.

The Gaineses lived in a typical South Philadelphia rowhouse on Wharton Street between 19th and 20th Streets. Everett Gaines was wary, though polite, when he greeted Shara. She had called in advance, so as not to impose. Called ahead, so father and daughter had several hours to become unnerved by another unexpected intrusion.

Ivy was sitting on a couch, which dominated a small, but immaculately clean living room. She was staring at the television, just as she'd done when the police had interviewed the family a month before.

The room was filled with pictures of Ivy at different ages. In many she was with her father, a third party having snapped the photo. Both smiling. Ivy swimming. Ivy in her basketball uniform. Ivy at a carnival — vanilla ice cream dripping down her chin — at the zoo, at the circus.

Even sitting, Shara could tell Ivy was tall and lanky for a twelve-year old, with mocha-colored skin like her father.

Everett Gaines was medium height, but lean like his daughter. She guessed him to be in his mid-thirties, though he had more than a touch of grey in his hair. His brown eyes looked tired and wary, tinged with a touch of apprehension, even fear. He ushered Shara into a small dining area.

"Coffee, tea, a soft drink, beer?" he asked.

"A beer would be fine."

She sat so she could keep an eye on Ivy. She wanted to see how the girl responded to her conversation with her father. Wanted to see if the vacant stare was an act.

"What can I do for you, Miss Farris?" Ivy's father asked, with a forced smile.

"Detective Briggs' lawyers wants to know how Biggie Shaw's victims have been doing since his death. The other girls have shown marked improvement, like weights have been lifted from their shoulders," she said with a smile. In truth, she hadn't spoken with the other families, but didn't think Everett Gaines had either. "How's Ivy?"

"Better. Improving," he said.

Each word seem measured, though he must have rehearsed how he would respond a dozen times.

"She goes to school. She listens. Speaks up once in awhile. She's still not her old self and remembers nothing of the attack."

Shara noted he put added emphasis on the last part.

Shara saw Ivy's eyes trying to take her in without giving herself away.

"She's still shy . . . no, that's not the word. *Fearful*!" he said loudly, as if discovering a word he'd been searching for, but hadn't been able to articulate until now. "Yes, fearful of strangers. Someone she doesn't know goes near her, she withdraws."

"Has she received help — counseling?"

"At school," he said with a shrug. "I can't afford nothing more, and I won't accept charity," he hurriedly added.

Her eyes on Ivy, Shara told Mr. Gaines about Alexis Briggs.

"Detective Briggs has a daughter close to Ivy's age — almost fifteen. She was raped just over a year ago. She was like Ivy is now. The animal beat her in the head with a brick *after* the rape," she added. "There was brain damage. She had been making progress — slow, but progress nevertheless, until her father was arrested. Now she's regressed."

Ivy turned away to avoid being seen. Shara thought she had seen the youth's eyes moisten. Ivy didn't want Shara to see her cry.

Shara went on. "Each day without her father must be an eternity for her. We've become friends," she said, turning for a moment to make eye contact with Everett Gaines. He had closed his eyes. She didn't think he wanted to hear what she was saying.

"Each day she seems more distant. I can't imagine what will happen if her father goes to jail. She'd been improving, like I said. Now, it's as if the life has been drained from her," Shara said, her voice breaking. "I'm sorry," she added, her eyes back on the father. "Kinda got side-tracked for a moment."

She got up and gave Everett Gaines a card with Briggs' attorney's number on it.

"If there's any improvement, I'd appreciate a call. Detective Briggs needs all the help he can get."

"He'll be in our prayers," Everett Gaines said, with difficulty. "In our prayers."

Ivy avoided looking at Shara as she left, but Shara could see tears on the girl's cheek.

She had planted a seed. How the Gaineses would respond, she wasn't certain. She did know Everett Gaines was a good man, and even a better father. She didn't know what she'd been expecting. Maybe she'd hoped he would turn out to be a bastard; a thug out for revenge. If so, she'd deluded herself. Taking him down would give her no satisfaction.

Shara spent the night in her car across the street from the Gaines' home. She slept in fits and starts, as always, and found herself in the woods again. When she awoke, bruised and aching, she saw cuts on her cheek and forehead in the car's mirror. She put it aside and waited for what the morning would bring.

At 7:45 a.m., Ivy left the house. She was *not* the girl Shara had seen the night before. There was a bounce to her step, and as Shara took her picture through a telephoto lens, life in her eyes; not the flat, vacant stare she'd greeted Shara with the night before.

She stopped by a house and was joined by another girl her age. Shara snapped more pictures of Ivy chatting and laughing with the girl.

At the schoolyard Shara took still more photos of Ivy interacting with the other children, focusing on the girl's face.

How difficult it must be, Shara thought, living a double life.

Shara was going to go home and develop her pictures, but decided to first see the school counselor.

When Audrey Cirillo greeted Shara, her eyes were bright and her smile infectious. She began talking non-stop before Shara could get a word in edgewise.

"Detective Briggs is a saint in my book. I'll testify to that if his lawyers want."

The woman looked nothing like the few photos Shara saw in her office. She was a good fifty pounds thinner, pale, even with makeup; literally a shell of herself.

The counselor saw her looking at the photos. "Cancer," she said. "Ovarian cancer, but it's been in remission three months, seven days and," she looked at her watch, "four hours, since my last chemo treatment. I'm not the woman I was," she said with a laugh. "*Literally*. But I'm alive. Even my hair's grown back," she said, tugging at her short gray hair. "Left my wig at home last week. I'm sorry, I'm rambling. It's just, well . . . I'm alive and it's grand."

"Why do you consider Detective Briggs a saint?" Shara asked, when the counselor finally wound down.

"For killing the bastard who raped Ivy Gaines. She'd been so withdrawn and unresponsive. I tried to talk to her, but she would stare past me. Then Detective Briggs killed that Biggie Shaw and overnight she began to show improvement. She's still withdrawn with adults. She

58

still won't share a thing with me, but her grades have picked up. And I steal a look at her at recess and see she's mingling with her friends, and that wonderful smile of hers has returned."

"So you approve of Detective Briggs taking the man's life without a trial." It wasn't a question.

"Don't get me wrong, Miss Farris. In the abstract I'm appalled. But in Ivy, I'm talking about a human being who was a tortured soul. If that monster had been taken alive and Ivy had to testify . . . I cringe at the thought. In *this* case Detective Briggs did the world a favor. He certainly helped Ivy on the road to recovery."

*   *   *

That evening, just after seven, Shara knocked on the Gaines' door, unannounced. Everett Gaines was clearly disconcerted to see Shara back. He tried to ward her off.

"I'm busy, Miss Farris. Can't we make this—"

"You lied to me last night," Shara interrupted. She held up an envelope. "Should I take this to the police?"

Everett Gaines hesitated, then ushered her in.

"Let's talk in the dining—"

"Ivy's part of this," Shara interrupted again. "Please, bear with me."

Gaines sighed and sat down on one side of his daughter, Shara on the other.

"The girl I see before me now and the one I saw this morning aren't the same." She opened the envelope and took out black and white 8x10 photographs she'd developed at home, and put one on the table in front of the couch. "She's not the same girl I saw with her friend . . ."

— put another photo down —

" . . . not the same I saw in the schoolyard . . ."

— three more photos —

" . . . not the same girl described by the school's counselor; an Ivy who's improving in class and interacting with her friends," she said, looking at Ivy.

"Maybe you'd better leave," Everett Gaines said, rising.

"And go to the police? Look, I'm sorry, but how long can your daughter go on with this charade? Imagine what it's doing to her. And when Briggs goes to prison—"

"Who says he will?" Gaines interrupted.

"He's going to cop a plea," Shara said. The man closed his eyes. "He'll be away from his daughter five, six, maybe seven years. How will Ivy feel knowing she's helped put an innocent man in jail? How will Ivy feel as *his* daughter withdraws from the world with her father lost to her? Is that your legacy to your daughter?"

Shara saw him cave then.

"Ivy, go to your room, okay," he said softly to his daughter.

There was terror in the girl's eyes.

Everett Gaines rose and led his daughter to the staircase. They hugged and Shara overheard him say, "It's time."

Shara had broken him, but holding back tears of her own, she felt no triumph.

SEVEN

MICA

Pleasure is pain. Pain is pleasure. Mica had learned from her clients the two could be one and the same. From what *some* considered pain, others derived great satisfaction. Pain *could* be pleasure. The greater the pain, for some, the greater the pleasure.

Mica was thinking how pain could lead to pleasure when an unmarked police car pulled up to her, at Myrtle and Third, two blocks from Maddy's house. Mica had taken a cab to Maddy's, but out of habit, had given an address three blocks from where she was actually going.

The driver leaned across and flashed his badge.

"Get in, sweetheart," he said.

Mica hesitated. She'd never been busted before. She wasn't a prostitute who worked the streets, nor a high-priced call girl who sometimes got caught in a police sting. The authorities, for the most part, turned a blind eye to the S/M Mica practiced. Her clients, demanding discretion, knew what buttons to push. Madeline Erskine had connections, as well. True, S/M *had* become trendy with clubs that catered to yuppies, rebels and amateurs alike. And there had been

61

some incidents involving these novices. A few had even died. Amateurs one and all. But Mica felt herself immune. Apparently, she was not.

"There's going to be a raid at your friend's house. Now get in." She did.

"Let me see some ID," he demanded, after he had driven several blocks and parked in an alley between Taft Avenue and Charles Allen Drive. Mica heard a dog barking in the distance, then another respond, and then a third dog. It was as if they were sending a chain letter.

The man's badge had said Ray Donato. His manner was brusque. His terse voice screamed *don't fuck with me*. He looked to be in his mid-thirties. His face was lean and unshaven, his black hair greased and slicked back. His brown eyes were predatory, immediately setting off alarm bells within Mica.

"Your fucking ID," he said, again. "Don't make me repeat myself if you want my help."

Mica handed over her wallet, her hands shaking. Donato clearly relished her discomfort, a sadistic grin baring his teeth, yellowed from years of smoking.

"So Terese—"

"Terése," Mica corrected, pronouncing the second syllable *ace*.

"Terése, then," he said, stretching her name out, rolling it off his tongue like a bowling ball. "Like I said, your friend's going to take a fall."

"What does that have to do with me?" Not having to shop her wares on the street, Mica wore a comfortable short-sleeved yellow summer dress. No way he could make her as a prostitute. If she didn't panic she could still talk her way out of an arrest. "Since when is it against the law to take a walk?"

"You got in my car fast enough when I mentioned a raid. I didn't even say who or which house. You want, we can go back. I think Mrs. Erskine will roll over on you in a heartbeat to save her tail. But maybe I'm wrong." He started the engine.

"Why warn me?" Mica asked, resigned to the fact she'd been made.

Donato turned off the engine, and now all Mica saw was a lecherous glint in his eyes.

"I was thinking we could reach an accommodation," he said, putting his hand on her thigh, quickly moving it up under her dress and ripping off her panties.

Mica slapped him in the face.

Donato slapped her back, and laughed.

"Feisty, aren't you. Like to play rough? Tell you what, bitch. Slap me, scratch me — hell, bite me. I'll slap, scratch and bite right back. It'll be a real turn-on."

He was on top of her now, pinning her to the seat. She clawed at his face and he tore at hers. She bit his lip when he tried to kiss her, and he bit her back, drawing blood. As he entered her . . .

— just as Ralph Danziger had done eight years before —

. . . she felt stirrings deep within. The wolf and her grandfather had been awakened. She hadn't summoned them. *Wouldn't.* Ray Donato, though, had brought out the beast in her — *literally.*

He climaxed, then breathing deeply and contentedly rolled off of her.

She sniffed him, and while his breath reeked of garlic — which she knew he'd tried unsuccessfully to mask with a breath mint — he wasn't diseased. She felt bloated and her stomach seized with cramps. If her period hadn't ended the day before, the cramps would have signaled its imminent arrival. She suddenly felt claustrophobic and nauseous. She thought she might get sick and puke all over him. Would serve him right, she thought. Might even repulse him enough to throw her out of the car. The feeling passed, though, as quickly as it came. She knew it had something to do with her long dormant inhabitants.

"We square?" she asked dully, wanting only be free of him.

"Not even close," he said, his grin more malevolent than ever. "This is how it goes down," he said, grabbing her by the face, so she was looking into his eyes. "I own you, bitch. I call, you come," he said and laughed. "*Come* in more ways than one. I'll have you until I tire of you, and that won't be for awhile, sweetheart."

"You're a crazy motherfucker," she said, unable to control her rage. "No way I'm going to be at your beck and call."

She twisted out of his grasp and tried to get out of the car.

Donato took out his revolver. He pointed it at her head. The smile never left his face.

"I *am* one crazy motherfucker, and you're a whore. A high-priced piece of ass, maybe, but a slut just the same. Now you're *my* whore."

"Fuck off," Mica said with disdain, ignoring the gun in her face.

"Don't believe I'll use it, huh? Think again."

He unloaded all the chambers, then put one bullet back in. He pointed the gun at his head and pulled the trigger, smiling all the while.

Click.

Pointed the gun at Mica's head. "Tell me you're mine."

When she refused, he pulled the trigger again.

Click.

Turned the gun on himself and pulled the trigger once more.

Click.

Shoved the gun under Mica's dress, resting the barrel against her genitals.

"Three left. Feeling lucky tonight?"

He *was* crazy, Mica now knew. Not just a bully, but certifiably in-need-of-a-padded-room insane. The wolf and her grandfather were now fully awake, yet they did nothing; not that she thought they would.

"I'm yours," Mica said, before Donato could pull the trigger. She had to stall for time.

"What? Can't hear you."

She saw his eyes were manic. They were glazed over, as if he'd lost all control; as if he wanted to see it through.

"I'm yours," Mica said louder.

"Not good enough."

"I'm yours, baby," Mica said, louder still. She caressed his face with a shaking hand. "I'm yours for as long as you want. Here, let me make you feel better."

The gun still resting on her genitals, she grabbed hold of his penis, standing at attention from his unzipped pants, and stroked it.

She could see him relax, but still she didn't like the feel of the gun against her.

"Eat me, baby," she said, soothingly. "Taste my pussy. Then tell me what you want me to do."

He removed the gun, bent down and began licking her vagina. She urged him on, talking non-stop, all the while looking for something to use as a weapon. She saw a crucifix hanging from a chain hooked over the mirror. While he feasted, she reached for it, but it was just beyond her grasp. She tried to shift, but he had her pinned. She reached again and this time her hand became a paw and she was able to grab the chain. *Her wolf within.*

"Now do me," he commanded.

"Do me one more time, please," she begged. "Flicking your tongue, it drove me crazy. Once more, please. Then I'll do you."

He laughed and lowered his head.

Mica quickly wrapped the chain around his neck. She looked at her hands and saw her grandfather's hairy arms and gnarled fingers. He had been in his seventies when he'd died, but even then he bragged he could still arm wrestle with the best of them. It was *his* hands which tugged at the chain until, like a knife, it sliced through Donato's neck.

He was dead even as blood gushed from his neck onto Mica's bare thighs. From just below her stomach, a wolf's head emerged and lapped up the blood. Mica sat watching, tasting the blood as it became part of her, wanting more.

She heard her grandfather's voice from within urge her to flee. She thought of going to the police. He'd raped her. Would have killed her. But to them, she was a whore who had killed a cop. No way would they believe her. She'd receive no solace from the police . . .

— just like when Ralph Danziger had raped her —

. . . only scorn.

Going to the police was out of the question. She'd heed her grandfather's advice and flee. She wouldn't be running away, though. She had unfinished business where Ralph Danziger had defiled her. She would flee.

Flee home.

E_{IGHT}

(DECEMBER 1998)

SHARA

Do the ends justify the means? Shara thought as she sat in the living room of Deidre's apartment, waiting for Deidre to arrive home. And what would be the price of duplicity?

As usual, Shara had let herself in. Twice before she had broken into the reporter's apartment. This time she used a key Deidre had given her when the two had worked together to hunt down The Nightwatcher. She had returned to Philadelphia, from her year in exile, with no place to stay. Deidre, too, had been alone. Her husband and young son had been killed in an automobile accident two years earlier. Her father-in-law, mentor and closest friend, Jonas Caffrey, lay comatose in the hospital after a stroke.

The bond they formed had been tenuous at best. At thirty-four, Deidre had been nine years older than Shara. And Deidre had lived a relatively trouble-free suburban existence, in sharp contrast to Shara, who was far more familiar with asphalt, street smarts learned from the homeless, a mother's neglect and the perversion of her half-brother. Their backgrounds were so dissimilar there was precious little common ground to share.

And there had been the deceit. Deidre may have brought it upon herself, but Shara had feasted on it. She had deceived Deidre as a novice reporter when she was eleven. She had betrayed her again when Deidre had attempted to track her before she killed her half-brother. She had duped her once more for good measure as she and Lysette plotted The Nightwatcher's surrender to the police behind Deidre's back.

Now despite the best of intentions she might have to betray her friend's trust again.

After Everett Gaines had confessed to her that he had killed Biggie Shaw, Shara couldn't just turn him over to the police. It was ironic that if Gaines had not been Briggs' mystery caller, had he killed Biggie Shaw as he tried to rape another child, he would have been hailed a hero.

Since becoming a bounty hunter, Shara had been allowed to view the world in terms of black and white. Bail jumpers, for whatever reason, were to be caught. It was up to lawyers and the courts to decide innocence or guilt. She quickly turned a deaf ear on any fugitive who pleaded innocence. A predator, she had only to hunt, capture and retrieve.

Suddenly the world consisted of shades of gray again which necessitated decisions that would hurt those she cared for. Biggie Shaw the villain was dead. In his wake he had left a host of victims, including Briggs and Everett Gaines.

Shara would adhere to her obligation to Alexis. Her father had not killed Shaw. He deserved his freedom. But Shara wasn't about to allow the system to swallow Everett Gaines alive, with Ivy Gaines further victimized and traumatized.

She had convinced Gaines to turn himself into Deidre, in the hopes that Deidre might champion his cause. But there was more on Shara's agenda. She held the city culpable for the lost innocence of Biggie Shaw's three foster children. Kimberly Watts would receive the absolution she sought from the mayor himself. The other two girls? Shara hadn't initially perceived them as victims. They held no animosity towards Shaw. They had willingly given themselves to him and held no grudge. But just because they weren't aware they'd been used didn't mean they hadn't been abused.

One of the girls had remained sexually active and would soon bear a second child out of wedlock. Shara feared for the other as well. They, along with Kimberly Watts, would be compensated, if Shara had anything to do with it.

Shara had visited two lawyers earlier in the day. Hunting fugitives, she had come in contact not only with bail bondsmen, but warrant officers at police stations in and out of the city, as well as a slew of lawyers. Where once Deidre had used her contacts to procure counsel for Lysette, Shara now knew lawyers far better equipped to help both Everett Gaines and Biggie Shaw's many victims.

She had gone to see Arnold Winkler first, mainly because his workday began at 8 a.m., a good hour or two before the lawyer she hoped would help Everett Gaines.

For Kimberly Watts and the other girls, she needed an attorney full of bluster, abrasive and arrogant; someone who couldn't be intimidated; someone a bit of a loose cannon, viewed as on the edge. Fuck with him and he would go public regardless of the ramifications. He didn't need courtroom skills or experience because the case would never go to trial. She wanted an alley fighter for a negotiator.

Arnold Winkler was such a pitbull. Ruthless and relentless. Shara had learned that, unlike television, most civil and criminal cases were resolved out of court. While the public knew lawyers of the rich and famous, far more cases were settled by a cadre of attorneys who made good money keeping their clients *out* of the courtroom.

Arnie Winkler fit the bill. At six-foot four-inches and well over three hundred pounds, with shoulder-length hair and a receding hairline, he resembled a Wrestlemania participant who had eaten himself out of the profession. He sported a perpetual five-o'clock shadow on an otherwise reddish face. His blood pressure, she thought, must long ago have hit the roof. And he was a sweater. While he wore expensive suits, tailored to mask his bulk, they looked like they'd been bought off the rack and stains divulged his most recent meals.

With a high-pitched voice, at odds with his size, you *didn't* want him to represent you in court. On the other hand, his opposition cringed when told he had taken a case. If he didn't break the lawyer's code of ethics, he certainly straddled the line and did so with delight.

He would go to just about any lengths for his client, and those who opposed him were fully aware of it.

He was eating a jelly donut when Shara was ushered into his office. She sat on his desk. Seated, looking up at him, she felt like a midget.

"How's it hanging, Arnie?" she greeted him.

"Can't complain," he answered while chewing on the donut.

"How would you like to take on the city?" she asked, coming right to the point.

He wiped his mouth with a napkin, then used it to wipe perspiration from his forehead.

"You've piqued my interest and you just walked in. You're my kind of person, Shara. Elaborate . . . please."

Shara told him everything.

"Someone's gotta pay, Arnie, and it sure isn't going to be Biggie Shaw. So, do they have a case?"

Winkler gave her a big grin, which only accentuated his many chins. "There's *always* a case, kiddo. A winnable case? That's another question. If you can substantiate all you say, the city will kiss my ass to keep it under wraps. Now tell me exactly what you want."

Shara had thought this out carefully. "A sizable cash settlement for the girls DHS gave to Shaw. For all intents and purposes they were running a brothel."

Winker laughed. "I like that. I'll use it, too, in my negotiations. Go on."

"Therapy for the girls, as long as necessary."

Winkler nodded.

"I see a direct link between DHS and Shaw having the balls to rape neighborhood girls," Shara continued. "The girls Shaw raped should share in any cash settlement and be provided therapy, as well." She paused to gauge his reaction.

"Your link is tenuous at best, but what the hell; in for a penny, in for a pound. They'll cave. Is that it?"

"No, two other items; one essential."

Winkler smiled. "This is going to be good, kiddo, I can feel it."

"The mayor — not one of his deputies — but the man himself must apologize to Kimberly Watts."

Winkler gave Shara a puzzled look.

"Kimberly feels she's sinned. She's damned in God's eyes. I told her she'd done nothing wrong; that she didn't need forgiveness. I don't think it took. She still feels consigned to hell. It'll eat at her, fester and torment her for the rest of her life. I'd ask for the Pope's or Cardinal's blessing, but that's unrealistic. But the mayor, face to face with Kimberly, taking responsibility. *That* and therapy and maybe she has a chance to feel redeemed."

Winkler shook his head. "So tough and gruff, I thought," he said, "but there's another side to you, kiddo. Am I right? Don't answer," he waved dismissively. "You understand me, Shara." He sat back in his chair. "The Pope, him I can't get. But the Cardinal . . . that's another story. Let's try for him and *settle* for the mayor."

Shara smiled. "*Settle* for the mayor. I like that."

"And your last request?"

"Not a deal breaker, but the DHS caseworker . . ." Shara said and paused. "One minute I feel for her. The next I wonder why the hell should I care. If she's not personally part of the problem, there's more she could have — *should* have — done. I leave it up to you, but if she can bring you dirt on her supervisors — help your case — can you see that she keeps her job?"

"I'll go for the whole ball of wax and see what we can get. The caseworker makes an act of contrition, as the Catholics say, I'll fight for her. She's gotta meet me halfway, though."

"Your fee—" Shara started.

Winkler again waved his hand dismissively.

"Fee-schmee. The fee will be included in the settlement. Now, you offer to let me pinch your pert little ass, I won't say no. Other than that, you've offered more than enough." He picked up a handful of papers and waved them in disgust. "I haven't kicked ass in I don't know how long. This will be my pleasure."

"You can have my pert little ass when you can catch me," Shara said with a smile.

"Can't blame a man for trying."

Half an hour later, she had given him all the specifics he needed and agreed to bring Kimberly Watts to his office at 3 p.m.

At the door she looked at him, as he attacked a cream-filled donut. "Thanks, Arnie. I owe you."

Again, a dismissive wave. "It's you *I* owe. Now off with you before I give chase for that pinch," he said with a wink.

For Everett Gaines, Shara chose a lawyer who was the polar opposite of Arnie Winkler; though as she thought about it, they shared more in common than either would care to admit.

For Gaines she wanted a lawyer *so good* in court the prosecution would be forced to offer a favorable plea. Douglas Frazier fit the bill. What made the DA's office grimace when facing Douglas Frazier was the passion and sympathy he exuded to the jury on behalf of his client. Shara had observed several of his closing arguments, and even if she were certain his client were guilty, she felt swayed by his conviction; and there was *no one* more cynical than she. Frazier had a lot going for him with Everett Gaines, and she felt the DA's office wouldn't want to lock horns with him in court.

Good as Frazier was with a jury, he was also a master at coaxing a favorable plea bargain. After all, he had no qualms taking a case to the jury, or so he inferred.

Shara had to admit she also chose Frazier because he was black. A former basketball star at the University of Pennsylvania, he'd only gotten into the school because of an academic scholarship. At six-foot two-inches, he was a good college point guard who knew he would never make it to the pros. He had no desire anyway. But dealing with the media after games, had been a good learning experience, he'd told her, for someone going into law.

With skin the color of chocolate mousse, clean-shaven and wearing suits that at forty-five years of age hid his still muscular body, he was non-threatening to white jurors. To blacks, he was a local success story: North Philly boy makes good, but doesn't turn his back on his roots. It didn't hurt that he was a good family man, with three children, which he somehow always mentioned in both his opening and closing statements.

Shara had gotten to know Frazier at a weekly poker game with Shelly Burke and Rudy. Burke was the bailbondsman who had given her her first big break; Rudy the bounty hunter who had been her mentor.

The fourth chair went to any number of people who happened to be available, and Shara had wormed her way into the games when she was in town.

Shara enjoyed the games as much for what she observed of the others as from the game itself. She saw that Frazier clearly had Shelly and Rudy's number. When the cards were going against him, he played conservatively, leaving just a few bucks shy of what he brought. When lady luck smiled on him he attacked with the same fervor he shared with a jury.

After losing one or two big pots, Shelly would throw caution to the wind, Shara noted, to regain the upper hand. Rudy was more cautious, but sometimes he, too, got caught up in the moment and on those days also went home a big loser.

Shara, for her part, enjoyed being one of the guys. The money she won or lost never reached higher than a few hundred dollars for the night, and she viewed it akin to paying her dues. When Frazier got on a roll, she tried to read him. She thought she could, but more often than not she went home far lighter than she had come.

Her meeting with Frazier was short and to the point. She laid out the facts and he agreed to represent the man, though he wanted to speak to him personally before formally committing.

"Who'll be paying his fee?" Frazier asked, as they finished. "I'll need a five thousand dollar retainer, which should cover the case *if* we don't go to trial."

"I'll guarantee the retainer," Shara said.

"Meaning what?"

"Briggs' defense fund has brought in a lot of money he won't need. Much of it is cash from people who wanted to remain anonymous. I'm hoping Briggs will offer to help Everett Gaines."

"Kind of like a political endorsement from a candidate dropping out of the race," Frazier said with a smile.

"Exactly. If he refuses, I'll pay — in cash."

"Then it's settled, again, after I've met with Mr. Gaines."

"Just one more thing," Shara said, as he began to rise, signaling the end of their meeting. Friendly as he was when they played poker, he was formal and all business on the job. No chit-chat. No ribbing. No jokes. Shara told him about the civil case. "Can you coordinate with Arnie Winkler?"

Shara knew some lawyers viewed Winkler with disdain, probably mixed with a healthy dose of envy. She didn't know where Frazier stood.

"Work with, no. Coordinate, surely. Arnie and I work different sides of the street, so to speak. He's a lot like you — transformed liabilities into assets. I respect that. He's not trying to be something he's not and he's not bitter that he can't spin his magic before a jury. We can co-exist," he assured her with a smile.

*   *   *

Now all Shara had to do was convince Deidre that Everett Gaines was another of Biggie Shaw's victims. She wanted to be straight with Deidre. Deep down, though, she knew if Deidre balked, Shara would pursue her own agenda, even if it meant further duplicity.

Shara came back down to earth with the sound of a key in the lock.

When Deidre entered at 4:10 p.m. and saw Shara she didn't look like a happy camper.

"What do you want, Shara?" Deidre said, without offering a greeting.

"Who says I want anything? Can't I just come by to visit?"

"Visitors don't break in," Deidre said, not taking a seat, keeping distance between Shara and herself.

Shara held up a key.

Deidre shook her head. "I gave you that key, what . . . six months ago, when you first came back. When you and Lysette moved into Jonas' apartment I forgot all about it. You can have a key and still be breaking in." She shook her head, as if talking to a child. "You haven't changed a bit," she said with hostility in her voice. "Friends don't invade your privacy. So, what do you want?"

Shara flipped the key to Deidre, a symbol of surrender. She didn't want an argument over a silly key. Didn't want an argument at all. She looked at Deidre curiously as the key bounced off her purse and onto the floor. Deidre looked at it, as if unsure whether to pick it up. Didn't, then glared at Shara. Why? Shara wondered.

"Why so testy?" she asked. "I was . . . inconsiderate, okay. But a tongue-lashing? Such hostility?" She shook her head in bewilderment.

"You just don't get it. What if I walked in with a man? You being here, it would be awkward to say the least. What if we were taking a shower? What if we were in the bedroom fucking our brains out and didn't hear you? Just because you don't have a life doesn't mean I'm not moving on."

"You're seeing someone?" Shara asked, filled with curiosity.

Deidre looked at her with exasperation. "That's not the point. You can't waltz in whenever you please like you own the place."

"You *are* seeing someone," Shara said. It was no longer a question.

Deidre looked at Shara, as if debating whether to open up, but finally relented. Her face lit up as she spoke. With no close friends that Shara knew of, Deidre must have been bursting to tell somebody. Suddenly, Shara's uninvited entrance was forgotten . . . if not forgiven.

"I'm seeing someone from work. There. Satisfied?"

Shara bent forward. "So tell me."

"He . . . Stuart, he's a reporter. He was originally from Philly, but moved to New York to run with the 'big dawgs' as he calls them. He worked at the *News* until there was a purge. Then it was over to the *Post* until politics there called for a house cleaning. Then back to the *News*. Six months ago he sensed another upheaval brewing and opted for stability here."

"Kind of like you," Shara said.

Deidre looked at her quizzically.

"You started at the *Daily News* and stayed there until . . . until you lost your family. You *must* have had other offers, but you opted for stability. Then a year at the mayor's office and back to the *Daily News*."

"So?"

"You're two peas in the same pod. You're both more interested in security than the free fall of risk-taking. Nothing wrong with that. Just an observation. Is it serious?"

"Serious enough that I think of him if he's not in my bed here, or if I'm not in his. I think of him — of his touch — and I get goose-bumps. I want to call him just to hear his voice. But I'm not going to jump in head first. This is the first time I've dated seriously since I lost my family. I'm kind of on the rebound."

"Rebound my ass," Shara said. "It's been three years. For once go with your heart."

"You're one to offer advice to the lovelorn," Deidre said, tartly, then laughed. "But enough about me. What *do* you want? I know you," she said with a genuine smile.

When she smiled, Shara thought Deidre Caffrey looked pretty. She could best be described as unremarkable. Medium height, with a decent enough body, though no one part jumped out at you. A nondescript face — a bit too pale without the right makeup. But her smile transformed her, as if it emanated throughout her entire body.

"I don't want anything. I *do* have something for you."

The smile left Deidre's face, replaced by an expression of stone. Shara couldn't blame her. The two had a history, after all.

"Briggs. I want you to help Briggs." She paused, but Deidre simply stared. "You never wrote anything about Briggs after he was arrested. Why? I knew he wasn't a friend, but you knew him. Respected him."

"My heart said he wouldn't have killed Shaw in cold blood. My head . . . ," she sighed. "The evidence against him was so compelling. And after what happened to Alexis still an open wound, it wasn't a stretch to imagine he could snap."

"He didn't do it," Shara said stating it as a fact.

"*You* know," Deidre said, with skepticism.

"I've found the killer. I did it for Alexis," she added.

Deidre shook her head. "Just like you. The police give up, but you're a hound dog. Give you a whiff and you dog your prey until you take him down. Again, why me? Why not turn him over to the police?"

"He asked to surrender to you. No, I take that back. *I* suggested he surrender to you. See, I'm being a good girl. No lies."

Deidre ignored the last. "In exchange for what?"

"Nothing, except that you hear him out."

"What aren't you telling me?"

"Shades of gray, Deidre, that's all. Hear him out, then decide for yourself how you'll write the story. He's not expecting special treatment. I think you'll find what he has to say . . . I don't know . . . intriguing."

"And you want nothing in return. I don't buy it."

"Peace of mind, okay?"

"No, more than that. He surrenders to me and you remain in the background, where you like it the most. *And*, you don't alienate the cops who look like fools. You need the cooperation of the police in your line of work. Make them look like assholes, you make enemies. You remain a shadow, you retain your credibility. Tell me I'm wrong."

Shara shrugged, as if she'd been caught with her hand in the cookie jar. Deidre didn't have a clue, but Shara would give her a small victory. If it opened a door for Everett Gaines it was well worth it.

"You got me, but I'm telling you, you *want* to hear this man's confession. It makes for a great story. No strings, though," Shara said, raising her hands in surrender.

"I'll hear him out," Deidre said with a sigh. "But just like you've told me often enough, whatever he says is fair game for me to use as I please."

She looked at her watch. "Have him down at the paper in an hour."

She picked up the key Shara had tossed her. "From now on you call ahead. Any possibility of a friendship ends the next time you enter my house unannounced. You know the way out."

She didn't wait for an answer, just walked to the bedroom. Probably to call her man, Shara thought.

NINE

In Deidre's editor's office — Deidre's office being a cubicle which afforded no privacy — Shara took the same seat she had when Lysette had surrendered to the police, with Deidre her conduit. For the next hour, she'd be little more than a fly on the wall.

"Mr. Gaines, how do I know you killed Biggie Shaw?" Deidre started.

Everett Gaines looked at Shara for help, but Shara remained silent. This was Deidre's show, on Deidre's turf. Her only role was that of an observer.

"Didn't Miss Farris tell you?"

"Look, Mr. Gaines," Deidre said, looking at him. They were both seated across from one another at a table her editor used for conferences. "Miss Farris knows her job. I have full confidence in her, yet if I run your story it's my reputation on the line. So *I* need some convincing. Tell me something only the police would know. Prove to *me* you're the killer."

He sat thinking for a moment, then brightened.

"The *gun*. I bought it on the street. Thought I'd be busted for *that*," he said, giving a bitter laugh. "I know this dude sold guns to just about anyone, but I imagined him a cop, just waiting to nail *me*. Anyway, the gun has two notches, like someone was keeping score. I didn't read anything about that in the papers."

"All right, Mr. Gaines," Deidre said. "I'll check it out later. I don't know what Miss Farris told you about me, but I'm not interested in a sad sob story. Even though Mr. Shaw may have been slime, you haven't reached a sympathetic ear. As far as I'm concerned you're a cold-blooded killer. I don't believe in vigilante justice," she said glancing briefly at Shara. "Convince me talking to you isn't a waste of time."

Shara hadn't seen this side of Deidre before. It was almost as if she were speaking to Shara *about* Shara. She was giving Gaines no slack. Treating him as if *she* were a cop. Though Gaines looked at her for solace, Shara said nothing, a mask of indifference painted on her face.

Whether it was Deidre's belligerence or unexpected hostility from someone he thought would be understanding, Everett Gaines looked like a cornered rat. He stood up, leaned across the table so his face was inches from Deidre's.

"Convince *you*!" he said, his voice simmering. "I'll bring my daughter in to *convince* you."

"No, *you* convince me Mr. Gaines," Deidre countered. "I have no soft spots in my heart for people who take the law into their own hands, and marching your daughter in here won't change my mind."

"You're cold," he said, shaking his head, and sat down. "Stone cold." He paused for a minute, then looked at Deidre. "After she was raped, my Ivy was a shell of herself. At home she stared vacantly at the television. At school when called upon, she didn't respond; not out of defiance, but she was reliving the rape and fearing that bastard Shaw would return. When she was given a test she'd turn in a blank paper."

"Sorry, Mr. Gaines," Deidre said. "Been there. Seen it — with Detective Briggs' daughter, as a matter of fact. But Briggs didn't shoot a man handcuffed to a fence, did he? I feel for you, I really do, but you had no right—"

"Ivy knew who raped her. *All* the girls did," Gaines said, interrupting her. He once again rose and began pacing the room, his eyes never leaving Deidre. "You know in the Mafia when they say someone is connected?" he asked.

Deidre nodded, but said nothing. Shara saw he had piqued her interest.

"Well, Biggie had friends and relatives — pushers, pimps, car thieves and ex-cons. Hell, he was a car thief himself. Boosted cars and everyone in the neighborhood knew he did. He told my Ivy if she dropped a dime on him, if he was arrested she was dead. First, though, they'd kill me, while she watched. Then they'd take turns with her. He was very graphic about what they'd do. Want me to spell it out for you Miss High-and-Mighty?"

"It's not necessary. Go on," Deidre said, and Shara could hear her voice breaking slightly. He'd reached her.

"Only *after* they were done violating her would they kill her. She told me this after the rape, then went silent. She was watching for my reaction. She saw me for the coward I was. I knew who Biggie hung with. I knew he weren't spinning no tales. They'd do it *and* enjoy it. And it gnawed at me each day; knowing who had violated my Ivy, yet too afraid to do anything. And Ivy knowing I couldn't protect her. You know what that does to a man?" he said, looking at Deidre.

*   *   *

Everett had gone back to work when Ivy returned to school, but his mind wasn't on his job. Coming home he would see Biggie Shaw. He thought the man deliberately sought him out to torment him.

"How's your daughter doing?" he'd ask, with a smile, his hand massaging his groin, and he laughed. "You make sure to give her my best, you hear."

The same thing for a week straight.

Then Everett thought Shaw had tired of taunting him. But he saw he was wrong. Saw Biggie eyeing Paula Carter. Same age as Ivy. She had gotten into some fancy private school in Center City. Her mother knew a ward leader who knew someone who knew someone else. Strings had been pulled and Paula no longer had to go to school in the neighborhood. Everett didn't begrudge her that. If he'd known someone, he would have done the same for Ivy.

Everett knew Paula would be next. He still had sick days and vacation time, and everyone at work had been really sympathetic. *Take all the time you need,* they told him. *Your family comes first.* He decided to keep tabs on Biggie. He didn't know what he would do if the man attacked Paula Carter, but he knew he couldn't let it happen.

He'd heard Mrs. Carter's car was in the shop, and she didn't have enough money for the repairs. Being in the seventh grade Paula wasn't eligible for free tokens so she had to walk to 22nd and Chestnut everyday.

For the first few days her mother walked her, but she had a job and couldn't walk her home.

Biggie didn't follow her *to* school. He would hang out in the crowded playground when school let out. There were plenty of parents around to pick up first and second graders. He just blended in, then followed Paula from a distance when she exited the building.

Instead of going straight home, Paula went to the Markwood Playground. The new equipment and frequent police patrols were a far cry from the neighborhood playground where addicts shot up, pushers plied their trade, and teenagers hit on anything with a skirt.

Paula seemed to lose herself on the swings. She'd pump higher and higher, sometimes staying on them for half an hour. Other times, she would give her swing to a younger child and gently push when asked. Most of the other kids were white, but no one shrank from her black skin. No panic-stricken mother demanded she stay away from her child. Paula would push a laughing child, a big smile on her face.

Biggie looked on, like Everett, close enough to see, yet not be spotted by Paula. The day of the attack it started to rain buckets without warning. The once-crowded playground emptied quickly with Paula alone by a building that housed bathrooms. At this time of year, they were locked.

Everett saw Biggie approach and knew what was to come next. He had called Detective Briggs a week and a half earlier. He'd seen an article about Briggs and how his daughter had been attacked. He knew the rage the detective must carry with him, if he were any kind of father. The same rage that coursed through Everett.

When he'd first called, Briggs told him it wasn't his case, yet he still gave Everett a number where he could reach him. Everett called that number now and told Briggs an attack was imminent. A plan had festered in his mind when he'd first started following Biggie. Though he didn't have the money to throw away, he had purchased a cellular phone. He was hopeful Briggs, seeing a child attacked — like his daughter — would snap and make sure Biggie Shaw never saw the inside of a jail cell alive. His own rage had been building only a few weeks. What must it be like for Briggs after more than a year, his daughter still little more than a vegetable, according to the papers? And the rapist had never been caught.

He watched as Biggie approached Paula. It looked like he was offering her a ride home. What did she have to fear? She knew him from the neighborhood. A charmer, especially with young girls, buying them ice cream and asking for nothing in return. With the playground deserted, he saw Biggie take out a knife and half drag Paula to a gate that led to the railroad tracks.

"C'mon Briggs," Everett said aloud, the wind-whipped rain almost blinding him. What would he do if Briggs didn't arrive in time? He touched the gun in his jacket pocket. Did he have the nerve? He didn't think so. Then he saw Biggie throw the girl down on the ground, weeds obscuring his vision. He *could*.

Would, if he had to. He couldn't just stand there, a voyeur.

He saw a car arrive and a man he recognized from the papers as Briggs get out. Saw him stealthily move towards the fence.

Move your ass, man! he wanted to yell out. Biggie could already be . . . but he tossed the thought from his mind.

He heard Briggs say something. Saw Biggie begin to run. Saw Briggs climb the fence and give chase.

"Shoot him!" Everett said aloud, but in the storm he couldn't be heard. "Kill him for your daughter. For Ivy."

He saw Biggie turn, then drop his knife and then Briggs was pummeling him. Saw him drag the unconscious body to the fence and cuff him, then run back to Paula.

No, Everett said to himself. *Don't you know Paula will never testify against him? He'll get off, free to rape again and again.*

Everett had made his way to the building Paula had sought for shelter. Now, crouched, he ran towards the gate, then through to where Briggs had left Biggie. He couldn't make out Briggs in the mist and rain.

He stood over the unconscious figure of Biggie Shaw, his hand on his gun. But, much as he wanted to, he couldn't. He cursed himself for his weakness and then saw Biggie open his eyes. Saw Biggie look up at him, blood flowing from his nose and mouth. Saw Biggie smile.

"How's that girl of yours, Everett?" he said, and coughed up blood. "Think I'll come around for seconds, soon as I'm healed."

Everett found the gun in his hand. Saw himself pulling the trigger. Saw Biggie's head explode; that damn smile wiped off his face. Then Everett ran.

＊   ＊   ＊

Shara saw Deidre hanging on Everett Gaines' every word. Convince her? He was doing a damn good job and had more to come. Shara had already heard the story.

"At home I told Ivy. She hugged me, cried, but now I was her savior. It wasn't just the rape. It was the fear that he would return. Seeing him every day strutting his stuff and no one could touch him. Seeing my helplessness. Killing him was the beginning of her recovery."

Everett had finally stopped his pacing. Now winding down he sat, eyes still glued on Deidre.

"When the police came to question me, I said I'd been with Ivy. She stared at the television when the detective spoke to her. When he turned away I saw her smile. It had been over a month since I'd seen that smile.

"They left, and she was almost her old self; proud she had duped the cops. Proud of her old man."

He'd run out of gas, but Deidre had questions for him.

"Why not come forward? Were you prepared to let an innocent man go to prison for something you did?"

"You don't get it, do you? I was caught between a rock and a hard place. Bad enough I come forward and Ivy ends up in foster care. No, I come forward and Biggie's friends and relatives make good on his threat. I didn't care what they would have done to me, but Ivy had been my life since my wife passed. In my mind," he said pointing to his head, "I was certain Detective Briggs' cop friends would cover for him. I was deluding myself, but you gotta understand it wasn't for *me*. All I thought about day and night was Ivy. Yet day after day dragged by and nothing. Knowing Detective Briggs was in jail was eating me up inside.

"Can't you see, though, I couldn't allow my Ivy to be harmed. You don't know these animals. Some are *worse* than Biggie. Every time my resolve weakened, I'd think of what they would do to my girl."

He paused, shaking his head, as if still debating with himself.

"I was almost relieved when Miss Farris found me out. I honestly don't know what I would have done if Detective Briggs was sentenced to prison. God forgive me, but I probably wouldn't have raised a finger. I know the contempt you must feel for me, but I was caught between a rock and a hard place. A rock and a hard place," he repeated, and Shara thought he was now talking to himself.

He looked at Deidre, but apparently there was nothing left to say. He just sat, as if awaiting judgment.

"What would you have me do, Mr. Gaines?" Deidre finally asked to break the silence.

"Tell my story. Nothing more. Condemn me if you want, but at least you got the truth. I'm not asking for anyone's forgiveness. I'm not asking that you help me. I just know you add the human element to a story. Maybe you can make others see my anguish. My dilemma. And understand my cowardice."

Deidre rose.

"I'd like to talk to Shara outside for a few minutes," she said, her voice no longer hostile.

"I'm not going noplace," he said, with a weak smile, looking old and worn.

"Can I get you something to drink?" Deidre asked, and Gaines shook his nead.

It was the first sign of compassion Shara had seen from Deidre.

Outside the conference room Deidre looked at Shara. "Is he the real deal?"

"The real deal," Shara said.

"You can corroborate his story — *all of it*?"

"That and more." She gave Deidre a copy of notes she had transcribed of all her interviews.

Deidre went through them quickly, then went over them again, commenting to herself out loud as she read. "Shaw a foster parent . . . *three times*! Jesus. . . . A wife that didn't exist. . . . He *told* Kimberly Watts what he did!" She shook her head in amazement. "Incredible," she finally said, when she was done.

"What do you plan to do?" Shara asked.

"For now . . . tell Gaines' story, when he turns himself in. He'll need a lawyer—"

"That's been taken care of," Shara said.

Deidre looked at her, but said nothing.

"Then I'll check out the rest," Deidre said, tapping the book Shara had given her.

"And . . . ? "

"Tell the whole sordid tale. Someone's got to expose DHS, or it will happen again."

"To expose DHS you have to parade out Biggie's three foster children. Haven't they suffered enough?"

"I won't divulge their names. They're minors."

"*They'll* know. Others will, too. There will be a feeding frenzy. You open up Pandora's Box, the rest of the media will want a piece of them," Shara said.

"So what would you have me do?" Deidre asked.

"Focus on Everett Gaines."

Deidre shook her head. "This story is much more than Everett Gaines. I'm not going to make any hasty decisions just yet. There's so much to digest. So much to follow up. You've done your job, now let me do mine. I'll tell the story, without interjecting my own biases. He'll come off sympathetic as hell, which is what you wanted. More than that I can't promise."

Shara sighed. She had tried. Almost gone too far, and aroused Deidre's suspicions. And she knew she couldn't bully Deidre. She would run with the story as she saw fit. Then again, maybe not. Her hand was on the doorknob when Deidre stopped her.

"What about Ivy?"

Shara smiled. Deidre had almost forgotten about the *real* victim.

"For the time being, she will stay with his in-laws. Gaines' wife died in childbirth. His mother's passed away and he never knew his father. His in-laws have health problems of their own, but for now they've agreed to care for her."

"At least she won't have to go to foster care," Deidre said, holding up the notebook. "I cringe at the thought."

TEN

Shara got precious little sleep that night. Asleep, she was back in the woods, chasing after the elusive blond; chasing herself. Awake, she awaited the call she knew she would be getting from Deidre. It came at 8:30 a.m. Less a call than a summons.

"Get your ass down to the paper now," Deidre said when Shara answered. There was a pause, then Deidre hung up.

Half-an-hour later Shara was back in the conference room, slouched in a chair across from Deidre. She would accept the tongue-lashing she knew was coming and hope for the best.

"You got some fucking nerve," Deidre said, her face red with anger. "You used me . . . *again*! I should have known last night. All this beating around the bush about what *I'd* do with the story, while you had it all planned out."

Shara looked up and Deidre must have thought she was going to defend herself. She waved her hand dismissively, then went on.

"I've just spent a wonderful forty-five minutes with your Arnold Winkler. You *did* hire him?"

Shara nodded.

"I don't like having my hands tied, Shara. You've put me in an awkward . . . no, an untenable position." She was no longer seated, but standing with her hands on the table staring down at Shara. "With the civil suit he's initiated, the way he tells it, if I go public about DHS he has no leverage. I go with *my* story, and I'm responsible for depriving Shaw's victims of remuneration and therapy. So I've got no story."

"No one's forcing your hand," Shara said, speaking for the first time. "I deceived you and I'm sorry—"

"I don't want to hear those words. You're *always* sorry when you stab me in the back. You don't seem to understand that with friendship comes loyalty. You want my friendship, want my trust, but it's a two-way street. You have to trust me, not go behind my back to manipulate me. You've never been loyal to me. And I always come back asking for more, fool that I am."

Shara had no rebuttal. What Deidre said was true.

"Write your story," Shara said. "You made no promises. I asked for none. You know how I feel. You're free to use whatever I gave you."

"*Bullshit*! You also know I don't live by your rules. I'm not going to see those children hurt for the sake of a story."

"So why am I here?" Shara asked, genuinely curious.

"So I can be rid of you once and for all," Deidre said. She paused and looked Shara in the eye. "You're a parasite, feeding off me, and I'm tired of being your host. Every time I put my faith in you, I'm rewarded by duplicity. It ends here. It ends now. Now get out."

Shara was shocked. She'd expected Deidre to be angry. She deserved Deidre's wrath. But she'd never assumed their friendship would be irrevocably damaged. She sat for a moment, unable to accept Deidre's dismissal.

"*Now!*" Deidre said, pointing towards the door.

Shara got up. *I didn't mean for it to turn out this way*, she was going to say, but knew it would ring hollow.

Deidre said nothing, just pointed to the door.

Shades of gray, Shara thought as she left. Deidre dealt in absolutes. Good and bad. Right and wrong. But life was shades of gray. It had cost Shara a friend, and she had far too few already. She had had her way with Deidre once again, yet she was more depressed than ever.

ELEVEN

The abruptness with which Deidre had dismissed Shara from her life left Shara numb. She'd expected the hostility, anger and bitterness, but after Deidre had vented, Shara thought she would be forgiven — as always. But this had a tone of finality Shara had never envisioned.

She walked aimlessly for hours, her mind blank to ward off the pain. Cramped sidewalks were teeming with Christmas shoppers. Shara often wondered why these people weren't at work. It wasn't just at Christmas. Whenever she was in Center City there were an awful lot of well-dressed people who *should* have been working. Parks were generally crowded, and not just with vagrants and retirees. For a city where white flight had accelerated to near epidemic proportions, regardless of attempts to lure people back from the 'burbs, the city always seemed bustling to her; with stores jammed, malls packed and thirty-something people with free time on their hands.

Don't you people work? she wanted to shout out any number of times.

Her mind in the clouds, she must have seemed a sight as she bumped into one person, only to stumble into another and be jarred by a third as she got in their path. "Pardon me" tumbled out of her mouth a dozen times, met by "Watch the fuck where you're going," "Get the fuck out of my way," or other similar terms of endearment.

Looking at her watch, she saw it was noon. She thought about getting a drink — several actually — but she had to be clearheaded when she picked Briggs up at Graterford Prison at four-thirty that afternoon.

She needed someone to talk to — a *friend* — and found herself in her car driving down City Line Avenue, making a right onto West Chester Pike in Haverford, approaching Club Aphrodisia and Lysette.

She hadn't seen Lysette in at least two and a half months — since she'd begun her new career — but Shara knew she didn't need an appointment. She knew Lysette would be there for her as she had been there for Lysette after she had been attacked by the albino.

Walking into the club, where she had been an assistant manager while Lysette had been in a coma, Shara instantly sensed something amiss. You work at a place for a while, you get a sense of its rhythm. The mood of the club had changed since she'd left; a subtle change to be sure, but one she noticed immediately.

She had enjoyed the month-and-a-half she'd worked at Aphrodisia. It had been a welcome diversion after several tension-filled months. And she'd found she was good at her job. She had a relaxed management style, yet still commanded loyalty and respect. New at the game, she readily delegated authority. As a result, others weren't aware of her shortcomings and, being able to make decisions, employees felt a greater sense of self-worth.

Moreover, she was a people person, when in her element. She regaled these upscale strippers — *exotic dancers* they liked to be called — with stories from her days at Frank's seedy strip joint on Market Street, where she'd danced. And she had tales about Jil, who had trained her and was now the manager of three clubs including Aphrodisia, that had the girls and bouncers alike in stitches.

Being a good listener helped, too. Girls with boyfriend problems, money problems and babysitter problems found a sympathetic ear. They told her of relatives and neighbors who snubbed them when they found out their daughter, cousin or neighbor was a stripper and how they felt conflicted. She heard them out, though she offered advice sparingly. Just getting their problems out in the open was a balm for their wounds, she found. She would get more credit than she deserved just by listening and asking the odd question or two that gave them pause for thought.

It was not to be her life's work — that she knew — but it was a massage to her ego to learn she was good at something other than hunting.

Lysette's management style must have been far different. Formal. Stiff. Strained. Those words came to mind, as Shara looked around, especially at the employees. They were going about their business as if looking over their shoulders for fear of being upbraided.

She saw Jil standing by one of the banisters, likewise appraising the workings of the club. Shara made her way over and the two women embraced. A former dancer herself, Jil still had a killer body, though she was approaching forty.

"And you, how are you doing?" she responded to Shara's question, looking at Shara with concern.

"Hanging in there," Shara shrugged.

"Never could bullshit me, Shara. Something's eating at you. Tell Mama."

Shara smiled as she recalled Jil's pet command. *Tell Mama*. When Shara was fourteen and dancing at Frank's illegally, Jil not only trained her, but looked out for her like a mother hen. When the weight of going to school and working to keep off the streets wore on her, Jil was always there with, "Tell Mama what's wrong." Just talking made her problems seem inconsequential. Jil, too, was a good listener.

"Ever do something you had to, something you knew was right," Shara asked now, "yet had to sacrifice something else you held dear?"

"I gave up my freedom for the security I have here, but that's not what you're talking about, is it?" Jil answered.

"You always could read me," Shara said with a weak smile. "I lost someone today — a good friend. I don't know if she'll ever forgive me and it hurts. I had no choice, though. I had to betray her for . . ." she shrugged, "the greater good, I guess. Still, she was a friend. And I'd done it before to her. Each time she bounced back. Today, though, she'd had enough of me. It hurts, Jil. Hurts bad."

"So you thought you'd come by and visit some old friends," Jil said. "Visit Lysette," she said, giving Shara a mock pout.

"Don't be feeling neglected, now. Yeah, I'm here to see Lysette, but spilling my guts to you *has* made me feel better. Just like in the old days."

She now looked to where Lysette was working the room, busily talking into a headset. "So, how's our girl doing?" she asked Jil.

"She's a work in progress, but more than holding her own."

"Then why are you here?"

"Making sure she's up to the task. It's my ass on the line. I'm leaving nothing to chance."

"She seems different than before," Shara said, her eyes on her friend. Lysette had been a dancer who was abruptly made an assistant manager when the media learned she was The Nightwatcher. With an impending trial Jil knew some overzealous photographer would be looking to take a photo of Lysette dancing nude. So Lysette had received a promotion, and a huge cut in pay, somewhat against her will. Two months later she was in a coma and Shara had temporarily taken over, as a favor to Jil.

"She is different," Jil said. "She's more hands on. She does more than she should — a lot on her own time — but she seems to thrive on it."

"There's more to it than that," Shara said. "Isn't there?"

"Well, she seems to need to be around others, though she's detached and aloof — if that makes any sense. With what she's been through, it's to be expected. Last time she was thrust into the job with no preparation. And she had other things on her mind. She was feeling her way around, walking on eggshells. She now knows with her celebrity status she can never dance again, yet she wants to stay in the business. She's taken her promotion more seriously this time around and is working at it just as she did with her dancing. This time she showed right away who was boss. Made an example of a couple of girls who had gotten into bad habits and the rest started to toe the line."

Jil took out a stick of gum. She had once been a heavy smoker, and when she stopped she still had to have something in her mouth. "She knows she's no longer one of the girls," she went on. "She's management, so she keeps her distance. It's not your style, Shara, but it seems to work for her."

"Then why do you sound like you miss the old Lysette?"

Jil shrugged. "She's doing a good job, but I wonder if she's getting any joy out of it. As a dancer and during her first stint as assistant manager, she laughed, teased and took teasing in stride. Now it's a job — joyless. Look, Shara, she needs balance. A little more of the old, a little less of the new. It'll come with time, believe me."

After saying goodbye Shara made her way over to Luther, head of security. She'd heard from management, and wanted to see if the employees felt the same way. Jil's words hadn't had the desired effect of assuaging her feeling that things weren't right at the club — weren't right with Lysette.

Luther — Lou to his friends, but Sweets to Shara — gave her a bear hug when she came over.

"You're a sight for sore eyes, Little One," he said, when he finally let her go. "And boney, as ever. When you gonna put some meat on those bones?" he asked, after scrutinizing her.

Only Shara called Luther Sweets and only he called her Little One.

Luther was a former Olympic wrestler who had joined the World Wrestling Federation, but hated the travel. Physically he looked a lot like Briggs — big, black, shaved-head and well-chiseled body — but behind the hard exterior, and when he was not on duty, he smiled often and eagerly. Unlike Briggs, he had a good sense of humor and didn't take himself too seriously. He was a Teddy Bear, albeit a lethal one.

"Our girl any different?" Shara asked, nonchalantly, looking at Lysette who was still pacing like a caged tiger.

"She's gone through hell, girl, so sure she's different. She's no longer one of *us*." The last he said lowering his voice.

"What's that mean?"

"She's less tolerant of mistakes and more likely to kick some ass if you cross her. Bullshit her and you're out on your behind. And don't be looking for sympathy because your old man dumped you."

"That doesn't sound like the Lysette I knew," Shara said.

"She's become a bit of an Ice Maiden. She needs to be around others, you know, but she's not part of what's going on. There's no desire to get close to anyone. But hell, who can blame her, after all she's lost. I don't know if I'd want to get close to people if I'd gone through what she has."

"So her management style is dictatorial; my way or the highway?" Shara said.

"That's a bit harsh," he said and mulled it over. "She knows what she is and compensates. She hired Grace," he said, nodding his head at a willowy blond with a headset on. "She's no great intellect, and she's not upper management material, but she's a real people person. When Lysette gives you hell, Grace provides a shoulder to cry on."

Luther stopped, looked at Shara and laughed. That was unlike Briggs, too. Sweets had a deep throaty laugh.

"Shit girl, I've opened up to you more in ten minutes than to Lysette since she's returned. You always were a good listener. Look, with time Lysette will thaw. At least that's my take. Got any jobs for me?" he added, flashing his smile.

Shara recalled taking Sweets on a job with her. She had been tracking a six-foot seven-inch lummox who had gotten into one too many bar brawls and had seriously injured someone. She'd hunted him down, but there was no way she could bring him in alone. She'd taken Sweets as backup, with a promise of a quick hundred dollars.

She had Sweets hide behind a dumpster while she confronted the fool, as he was urinating in an alley behind a bar he'd just left. She wanted to take him in without Sweets' help. She kicked him in the balls, then used brass knuckles to hit him in the solar plexus, but he had laughed, picked her up and thrown her into the dumpster.

Saying to hell with her wounded pride, she'd called for the cavalry — Sweets.

Sweets let the other man be the aggressor, and soon he tired himself out without so much as connecting with Sweets once. Sweets then made quick work of him, without doing any real damage.

On the way to the police station they both sat in the backseat of the car talking good-naturedly about boxing and wrestling. Ended up pals.

Since then Shara had used mace, stun guns and anything else available to get an edge. She didn't really need Sweets, but every so often threw him a bone, because he got off on the action.

"I may soon have a partner, Sweets. Big as you, but not as good-looking," she said with a smile. "And not as good company," she added. "If it doesn't work out, you'll be the first to know. Promise."

Lysette must have seen them talking, because Sweets abruptly was listening intently to his headset.

"Gotta go, Little One," he said, his smile gone. "Got orders from the boss — for the both of us. Me, back to my job, you to the Queen's office."

Shara followed Lysette into her office on the second floor in silence. Lysette had eyed her suspiciously when she approached. Unlike with Jil or Sweets, there had been no greeting, no embrace after a long separation among friends. When Shara had approached, Lysette simply turned around and led the way. *Ice Maiden* Sweets had called her. What the hell had gotten into her? Shara wondered.

Lysette let Shara go into her office first, not to be polite but, as Shara observed, so she could keep the door slightly ajar. Shara remembered both Jil and Sweets saying she had to be around people. And the long hours. She didn't want to be alone. She was still haunted by her demons, Shara thought.

"You checking up on me, Shara?" Lysette asked accusingly. No *how are you. How have you been. You're looking good* or *a sight for sore eyes*. No smile, just the accusation. And she played with a lock of her hair with her finger, something Shara had never seen her do before.

"You mean with Sweets?"

Lysette looked at her quizzically.

"Luther to you. I worked here for almost three months, remember. Sweets . . . *Luther*, was a shoulder to lean on. Where I danced, the owner was the bouncer, a dancer's best friend. Here, Sw — *Luther* filled that role for *me*."

"And Jil?"

"Christ, girl, I knew Jil long before you. I told you she trained me, but she was much more. I put up a good front, but at first I was scared shitless. One of the men I was dancing for could attack me like the bastard who killed my friend. Jil was my security blanket. She was more of a mother than my biological mother. I shouldn't say hello to them?"

"So you *weren't* checking up on me?" Lysette asked, apparently not mollified.

Shara had come in need of a friend after losing Deidre, and here she was facing an inquisition instead. Control your temper, she told herself before answering. And be straight with her.

"I won't lie to you. Sure, I asked about you. I was concerned . . . *as a friend*. Satisfied?"

"Did I pass muster?"

"You did with them."

"What's that mean?"

"You no longer talk *to* people, but *at* them. You spend most of your waking hours here. You're aloof—"

"I admit I'm not the same naive woman who managed the club the first time," Lysette cut in. "I was plucked out of my element and thrown to the lions against my will. So, I was close with the girls, with the help, with Luther. But I was wrong. I'm no longer one of them. I'm management and I have to maintain a distance. I can't be their friend and their boss. Hell, I'll have to fire some of them. If I act like I'm their friend, then can their sorry ass, it's like I'm stabbing them in the back."

"So you become a queen bitch?" Shara shot back and instantly regretted it.

"That what Jil said? And Luther?" she asked, that lock of her hair wrapped tightly around her finger.

"No, I'm talking about the person speaking to me now. God, girl, you've changed."

"Damn right. And for the better."

"What about your past?"

"What about it?"

"You're in denial."

"Because I want to move forward?" Lysette said, with venom. "Sorry, Shara but I want to outrun the horrors of my past, not relive them. I'm not the Lysette you left three months ago."

"Tell me," Shara said with sarcasm.

"I'm *becoming* Lysette," she said, ignoring the remark. "The Cassandra in me had been coming out; a woman with self-confidence to balance the straight-as-an-arrow Lysette. Then I found the Angel in me — brash, devilish, selfish. She's part of me, too. I'm trying to get comfortable with all of them, because they're all me."

"At the expense of those who helped you before your *becoming*?"

"If need be," she said, with no trace of emotion in her voice, looking directly at Shara, as if waiting for a challenge.

"What about Alexis? You've totally abandoned her."

Lysette had been the first to take Alexis into the healing woods. Shara had assumed the task when Lysette had gone into her coma.

"She's a child. I reached out to comfort her. She has you now. She no longer needs me."

"And me?" Arguing about Alexis was fruitless.

"You saved my life — my sanity — when I could have gone into the attic of my mind for good. For that I'll always be grateful. But you're looking for a soulmate; someone to share with, someone just like yourself. And that's not me. My secret's out. I have nothing more to hide, nothing to share. We're not as much alike as you'd like to think. Look, I don't want to hurt you, but I can't be what you want — what you *need*. I don't want to share your angst, your misery. I know it's being selfish, but it's what I need now to be me. To *become* Lysette. And right now that means excluding you."

She got up before Shara could reply and walked towards the door.

"I've got a job to do. Search my desk if you want. Poke around the club to your heart's content. Look for something to tell you I've gone off the deep end, if it helps. Then leave me be."

With that she left.

Shara was devastated. First Deidre — with justification — and now Lysette in the same day. She felt like a leper, being shunned by all she held dear.

She walked out to her car and tried to start the engine, but her hands were shaking so badly she couldn't turn the key. She sat and cried.

*   *   *

Watching from the dance floor, Lysette saw Shara leave. She wondered why she had snapped so at Shara, for all intents and purposes severing their friendship. It was the Angel in her, she knew, speaking through the tough-as-nails take-no-prisoners Cassandra.

Lysette had just been along for the ride. In becoming Lysette she had difficult choices to make. Angel was the most selfish element within her; that part of her who had lost out on her adolescence and most demanded moving forward. And the Angel in her was right. Sure Shara had done so much for her; had been there for her. But she couldn't live in the past. It was time to move on and Shara wasn't ready to do so. Shara would hold her back. Shara would dwell on the past, the darkness within Lysette that had three times threatened to consume her. Angel wouldn't allow that.

Lysette turned away from the door, and got back into the rhythm of the club. A chapter in her life had ended. She was one step closer to *becoming* Lysette.

* * *

Shara wasn't immediately aware of Jil's presence. She was startled to see her, looking at her with a sad smile.

"I've only seen you cry once before," Jil said.

Shara looked at her. "It's not something I do often. I honestly can't recall the last time I broke down like this."

"I do. Not when the first Shara was attacked. Not when she refused to go to the hospital. Not when you couldn't nurse her back to health. Not even when she was buried. And not when I trained you and did all in my power to dissuade you from dancing."

Shara could see Jil's eyes go moist, as she continued.

"No, I saw you cry after your first night on stage. I didn't intrude. You had to grieve and grieve alone. That first night was your release, and you could mourn the loss of your friend."

Shara shook her head, and composed herself.

"I wasn't grieving for her, Jil. She made me promise not to before she died. It was then, after that first night dancing, I *knew* I could go on, as she would have wanted. And only then did I realize how alone I was. I had no one to share my triumph with, my fears, my joy. The only person I could ever confide in was gone, and a loneliness you could never imagine engulfed me. If I were Lysette, I would have retreated to my attic."

"And now?"

"I'm alone again. I thought Lysette . . . ," she started, then paused, and tears again threatened to break out. "But Lysette wants to bury the past and I'm part of that past."

"There's me," Jil said, and Shara thought she detected a sadness in her voice, almost a longing.

"You were always there for me, Jil, but I don't know . . . maybe it's the difference in our ages or your self-assuredness, but I look at you as a mother figure," she said with a forced laugh. "There are just some things you don't tell your mother."

Jil squeezed Shara's arm. "I'm here if you need me."

Shara held on when Jil attempted to let go. "My life's a mess, Jil. What do I do?"

"You go on, Shara. You just go on."

Still Shara wouldn't let go.

"Keep an eye on Lysette, will you? I don't like what I see. She's ripe for another fall."

Jil shook her head. "I'm concerned, too, but she's strong like you, in a different way."

"Keep an eye on her, nevertheless. You know how to reach me if she crashes."

Jil gave Shara a kiss on the cheek. "Have no fear. I watch after *all* my children," and she walked back to the club.

Shara sat in her car, but shed no more tears. She knew Lysette hadn't been entirely off base. Shara *was* looking for a soulmate. She was looking for someone who shared her pain, someone with secrets that couldn't be revealed to anyone but her. Lysette no longer fit into that category. As much as they had in common — childhood trauma, rape, a killing spree — they were different. Lysette hadn't stalked. And she had purged herself of her demons. Shara's demons still haunted her; ruled her.

Shara had hit rock bottom. She had tried desperately to rebuild her life. With her half-brother dead, she *should* have been able to move on, but she seemed mired in cement. Worse, those she had allowed to get close now turned their backs on her. The optimist in her said she had nowhere to go but up. The pessimist wondered.

Shara thought about returning to her home, to her playroom, but it was time to pick up Briggs. With concentration, though, she was able to go through a workout in her mind.

While built to keep her in shape, Shara found her playroom most useful whenever life sent her sprawling. And if she ever needed the playroom, it was now.

She had constructed it herself over a two month period, shortly after moving into her home. It had cost nearly $100,000. She made the money on the stock market. Her year in exile, as she liked to call it, had been spent as a deputy sheriff in a small town just north of Allentown, Pennsylvania.

She had felt like a fugitive in the Witness Protection Program. She spent a lot of her time by herself, with herself, trying to better get to know herself. Only now did she understand she hadn't gotten to know herself at all. She had socialized, but only minimally to avoid suspicion, and had made no close friendships. Most of her time she had spent educating herself.

Shara had taught herself almost all she knew. There were no colleges that taught stripping. You learned on the job. There were no trade schools you could major in murder, yet she had committed six undetected. And she'd taught herself most of what she knew about computers. Her hobby in exile, though, was playing the stock market. She'd read every book she could get her hands on, scoured the pages of *The Wall Street Journal* and *Business Week*, listened to radio programs where so-called experts analyzed specific stocks and trends. She had spent countless hours on the Internet, reading and chatting anonymously with others.

She had then applied what she'd learned, first as a game without actually committing any money. She found she had an aptitude for sensing mergers before they were actually announced, as well as recognizing trends such as the tremendous growth of the Internet. With growing confidence, she began to invest her savings and salary, seeing her money double, triple, even quadruple within a short period of time. She could have made a fortune, but she had no real use for money and, being self-destructive, she had sometimes taken risks that had backfired.

When she had returned to Philly, her needs had changed and she invested more cautiously. Her home was paid for by the market and so was her playroom. And, when she needed money quickly, she used another acquired skill — hacking. No matter how often the media trumpeted the lack of privacy on the Internet, advice was ignored. If Shara *knew* a company was going to merge, for example, and she needed to know when to strike, she would just read the e-mail of company executives. Even those who took precautions at the office, were seldom as vigilant at home. Shara thus knew when to buy, got the money she needed and got out, even if the stock hadn't reached its peak. She wasn't greedy. She wasn't into having a good deal of money for the proverbial rainy day, just for immediate needs. Anyway, it was more fun playing the game all over again when she needed money.

It was how she planned to pay Briggs, if he accepted her offer.

Money wasn't an issue for Shara. It was simply a means to an end.

She had seen the need for someplace to exercise in her home, initially because she abhorred the fake camaraderie at local athletic and health clubs. She didn't want to exercise with others. She didn't want to be hit upon at the co-ed clubs and she was even less interested in trading gossip with women at clubs that excluded men. And no club could give her the intense workout she desired. She craved exercise for the soul as well as for the body.

Just as with the stock market, Shara had taken a self-taught crash course in electronics and soon she was transforming her entire basement, leading up to a room on the first floor. She referred to her creation as her playroom. It was as much an obstacle course as a room for physical fitness and could be deadly. Only she could get into it by using her palm print. And once in, she couldn't get out until she completed the regimen. There was no-fail safe device, no kill switch, no safety valve. Once in, she had to successfully complete her routine or die.

The basement walls were covered with thick foam padding, painted over with a mirror-like substance, so she was always eyeing herself. Naked, so she could see the tattooed eyes that symbolized the destruction of her tortured youth, she began boxing herself in the mirror, working up a good sweat.

But what was boxing without an opponent, a worthy adversary? She would next harness herself so she could move laterally and forward, but back only a few inches. A dozen fists flew at her from one section of the wall, sensors determining her body position. If she fought defensively, the fists were programmed to become more aggressive. Only when she gave as good as she got was she equal to her opponent, the image she saw in the mirror. She would hit herself, inflict punishment on herself or literally be pummeled by the Shara who stared back at her.

Music blared from speakers she had set up. Her anthem was Gloria Gaynor's "I Will Survive."

Once out of the harness, the room was programmed to give her exactly one minute to recuperate and get water before she met her next obstacle; flying styrofoam and whiffle balls, wrapped with foam used to make Nerf balls. Balls whizzed by her from the ceiling while others attacked from the floor. Those on the ceiling, guided by sensors, were aimed at her head and body. From the floor leather whips flew back and forth to ensnare her like the tentacles of an octopus. She had to be agile enough to keep away from the tentacles from below and bat away flying fists from above.

After thirty minutes it was time to go up to the next level by climbing a staircase similar to a stairmaster. The stairs moved like a windmill, propelled by her own motion as she tried to climb. If she wasn't up to the task, she would never reach the top.

Having left the basement, she was in a target room. Facing her would-be targets of herself that appeared at random from anyplace in the room. Equipped with a laser gun, she had to destroy versions of herself before they returned fire. When she was hit, it was with a numbing electrical current. Once she had defeated herself, her opposition then assaulted her with whiffle balls, the final test on the obstacle course. Sweat would be pouring from her and she'd be sapped of energy, but she would have to go on. The balls shot at her could cause serious damage.

She had only a heavily padded mitt to bat the balls away.

To her left and right were handguns she could use to shoot balls at the target in return. They were held in place by electromagnets, and without warning a bell would ring, giving her five seconds to retrieve a gun and fire at her assailants. She had but ten balls to hit each of the ten targets on her first attempt, with no margin for error. She had never been successful. Intermingled with the images of herself firing at her were innocents — Deidre, Lysette and Alexis. If she missed herself or mistakenly fired at one of her friends who had no weapon, she would have to start anew. More balls were launched at her each time at greater velocity. The balls would pelt her, with only the mitt for protection, the bell giving her five seconds to get the gun. This time the gun contained eleven shots, allowing her one miscue. And on and on, until she had twelve, thirteen or fourteen shots. The tradeoff for more bullets was she would first have to withstand a fusillade of shots aimed her way with increasingly greater force.

When she finally destroyed the ten images of herself, the door allowing her to exit the room would open, leading to a shower.

Her playroom; a survival course for the damned. Defeat herself, she felt, and she could meet anything thrown at her on the outside. Physically, maybe, but it hadn't prepared her for the emotional assaults she had faced that day.

Only she knew of its existence; and, of course Alexis. And Alexis' knowledge of the playroom had almost severed another relationship.

She had been in the woods with Alexis after capturing a fugitive several months earlier.

"Show me your playroom," Alexis asked, in her flat, emotionless voice. Her eyes, though, were filled with curiosity.

"What are you talking about?" Shara asked, knowing exactly what Alexis was referring to.

"Your playroom. Pleasure and pain." She paused, in thought. "No, pleasure *is* pain," but her eyes showed confusion. Then finally, "Pain is pleasure," and she repeated it over and over, as if she'd had a revelation.

"Don't go there, Alexis. Let it be."

"Pain is pleasure? Show me." The words carried no emotion, but her eyes were beseeching.

Shara was suddenly furious. "*Everyone* deserves their secrets,

Alexis, yet I can hide nothing from you. You're always peering into my mind, girl. Can't you tell when you should let something be?"

Alexis said nothing, but Shara saw the pout of a child in her eyes.

"Fine. Let's go, then. Now!" She led Alexis out of the woods, the only place she could communicate like a normal human being. Shara wanted Alexis to feel the pain of being unable to communicate, to feel the helplessness that drove the girl to distraction. Out of the woods, Alexis was totally dependent on Shara. The woods were her salvation, and Shara now shamelessly deprived her of what she'd longed for to make a point.

She took Alexis to her playroom and put her in a corner where she would be safe. She wondered if she had constructed this one area, knowing one day she would bring Alexis here. She had never availed herself of this sanctuary. It would have been a sign of weakness.

She began boxing herself in the mirror, all the while berating Alexis.

"Everyone, Alexis . . . needs their space."

Jab. Jab. Punch.

"We all need privacy. All need secrets . . . we share with no one until we're ready."

Jab. Jab. Punch.

"I don't need you constantly dissecting me."

Jab. Jab. Punch.

"Let me have a little piece of me for *me*." She looked at Alexis, staring at her. "Sometimes, Alexis, I need you to leave me the hell alone."

Jab. Jab. Uppercut.

She went through her routine in the basement, then carried Alexis up the steps that were like climbing a down escalator. What a fool she had been, she thought. What if she couldn't make it up the stairs with Alexis? There was no way she would ever leave Alexis alone in the basement. They would both survive or perish. *What a selfish bitch you are, Shara*, she thought.

She closed her eyes and climbed, ignoring the pain and finally reached the top.

The target room was just as dangerous for Alexis. Shara could deflect the balls with her mitt, but she would have to leave Alexis to get the gun. Alexis would be defenseless.

"Curl yourself into a ball when I go for the gun," she told the girl.

The bell rang and Shara was separated from Alexis, knowing every shot must be on target. This time it had to be ten out of ten. But her concentration suffered with the presence of Alexis and she unintentionally shot the figure of Alexis.

Balls bombarded both Alexis and Shara. She couldn't shield Alexis or she'd be out of reach of the next gun.

She had to ignore Alexis. Stay focused. Ignore her friend to save her friend. The bell. The gun. She had eleven shots now, but needed only ten. She was no longer fighting for herself.

She guided Alexis out of the room, bypassed the showers, and sat Alexis on a couch in the living room.

"I'm sorry. I don't know what got into me," Shara said.

"I got into you," Alexis signed, though her hands shook. "I asked for too much. Wanted too much of you. You're right, I allow you no secrets. But I can't help myself. I have no on and off switch. But being down there with you was exhilarating. So much better than reading your mind. I *saw*. For you pain *is* pleasure."

Shara hugged Alexis, not wanting the girl to say more. Her gift was her curse, and would destroy her if she couldn't master it.

Their bond had been strengthened by the incident. Alexis had seen Shara's rage. It was one thing to peer into another's mind, to know there was fury within, quite another to experience that rage firsthand.

A bounty hunter, she now had a way to release her pent-up frustration. Yet she *had* lost control when she felt Alexis had probed to the depths of her soul. Deep within, though, the need to protect Alexis had won out over the rage.

Reading her mind, Alexis signed that she understood.

Shara knew she could never again allow her rage to consume her as it had that day. She could never put Alexis — or anyone close to her — at risk again.

Now Shara had lost Deidre and Lysette. And she could still lose Alexis if Briggs, now without a job, relocated. What she had to do now she would do for Alexis. For without Alexis she would be hopelessly adrift and eventually lost.

T W E L V E

MICA

Flee, Mica thought, as she packed her knapsack. She still couldn't believe she'd just killed a cop. And she *wouldn't* allow herself to dwell on what he had done to her.

Oddly, the thought of leaving Atlanta — home for eight years — didn't disturb her at all. It wasn't because of the city or its people, but rather it had never been more than a convenient place to disappear after she had run away from home. She'd never given the city a chance to become her home.

She thought fleetingly of Rainy Day Records, the *one* store in Atlanta where she had felt welcome, located on Peachtree north of the Amtrak Station. The store now stood shuttered.

One of her first purchases, after she'd left Colleen's to make it on her own, had been a record player. Later, she could afford — and did buy — a tape deck and CD player, but she'd grown up with a record player that played now almost non-existent vinyls. It was the only thing from home she'd allowed to intrude upon her new existence. The sound of tapes and CDs somehow didn't quite sit right with her.

Both she and Jeremy often spent time browsing through the bins at Rainy Day Records, which was literally a hole-in-the-wall store that had opened without fanfare. It was one of those stores that didn't seem to belong in the company of the pubs, restaurants and clothing stores that dotted the block. Actually, it belonged in a different era, Mica thought.

The property itself was not conducive to anything other than a small record store or comic book shop. It was as if the surrounding stores had been built and, due to some quirk or engineering error, there was a wee bit of space remaining; not enough for a restaurant, but too much to remain uninhabited.

Rainy Day had these incredibly narrow aisles that had customers holding their breath to pass by one another. When it had opened it had carried *only* vinyl records picked up at yard sales or special ordered. Over the years tapes and CDs had first intruded, then swallowed up half the store. Still, the owners seemed intent on fighting the losing battle against the total elimination of vinyl. They were always on the prowl for records, which brought customers back several times a week, lest they miss out on a bootleg or rare pressing of an album.

The clientele was fiercely loyal. Mica saw many familiar faces when she and Jeremy ventured into the store; fellow vinyl-holics, looking for a rare gem that appeared almost by magic. Though Mica seldom spoke to her fellow diehards, they would acknowledge one another with a smile or a nod. An anarchistic little community.

Perry and Marsha — she'd never caught a last name — who owned and ran Rainy Day, knew all the clientele on a first name basis. Both in their early-thirties, they looked like stereotypical Greenwich Village hippie-wannabees who didn't want to get a *real* job. They just wanted to make ends meet doing what they loved most. Perry sported a Jerry Garcia beard, dotted with whatever food he'd had for breakfast or lunch and wore a tight-fitting short-sleeve t-shirt, even in the winter. His wife Marsha had been pregnant as long as Mica had known her. She now had five children, with another on the way. During the last few months of any given pregnancy Marsha would be unable to negotiate the store's narrow aisles. She would plant herself on a stool, her youngest child on her lap sucking on a bottle or teething ring, and ring up purchases on one of those old manual cash registers; the ones where you had to use your mind to figure out how much change to give a customer.

Mica loved challenging Perry with special requests. While she would shrug whenever Perry asked how, she had fallen in love with reggae music. Many of the albums she desired were unavailable in CD format. Bootleg Bob Marley records, Marcia Griffith, Carleen Davis, Derrick Morgan; some Jamaican reggae artists cut several records a year and *only* on vinyl. Somehow, Perry had been able to get them all — with one exception. Before the store had closed, Mica had read a review praising a new Jamaican female artist Ivanay, whose album *Empower Me* was on an obscure Kingston label. She had set Perry on the trail of the album and he had searched in vain for it for six months.

Mica had ribbed him unmercifully, each day, as she stopped by and he gave her a forlorn shake of the head.

Then, four months ago Rainy Day Records had suddenly closed — without so much as a going out of business sale. It was appropriate, Mica thought; leaving like a thief in the night, just as they had entered.

Though dust and grime now covered the narrow front window, Mica could still see bins with a smattering of CDs. She had heard Perry and Marsha had left for South Florida to dabble in the drug trade. Mica wasn't all that surprised. There was nothing PC about Rainy Day Records. Cigarette smoke filled the store, and there was more than a faint aroma of pot. Perry and Marsha had taken their children and vinyls, left the CDs and tapes, and vanished.

Passing by the abandoned storefront each day reminded Mica this was the only store in the city she'd allowed to worm its way into her heart. She often wondered if someplace in southern Florida Perry and Marsha had recreated her favorite store, complete with its logo of a turntable with a lightning bolt striking it. She wondered, too, if Perry was still on the hunt for Ivanay.

With Rainy Day Records gone, there was precious little in Atlanta she would miss.

Her only misgiving was leaving Jeremy. He had been the *only* person she'd let get close to her and, even with him, it had been out of necessity. She had kept him at arm's length at first. They were friends, but not too close. It was only after their first February together that their relationship evolved. What she'd wanted was purely physical — unadulterated and uncomplicated sexual gratification — but she had found it impossible not to bond emotionally. Something about Jeremy inspired trust. She felt a connection to him she shared with no other.

Other than Jeremy, there was no one. She would miss her mentor Colleen but over the years they'd had less contact. Moreover, there had never been an emotional attachment. As for her clients, Mica knew they would miss her, but quickly move on. In a few months, she would be an answer to a S/M trivia question.

Distance without emotional commitment was what Mica had wanted because of Ralph Danziger. No, not just him, she corrected herself. He had been the catalyst, but the town of Emory itself had left her an emotional cripple. She'd just never realized how empty her life had been until tonight.

She'd returned home, and only when removing her blood-soaked clothes had she realized she still clutched the chain and crucifix she'd used to kill Ray Donato. Discard it was her first thought. Damning evidence, the murder weapon. It hadn't been murder though, she chided herself. Self-defense. And she sensed she would need it again. She washed off the blood and put the chain around her neck.

She was also aware that she alone wasn't making decisions for her. The wolf within had been awakened. So, too, had her grandfather. Within, there was an uneasy truce, for the moment, yet Mica was aware each was defining its turf; vying for a piece of her. Mica remained in control, but at times it seemed she was at the whim of the other two, and she actually welcomed their presence and intrusion.

She was acutely aware of this as she packed. It wasn't Mica who chose to take only a knapsack, but she *knew* it was the right thing to do. It wasn't Mica who stuffed jeans, sweatshirts, sweaters and two pairs of sneakers into the knapsack. And the jeans . . . most no longer fit her. Some she had purchased as much as five years before. She was a pack rat, she was the first to admit. Though she brought in more than she could spend, she only discarded what couldn't be salvaged. Jeans worn at the crotch, she would patch. Those with holes in the knees, she would cut into shorts. She had arrived in Atlanta scrawny and had since put on some weight; not much, but the jeans she now packed were at least a full size too small. She packed them just the same.

Dresses, shoes, jewelry — worth thousands of dollars — she gave no consideration. Makeup? Unnecessary. Her S/M toys? Part of a past she would never revisit.

The last item she packed was five thousand dollars in cash; twenties, fifties and a few hundred dollar bills.

Mica had $30,000 in her loft. It wasn't that she didn't believe in banks. But large deposits from working at an art gallery might arouse the suspicion of the IRS. She deposited just enough in a checking account in Terése's name to pay her monthly bills. While she co-owned the art gallery with Colleen, her name appeared on no papers. She had a verbal agreement with Colleen, as good as any contract. The rest of her cash she hid behind an air conditioning vent in the kitchen. Only a meticulous search would uncover it. A search like the police would make once she was identified as Donato's killer.

She put the remaining $25,000 in a box and dashed off a note to Jeremy. She noticed even her handwriting had changed. Some had likened her handwriting to calligraphy. She took pride in personalizing invitations she wrote for gallery events. There was always a brief personal message or endearment to everyone she invited.

Her note to Jeremy now was rough and raw. She couldn't tell if it was her grandfather's influence, the wolf's or both.

> Jeremy,
> You alone know I had no choice. February will be awful without you. See Colleen if you need anything.
>
> T

Along with the money she placed receipts for the paintings Jeremy had painted, printing on each "Property of Jeremy."

She wrote a short note to Colleen, telling her Jeremy controlled her half-interest in the gallery and to give him money he required. She trusted Colleen like a sister and felt content Jeremy would never go wanting.

Knapsack on her back, box under her arm she left, without turning back to give eight years of memories a final glance.

There was unfinished business to take care of at home.

She mailed the letter to Colleen, then dropped off her package to Jeremy at his loft a few blocks away. She left it outside his door. There was no way she could face him to say goodbye.

A part of her wanted to just begin walking, but to get to where she had to she knew she would need to take her car to get out of the city. An inconspicuous Ford Taurus it had dings and dents that also discouraged would-be car thieves. She drove east, north, northeast, east then north. She was oblivious, feeling like an abandoned cat who would somehow make her way home. Soon she passed an abandoned tannery — a huge bleak structure that seemed to scream *stay clear* — and a mile further, Lake Lanier. She got out, placed a heavy stone on the accelerator and watched the car plunge into the lake, where it was soon swallowed up. She stared at the woods that now surrounded her, entered them and felt immediately one with the forest.

She didn't look down as she walked, unafraid of tripping over a fallen tree or other obstacle. She had given herself to the wolf. Her mind drifted back to Ralph Danziger.

THIRTEEN

Mica had a three mile walk to school. There was no busing in Emory. A few kids rode bikes, fewer still were driven by their parents in pickup trucks. Most, like her, walked to school.

That day a driving rain fell, making her umbrella virtually useless. The mid-September rain felt good, but she had no change of clothes and didn't want to spend the day drenched. Worse, her mother demanded she wear a dress. Mica had worn baggy jeans or overalls most of her life. At sixteen she had been a late-bloomer. She had only had her first period a few months before, and to her mother it signaled a momentous shift in her life. She was now a woman and she would dress accordingly, even if it were only a simple, drab gray dress her mother had sewn for her.

Her mind occupied with keeping dry, she hadn't heard the horn until the truck had pulled alongside of her. Ralph Danziger yelled through the wind, telling her to get in. She debated with herself for only a moment, lightning and the peal of thunder making the decision easy. It wasn't as if Ralph Danziger were a stranger. In fact he was her closest neighbor, though he lived a full half-mile down the road.

He gave her one of his patented smiles when she got in. Ralph Danziger smiled a lot. People liked him. She had nothing to fear. He had to be in his forties, she thought, though she was certain he dyed his hair black to appear younger. It was *too* black to be natural. He was a large bulky man, muscular from working his farm, with only his son to help. He certainly wasn't handsome; his face was bloated and red. She saw the bottle of beer in his hand and recalled having heard he drank too much. Most prominent and disturbing was his nose. It was bulbous with deep pores that reminded her of a wasp's nest. He was wet from having worked in the rain. The smell of rain and perspiration was unbearable. She opened the window, even though the rain soaked her light sweater.

"You're looking fine, child," he said, offering her his bottle, which she declined. "Scrawny, all skin and bones before the summer," he went on. "But now, you're a woman."

She said nothing.

"Got you a boyfriend?"

"No," she said, without elaborating. Until recently she hadn't thought much of boys, in the sense Ralph Danziger meant. Before her period, her two older brothers hadn't given her a second look when she entered the kitchen. She had been a tomboy, with a body to match and hadn't drawn much attention from the boys at school. Only in the past few months had she had . . . fantasies, she thought, searching for the right word. It must be something to do with having her period, she decided, not even considering broaching the subject to her mother. She would look at some boy in class and feel faint stirrings. A boy would look at her with more than a glance and she'd blush, not knowing why.

"You gonna have boys all over you in no time, if you keep growing like you are," Danziger said, his eyes on her instead of the road. "Time you learned what it takes to please a man."

She wasn't sure what he meant, but she didn't like the smile on his face.

He pulled the truck off the road and under some trees. Before she could react, he was on top of her, kissing her and touching her all over. She tried to fend him off, but with his bulk, and having been caught off guard, she was helpless. She screamed, ranted and raved at him, but he only laughed in return.

"Scream all you want, girl. No one to hear you, especially in this storm."

When he roughly entered her, she cried out in pain, then simply cried in shame as he grunted with each thrust. Done, he got off of her, as she lay huddled, crying.

"C'mon, girl, that wasn't so bad, was it? Hell, it was good for me," and he laughed again.

Mica yanked the door open and stumbled out of the truck.

"C'mon Mica, don't go away mad. I'll drive you to school now. You'll catch your death in that rain," followed by more laughter.

Mica ran the half-mile home, bursting into the kitchen, unable to speak. She hadn't stopped crying, and she couldn't catch her breath.

"You hurtin', child?" her mother asked, waiting for her to speak. A moment later her father came in looking worried. Mama never panicked, Mica knew. Took everything in stride. After all, it wasn't as if Mica was comatose or bleeding. She kept on with her sewing, only occasionally glancing at her daughter. "You fall or something?" her mother pressed, her voice calm.

Mica finally composed herself.

"Ralph Danziger . . . he . . . raped me," she said, and began crying again.

Her mother sighed, put her sewing aside, came over and hugged Mica stiffly.

Her father left the kitchen.

"Where's Pa going?" Mica asked.

Mica knew her father loved her, but he had never been overly demonstrative. He had become even more distant lately, when her mother started having her wear dresses. Before, she worked side by side with her brothers doing chores. All of a sudden, those chores were no longer hers. She was given women's work to do.

"You know your father," her mother said. "This here is a woman's problem. Your Pa takes care of the boys, and I deal with female concerns, like when you had your period."

"Is he going after Mr. Danziger?" Mica asked.

"You and I are going to have a talk before anyone does anything," her mother said.

Anna Swann was a stern woman who seldom smiled and didn't do much talking, so what she did say took on extra meaning. Mica had long ago learned not to argue with her mother. It was akin to spitting in the wind. Long as Mica was living under her roof, she would listen and do as she was told. Mica knew it would do no good to nag or pout or try to reason with her mother. A decision made meant the end of any further discussion.

"Now tell me what happened," her mother told her.

She did. "Are you going to call Sheriff Fallon?" she asked when she'd finished.

"We're not calling *anyone*. Danziger will deny it, or worse say you led him on. Now listen and listen good. A girl in a small town like Emory, your reputation is all you got. Word spreads that Ralph Danziger had his way with you, boys'll think you're easy. You done it with Ralph Danziger, you'll do it with them. Boys'll spread stories 'bout you and them, even if they're not true. You'll get a reputation like Sarah Huggins, and no boy will want to marry you. No good at all will come from telling the world what he done to you. Things like this happen to a woman. You got to have the strength to put it behind you. Understand me?"

Mica knew her mother wasn't asking for her opinion. As far as her mother was concerned there had been no attack, and her mother wanted to hear no more of it.

"Yes, ma'am," Mica said, unable to make eye contact.

"Good. Now go up, take a shower and put some dry clothes on. I'll write you a note for your teacher. Tell her you has cramps," she smiled thinly. "Woman says she had cramps, there'll be no questions."

Finished, she went back to her sewing. She said nothing when Mica came down wearing jeans.

Forty minutes later Mica reached a crossroads. To her left was the school. To her right, the sheriff's office.

She went right.

At the sheriff's office, one of the deputies, Tommy Boyd, greeted her. Tommy was only a few years older than Mica. No way was she going to tell Tommy what had happened.

"What can I do for you, Mica?" he repeated when she asked to see the sheriff.

"I gotta see the sheriff."

"What about? He's a busy man."

"None of your damn business, Tommy Boyd. Nothing ever goes on in this town. What's he busy doing? Cutting his toenails?"

She wasn't aware her voice was rising until the sheriff came out of his office.

"What all the fuss about?" he asked, looking at Tommy.

"I gotta talk with you, Sheriff. It's private," Mica said.

Dan Fallon looked at her and must have seen something in her face.

"Come back to my office, Mica, and tell me what's got you so lathered."

In his office, Mica told her story; almost word for word what she'd told her mother. And, like her mother, he didn't interrupt with questions until she was finished.

Mica knew the sheriff like most of the kids in town knew the sheriff. They *saw* him around. At her age, you didn't want to be seeing the sheriff for much of anything else. His father had been sheriff and Fallon had taken over five years earlier, after a fall from a horse had left his father paralyzed. She knew he was forty-five because there had been a big party for him over the summer. He was a big stocky man, who liked his wife's cooking a bit too much.

He was proud of his position in the community. His uniform was always neatly pressed. She recalled seeing him a few weeks earlier, when it had been dreadfully hot. There had been a patch of sweat on the back of his uniform. Half an hour later, she had seen him again, and it was gone. He had changed uniforms. Hot August days, she imagined he changed his uniform quite often. He was not one to look slovenly.

When she finished her story, Sheriff Fallon looked at her closely for a moment, as if deciding whether to believe her or not.

"You tell your parents what happened?" he asked.

She couldn't tell the truth. If she *had* told them and they *had* supported her, they would have been with her now.

"No, sir," she said, thinking it best to keep her answers simple.

"I thought you said you were wearing a dress when he attacked you?"

"I was." *Keep it simple*, she reminded herself.

"You're not wearing a dress now. How's that?"

"I . . . I *did* go home to change. But I told my ma I'd fallen in some mud."

"I see. Did anyone see you get into Ralph's truck?"

"No, sir."

"Did you scratch him — maybe leave a mark on his face?"

"No, sir. I told you, he surprised me. I couldn't move."

"Did he hit you? Leave any marks on you?"

"No, sir."

"Anyone see you on your way back home?"

"No, sir," she said, wondering where all these questions were leading.

"Well now, Mica. This is a serious charge, you know that?"

"Yes, sir, I do."

"You sure you want to be stirring up this hornet's nest?"

"I thought about it long and hard, sir," she said. And she had, especially since she was defying her mother. "He raped me and I don't want him to get away with it."

"Okay, then," he said, offering her a smile. "You stay here. I'm going to have a talk with Ralph. Get to the bottom of this."

Half an hour later she heard Ralph Danziger's voice. She heard the sheriff greet him all friendly, then the two of them disappeared into another office. Mica had heard the sheriff tell Tommy to take his break and bring back some donuts and pop for Mica when he returned.

Mica left the sheriff's office and listened outside the room where he and Ralph Danziger were speaking.

"You done it now, Ralph," she heard the sheriff saying. "I told you before you gotta curb your appetite for young pussy."

"You know I mean no harm, Dan," Mica heard Danziger say. "I'd a little too much to drink . . . saw her looking so grown all of a sudden. You know I like the young ones . . . I didn't hurt her, though."

Mica could hear panic rising in his voice.

"What you gonna do, Dan?" she heard him ask, almost a plea.

"Make it go away, Ralph," Mica heard him say, sounding irritated. "But let this be a warning. Times are changing. Even here. You got the hankering, you go to Sarah Huggins. For $10 she'll rock your world," he said, and laughed, with Ralph Danziger laughing along with him.

Mica returned to the sheriff's office when she heard someone getting up. The sheriff didn't return for another five minutes. He came in with a tray of donuts and a can of Pepsi. She declined his offer of one. And, no, she wanted nothing to drink.

"We have a problem, young lady," he finally said. "Ralph Danziger says it never happened."

"Bastard," Mica said, aloud, referring to *both* Danziger and the sheriff.

"He says he never left his farm. Says his son would vouch for him."

Mica didn't know what to say. She knew the sheriff was lying, so it would do no good to contradict him.

"And I got another problem," he said. He looked Mica square in the eye. "You lied to me."

"No I didn't," Mica said before he could go on.

"I called your father," the sheriff said, then seemed to be waiting for Mica's reaction.

"Oh, that," Mica said, looking down at her lap.

"You *did* tell your parents what happened. Or, at least what you *say* happened," he added.

"It *did* happen," Mica said weakly.

"Look at it from my point of view, Mica. You have no witnesses. Neither you nor Ralph Danziger have any marks to suggest a fight. Ralph denies *anything* occurred. Your mother says you took a shower, so I can't even have a doctor examine you to corroborate your claim. And, you lied to me. What would you do if you were in my shoes?"

Mica said nothing. Knew it was useless. He'd told Ralph Danziger he'd *make it go away*.

"I suggest you heed your parents' advice," he went on, when she said nothing. "You don't want people talking behind your back. Go home and think it over. If your parents want to file a complaint, there'll be a full investigation. I promise. How does that sound?"

Mica shrugged indifferently. She felt deflated. She had already defied her mother. And her mother *never* changed her mind once she'd made a decision. Worst of all Ralph Danziger would go unpunished.

The sheriff had Tommy drive her home, as the rain hadn't abated.

When she walked into the kitchen, her mother was still at the table sewing. Her mother said nothing when she entered. Her mother's face betrayed no emotion. If she were upset with Mica, she hid it well. Mica knew as far as her parents were concerned, *they* had put the incident behind them, and they expected Mica to do the same.

Easier said than done, Mica thought over the next several days. At night she had trouble sleeping, afraid she would have nightmares of the rape. And when exhaustion took hold, she *did*. In her dreams, she fought back valiantly, scratching and gouging Ralph Danziger's eyes so he would never see again. Awake, it ate at her that she *hadn't* fought back. Revenge was all she could think about.

At school, she thought everyone knew. Two girls talking; it had to be about *her*. Boys giving her the eye. *They* knew. She would look at herself in the mirror in her room, both clothed and naked, wondering what gave her away.

On the third day after the attack, when she got to school, small groups of students were abuzz. She had stayed clear of her friends since the attack, afraid she would betray herself the first time she opened her mouth. Now she went over to Cynthia McCoy to find out what all the fuss was about.

"Ralph Danziger is dead," Cynthia told her. "His tractor flipped over and . . . his skull was crushed," she added, looking pale all of a sudden.

"I heard he was drunk as a skunk," Tiffany Anders said. "Probably didn't feel a thing."

Mica went outside and burst into tears. Her friends came out to console her, but they didn't have a clue *why* she was crying. It was neither grief, as her friends thought, nor relief that her ordeal was over. She shed tears of rage. *How dare you die, Ralph Danziger, before I've settled my score with you* she wanted to scream out. She'd imagined his death at her hand a thousand times, and now there was no way to vent her wrath. He had cheated her. God had cheated her. No, she corrected herself, God had *abandoned* her.

Put it behind you, she told herself in the days that followed, but she couldn't. At night she would see his crushed skull in her dreams. He'd be leering at her, brain matter dripping down the side of his face.

"What you gonna do to me now?" he would ask, laughing. "Can't do *nothing*, can you?"

At school, she was more certain than ever that others knew he'd raped her *and* gotten away with it. Twice she had gotten into fights with other girls. Twice she'd visited Principal Williard and been warned.

When Josh Farrell snapped her bra in the lunchroom, as she walked by him on her way to throw away her uneaten lunch, she could take no more. Without thinking she picked up a soda bottle from the table and smashed him in his face. She raised the bottle for a second blow, but the sight of blood streaming from his nose and the terror in his eyes made her pause. She dropped the bottle and walked directly to Principal Williard's office. She took a seat and awaited her punishment. She was surprised when the principal simply told her to go home for the day and return with her parents the next morning. He was on the phone, calling her parents, when she left.

Her parents said little, after she told them what had happened. Her father, who had come home from the hardware store he owned in town listened and then left.

Her mother shook her head. "When you gonna stop reliving a past you can't alter? It's time to move on."

As usual there would be no discussion.

At Principal Williard's office the next day, her parents sat on either side of her, as the principal passed judgment.

"I don't know what's come over Mica lately," he said, looking at her father, as if she wasn't there, "but it stops here."

A thin, little man, with a bowtie and receding hairline, his deep commanding voice seemed to Mica totally at odds with his stature. It was that authoritative voice, along with steely gray eyes that held no compassion, that students feared. Frail as he looked, he could intimidate just about anyone with a stare and a few carefully chosen words.

"Aside from any punishment I mete out, I would strongly advise Mica receive professional help for whatever ails her," he continued.

"What about the boy?" her father asked, surprising Mica.

"He suffered a broken nose. It could have been far worse. *Then* we'd be dealing with the police," he said, glaring at Mica's father.

"You misunderstand me," Mica's father said. "You're going to punish my daughter. What about the boy?"

This was Mica's father as she had never heard him. He seemed unfazed by the principal, intent on protecting *her*. It was as if he were a total stranger, and Mica could have hugged him then and there for standing up for her.

"He hasn't suffered enough?" the principal asked in astonishment.

"He provoked Mica," her father said, "pulling her bra strap. Her response was purely instinctive."

"What the Farrell boy did was in bad taste, I'll admit that, but it's not the first nor the last time it will occur. Childish antics, to be sure, but certainly not meriting Mica's response."

Mica's father took out several folded pieces of paper from inside his suit pocket and passed them to the principal. "I spoke with an attorney, sir, and what the Farrell boy committed was sexual harassment. As you can see, in other cases the offender was punished. Sometimes severely. And in several cases the parents sued the school."

Williard gave Mica's father an incredulous look. "You'd have me do nothing to Mica?" he asked.

"No," her father answered. "Mica's response was inappropriate, but before you persecute her consider the ramifications."

Williard looked at Mica's father for several moments, as if debating whether to call his bluff, then seemed to come to a decision. "No one wants to persecute your daughter, Mr. Swann. Considering that the Farrell boy initiated the . . . incident, I don't think a three day suspension for Mica is excessive. Do you?"

"And the boy?" Mica's father persisted. "He *did* provoke Mica. You could send a message to those who would sexually harass the girls in your charge."

Mica could swear she saw the principal do a slow burn. He cleared his voice before responding. "Five days for the Farrell boy." It was a statement, but almost sounded to Mica like a question.

"We can live with that," Mica's father said, rising, again to Mica's shock, indicating to the principal the meeting was over. It seemed to Mica the world had been turned upside down and inside out like an episode of *The Twilight Zone*.

"Mr. Swann," Williard said, as Mica's father turned to leave. "I still believe your daughter needs counseling. She was provoked *this* time, but I can assure you there will be no leniency in the future. She steps out of line again and she's out. Do I make myself clear?"

Mica knew it was an effort to save face. Knew, too, that Williard meant what he said. Her father seemed aware of this.

"I'm not one of your students, Mr. Williard, and I won't be bullied. We'll consider your advice, but I don't respond well to threats. Do *I* make myself clear?"

Williard said nothing. After a moment, Mica's father led her family out of the office.

No one said anything on the way home. Mica's thoughts were on her father; not just for standing up for her, but how forceful he had been. It wasn't like him at all. He wasn't a timid man, especially when dealing with her two brothers. But she'd never seen this side of him. It suddenly dawned on her. With Williard, he'd acted as her grandfather would.

Her grandfather had owned a lumber mill, and Mica heard he took no crap from anyone. He had been sorely disappointed when his son decided against taking over the business. He was disappointed that his son's only ambition was to own a hardware store, make a decent living and be home on time for dinner each night.

Today, her father had acted like Augustus Swann and Mica finally understood. He might not have been affectionate towards her, but she was his daughter. Back him into a corner, as Williard had tried, and he would protect his child to the death. She had never been so proud of him and wished she could put it into words. But she remained silent.

Coincidentally, when they arrived home, Augustus Swann was there to greet them. Father and son talked for a few moments and then Mica's grandfather came over and gave her a bearhug.

"I hear you have a three-day vacation," he said with a wink.

Mica blushed and her grandfather laughed aloud.

"I had my share of *vacations* when I was your age. What say you and I go camping? You know, just the two of us get away from it all for a bit?"

Mica looked at her father, who nodded. Her mother didn't look too happy, but she deferred to him.

Mica was thrilled. She didn't know, then, that her grandfather had special plans for her *vacation*.

F OURTEEN

(DECEMBER 1998)

SHARA

Shara was waiting outside of Graterford Prison with a pepperoni pizza when Briggs emerged. He was both a free man and unemployed. She had an offer for him, but needed to speak to him alone. She wanted to plant the seed before he saw his family, then see if it took.

Vivian Briggs had readily agreed to allow Shara to pick up her husband, and Briggs had been agreeable, as well. After all, Vivian wanted to plan a *proper* welcome for her man.

Shara handed him the pizza when he got in the car, before he could say anything.

"Alexis said this is what you missed most . . . the *food* you missed most," she corrected herself. "Said to save her a piece, by the way," she added with a smile.

Briggs dug in as Shara began to drive to Southwest Philly, where Briggs lived.

"How do I thank you?" he asked between bites.

"By offering me a piece," she said, looking at the pizza she had bought at a no-name pizzeria. No Pizza Hut, Domino's or Papa Johns. This was true Philly pizza, grease and all.

Briggs gave her a slice, which Shara quickly devoured. Seeing Briggs eating, she was reminded she hadn't eaten all day what with her confrontations with Deidre and Lysette.

"So tell me, how did you prove in a few days what my people on the force couldn't in a month," he asked, still chewing on a piece of his pizza.

It was an overcast day, not unlike the day that had landed Briggs in jail, Shara thought. Briggs didn't seem to notice.

"I *knew* you were innocent. They assumed you were guilty. They did some cursory canvassing, but never dug beneath the surface. Since I knew you didn't kill Biggie Shaw, I had to come up with an alternative. The call you received that first alerted you to Shaw had to come from someone with his own reason for wanting Biggie taken down. Once I saw Biggie had three foster children — *all* teenage girls — it was simply a matter of connecting the dots. Everett Gaines knew you were ripe to go hard on Biggie . . . kill him in self-defense. It was never his intention for you go to prison. Things just didn't work out the way he'd hoped."

"It couldn't have been as easy as you make it sound," he said, looking at her.

A few drops of rain fell on the windshield. Mid-December and still it was fifty-five degrees. Shara wondered when winter would shake fall. So far, winter was fighting a losing battle.

"I'm not a cop, Briggs, and that helped a lot. I was able to cut corners. I didn't have to worry that what I found out would be inadmissible in court because I didn't follow proper procedure. I talked to minors without their parents' knowledge or consent. I lied and deceived. Do you think less of me because I bent the rules?" she asked, genuinely curious.

"The ends justify the means is what you're saying," Briggs said, and Shara could hear his condescending tone. She'd heard it before. Law enforcement looked down on bounty hunters, even though people like her provided an invaluable service. They captured fugitives *already* apprehended by the law.

"You're not one to talk," Shara answered, miffed. "You cut more than your share of corners in this case alone. When Everett Gaines first called you, you didn't report it. The afternoon of the attack you didn't call for backup. And was beating the crap out of Biggie Shaw following proper police procedure?" she added with sarcasm. "You hired me because I played by my own set of rules. You counted on it. So cut the holier-than-thou bullshit."

"You're right. I'm not one to talk. Still—"

"I almost let Gaines walk," Shara interrupted. "If it weren't for Alexis, you might still be in jail."

"But *he* killed Shaw."

"He was as much a victim as you were. What I had to wrestle with was with Biggie dead, there were no villains. Only victims. Too many victims," she added, speaking as much to herself as to Briggs.

"That's why, except for Alexis, I would never have gone near your case," she continued. "As a bounty hunter the people I track down have fucked someone over. They're guilty of fleeing, plain and simple. And some are bastards I'd hunt down for free; murderers, child-molesters, people who swindled retirees out of their life savings. This was different. There was no satisfaction in bringing Everett Gaines down. The irony is, if you had been another minute or two, he would have killed Biggie to save the girl and would have been hailed a hero. Instead, he'll go to prison and his daughter loses a father. No justice in that. Can you understand how I was torn?"

Briggs shrugged. "As a cop, I don't have that luxury."

"You're not a cop anymore, though, are you?" she corrected him.

"It's gonna take a while for that to sink in. I guess I always held out the hope I'd be allowed to remain on the force if the killer was caught. A reprimand, suspension, even a transfer, but I'd still have my job. I'm just beginning to realize that I was deluding myself. My fate was sealed with the department the moment I admitted I beat an unarmed Shaw."

"So tell me, what did your lawyers work out?"

He didn't answer her right away. He had more on his mind and was intent on getting it out in the open. "It's been a dizzying few hours. Last night I was considering taking the plea the DA offered," he said and paused. "No offense, but I didn't have much faith in you. I underestimated you."

"A lot of people have underestimated me. It's a liability I've turned into an asset. But go on."

"Then this morning I had all these decisions thrust upon me. To cut to the chase, I go away quietly — resign from the force. No interviews. No book about my years on the force. Nothing to draw attention. In exchange, I get my pension. Hell, I *did* put in my twenty. The FOP agreed to extend Alexis' medical coverage for therapy for as long as necessary. And all charges against me were dropped. Biggie Shaw's not going to complain about the beating I gave him. Seems everyone just wants to make believe nothing happened. Any of that your doing?" he said, looking at her.

Shara shrugged. "Not intentionally. The city's facing a civil lawsuit from the girls DHS gave to Biggie. Philly's making strides combating crime, haven't you heard?" she said sarcastically. "The streets downtown are relatively safe. News reports to the contrary would have hurt the city's image, as the city courted conventions and tourists. What happened to Alexis and all of Biggie's victims would have been a PR nightmare. And I don't think the city will want to march Everett Gaines into court either. So having you resign quietly and fade into the woodwork makes sense. By the way, I heard your defense fund is footing Gaines' attorney's bill," she added.

"Tell me that's not your handiwork," Briggs said, beginning to relax.

"Either that or it would have come out of my own pocket."

"No shit," Briggs said, again looking at her, in surprise.

"I told you," Shara said, her voice rising, "Everett Gaines is as much a victim as anyone. I brought him down, but I wasn't about to let him drown. He won't be wanting for a good attorney, regardless of who has to pay."

The rain fell heavily now. Shara wondered if Briggs were reliving that afternoon by the railroad tracks as he looked out the window.

They drove in silence for a few minutes. Her time alone with Briggs hadn't gone as she'd scripted. She and Briggs were like oil and water. They had spent the entire drive sparring. A part of her wanted nothing further to do with Lamar Briggs. Yet she owed it to Alexis to at least try to find some common ground. She would make her pitch and live with the consequences.

"So what are you going to do now?" she asked. "About a job, I mean," she added.

"To tell the truth, I haven't given it a thought."

"Maybe it's time you stopped feeling sorry for yourself and started thinking about your future. You have to supplement your pension."

He shrugged. "I have no interests outside of policework. No expertise like other cops who retire after their twenty."

"You could become a security guard," she said jokingly, but saw by the glare he returned he wasn't in the mood.

"I think not. I need something to exercise my mind."

"So become a private investigator."

"And make surveillance my life? No way."

"What does that leave?" Shara asked.

"Relocating. I read the papers. Most cops applauded my actions, even when they thought I'd killed Shaw. Another department might hire me," he said. To Shara, he sounded neither confident nor thrilled at the prospect.

As far as Shara was concerned relocation wasn't an option. Alexis' continued improvement was contingent on time spent in the forest in Cape May. Relocate and there would be no further healing. For all Shara knew, Alexis might regress.

"You'd leave Philly? I thought the city was in your blood."

"Do I have an alternative?" he asked morosely.

"Come work for me," Shara said, then paused to let it sink in.

"Me a bounty hunter? You gotta be kidding."

"Indulge me, okay?" Shara asked.

He shrugged, his eyes on the rain slapping against the windshield.

"What I do isn't a hell of a lot different from what you did. Only I've got freedom, more money and control of my life. I have no superior to answer to. I'm my own boss. Imagine being a cop without the bureaucracy, without the political bullshit and the personal agendas of a half-dozen superiors. *That's* what I've got. And like I said before, I don't have to follow procedures which constantly handcuff you. No search warrants. No need for parents to be present when I speak to minors. Illegal wiretaps? Frowned upon, but I can do it. My prey is already a fugitive. He has *no* rights. The system works *for* me, not the other way around."

"But the money's not guaranteed. I've got a family to consider."

"I'd guarantee the money. Look, most fugitives are caught. They fucked up in the first place and were captured. Flight isn't often planned, and they make mistakes. Plenty of them. I'm not asking you to take any risks. You work for me, I'll pay you what you made as a cop. For every capture, you get forty percent after expenses and any advance. Not including your pension, you work six months and you'll make as much as you made as a detective. That leaves six months to be with your family."

"You make it sound tempting, but hunting fugitives—"

"It's not being a homicide detective, right?"

"I know beggars can't be choosers, but where's the challenge?"

Shara smiled. "*I* don't do it for the money, and I take only enough fugitive retrievals to make ends meet. The challenge, and the possibility of big money, comes from privately-funded rewards."

She paused. If he asked her to elaborate, she would know she had piqued his interest.

"What are you getting at?" he asked.

"Families, neighbors, corporations, interested parties, even strangers put up rewards all the time. A child disappears. A runaway? Maybe. I get paid to find the kid, not necessarily return him. The family just wants to know he's safe. A husband goes AWOL. The wife wants him found for any number of reasons; love being only one. And cold cases. As a cop you could devote only so much time to a case. Some eventually get buried. Rewards are posted. These are the cases I hunger for. These are the cases you caught once or twice a year, if you were lucky. Fugitive bounties fund the cases that pose a challenge; that get the adrenaline pumping. That's what I'm offering."

"Sounds like you do well enough alone. You don't need me. I'm not looking to be a charity case."

"You're a pigheaded son-of-a-bitch, you know that? A self-centered one at that," she added. "I'm not offering charity. You've heard the bright side, but I've faced problems, especially being a woman. Most of what I do I *can* do alone. I can follow the paper trail, work snitches, conduct surveillance — the whole ball of wax. But the capture . . . sometimes the dude's six-four and three hundred pounds. Tough as I am, I'd get thrown around like a pillow. I need backup. I need muscle."

"You're talking ten, twelve, fifteen days a year tops you'd need me. That's not going to feed my family."

"Let me finish, damn it," Shara said and paused to regain her composure. "I've also run into trouble with local authorities. Once I brought in a bench warrant and told the locals where the perp was. *They* collared him, out of pure spite. Shit happens. I can accept it; learn from it. Still, it hurts. Another time I brought a fugitive in and the locals took credit. Later I found out they suggested the bondsman make a *donation* to the department. *My fee.* For future cooperation. That's where you come in. You give me instant credibility. Like you said, cops applaud what you did. They're not going to fuck with one of their own. I don't call that charity."

Briggs was about the say something, but Shara held up a hand.

"You're also one hell of a cop. Together we can more than double the number of cases I now work. That leaves more time for those challenging cases that bring in the big bucks and leaves more time to be with your family. Simply put, Briggs, you'd be one hell of an asset."

Shara saw Briggs was no longer looking out the window, but at her.

"I don't want an answer now," Shara continued, before he could respond. "You owe it to your wife to talk it over with her. Christmas is in two weeks. Think on it. Mull over your options, then decide. Something better comes along in a few months, run with it. You're under no obligation.

"You're quite a saleswoman," Briggs said with a smile.

"Part of my charm."

Shara had pulled up to Briggs' house. Any questions he had would have to wait. Reservations he had, he would have to work out in his own mind and with his family. She *didn't* really need him. She didn't know if she could work with someone else. She had always done things her way. And she was set in her ways. Still, she owed it to Alexis to give it a try.

"I'll let you know," he said, as he opened the door. "Thanks for the offer. Thanks for saving my ass," he added hastily and got out.

"Briggs," Shara called.

He turned around, and she could see the rain dancing on his bald head.

Shara held out a box. "Alexis is expecting a slice of pizza. Don't disappoint her."

He took the box. She held onto it for a moment. "Be there for her, Briggs. You'd be going to prison if it weren't for her."

He said nothing, but nodded in acknowledgment.

Shara drove away. Alone. Maybe working with someone wasn't such a bad idea, after all, she thought. She had been alone for too long and at times made for lousy company.

FIFTEEN

(SEPTEMBER 1990)

MICA

Mica watched her grandfather as she set up the tent where they'd made camp. He sat shirtless, with his feet crossed, looking into the woods, as if expecting someone. He was seventy-one and looked every bit his age, though he was fit and Mica hadn't known him to be sick a day in his life. He was tanned and weathered from a life spent outdoors. His once blond hair, which he tied in a ponytail, was now white, and with it hanging loose he looked like an American Indian.

Mica saw very little resemblance between her father and grandfather. Where her father's eyes looked soft and unfocused, Augustus Swann's had a hardened edge that bored through you.

His face and torso had fine scars, which he likened to a roadmap of his life. He'd been a wild one, he had told her, and not just in his youth. He had drunk too much, been hot-tempered and too often settled even the pettiest of disputes with his fists, or any other object that was at hand. Her father, on the other hand, to her knowledge had *never* resorted to fisticuffs to settle a quarrel.

Her grandfather had owned a lumber mill in Emory which he had sold eight years earlier, having finally given up trying to convince her father to take over.

For the past ten years he'd taken Mica and her two brothers camping several times a year. He loved the woods. Her brothers enjoyed the hunting. She adored the man, the only member of her family who listened to what she had to say — who didn't dismiss her as an annoyance. She knew the feeling was reciprocated. She had always been his favorite. She hadn't thought much about it then, but lately she considered it might be because he had never had a daughter to dote on. Or maybe she reminded him of his wife who had passed away just before he sold the lumber mill. Her last theory was that he had been disappointed in his son, and her brothers were very much like him.

Whatever the reason, she got more attention from him during the camping trips than she got from her parents the rest of the year.

Her grandfather had changed abruptly five years before. Mica could still recall the day she'd first noticed. His pickup packed for a camping trip, Mica's brother had asked where the rifles were.

"We're not going hunting this year," he'd said gruffly. He had a sandpaper voice from many years of smoking. Except for when he was in the woods, she seldom saw him without a cigarette dangling from his mouth.

"What are we going to do? Sit around the campfire and tell ghost stories?" her older brother Michael said morosely.

"We'll fish. We'll track animals, but there's to be no more shooting animals," he'd replied.

"Why the hell not?" Mitchell, a year younger than Michael had asked.

Her grandfather didn't mind the profanity. Actually, they didn't curse around their father. He taught them manners and frowned on vulgar language. Their grandfather's language had always been salty, Mica had heard her mother say disapprovingly more than once. She couldn't change her father-in-law, but she wanted them all to know he was not to be emulated. Around him they talked like most kids when unsupervised in the schoolyard, spicing their vocabulary with a hell, a damn or a shit.

He had looked at the three of them and patiently explained.

"Humans are the only animals who kill for sport. And where's the sport in shooting a deer with a rifle? If you want sport, hunt after a deer with a knife. What you kill you eat. No killing just for the sake of bragging to your friends."

That had been the last time her brothers had gone camping with them. And, truth be told, Mica was glad she had her grandfather all to herself. She found he opened up so much more without her brothers present.

He had even taken her hunting for deer with a knife. He would tell her to stay well back and observe. He would sneak up on a deer and pounce. The first four times he had been unsuccessful, the deer bolting before he got close enough for the kill. He hadn't been perturbed, though. Only on the fifth attempt had he been successful and the buck had kicked him in the ribs before succumbing, leaving a hoof print that looked like a tattoo. Later she found out he'd broken two ribs.

"I could never catch a deer like that," she had told him, as he skinned the animal before cooking it.

"That's why I had you watch. You watch, you learn. It's like wolves. Cubs have to be taught how to hunt. And, like me, they fail more often than they succeed. Until ready to hunt for themselves, wolves share with the rest of the pack. Not just the young, but the old and infirm, as well. There's a lesson to be learned from that."

She had never killed a deer, but he often let her help in the hunt. They would approach from different sides. If there was more than one deer, she would bluff a charge. Her grandfather would look on for the most vulnerable. *That* deer he would pursue. Later, she would creep up and intentionally make noise, so the deer would flee, often right into the path of her grandfather.

Now, she set up camp while, she assumed, he rested. He had helped until she could do it alone. He was big into self-reliance. Often he had told her you only had yourself to rely on.

"I was never good at delegating authority at the lumber mill," he told her. "I did it because I had to. But when I managed to sneak away from my office — some inner voice pulling me — sure enough, more often than not my foreman would disappoint me. I *knew* if I did it myself, it would be done right. I've never had much faith in others. I ended up double-checking everything myself, and spending more time than if I hadn't put someone else in charge."

Then, his voice would soften. "You, though, you're not like your brothers, always taking the easy way out. You do it right. You, I would trust to guard my back. I can't say that about many others."

Finally finished setting up the tent, her top coated with her own perspiration, she saw a wolf — big, gray, like ash — standing proud looking at . . . no, she corrected herself, looking *through* her grandfather. He glanced at the animal, but refused to make eye contact. Its most distinguishing feature was an ear that looked as if it had been mauled, possibly doing battle with another wolf or some prey it had underestimated. Though her grandfather's back was turned towards her, he seemed aware what she'd seen.

"Hush, child. He's a friend. Stay where you are and do *nothing*, no matter what happens. Watch. Observe. Learn."

Her grandfather got on his stomach and began whining and whimpering, like a dog. The wolf approached, glancing at her once, then dismissing her. The wolf didn't approach with stealth or caution, and his body language was not that of an animal preparing to attack.

Mica was confused.

As the wolf got closer, her grandfather rolled onto his back. The wolf came over to him and growled, while her grandfather responded with a plaintive whine. He licked her grandfather's bare chest, sniffed at his groin, then put his mouth over her grandfather's mouth.

Mica had to bite back a cry of warning. *Do nothing*, he'd told her. *Watch. Observe. Learn.*

She knew her grandfather well. Knew to heed his words — out of respect, not fear.

Her grandfather, now back on his stomach raised himself on all fours, but remained lower to the ground than the wolf. He whined, nuzzled the wolf with his nose, then licked its ears and neck, but never made direct eye contact.

Seemingly tiring of the attention, the wolf made its way back into the woods. Only when it was gone did Mica move.

Her grandfather was again sitting.

Mica looked at her grandfather's face, where it looked like the wolf had bitten him. Saw no marks at all.

"I don't understand. I don't understand at all. There are no wolves here. They're extinct in Pennsylvania. We learned that in school."

"Wolves *are* extinct in Pennsylvania," her grandfather said, with a gleam in his gray eyes. "Yet that wasn't a big dog, I can assure you."

"Is he yours?" Mica asked, trying to make sense of what she'd seen.

"He's family, but he's not mine and I'm not his."

"What were you doing?"

"Within a pack there is one dominant male. All others are submissive to him. Sometimes there'll be a challenge to his dominance. Except for that, what he says goes, so to speak. All others submit to him. That's what I was doing."

He took one of her hands in his own. She'd noticed many times how big they were. And while his fingers were gnarled from age, working with them all his life, or maybe from arthritis, his palms were soft.

"He didn't bite me. It's his way of showing his dominance, but there's no intent to injure."

"How did you meet him?" Mica had dozens of questions.

"It's not a story for now," he said with what she thought was a twinge of sadness in his voice. "There are other, more important things we have to discuss. Let's fish, then talk over dinner."

They were silent as they ate. It was a comfortable silence, so unlike the silence at the dinner table at home. Her parents didn't believe in small talk at meals.

When they were done, they sat by the fire. He smoked a cigarette. Even in the woods he smoked after meals. It was just after 6 p.m. and still light.

"I know what happened to you, Mica," he finally said. "I'm not going to tell you I know how you feel. I'm a man. I *can't*. But I would have thought that with him dead, you would have felt relieved. You would have been able to go on with your life. He is no longer there to haunt you. Yet he's with you still, isn't he?"

"His dying, Grandpa, was the *worst* thing that could have happened,"

Mica told him. She had spoken to no one about how she felt, yet she freely opened up to him. "I planned his death — or at least revenge — over and over in my mind. I would have gotten back at him somehow. It wasn't just wishful thinking."

He nodded in understanding.

"With him dead, I feel cheated. It's like he's laughing at me. He had his way with me and now knows I'm helpless.

Her grandfather sat for a few minutes in silence, his eyes closed.

"I should have known," he finally said. "It's called closure." He paused, in thought for a moment. "They teach you about the war in Vietnam in that school of yours?"

Mica nodded.

"The remains of many soldiers were never found. Some families still hold out hopes they're still prisoners, but many *know* their sons are dead. Yet twenty years later, they're still pressing the Vietnamese government to locate their bodies. Some can't get on with their lives because they lack closure. It's the same with you. You're mad at the world, aren't you?"

"Yes. Mad at the world. Mad at myself for not putting up a better fight. Mad at Mama and Papa for wanting me to put it behind me. Just plain mad."

"That feeling I *do* know. It happened to me ages ago. I had forgotten about the need for closure," he said, almost to himself.

"What happened to you?"

"Long before I bought the lumber mill, I was up for the foreman's job, an important stepping stone. John Lathan got the job, though I was more qualified. I found out he was sleeping with the boss's wife. She put in a good word for him and I was bypassed. I can still taste the fury I felt. Three days later he died in a freak accident at the mill, and I was made foreman. But I still had this rage within me. Like you, I'd been robbed of the chance to avenge myself. Because of my anger, I was a lousy foreman at first."

He took a last deep drag on the cigarette and tossed it in the fire.

"I was too demanding, distant, short-tempered, gruff and vindictive. I was in danger of losing the job if I didn't change, but I didn't care."

"How long did it last?" Mica asked.

"Until I got revenge."

"But he was dead," Mica said, confused.

"The woman wasn't. She made a play for me. I took a chance and told her husband — my boss. He almost fired me on the spot. But I could see in his eyes he knew it was true. We set her up. He found her in a hotel room waiting for me, only I never showed. It was the same hotel room she had been at with Lathan."

The sun was setting, and there was a chill in the air. Her grandfather, who still hadn't put on a shirt, wrapped a blanket around him.

"He said nothing to me, but a week later I got a raise and a bonus. He had thought I had done the honorable thing, but honor had nothing to do with it. It was self-preservation and revenge. Once she got her claws into me, I would have become her prisoner. And she as much as Lathan had cost me the job in the first place. I had closure and became the foreman I should have been. Tough, demanding, but fair."

"There's no one for me to strike back at," Mica said after a few minutes of silence, as depressed as ever. "I understand the need for closure, but what can I do?"

"You've got to purge yourself of him, Mica. You have to understand that every time you strike back at him by getting into a fight, he's raping you again. Raping your soul, not your body, which is far worse. If you don't get him out of your system, he'll consume you. *That*, I know. I've been there."

"But how? I want to let him go. I really do. I try, but I can't."

"Come," he said, and Mica followed him past the tent to the edge of the clearing. Hanging from a tree was a punching bag with a full-sized picture of Ralph Danziger fastened to it.

Mica gasped when she saw him and began to tremble.

"He's dead, Mica," her grandfather said, "but you can beat him out of your system."

He held out a pair of boxing gloves for her.

"No," she said. "I have to feel him. No gloves."

Her grandfather dropped the gloves.

"Beat him till he's out of your system."

"How long?" she asked.

"As long as it takes."

"Will you stay with me?" she asked, her eyes not leaving the picture of Ralph Danziger.

"This is between you and him. I'd only be an interloper. Time for me to get some sleep anyway. I'm not as young as I used to be. We'll talk when you're done."

He gave her a kiss on the cheek and went to the tent.

Mica had never been taught to box. Her fights at school mainly involved pushing and shoving and posturing, much like bench-clearing brawls at baseball games she had watched. Everyone got into the action, but precious few punches were thrown and even fewer connected.

Mica now flailed away at the punching bag, with little effect. She hurt her hands more than the figure of Ralph Danziger on the bag. In her mind, his attack on her was replayed, and she could feel the rage in her swell. She swung wildly, missed and fell. Got up and began hitting the bag again, smelling his foul breath and the rain and perspiration that had covered him. She swung with all her might, but the bag barely moved. Then she heard him mocking her.

"Think you're hurting me, sweet thing? Give me your best shot."

"Couldn't fight me off then. Can't now."

"*Didn't* want to fight me off, then. Don't want to now."

"You wanted it. Asked for it. *Begged for it!*"

"Want me to do it again? Felt so nice, you want me twice."

Each sentence was punctuated by laughter as she swung, missed, swung, slipped and fell, swung, but couldn't shut his face.

Then there was another voice in her head — her grandfather's. He had never taught her how to fight, but now she heard his words and heeded them. She jabbed instead of swinging with all her might. He spoke to her of balance so she could deliver her blows with force. Soon she was into a rhythm.

Jab. Jab. Jab. Punch

Jab to the body. Jab to the body. Jab to the body. Uppercut to the face.

With growing confidence she began delivering punches with force. Soon Danziger wasn't leering at her anymore and his constant chatter was replaced by cries of pain. Finally, he fell silent and she knew she'd triumphed.

She was unaware how long she had pummeled him. She'd been so completely within herself, so focused on destroying him, hours could have passed for all she knew. When she looked at the figure on the punching bag, it was covered with blood. At first she thought it was hers. Her knuckles were red and raw, but the blood on them wasn't hers alone. Looking at what was left of Ralph Danziger, she knew the blood had to be *his*, impossible as it seemed. Where his face had been, blood dripped in a steady stream, as if from the punching bag itself.

Mica ran to tell her grandfather; let him know she'd shut Ralph Danziger's trap for good.

He was asleep on his side, his back facing towards her. She gently shook him by his shoulders and he fell on his back. His face had been beaten to a bloody pulp; beaten so badly she could hardly recognize him. Yet, while his lips were cracked and bloodied, there was a strangely serene expression on his face.

He had gone to sleep without his shirt, and she could see his body was horribly bruised, as well. Still she shook him to awaken him, without success. Her hand shaking with dread, she felt for a pulse. There was none.

He was dead.

She had killed him.

Panic gripped her and she ran. Ran to get help for her grandfather, though she *knew* he was dead. Ran, because as much as she loved him, she couldn't stand the sight of his bloodied body. Ran, because she had killed the person she had loved most. Ran, with no sense of purpose, with no sense of direction. Just ran.

Deep within she knew he had sacrificed himself so she could get on with her life. She knew this in her heart, but her mind screamed something entirely different. *You killed him. Beat him to death, as you would have Ralph Danziger.*

She ran further into the woods, unable to get her bearings. All she had learned from her grandfather deserted her. Try as she might to figure out where she was or how to backtrack to camp, her mind would wander. She saw herself pelting Ralph Danziger, then beating her grandfather. Saw the blood oozing from the punching bag. *Her grandfather's blood.*

Disoriented, she would stumble and when she would get up she wouldn't know which way she had been running. Soon she was shivering. She realized she wore only her jeans and a bra. Sometime, she dimly recalled, she had taken off her sweatshirt as she beat Ralph Danziger. Its bulk hadn't allowed her to punch with any force. Now, though, she was cold. She knew if she didn't find shelter for the night she might die.

She abandoned her flight and just stood a few minutes, waiting for the panic to subside. Her grandfather had given his life for her. His sacrifice would be in vain if she perished.

Soon her mind cleared. She was once again able to discern sounds of the forest that had always comforted her; the wind rustling through the trees, grasshoppers and other insects, an owl. She knew what had to be done. Her grandfather had taught her, after all.

Using her hands she dug a shallow ditch. She pulled branches from trees and gathered leaves. She coated the ditch with leaves and with vines tied branches together to form a makeshift blanket. She lay in the ditch, covered herself with her blanket of branches and soon fell into a dreamless sleep.

When she awoke it was daylight. Six feet from her was a wolf. No, not *a* wolf she thought, but *the* wolf who had visited the camp the day before; the wolf with the horribly deformed ear. She instinctively knew it wasn't there to harm her, but to protect her. She knew there was something more, but she couldn't quite grasp what it was.

She remembered what her grandfather had said the day before. She wouldn't make any sudden movement. She wouldn't appear threatening, but would be submissive. She whined, as her grandfather had done. She remained low to the ground and didn't stare at the wolf, just shot it quick glances. She saw its predatory yellow eyes. Looked again and its eyes were now gray, like her grandfather's. Their color kept fluctuating; the yellow of the wolf, the gray of her grandfather, as if trying to send her a message.

Suddenly she knew. Somehow her grandfather's . . . *spirit* or *essence* was within the wolf. She didn't say the words aloud, but the wolf nodded, then pawed at the ground.

Mica stood up and held out her hands, ready to embrace the creature.

The wolf lunged at her, and as it made contact became one with her. She was still standing and the wolf was gone. *Not gone*, she thought, but a part of her. The wolf, her grandfather — now both a part of her.

She allowed the wolf to guide her back to camp, no more than ten minutes away. For all the running she had done, she had gone in circles. The punching bag was gone. Had it ever been there, she wondered? Tentatively, she made her way to the tent. Her grandfather lay there dead. There was no blood, no bruises on his face or body. His face was serene, as if he had died in his sleep.

She sat and nestled his head in her lap. While she knew his spirit was within her, knew he'd given himself willingly to spare her further pain, she already missed him terribly. She cried for hours. Cried until there were no more tears. Then she cried some more.

Finally, she felt a stirring from within. She *should* have gone to the pickup and with the CB called for help. But it wasn't time. First there was the need for food, the need to hunt — to prove herself worthy to her grandfather and the wolf within.

With only a knife, she ventured deep into the forest, and finally came upon three deer by a creek. As she had been taught, she charged, watching the three deer as they fled. One hobbled slightly, as if from a leg injury. She spent the better part of the day tracking it, her sense of smell suddenly heightened. Three times she came upon the lame deer, but didn't attack. Instead, she would run straight at the deer, who scurried off. She saw it again half an hour later, but this time she approached with stealth. This time when she attacked, it was within her grasp. This time she cut its throat before it had a chance to react.

She lifted her prey onto her shoulders and with difficulty made her way back to camp, arriving at dusk. Exhausted, she was too tired, and too hungry to skin and cook the deer. With her knife she slit open its chest. The wolf within feasted for the three of them. Sufficed, she slept and learned how her grandfather and the wolf had met. It was something she *had* to know before she left the forest. Her grandfather told her.

*   *   *

After Augustus Swann had sold the mill he had, for the most part, shunned people. His wife dead, his son a disappointment and his grandsons no better, he was sorely disheartened in mankind as a whole. Too many men at the mill put in just enough work to collect their paychecks. Unless he offered monetary incentives, few did more than they were required. Others didn't put in enough work, then took it personally when Augustus fired their sorry asses. They acted as if they were owed a job whether they worked at it or not.

With the mill sold, Augustus spent a lot of his spare time with Lonnie Peterson. Lonnie, who had just turned twenty-four, wasn't as much a friend as an interesting specimen, and the two got on better than most. Lonnie had spent five years after high school studying wolves in northern Minnesota. He told Augustus he really got off on the creatures. So much of the myth about them was a crock of shit, he said. Wolves, he told Augustus, were more human than most people. His only problem, Augustus soon learned, was that Lonnie was a sick sadistic motherfucker.

Each winter, Lonnie would illegally transport a two- or three-year-old wolf back to Emory with him, though he never explained how. He would put a homemade radio collar around its neck, so he could pinpoint its location, then let it loose to hunt. He would befriend the creature, adopting a submissive role.

After a hunt, he would keep the wolf penned behind his house, with an eight-foot fence to keep it from escaping.

"It's for his own good, man," he'd tell Augustus. "Let him in the forest and some hunters will kill him for sure. I can't have that. When I'm good and ready, *I'll* kill the fucker."

Augustus thought Lonnie was just shitting him. No way he would kill a creature he'd befriended.

Sure enough, though, after about a month, when the wolf truly trusted Lonnie, he turned on the animal. He would challenge the wolf, just as in the wild where wolves often fought one another for dominance.

Augustus would watch as Lonnie, with thick padded clothes, gloves and a mask to protect his face, would spar with the wolf, finally forcing it to submit. Then Lonnie would free the animal and track it down. With Augustus at his side, he would hunt it to ground and shoot it, a big grin on his face.

"You're one crazy motherfucker, Lonnie," Augustus would tell him, though looking at the dead animal he also felt shame and revulsion. Some fear, too. He didn't doubt that if he posed a threat Lonnie would turn on him without a thought.

"Got that right, old man," Lonnie answered. "Don't you love it, though? One day I'm his best friend. The next I turn on him and destroy his spirit. Killing him is the *humane* thing to do after I've fucked with his mind."

Sadly, Augustus thought, Lonnie really believed he'd done the creature a service.

Augustus' own problem was that each year he was learning to respect the wolf more. Sure, wolves would fight for dominance, as the leader grew old and could no longer command the others. But, as a group, he felt them far more humane than humans. He'd let Lonnie have his way for three years, mainly out of fear and self-preservation, but then Lonnie brought back a female, unaware she was pregnant.

"Shit man, no way I can let her give birth, Augie," Lonnie told him when he found out. "She would be as protective of her cubs as you are of your son — maybe more so. Best if I kill her now."

Lonnie came out the next day to find the female had escaped, and its radio collar now malfunctioned.

He smiled at Augustus, unaware the old man had freed the wolf and cut off its collar.

"We'll just have to hunt her down the old-fashioned way, Augie. No big thing." He gave Augustus that grin of his that signaled he wasn't just sadistic, but insane.

Lonnie didn't find the female for five weeks, by which time she'd given birth to her cubs. Augustus, hoping the wolf had left the area, stopped hunting with Lonnie, who was clearly obsessed. When he found the den, he came running to get his friend.

"Yo, Augie. Found the fuckers. It's gonna be so fine. She gave birth to five little fuckers, and they're right outside their den — a cave I just lucked upon. I tell you, if I wouldn't get into trouble with the law, I'd let them be. They're already playing games and defining their roles. Shame we gotta waste them."

Augustus went with Lonnie, but he wasn't about to shoot any wolf cubs. He tried unsuccessfully to convince Lonnie to trap the cubs and transport them back to Minnesota. Lonnie would have none of it.

Behind some rocks, overlooking the den, Lonnie pointed to the cubs. Several rested, while two pawed at one another.

"Take your pick of the litter, Augie," Lonnie said. He began picking the cubs off one at a time. When he'd shot the last cub, the mother, who had to have been out hunting, lunged at Lonnie from behind. They both rolled down the embankment, with Lonnie finally tossing the female off of him. He shot her as she charged again. She sank her teeth into his neck before dying, her body resting on top of his.

Augustus made his way down to them.

"Augie man, get this bitch off me before I bleed to death," Lonnie said with difficulty.

Augustus saw blood gushing from Lonnie's neck. Saw that Lonnie was too weak to push the seventy-five pound wolf off of him. He decided to let nature take its course.

"Not gonna do anything for you, Lonnie. You made your bed, best you sleep in it. You make it back to your cabin, that's fine with me. You up and die, makes no nevermind to me neither. By the way, son, I set the female free and cut off her collar. Least she had a fighting chance."

Augustus sat and watched Lonnie bleed to death. For a while Lonnie begged Augustus to help him. Then he tried to extricate himself, but he'd lost too much blood. He spent his last minutes cursing Augustus.

"A waste," Augustus said, just before Lonnie died. "Up and dying and all you can do with your last breath is cuss me out."

He buried Lonnie and the wolves deep in the cave; all the wolves save one. One had been too clever for Lonnie. He'd been grazed. The bullet had torn off part of its ear. He'd played possum, watching Augustus watch Lonnie die. He still didn't move as Augustus buried Lonnie and its mother, brothers and sisters. He had been the biggest of the cubs and most likely would have been the dominant of the pack.

Augustus lay with the injured animal after burying the others. He took on a submissive role. Hours later, the wolf whined in hunger. Augustus left and shot his last deer. He returned with it, chewed some meat for the cub and spat it out.

The two formed their own pack, with Augustus the submissive male. Over the next five years he would spend most of his time in the woods with what he considered his brother. He shunned human companionship, with the exception of the camping trips he went on with Mica. He might not have redeemed himself for his often inhumane behavior, but it was a start.

So was his sacrifice, so Mica could be free of her demons.

It was the last she had heard from her grandfather until the rape in Atlanta.

*   *   *

Mica awoke the next morning with a new understanding of her grandfather. He was a far more complex man than she had imagined. He'd always been her *grandfather* — the only member of her family to treat her with kindness and respect. But she had always viewed him as old, wise and kind. She couldn't fathom he'd been headstrong, reckless and ruthless. She had never considered that he had had much of a past. Maybe, she thought, that was how most children viewed their grandparents. They came with gifts, smiles and open arms, but unlike parents, never had to discipline or expose their true selves. Mica now knew her grandfather to be full of secrets and contradictions. Seeing him for what he was, though, only made her love him more. He was flesh and blood like her, no longer the caricature of the kindly and wise grandfather she'd known.

She could have gone to the pickup to call for help, but she decided to wait and be rescued. She wanted her parents worried when she and her grandfather didn't return as expected. Maybe they would open their eyes and not view her as just another piece of furniture.

A day after she *should* have returned, Mica prepared for her rescuers. She had feasted on raw meat for two days, but now cooked a portion of the deer and left it hanging near the fire. She unhooked one of the cables that ran to the battery in the pickup, so neither the engine nor the CB would function.

She was sitting by her grandfather when her father, Sheriff Fallon and a host of others finally found her.

She had an explanation for all their questions. They were accepted without question, for she was merely a helpless girl paralyzed by the death of a loved one. What fools they were, she thought, still living in a fantasy world ruled by men.

Little had been said at home when Mica returned. There was perfunctory mourning, but no real grief. In some ways Mica thought her father was more like *his* father than he would ever want to admit. There had been no love lost between them in life. Now her father refused to make peace with him in death.

Only her mother had words for her . . . and not too many.

"If you had put it behind you, your grandfather would be alive today," she'd said tartly, at his burial.

Her grandfather had been wrong about one thing, though. Mica *hadn't* been able to purge herself of Ralph Danziger. He didn't prey on her mind constantly, as before, but she felt his presence each day as she passed his farm on her way to school.

And the kids at school treated her differently, upon her return. She hadn't come back until after her grandfather's funeral. When she returned, Josh Farrell had been back for several days, talking about her behind her back. Yet he steered clear of her. For that matter, everyone did. She scared them, it finally dawned on her. She wasn't the Mica they had grown up with. She was changed. Had changed before she'd been suspended, compliments of Ralph Danziger. Changed even more upon her return. She was no longer one of them, and she was shunned — even by Cynthia and Tiffany, who had been her closest friends.

Like a pack of wolves, they turned on one of their own; a square peg who wouldn't fit into a round hole. Worse than outright ridicule or hostility, they simply ignored her.

With no reason to stay in Emory she had fled.

Now, eight years later, she was fleeing again, but this time back *to* Emory. It wasn't a longing for home. She acknowledged no home. *Home* was a place of love and fond memories. She had precious few of those.

She had buried Ralph Danziger deep within, but hadn't purged herself of him. To go on she needed the closure her grandfather had found. Only now was she aware closure had always been within her grasp, back in Emory, but she had let it slip away out of childish ignorance.

SIXTEEN

(MARCH 1999)

SHARA

Shara and Briggs sat in the spacious living room of Estelle Winston's home on Philadelphia's Main Line. It was technically a part of Philadelphia, but a Philadelphia most only dreamed of. The Winston home wasn't an estate, but Shara thought it was damn close. Huge as it was, its only occupants were Estelle Winston and the help.

Shara had seen one of those long mahogany tables in the dining room and recalled numerous movies where one person sat at one end of the table and another at the other end, barely within shouting distance of one another.

Two and a half months had passed since Shara had made Briggs the offer of a job. He had accepted — "on a trial basis," he said — without explanation. Maybe it was because his options were so limited, Shara thought. Maybe because he was loathe to relocate. Or maybe Alexis had interceded. Whatever, the next two months had been dizzingly satisfying.

Shara vividly recalled the day she'd marched Briggs into Shelly Burke's office. Burke was nothing like the stereotype of the bail-bondsman. He wasn't the flabby, cigar-chomping, foul-mouthed bozo dressed in a shabby silk suit, shiny from too much wear. He wore an Armani suit, obviously tailored to fit his six-foot frame. A dark-skinned black, his hair was cropped short, as was the beard that covered his face. He could have worked for a Fortune 500 Company.

A man who guarded his innermost thoughts, Burke was clearly nonplused and duly impressed by the appearance of Shara's new associate. She almost thought he would ask for Briggs' autograph.

Her stock immediately rose, not only with Burke, but with every other bondsman Shara worked for. And those she didn't work for were *now* clamoring for her services.

As well as she performed on her own, she was still a woman at a man's job. There was always a reluctance to give her the toughest nuts to crack. With Briggs, a proven investigator — and a high profile one, at that — she was now a major player with so many contracts offered, she could pick and choose.

Both she and Briggs grudgingly admitted they made a good team. Often they worked on cases separately, at least on the preliminary paper trail. Shara used her computer skills to get from point $\underline{A}$ to point $\underline{B}$, while Briggs pounded the sidewalks. Neither, though, was reluctant to ask for the other's help. At some point they would join forces for the capture.

Just as she had predicted, there was newfound respect bestowed upon her when she entered a police station with Briggs, though at times it was as if she weren't there. Had she cared how others perceived their relationship, she might have been jealous. To *them*, Briggs was the brains and brawn and Shara mere window dressing. Briggs knew better and often told Shara so, apologizing for the lack of respect accorded her by law enforcement officers.

Shara wouldn't have it any other way. She was able to maintain the low profile she desired, yet pursue her quarry, which had become a biological imperative. She would be the first to admit earning Briggs' respect was more than just icing on the cake, but widespread recognition from others she shunned.

Still, Briggs was constantly agitated at the way she was ignored.

"They treat you like a house slave. Talk about you to me, with you right there. Why don't you let me put them in their place?"

"What good would it serve?" she would say. "If it makes our job easier, I don't care how they perceive our roles. I'm into self-gratification, and the money we're making ain't half bad," she added, staying in character. She didn't want Briggs to know just how little the money meant and how important the hunt itself was to her.

In mid-January, she had been summoned by Arnie Winkler and Douglas Frazier. All smiles, they'd told her their *coordination* had in fact turned into a *collaboration*, with a slam dunk victory. Everett Gaines pleaded guilty to manslaughter. While sentenced to two and a half to seven years at a minimum security prison, he would likely serve no more than a year.

Biggie's victims would share in the city's offer of $500,000, with therapy for all as long as necessary. And Arnie had been surprised that while the mayor himself balked at an apology to Kimberly Watts, His Honor had prevailed on the Cardinal to intercede.

"They're both political animals," Arnie told her. "There are no freebies. The mayor gets off the hook and the Cardinal gets an IOU for something he would have done anyway. He was genuinely moved by Kimberly Watts' religious convictions and concern that she had sinned."

Arnie also smiled when he'd told Shara about Danielle Jamieson.

"You backed the wrong horse, there, kiddo," he said, still chewing on a Tootsie Roll that Frazier kept in a jar, along with other candy on his desk. "She played you. The mayor is already making good on his word to reform DHS, and clean house if necessary. Seemed, though, that Jamieson was *part* of the problem. Did you check out her file?"

Shara reluctantly shook her head.

"She wasn't an accomplice of Shaw's. I'd considered the possibility at one time, but he was out of her league. She cut corners, though. She'd been reprimanded a number of times. Still, I gave her a chance, but she brought me nothing. Problem was, she knew all too well her co-workers had plenty of dirt on her. If she dimed on them she would have been bitten in the ass, giving her little credibility. Give her her due, though. She got engaged a week before we settled and up and quit. The woman ain't no fool."

Shara had no trouble swallowing her pride. Arnie's thoroughness had prevented a major embarrassment. She had left feeling better about herself than she had in a long time.

Shara had also sensed when it was time to cease hunting fugitives and offer Briggs one of those challenging cases she had spoken of. Two months of steady work and good pay had proven to Briggs that Shara's claims hadn't been bogus. Still he seemed a bit antsy. Hunting fugitives held little appeal for him.

Before confronting Briggs, Shara had taken Alexis to the beach, into the forest where, as usual, she appeared all but healed. She had shown Alexis three files. Her plan was to allow Briggs to decide which case to take, but Alexis had startled her.

"This one's your dream," she said, after looking through the file of a woman who had killed a nineteen-year-old boy after he'd apparently picked her up hitchhiking. "The woods. The manner of killing. *She's* the woman of your dreams."

"Will your father go for it?" Shara asked, wondering now if she should allow him to choose.

Alexis tapped Shara on the forehead, as if she were a child.

"L-l-look at the cases you chose." At times, she still stuttered, as her churning thoughts outpaced her ability to express them. Shara knew this exasperated the girl, but she seemed to have learned to accept her limitations — even in the forest. "A missing child, an embezzler and . . . a murderer. Anyone home? My father was a homicide detective."

"It wasn't intentional," Shara said with a smile, feeling embarrassed. But, she wondered if she had unconsciously made his choice simple. She *now* saw the parallels between the case and her recurring dream. But in choosing the case, she had been more concerned that it was a homicide. It was an itch Briggs could scratch, if he so desired.

"You'll find out about yourself by capturing . . . no, that's not it," Alexis said, closing her eyes, trying to find the right words. "You'll find out about yourself in hunting her down. She's not you and she's not what you think you're looking for."

"Pray tell, what am I looking for?" Shara asked, with a forced smile. She didn't know if she wanted to hear what Alexis had to say.

Aside from her psychic powers, Alexis' instinct and intellect had been stimulated by her attack. She wasn't your normal fifteen-year-old. Intellectually, she could have been a post-graduate student at college. Shara sometimes didn't particularly like Alexis analyzing her motives, but more often than not the girl was right on target.

"You want a twin . . . an emotional clone; someone you can share your world with. I wish I could be that person, but you won't let me." It was a statement of fact, not a rebuke, Shara saw from her eyes.

"That's not it, Alexis," Shara said, in protest. "You're ten years younger than me. If I were forty and you thirty, it wouldn't be a bridge we couldn't cross. At fifteen, you haven't experienced life yet. And you *know* it bugs me to no end that there's nothing I can keep from you. I trust you like no other, and I blame myself, but to me you're my younger sister."

"I know," Alexis said, and Shara could detect a hint of sadness in her voice, "but she's not the one either, and I don't want you disappointed."

"How do you know she's not the one?"

"You're looking for someone you can't find. But in hunting her you'll learn more about yourself. That's what I think your dream means." Alexis closed her eyes, looked up and seemed to be listening to some voice only she could hear. "These woods have something to do with your dream."

"What do you mean?"

"You said it yourself. These are healing woods, but not just for me. For you, too. Your healing doesn't come from being in the woods. It comes from hunting this girl down. The woods . . . I think . . . have given you a link with this girl so you can help yourself. How else can you explain your dream and the coincidence of choosing this particular file?"

Shara shook her head in wonder. "You're wise beyond your years, Alexis."

"What else do I have to do with my days?" Alexis asked. Though there was no emotion in her voice, Shara saw the melancholy in her eyes. It was sometimes difficult for Shara to remember that life was literally passing Alexis by. Others her age were dating — some doing far more. Some were involved in high school extracurricular activities that would help shape their lives. Others were thinking of college or otherwise planning their futures. Alexis, by contrast, sat at home.

Learning sign language and navigating successfully from one room to another were her triumphs. Shara didn't need psychic abilities to know these lost years weighed heavily on Alexis, as did the loneliness. In a sense the woods were a tease, a glimpse of what could be. Alexis put up a good front, but there had to be times when she despaired she would never lead a normal life.

Shara wanted to say something to ease the pain she knew Alexis felt, but was at a loss as how to comfort her. So she remained silent.

As Alexis had predicted, Briggs took all of thirty seconds to choose the homicide. Shara saw he was almost foaming at the mouth, and it had nothing to do with the $30,000 reward.

And now they were at Estelle Winston's house to get as much information as they could. Estelle Winston had been initially reluctant to see them when Shara had called.

"I've had my share of private investigators. You're wasting your time."

"We're not private investigators, Mrs. Winston," Shara had told her over the phone. "We're after the reward. We don't get a penny without a capture."

Her interest apparently piqued, Estelle Winston had agreed to meet with them.

Shara saw in Estelle Winston a woman used to intimidating others. At almost six feet, she could look Briggs in the eyes and stare Shara down. While thin, she had broad shoulders. And while Shara could imagine her friends getting face lifts and other operations to steal away the years, at fifty-five Estelle Winston seemed comfortable with the equipment she had been born with. Her nose may have been too long and too narrow, her eyes a bit pinched, but she wasn't someone out to recreate herself. There was also a profound sadness about her. She was now utterly alone; no husband and her only child dead.

A servant seated them and Estelle Winston waited ten minutes to make her entrance. Shara knew this was calculated. Everything about Estelle Winston was calculated. Shara would have to get under the woman's skin, if they were to learn anything.

"You must be Detective Briggs," she said, as Briggs rose and shook her hand.

"*Mr.* Briggs, regrettably," he corrected her with a weak smile.

"I've heard about you. Did you kill that horrible man?"

"I've been exonerated," Briggs answered.

"That's not what I asked. Power, influence or money, Mr. Briggs. A combination of one or all can set a murderer free."

"I'm not a murderer, Mrs. Winston."

"I'll take you at your word, then."

Briggs introduced Shara, whom Mrs. Winston gave the once-over and dismissed.

Shara and Briggs had discussed their approach earlier. Briggs was to take the lead. Shara would observe, remaining in the background.

"As I told your Miss Farris on the phone," she said, her eyes on Briggs, "private investigators are akin to used car salesmen. They string you along, then screw you in the end."

She sat with her hands clasped in her lap so as not to betray any emotion, Shara saw.

"We're not private investigators. And, as Miss Farris told you, we don't want a penny of your money until we find your son's killer."

"What are you then?"

"Independent contractors, Mrs. Winston," he said. They'd agreed this was the best term to use. "We take what is called a cold case — one the police are no longer actively pursuing — and solve it for the reward."

"My son's murder isn't a cold case," she said tartly, her eyes focused on Briggs.

"The police aren't actively investigating it," Briggs said, without much confidence.

"The FBI is."

"The FBI?" Briggs asked. "Why would they get involved?"

"The woman has murdered more than once — in another state, which, according to the agent who spoke to me, makes it a case for the FBI."

Briggs looked at Shara, as if to ask whether he should go on, but Shara remained expressionless.

"Why the reward, then? And, why hire private investigators? Seems like you're throwing your money away."

"I wasn't pleased with the FBI's lack of progress," she answered without elaborating.

"Would you be willing to share with us what the private investigators learned? It would save us needless duplication," Briggs added.

"I see no reason not to." Mrs. Winston gave Briggs a folder that had been on the table beside her.

Briggs thumbed through it, then passed it to Shara, who saw that Mrs. Winston once again had her hands clasped in her lap. *What are you holding back?* she thought. *What don't you want us to know?*

"You didn't get much for your money," Briggs said. "I can understand your frustration."

Estelle Winston stood. "If that will be all —"

"We haven't begun," Shara said, speaking for the first time. "Do you really want your son's killer found, or is the offer of a reward to soothe a guilty conscience?"

"The reward is sincere, and I don't like your tone," she said tartly. She sat down again, her hands clasped more tightly than ever.

"From these reports, you don't seem to have given the private investigators much to go on. Had your son been in trouble with the authorities?" Shara asked.

"He had no police record."

Now who's being evasive, Shara thought.

"I'm not asking if he had a record. As you said earlier, people of great wealth have a way of making problems, let's say, disappear."

Estelle Winston stood again. "I don't need your insinuations. My son is dead. It is *he* who is the victim here."

"Then help us find his killer. When did Steven's father die?" Shara asked, softening her tone.

"When Steven was three," she answered after sitting down, her eyes now on Shara. "Paul owned a computer software company. He was a visionary. He knew well before most how computers would revolutionize our lives."

"And you took over when he died." It wasn't a question.

"Yes, and the company prospered more than ever," she said proudly. "Paul knew computers. I knew how to promote his ideas. I hired people with Paul's vision, but all financial decisions — actually *all* decisions relating to promotion, direction and expansion — were mine. We branched out into the Internet several years ago. Everyone hopped on the software bandwagon, but the Internet was relatively unexplored."

"Which didn't leave you a lot of time to spend with Steven. He got into trouble, didn't he, to get your attention."

"He was rebellious, even as a child, yes . . . but never anything serious. Just enough to embarrass me so I'd be forced to spend time with him. Don't condemn me, Miss Farris. Steven was well cared for and wanted for nothing. You, of all people, should know a woman in a man's world has to work twice as hard to earn the respect of others. But Steven was never wanting."

Shara let it pass, though it was clear the woman didn't have a clue. Money couldn't buy love. Shara had grown up without money *and* without love. It was a mother's love, though, she missed most.

"And as he got older, he still got into trouble."

"Unfortunately Steven didn't know what the word 'no' meant," Mrs. Winston admitted "And money made his problems disappear. He thought he was immune."

"What sort of problems, Mrs. Winston?"

"I don't see —"

"Problems of a sexual nature, Mrs. Winston," Shara said. The facts of his death indicated she was on the right track.

"There were accusations of impropriety, yes."

"That went away with money. And lately?"

Estelle Winston looked deflated.

"Steven was into kinky sex, Miss Farris. Is that what you want to hear? Sex with two partners. Sex with twins. Sex with a mother and daughter. Here under my roof. What does that have to do with my son's death, for God's sake?"

Shara could see the woman's hands clasped so tightly, they were bone white.

"And the night of his death?" Shara asked, ignoring her question.

"He would frequent titty bars," she said, with distaste. "There was one near the airport where the women wore *nothing*. Sometimes he would take a girl there. Sometimes he would bring back one of the dancers for his own private show. Steven always got what he wanted."

"But the police ruled out these women as suspects?"

Mrs. Winston nodded. "He must have picked up a hitchhiker," she said. "He'd do that, too. A pretty girl hitchhiking, Steven told me, was advertising she was on the prowl. Steven, you see, liked to talk about his sexual conquests. He knew it embarrassed me. He was always looking for a challenge. Someone who might resist his charms."

"And he would still get what he wanted," Shara said, not expecting an answer.

Estelle Winston glared at her.

"This time someone fought back, didn't she? Wouldn't allow herself to be raped," Shara said.

"My son was no animal," Estelle Winston said, her voice rising.

Shara noticed she didn't dispute her use of the word rape.

"Maybe not, but you indulged him to make up for your lack of attention. And when he got into trouble, money and influence made the problem go away. It made him feel omnipotent and cost him his life. And now you want your pound of flesh."

"Do I disgust you, Miss Farris?" Estelle Winston asked, regaining her composure.

"Not as long as you can acknowledge what motivates you."

"Guilt, Miss Farris. Are you satisfied?" She paused a moment, then gave Shara a tight smile. "You're a shrewd judge of character. I underestimated you — something I seldom do. You got me to admit things I hadn't wanted to admit to myself. I was selfish and overindulgent, and yes, it cost me my son. He wanted my love, but I never had the time. My legacy to him was the notion that you could buy your way out of whatever you got yourself into. I was wrong. I want that woman to pay. Just as important, though, I want to know why she had to kill my son."

"I think we have all we came for," Shara said, rising, and Briggs followed suit.

Seated, Estelle Winston looked at Shara. "He's in this for the money," she said, acknowledging Briggs with a quick glance. "You're in it for . . . the pleasure. No offense, but he's the brains and brawn.

You're the heart. You come to a fork in the road, your will shall prevail. Wait a moment . . . please," she said, getting up, and leaving the room.

She came back a few minutes later with a check, which she handed to Shara. "I want your best effort. I don't want you cutting corners for lack of funds."

Shara tore the check up without looking at it. "We're not working for you, Mrs. Winston. If we accept the check you own a part of us. You'll hear from us when we find your son's killer. We'll show ourselves out."

They were silent until they got to Briggs' car.

"What the hell was that all about?" Briggs asked. "One minute she's talking to me, the next I'm a piece of furniture."

"She was taking my measure," Shara answered. "She mistakenly took me for a glorified secretary. You, after all, have all the credentials."

"You went for the jugular — maybe more so than was necessary."

"It *was* necessary. I put her on the defensive, something she's not used to. You saw the reports from the private investigators. She told them squat about her son. No wonder they got nowhere. I got us the information we needed, and I got her goat, as a bonus."

"You don't like her, do you?"

"I have nothing against her personally. I just can't stand people who use money to buy love. And I can't understand parents who neglect their flesh and blood and are shocked when they come to a bad end. Estelle Winston created a monster. She must accept responsibility."

"What we now know puts a whole different spin on the case. It's *not* a cold case," Briggs said. "The FBI is actively working it. Doesn't that violate your rules?"

"I have no rules, Briggs. Guidelines, yes. Steven Winston was killed two and a half months ago, and the FBI has nothing. I call that a cold case."

Shara couldn't tell him what only she and Alexis knew. Shara couldn't abandon the case. It literally haunted her dreams. She had to see it through.

"Okay, then I suggest we go see the FBI agent in charge — Claire Cleary, according to the notes. I've worked with her on occasion. Has a chip on her shoulder, but she's competent."

"Don't all us women have chips on our shoulders?"

"I used to think so," Briggs readily admitted. "Lately, though, I've been paired with nothing *but* women. Caffrey, Rios and now you. I'm no expert, but the three of you are far different than Cleary. She's referred to as 'cc Cleary' — as in carbon copy Cleary. She wants badly to be a member of the club, but doesn't get the respect she merits. She also wears her bitterness on her sleeve. If we try to circumvent her, she can tie us in knots with a single phone call. Show cooperation and she can just as easily open doors for us."

"What do we have to offer in return?" Shara asked. "She doesn't sound like the type to share if there's nothing in it for her."

"We share information."

"I don't want the FBI dogging us and scaring away the prey," Shara said.

"Not to worry. Cleary will toss us a few bones, nothing more. We, in turn, do the same."

"Sounds like a plan," Shara said.

"This time, though, let me do the talking. I *do* know Cleary. And the two of you in an alley fight I can do without."

"No promises," Shara said, with a smile. "But I'll *try* to be a good girl."

SEVENTEEN

(AUGUST 1998)

MICA

Mica met Shara, in a manner of speaking, on her first day of flight. She had little knowledge of traipsing through the woods that first night out of Atlanta. Her grandfather guided her northward through the woods, while the wolf led her safely through the forest. Mica had given herself to memories long ago locked away. Ray Donato had been the proverbial key that unlocked the door.

She could go only so far so fast. It was *her* body, after all, and she was not content to be a silent partner in her pilgrimage for redemption. She was not yet up to the pace demanded of her. That would come with time, but as dawn approached, she knew she could go no further. Her mouth was parched, her stomach screamed and her legs began cramping. She had to find shelter before her body betrayed her.

A motel? No, not until she knew if the police were on her trail. A cabin then, she thought — a summer home, unoccupied, as families prepared for the post-Labor Day return to the grind. She had passed several, but they were not yet deserted.

Finally, though, she came upon one she sensed fit her needs. She broke a window pane and let herself in. She checked the refrigerator

163

and found it empty. *That* was the tell-tale sign. You leave at the end of the summer, you clean out the fridge. If you return for a long weekend, you bring only what you need. There was, however, plenty of canned food and the electricity hadn't been turned off.

She wanted food. A shower. Sleep. Most of all sleep, but first she had to find out what the police knew. It was almost 6 a.m. She turned on the small portable black-and-white television, but kept it low, in case anyone happened by.

Ray Donato was the lead story.

"Police remain tight-lipped regarding leads in the brutal death of vice Detective Ray Donato," a female reporter began grimly. "Donato, a fifteen-year veteran on the Atlanta Police Force with numerous commendations, was found strangled to death in his car last night at 10 p.m., according to police sources."

There had been no witnesses, Mica learned, and no identification of the alleged assailant. She saw no picture of herself staring back at her from the television. There wouldn't be. She had *never* allowed herself to be photographed in Atlanta, except by Colleen for her new identity as Terése. She didn't know why at the time, but within she must have known the inevitability of her return to Emory. Jeremy's paintings would have been useless, as well. She had left fingerprints in Donato's car, but having never been arrested they couldn't be used to identify her until they could match them to those at her loft.

What surprised her, though, was no mention of a raid at Madeline Erskine's. The police weren't total fools, and the media had its *anonymous sources* within the department. A raid on a S/M den and the killing of a vice cop the same night in such close proximity. It was a connection the media wouldn't have overlooked.

It suddenly dawned on Mica that Donato had been lying about the raid. There *may* have been a raid planned, but Maddy's clientele were as influential as hers. If one had been proposed, it would have been scuttled. Donato had been out on his own. She could have killed him for his duplicity, she thought, then laughed out loud. *She had*.

Sleep beckoned, but her stomach protested. Food and a shower first. She ate dry cereal and canned fruit. Walking to the bathroom, her legs felt like jelly. She lay down on the bed for a moment. How she wanted — *needed* — a shower. A few moments of rest. A shower. *Then* sleep. A shower, then . . .

Asleep, she dreamed.

She was in the woods, naked, being pursued. She didn't turn around to look at her pursuer. It wasn't necessary. Her grandfather and the wolf saw her; were her eyes. A woman was chasing her. Her pursuer was shorter than she was and lean, with a tawny complexion and dark hair. But so many eyes. She was tempted to look behind her, doubting what she saw without having to look. *Fourteen eyes followed her every move.*

Then she realized that only two were real. The others were tattoos on the woman's breasts, as, like her, the woman was naked.

Coming to a stream, Mica crossed without hesitation. She had never been a good swimmer, and the wolf was far better suited to land. The figure behind made up ground and made contact, just as she slid down an incline into far deeper water. She felt the other woman's nails tear at the skin of her shoulder blades. As they struggled towards the surface, Mica turned to face her pursuer. As they broke the surface, she was staring at herself.

Her grandfather began to choke her look-alike and the woman began to go limp. She demanded her grandfather stop and he reluctantly complied. Mica dragged her semi-conscious clone to land, and was no longer looking at a mirror-image. Tawny skin, dark hair, brown eyes and the tattoo. Mica fled, knowing the other — *Shara*, her mind screamed — was too weak to follow.

The next moment the forest was gone and she had walked through a wall into a room where a figure was stirring on the bed. *Shara*, her mind whispered. Mica felt terribly exposed, as mirrors surrounded her from every wall, as well as the ceiling. When the figure awoke, she would be immediately spotted. But glancing around, Mica saw no reflection.

Shara turned on her back and looked at the mirror on the ceiling. She saw what Mica saw; her wounds from the chase in the forest began to heal.

Mica felt herself being sucked back through the walls, back into the forest where she was now alone. She screamed in frustration. She had wanted to make contact with this stranger, but hadn't been allowed.

Screamed again and awoke.

Awake, her shoulder felt raw, as if she'd been scratched. She went to the bathroom and looked in the mirror. There were fresh marks on her shoulder, but as she peered at them they began to heal. The pain subsided. Then the wounds completely disappeared.

A shower, she thought. No. Not yet. What she'd experienced while asleep was more than a dream. She had to puzzle it out before anything else.

Looking at herself, she realized she was naked. She was certain she had been clothed when she'd fallen asleep. She stumbled out of the bathroom, her legs still weak from her actual journey through the woods, and saw her clothes neatly folded by the bed. Mica *never* neatly folded her clothes when she returned from a S/M session. All she wanted was a shower. Her clothes littered each room as she undressed. After a shower, sleep was all she desired. It wasn't until the next morning that she would pick up after herself. So, why the clothes piled neatly now?

She shook her head in bewilderment. It wasn't significant.

What intrigued her most was the woman — *Shara*. She'd been chased . . . no, *hunted*, something within corrected her. Shara had . . . no, she corrected herself again, Shara *would* come after her. Not yet, though. When, Mica didn't know, but this woman was a predator and Mica was to be her prey.

But why had she seen herself when she had stared at Shara eye-to-eye in the stream? And why had her grandfather tried to kill her?

She and this Shara must have something in common, she reasoned. That's why she had seen herself when she'd faced Shara in the water. This Shara must have been plagued by memories similar to her own. This Shara hadn't been able to exorcize them, so her grandfather decided she must die. He must have feared that she, too, wouldn't be able to purge herself of her guilt and rage, even after she avenged herself. Having failed once again, with no one left to strike out at, might Mica succumb to self-pity with suicide the only way out?

All these thoughts ricocheted in Mica's mind. Every answer brought a new question.

What Mica did know was that somehow she and this Shara were inextricably linked. She likened it to making a phone call and crossing lines. She would hear a third party. This link wouldn't be broken, though, she was certain. When she stood in Shara's room, it had had a different feel than the rest of her dream. She — or an extension of herself — *had been in that room.* Had she wanted, had she been given more time, she could have touched this woman.

Was this Shara aware of her, she wondered? Not to the extent Mica was aware of her adversary. And that was the word — *adversary* — that best suited her, Mica decided. They would cross paths. Shara *would* take up the hunt. Mica would be prepared. She almost looked forward to their combat, to their eventual meeting, and to Shara's ultimate defeat. A worthy adversary, Mica thought, as she sunk into a dreamless sleep, but one doomed to fall short of her prey.

EIGHTEEN

Shara was aware Briggs was worried she would overreact when they met with the FBI agent, the one with the chip on her shoulder. Walking into the building that housed the U.S. Attorney's Office and FBI on Fifth and Chestnut Streets, Briggs had reiterated what he'd hoped to accomplish for the sixth time.

Shara couldn't blame him. For the first time, with Estelle Winston, Briggs had seen a side of Shara he wasn't aware existed; Shara the predator. He had seen the Shara who would go to any lengths to get what was necessary. The end *did* justify the means. He had seen Shara not only destroy the woman's carefully constructed facade, but then intentionally inflict pain *after* it was no longer necessary. He had seen Shara strip the woman of her dignity; forced her to look at the monster *she* had created. He'd seen Shara get off on bringing Estelle Winston down a notch or two. It hadn't been a pretty sight for him, she imagined.

Get used to it, Briggs, she thought.

She'd been on her best behavior for over two months, as she made hunting fugitives seem a rewarding alternative to any other job Briggs might be offered. She would have allowed him to puzzle out this case, as well, but the stakes had risen when she discovered the woman they were after was that of her dreams.

If she shattered the illusion of the competent, but compliant bounty hunter she had carefully crafted, so be it. *In her hunt, she would learn something about herself*, Alexis had said. Briggs would have to bear with her, follow *her* lead, bend to *her* will.

While her dreams had been intensifying for weeks now — like sitting in the first row of a movie theater — there had been a subtle change the night before. For the first time she could actually feel the presence of the woman she pursued *after* she awoke. She had looked at all the mirrors in her room, but had seen nothing. Still, she felt a hand reach out and almost touch her. Now actively pursuing her quarry, their relationship had altered. For the moment she was content to remain the voyeur, but it wasn't in her nature to be passive. At some point she hoped to take control of the dream; to work it to her advantage.

She also had to be ready for some verbal acrobatics with Briggs. There was no way she could convince him that something she learned couldn't be explained by traditional investigative techniques.

Today he needn't have worried. Estelle Winston they would never question again. Shara had but one opportunity to get what she needed, and with Briggs unsuccessful, she had interceded. With this FBI agent, Shara was merely there to observe; to look for chinks in her armor, maybe gather ammunition for a future confrontation. No matter how frustrating the woman might be, Shara would hold her tongue.

Special Agent Claire Cleary rose and gave Briggs a tight smile, as they shook hands. A firm handshake, like a man, Shara thought, when Briggs introduced her. Like Estelle Winston, Cleary all but ignored Shara when they were introduced.

"I don't know whether to offer congratulations or condolences, Lamar," she said when they were seated. "I'm genuinely sorry no way could be found to keep you on the force. I didn't have to pussyfoot around you. You never felt threatened by me as an FBI agent or as a woman. I can't say that for many."

Shara thought the woman was full of herself. She liked to hear herself talk, and given the opportunity would have gone on for another ten minutes.

She was in her late forties and not unattractive. Shara could see, though, that she worked at projecting an image that intentionally obscured her sensuality, from her short-cropped brown hair to the masculine pants suit that all but obliterated her figure. Shara saw a woman trying to hide her femininity; to be one of the boys.

In the past two days she had seen two successful career women, but they were as different as night and day. Estelle Winston had exuded confidence and authority, except when discussing her son. Claire Cleary saw opportunity for advancement passing her by and was recklessly and ruthlessly intent not to allow that to occur.

Shara had already taken the woman's measure. She would enjoy knocking her off her lofty perch . . . when the time came.

"So I hear you're a bounty hunter now," she said, not hiding her distaste.

"You do your homework, Claire," Briggs said, finally able to put an end to her monologue. "Know your enemy, right?"

"That's unfair. Why all of a sudden are we enemies?"

"Figure of speech, Claire. I'm hoping for the opposite, actually."

"Why are you interested in the Winston case?" Cleary asked, seemingly tiring of the foreplay. "There's no fugitive with an out-standing warrant."

"Your sources are passing you old news," Briggs said with a smile. "We don't solely pursue fugitives. There's more money in cases with a reward from a private source. Estelle Winston wants her son's killer and, no offense, she's betting $30,000 we can find her before you."

"But it's an active case, Lamar. Reward or not, I can't have you interfering."

"C'mon, Claire, the woman hasn't killed in three months. August, September, October, November — it was like clockwork. Then nothing and here it is March. I call it a cold case, unless there's something I'm missing."

Shara saw Cleary hesitate a moment. How much to divulge, she could almost hear the woman debating. She appeared ready to bite a nail, then abruptly forced her hand from her mouth. Her nails were bitten to the quick, much like Shara's. With Shara it was rage and anticipation that was the cause. With Cleary, it was a nervous habit, a sign of insecurity.

"You've got a point," she finally said. "We have hit a wall, so to speak. Now," she said, leaning forward and looking directly at Briggs. "Why should I help you? What's in it for . . . us?" Shara knew she meant, *what's in it for me?*

"Pardon my arrogance, Claire, but you know I'm a straight shooter. We'll find the woman, with your help or without it. All we want is the reward, no notoriety. We can turn her over to the local authorities and they can be showered with praise, or we can turn her over to you, then vanish. Help us and we owe you. It's as simple as that."

"I like your honesty, Lamar. I'll share what we have, though it's not much."

"And make a few calls so we can check out leads without butting our heads against the wall."

"That too can be arranged."

She opened the file and gave a crisp, succinct report.

"Terése Richards was a high-priced call girl who, oddly enough, had never been arrested. Detective Ray Donato in Atlanta somehow stumbled onto her and she apparently panicked and killed him. Left fingerprints all over the car, which allowed the locals, with *our* help, to locate her.

"She has killed three times since — once a month, like you said. She hitches a ride and strangles the driver. She was headed north when we lost track of her."

Cleary made copies of the police reports for each of the homicides and passed them to Briggs, along with a police composite sketch of the woman.

Briggs looked them over and handed them to Shara. He winced as he gave them to her, knowing her reaction the last time he had handed her bare-boned reports which hid more than they told. He was expecting an outburst from her, she knew, but she merely perused the reports and remained silent.

Briggs *almost* audibly sighed.

"No motive has surfaced?" Briggs asked.

"Personally, I think the Donato killing wasn't planned. A panic reaction, like I said before. And there are precious few female serial murderers, so developing a profile is difficult. I'm sorry I can't be of more help," she said, rising.

"Let me know who you want to speak to and I'll grease the wheels. I would hope you would pass on anything relevant you might learn. This isn't a competition after all, Lamar. The cop in you wants her in jail before someone else dies. I know $30,000 is a big chunk of change, but can you put a pricetag on a human life?"

"We appreciate your help, Claire. We'll be every bit as forthcoming as you've been, if that puts your mind at ease."

*   *   *

They walked to a park at Fifth and Chestnut in silence. They had in many ways come to understand one another's manner of processing information over the past months. Each was digesting what had been said — and left unsaid — and was waiting for privacy so there would be no interruptions. Shara the lifetime loner was becoming a team player . . . with Lamar Briggs, yet. What's the world coming to, she wondered, and smiled inwardly.

March had been relatively mild so far. The pessimist in Shara had expected one of those late-winter snowstorms that paralyzed the city for a week or more, since all winter there had been nothing but rain. Today it was not only mild, but the sun was shining.

Seated, Shara was smiling.

"Something funny?" Briggs asked.

"That parting shot of yours was classic."

Now it was Briggs' turn to smile. "Well, she *wasn't* particularly forthcoming. I'm a bit disappointed, to tell you the truth. Cleary must want this one bad. Those police reports," he said, shaking his head in exasperation, "were expressly written for us and nosey journalists. I wanted to call her on them, but it wasn't worth starting a fight. You, by the way, were a model of decorum," he said, again flashing a smile; a genuine one — one which Shara saw too little of from the man.

"What did I tell you? We *did* get what we came for — names, places, dates, and for a while she will keep her word and allow us to poke around with her blessing," Shara said. "So, mission accomplished."

"She's holding something back," Briggs said.

"Like what?"

"What our killer's been up to the past three months," he said. "She knows, but she ain't saying."

"You've dealt with the FBI. Why the secrecy?"

"Something to offer us later, as a *quid pro quo*. You never know, we just might catch a break. I get the feeling Cleary feels this is a make-or-break case for her. I know she's been bucking for a promotion for . . . well, for a long time. She's competent, but not overly imaginative. And she doesn't command a hell of a lot of respect. Worse, she's aware of it. If she can use us to solve this case, it could do her a lot of good. By the same token, if we deliver the killer, she's a failure."

"So we gotta watch our backs with her," Shara said.

"Yeah, and beat her to the punch by finding out what our girl's been up to or Cleary will cut us off at the knees, if we become irritations. She can deny us the access we need."

"You're so devious, Briggs," Shara said. "It's a real turn-on, you know."

Briggs flushed. To hide his embarrassment he went on quickly, not looking at Shara. "We find out what she's been holding back, we can tell Cleary to go fuck herself. You know, no more cooperation from *us* unless she provides us with something juicy."

"You *are* getting the hang of it," Shara said, then paused. "I figure we have two weeks before she strikes again."

"Which means Cleary will drop her little morsel in one week if we don't find out first. One of us has to go to Atlanta," Briggs said. "I assume—"

"You go to Atlanta," Shara said, and by his expression knew she'd surprised him. "You'll be dealing with cops — your strong suit. Why was Donato killed? Why was this Terése unknown to the police? Who the hell was the woman? You'll be in your element."

"And you?"

Shara looked at her partner — for she now considered him an

equal, not an employee. "It's time I came clean. And you won't like what I'm going to say—"

"You haven't been jerking my chain; holding back on me?" Briggs interrupted, his voice full of suspicion.

"That's not it at all. Look, long before we took this case I'd been having dreams about this woman."

Shara saw Briggs roll his eyes.

"Let me finish, then ridicule me." She paused, took a deep breath, then went on. "Alexis says this is the woman from my dreams. There's some psychic connection."

Shara now took out the police composite of Terése Richards.

"I've seen this woman in my dreams. She's leaner, maybe from being on the run, but it's her. I want to go to Dismal, Virginia and see if I can get a handle on her. I want to get inside her head."

She fell silent, waiting for Briggs' reaction.

"You're right. I *don't* like it. I'm a cop, even if I'm not on the force. I still think like a cop is what I mean. I can accept hunches. Gut reactions. Instinct. Call it what you want. But a *dream*. A *psychic connection*. You lose me there," he said, shaking his head wearily.

"So call it a hunch, if it will make you happier," Shara said. "I just wanted to clear the air. I tell you now, at least you can come to grips with it as you see fit. Problem is, now that we're on the case, this feeling of her presence is getting stronger. I don't want it to come between us. It's out in the open, all right? Deal with it. Even if you don't believe a word I say, it makes sense to check out the killing in Dismal. We know Steven Winston probably tried to rape her. We'll have Donato and," Shara paused and opened the file, "Kenny McIntyre, from the Dismal crime scene to compare. We connect the dots and get a bead on this woman. We learn as much, maybe more than Cleary. Whadda you think?"

"Sounds like a plan," Briggs said glumly. "Try to dig up some facts, though, without resorting to a seance."

Now Shara could detect the sarcasm in his voice. She wished she could drag him to the woods in Cape May, and he could see Alexis, almost healed, and grasp her psychic abilities. But he wasn't ready yet. Maybe never would be. It really didn't matter. This was, after all, about her and this Terése.

Something about the name bothered her, but she would wrestle with that later. *In hunting this woman she would learn about herself.* Whether Briggs believed her or not was irrelevant. Instinct — the kind Briggs believed in — told her she would learn a lot about her quarry in Dismal . . . and maybe something about herself in the process.

NINETEEN

(AUGUST–DECEMBER 1998)

MICA

A sense of lethargy surrounded Mica over the next several days in the cabin. She'd slept twenty-four hours straight, yet when she woke up, her body throbbed and all she wanted was to sleep again.

Television reports hadn't uncovered anything new of substance. She *should* be on her way, she told herself not only to get distance between herself and the Atlanta police, but to begin her trek to Emory. The cabin was a safe haven that beckoned her every time she prepared to leave.

Finally, on the fourth day, she was identified. The TV showed an ashen-faced Madeline Erskine being led by police to a patrol car. Unlike most alleged criminals, she didn't shield herself, but held her head high.

"Good for you, Maddy," Mica said, aloud.

"Early this morning," the same reporter who had followed the story from its inception told viewers, "Atlanta police raided the S/M dungeon of Madeline Erskine, arresting the thirty-eight year old mother of three on charges of prostitution and child endangerment—"

"Prostitution! Child Endangerment!" Mica said to the screen. "What a crock of shit."

Maddy had three children — daughters sixteen and thirteen and a son, ten. But she would always send them to friends when she had "guests" over. Mica felt confident Maddy's children hadn't witnessed any of her S/M games. She also knew, deep down, this was a ploy by the police to get information from her. The reporter confirmed her suspicions.

"Late this afternoon, police finally identified the alleged killer of Detective Ray Donato . . ."

Mica saw a police composite of herself on the screen and almost burst into laughter. She could see herself in the drawing, but just barely. Either the artist lacked the requisite skills or Maddy — and any others who had been questioned by the police — had deliberately provided a description that bore little resemblance to her.

Cameras then panned to the building she lived in.

"According to the police, Terése Richards lived in the loft of this building. Neighbors haven't seen her since the night Detective Donato was brutally murdered."

There were interviews with neighbors, most of whom Mica hardly knew other than to exchange hellos.

" . . . such a nice woman. Kept to herself, but polite . . ."

"No, if she was a prostitute she didn't bring men to her loft . . ."

"Who would have thought? She'd never raised her voice, much less resorted to violence . . ."

Thank goodness there was nothing about Jeremy, Mica thought, as she flipped off the television.

A sense of urgency arose within her. It *was* time to leave. She'd regained her strength. She would continue her trek through the woods, but this time she'd pace herself. Though well-conditioned, she knew she would be using muscles unaccustomed to such stress. She would have to slowly work her way into shape. Mica could put herself in the wolf's hand, but *she* would determine when to rest, when to stop and the pace of her journey.

She made her way north the next two weeks, finding cabins along the way where she stayed overnight. Often, there was canned food for sustenance. She'd found a Walkman at one cabin and listened to the news. Police had no leads on her whereabouts. After a few days a new horror made her old news.

She continued on until her period arrived. She'd always been regular — every twenty-eight days. She had wondered if, with the wolf and her grandfather now awake, her body might readjust, but right on schedule she had felt the telltale cramps and bloating.

Just before she began to bleed, she gave herself to the wolf. She sensed some need, and instinctively knew he would make sure she wasn't harmed. Shelter was a small cave. She began to bleed just after she'd located it, cursing herself for not having brought any sanitary napkins.

"I'm yours. Knock yourself out," she said aloud to the wolf.

Sometimes she thought it was good not to have to make decisions. Now she peered from within aware, but having passed the torch for the five days of her period.

She shed her clothes and urinated around the area near the cave; a combination of urine and blood. Staking out her territory, she knew, letting other animals know to keep away or suffer the consequences.

Over the next five days, she alternately slept and hunted. She hadn't thought she needed the rest, but she had. A part of her longed to go to a nearby creek to bathe, but she didn't. She knew she'd smell rank to others, but her smell was like an exotic perfume to her senses. She caught several rabbits which she brought back to her den and ate raw.

The Mica in her thought she would feel exposed, roaming the area around her den in the nude. While not inhibited by nature, she feared the reaction she'd receive if she ran into hunters or bikers. She was, after all, wanted by the police, and she should have taken extra precautions. But oddly, she never felt so liberated. Maybe it was the wolf within, but she felt at home in the woods, and clothing was unnecessary. And, just as on the night her grandfather had died, she dug a ditch, lined it with leaves and covered herself with a blanket of branches when sleep beckoned.

On the fifth day, the bleeding ended. Before putting on her blood-caked jeans, she urinated on herself, the warm liquid coating her legs like a second skin. Her jeans, which had fit snugly when she'd left Atlanta were loose. Now she knew why she'd chosen the other jeans in her backpack. She'd lost weight and now they'd fit. With no underwear, she put on a sleeveless t-shirt that clung to her body.

She was aware the wolf had given itself over to her grandfather. There was something *he* had to accomplish. Again, Mica gave up control. Before leaving her den, she looked at her image in the creek. She still hadn't bathed in over a week. Her hair was unruly, stringy and full of dirt and sweat. Her face was gaunt. Her body, while lean, was toned, even muscular from weeks of traipsing through the woods. She hadn't shaved in close to two weeks and hair sprouted from under her armpits; more hair than normally would have grown during that period. It was the wolf within her. And her rank odor, while appealing to her, would surely make others wince. In short, she was sexually alluring, yet repulsive.

She made her way out of the woods to the roadway at dusk. It was a lightly-traveled road. Her grandfather wanted something, but what? she wondered.

A car stopped and she hopped in. With darkness approaching, in her tight jeans and revealing top, she must have appeared sexy, even easy. The teen who picked her up — zits covering his face — looked uneasy.

"Where ya going?" he asked.

"North," she said. She'd put her backpack in the backseat, but found herself grasping the chain with the crucifix she hadn't touched in a month.

He talked non-stop for a mile or two, about his girl and his job with Pizza Hut, while giving her quick glances. Mica remained silent. He abruptly pulled over to the side of the road.

"I'm sorry Ma'am, but . . . this be as far as I'm going."

Mica gave him a knowing smile, got out, hearing him apologize again, but he peeled off as soon as she had shut the door.

The next driver, a salesman, seemed more at ease. He was in his late forties, twenty pounds overweight, and not-too-pleasant on the eyes. His short black hair had bits of gray.

"Kind of gamey, aren't you?" he said, rolling down his window. "You into going natural? Not that I mind. Find it a turn-on, to be perfectly honest."

This was the one, something told her, though she wasn't sure just what her grandfather wanted.

He, too, drove only a few miles, then pulled over to the side of the road. He didn't make excuses. He didn't ask her to get out. No, he wanted something from her. Wanted *her*.

"How about you pay me now, then we can drive on till I have to turn off," he said.

"Pay you what?"

"Don't play hard to get now, honey. We both know, rank as you are, I want you and you want me."

"I don't want any part of you, mister," Mica said "All I want is a ride."

While she spoke, he placed his hand on her leg, then cupped one of her breasts. She slapped his hand away, but he grabbed it.

"I don't think so," he said, squeezing her hand until it ached. "You want rough, I'll give you rough." He slapped her across the face. The smile he had previously displayed now turned hard. His hand again cupped her breast. He grunted as he unzipped his pants.

"Please stop," Mica said, giving him one final chance. "I want to get out."

He ignored her, ripping her t-shirt when he couldn't pull it over her head.

"All right," Mica said, sounding resigned. "I'll give you what you want." She pushed his hand off of her and unzipped her jeans, so he would think she had given in. She pulled her jeans down, exposing her thick pubic hair, mottled with blood, piss and dirt from over a week without bathing.

"Eat me," she said, "then I'll do you." She wasn't asking. With her having seemingly assented to his assault, he did as he was told.

Without a word he bent down, and as he did she coiled the chain around his neck and jerked once. As with Donato, it was her grandfather's strong hand, and as with Donato she had severed his jugular and he was dead, even as blood spurted onto her breasts and exposed genitals. And, as with Donato, she saw the wolf's snout emerge — this time from her vagina — and lap up his blood.

Making sure no other car was approaching, Mica got out and ran back into the woods. Her grandfather having got what he wanted, he now acquiesced to Mica, who now wanted only to flee, find a body of water and bathe. She made her way north for at least twenty minutes, found a stream and, walking against the current, made her way upstream. There would be no way to trace her scent.

Finally feeling safe, she took off her clothes and washed. She tied her bloody jeans and tattered top around rocks and saw them sink to the bottom. Shivering, she put on a new pair of jeans and a sweatshirt, then walked for another three hours before finding a vacant cabin to spend the night.

She was tired and angry. Why had her grandfather forced her to be humiliated? Why had he the need to kill? It wasn't the Augustus Swann she'd known, but then again, she recalled feeling that her grandfather had a dark side she had been largely unaware of.

Too exhausted to fight sleep, she went to bed. In a dream her grandfather provided some answers.

*   *   *

Augustus Swann cheated on his wife only once. He'd played the field until he was twenty-eight, but Ashley Ross won his heart and soul within two weeks. They were married six months later. Not yet fore-man at the lumber mill, he and a half-dozen other workmen would go for a few drinks after work at a bar conveniently located across the street from the mill.

Ruth — that was all he knew her by — a buxom redhead, had made a move on him on numerous occasions, but he had no desire to betray Ashley for a night of passion. While Ashley was no tiger in bed, she gave herself freely and often, and Augustus was never wanting. Yet one night, after a few too many drinks, he woke up at 2 a.m. to find himself in Ruth's bed.

He'd dressed and rushed home — shame washing over him in waves — to find his house had been broken into. Ashley was in the kitchen naked and unconscious; having been raped and repeatedly beaten. Doctors had found semen from at least three men in her. She lingered between life and death for three days before waking.

She'd told both Augustus and the police that she couldn't remember anything of the attack. She had been cooking dinner in the kitchen, waiting for Augustus to get home, then woke up in a hospital bed.

Though she never changed her story, deep down Augustus was certain she knew her assailants. She was afraid to name them for fear of what he would do. Gentle as he always had been with her, he was easy to anger. Before his marriage he had spent any number of nights in jail, cooling off after a barroom brawl. If he ever found out who had assaulted her, he vowed to kill them, after cutting off their testicles and feeding them to the bastards.

She knew this was no idle threat. She didn't want to lose her man, Augustus rationalized, so she maintained her silence. It made him love her all the more and deepened his shame.

Nine months later she gave birth to Mica's father. While not his child, Augustus had raised him as his own. It had been a difficult childbirth; he was to be their only child.

The rage that had simmered within Augustus soon exploded. *He* knew his son wasn't his flesh and blood. And God had further punished him for his one transgression, by not allowing him to sire a child of his own.

He stayed out at night later and later, turning to alcohol to soothe his conscience. Unable to control his inner turmoil, for a while he became abusive towards Ashley. In a perpetual drunken stupor he would hit her when she was slow to heed his commands; hit her when she wouldn't hold her tongue in an argument; hit her if she ignored him when they would quarrel. She took his abuse for two years.

He only woke up when she finally left him, taking her son with her to her parents.

"You get help, Augustus. You come back the man you were or you'll never see either of us again."

He hadn't known what loneliness was until he came home at night to a house without Ashley. He was never one to seek the help of others, and he didn't seek professional help now. He went cold turkey; then remained sober for six months before calling Ashley. He'd told her he didn't want to see her until *she* could trust him again. They talked on the phone nightly for a month, and then she returned.

He never laid a hand in anger on her again. He had done the best he could with his bastard son, but the boy wasn't at all like Augustus. He had no drive, no ambition, no passion. He was neither scholarly nor an athlete nor particularly good with his hands. He just *was*.

Had Augustus been able to mold his son in his own image, it wouldn't have mattered that he wasn't really his child. Had he had Ashley's lust for life, good humor and charm, he would have embraced him as well. But the youth, so unlike either of his parents, was a constant reminder of his betrayal. And when he married, he chose someone much like himself; humorless, dour and unfeeling — the polar opposite of Ashley.

And his grandchildren, save for Mica, were just like their father. Mica, somehow, not only had Ashley's sky blue eyes and long-flowing golden hair, but her smile and personality. In Mica, Augustus saw Ashley, the child he had never sired.

When Ashley died, never having revealed who had attacked her, it was only Mica that kept Augustus from lashing out, from falling apart. He had kept his rage bottled within for thirty-five years, but it had always been a constant companion. And now that Mica had been defiled and he was once more awakened, it was his time to avenge himself against predators like those who had ravaged his Ashley.

*   *   *

Mica awoke in a sea of tears. She'd *wanted* to know why her grandfather had the need to kill, but now that she knew it disturbed her even more. She now understood, too, why he had sacrificed himself to save Mica from the anguish she'd gone through after she had been raped by Ralph Danziger.

She wished she'd gotten to know her grandmother better. She had only been eight when Ashley Swann had died, too young to appreciate what a woman she had been. Had she lived, Mica would have confided in her after Danziger had attacked her. She was sure her grandmother would have stood by her side, much as her grandfather had.

She couldn't deny — *wouldn't* deny — her grandfather his revenge, for her mission was no different. But she wished she had someone with whom she could share her churning emotions. She wished she had reached out to Jeremy, who had also bottled up secrets that tormented him. She wished she could reach out to this stranger, Shara, who, instinct told her, shared her pain and might be able to understand and offer solace. But Shara wasn't ready yet. For now, Mica's only companion was herself.

She had followed the same ritual the next month; traveling through the woods, finding unoccupied cabins for food, recuperation and shelter. By the end of October she was somewhere in Virginia. She recalled she had skirted Virginia Beach, a city too large for her tastes. As her period approached she had found a lair, not too far north of the city. After her period she had once again killed at her grandfather's whim.

Against her better judgment she had traveled again, into November. She'd wanted to stop; *not* to abandon her mission, but to rest. The constant travel through cold, biting rain that would soon turn to snow was almost too much for her.

She was exhausted, lethargic, even delirious at times, yet she plowed on.

From the outset, she had been driven by forces she was having difficulty controlling. Doing the bidding of those within her in November had been a mistake, she knew, but she felt helpless. Twice she had collapsed in the forest, once awakening under a quilt of snow. The week of her period had been unbearable. Every muscle ached, and she'd been unable to catch any animals. She ate berries and insects, only to vomit what she had eaten after it sickened her. She'd spent most of the week cowering under leaves, her body shivering from the cold.

She beseeched her grandfather to abandon his search for that month. *I'm so weak*, she told him. *I don't have the strength to fight your battles.* But he wouldn't be denied.

Her senses had been refined over the past two months. She recalled the teenager who had given her a ride. She'd known when she got into the car he wouldn't attack her. Now, she didn't have to wait to get into a car. An automobile, pickup or truck would stop, and she could smell, almost immediately, whether the driver was a predator, or just someone out to help a stranded traveler.

She emerged from the forest on Route 291, just outside of Philadelphia, near the airport. The city's lights beckoned, but first, her grandfather demanded a sacrifice. She tried to fight him, making no attempt to hail the few passing cars as they approached.

Then a car slowed, as it came abreast of her. She could barely concentrate to hear his words.

" . . . not wait all day . . ."

"Get the fuck in . . ."

She found herself in a car, yet she wanted to flee. This . . . boy, possibly still a teen, reeked of evil, just as she stank of blood, piss and sweat. He was not like the others, she sensed. Her stench turned him on. He drove for less than a quarter of a mile, before pulling over under some trees. She wondered why he wanted her. He was handsome. He certainly wasn't wanting for female companionship.

"My name's Steven," he said. "What's yours?"

She was stunned. Why tell her his name if he planned to attack her? She kept silent.

He slapped her. Slapped her roughly. His sudden viciousness so stunned her, she dropped the chain she clutched. In the dark, she couldn't see it, couldn't find it with her hand.

"Your name, bitch," he said again, raising his hand, as if to strike her.

"Mica," she said, figuring why not tell him the truth. One of them would soon be dead.

"Know why I'm telling you my name, Mica?" he asked, rolling her name off his tongue with relish.

"You're going to kill me," she answered dully.

He laughed. "What do you think I am, an animal? No, I *get* what I want, and as funky as you are, I want *you*. Want you because of the funk. Because of your stench. I'm going to lick you clean, then fuck your brains out. And you'll like it and beg for more."

"Full of yourself, little man, aren't you," Mica said, her right hand still searching for the chain.

He slapped her again.

"It's Steven."

"Full of yourself, *Steven*. You can fuck me, but you can't make me enjoy it."

He took out a roll of bills and flashed them to her.

"This says you'll enjoy it . . . or at least fake enjoying it. Makes no never mind to me."

"You don't want me, Steven. Trust me. Let me out."

He slapped her again, then kissed her. She bit him and like Donato, he bit her back and laughed.

Where the fuck is the chain? she said to herself. *It can't be under the seat.*

His hands were yanking down her jeans.

"Hairy, aren't you?" He pulled at her pubic hair, and she yelled in pain. Then his fingers were inside of her. Rough. Hard.

Without warning, he uttered a scream of terror and withdrew his fingers, bloody and raw.

The wolf had bitten him, sensing her danger.

"What the fuck you got in there, a mousetrap? You goddamn bitch." He punched her in the face with his other hand. Hit her so hard she almost lost consciousness. He tried to punch her again, but her arm was now a wolf's paw, and she slapped him away.

With her right hand, she finally found the chain. She looked in his face and saw he was crazed. Even with the chain she feared for her safety. She had to regain control.

"All right, Steven. I'm sorry," she said, soothingly. "You're right. You *do* get what you want. I don't want to be hurt anymore."

As she talked, she pulled his zipper down and removed his penis from his pants, stroking it gently.

"Eat me. Eat me now. Make me enjoy it, Steven."

He gave her a smile, bent down and she had the chain around his neck. Her grandfather pulled the chain tight, but not tight enough to bite into his skin. She knew what he wanted of her. She looked at Steven, his eyes bulging; real fear in his face, possibly for the first time in his life.

"You get what you want, right, Steven?" she asked. "If I spare you, you'll give me all your money, right?"

He nodded.

"Then tomorrow, you'll fuck with someone else, isn't that right? Money's always got you what you wanted." She paused. "Not this time, lover."

Her grandfather tightened the chain slowly. He wanted Steven to suffer. So did she. Just before he stopped breathing, his face turning blue, her grandfather pulled sharply and, as the blood flowed, the wolf fed.

Getting out of the car, Mica stumbled into the woods and came to a body of fetid standing water. Too tired to move on she bathed in the water that smelled as rank as she did. She didn't care about accumulated dirt from the past week. She had to get Steven off of her. She couldn't allow his vile blood to seep into her pores. Even the wolf hadn't fed with relish. It was as if Steven's blood repulsed him, too.

She changed clothes and made her way to the city. There would be no more debates; no more acquiescing to her grandfather. It was winter — well, it *felt* like winter, even if the calendar said otherwise. She would never make it to Emory if she didn't hole up for the winter. And where better to disappear than in a city like Philadelphia.

She was no stranger to the city. Her parents had taken her to the city a number of times. Funky as she now looked, she would blend in on South Street. From there, with some decent food and the cold thrust from her bones, she could decide where to crash for the winter.

TWENTY

Shara wasn't certain what her trip to Dismal would accomplish. The crime scene was three and a half months old, after all, yet she was drawn almost against her will. It was true, as she'd told Briggs, instinct demanded being where Terése had been. Only there would this woman allow Shara to crawl inside the deep recesses of what must be a tortured soul.

It was something Deidre had been particularly good at; thinking like her prey. The random thought of Deidre wasn't comforting. Deidre lost to her. Lysette lost to her. Who replaced them? Briggs, she thought, and laughed aloud. No, she would banish all thoughts of Deidre and Lysette, at least for now.

Drawn almost against her will. The thought kept popping into her head as she drove south. Dismal was located, she'd been told when she had called the local police department, halfway between Isle of Wight and Virginia Beach. *Dismal*, she thought. It sounded like a name from the Old West. With such a name, the only tourists she could imagine visiting were the sick and depraved. "Me and the kids, we done went to Dismal and had a swell time," she could imagine someone telling their friends and drawing stares. She only hoped the local police weren't . . . well, *dismal* at their job.

When she was twenty minutes away from her destination Shara began seeing images of which at first she could make no sense.

A car. A man and a woman inside. The man with a gun. Pointing it at himself, then at her, at himself, then at the woman again. A chain — with a crucifix dangling. The chain around the man's neck. Blood. Blood over the interior of the car, splattered over the woman. Shara could smell the blood, taste the blood, even feel the blood seeping into her skin . . .

A horn interrupted her thoughts, and she saw herself driving on the wrong side of the two-lane highway towards an eighteen-wheeler. She veered to the right without thinking, narrowly missing the onrushing truck, whose driver continued to blow his horn in irritation long after it had passed.

Shara pulled over to the shoulder. Sweat was pouring from her like a balloon that had sprung a leak, and she was shaking uncontrollably.

The images had been so vivid, so intense, it was as if Shara had been there. *Where?* her mind screamed. "Atlanta," she answered aloud. She had seen the attack on Terése. Seen Terése kill the cop *in self-defense.*

She had received the images like downloading files from a computer. They had been fragmented, and she'd experienced in seconds what must have transpired over a fifteen-to-twenty-minute period. Now, though, with the images a part of her, she could view them at will; pore over each of them, if she wished. They were still disjointed — maybe a dozen photographs, yet to Shara a full-length film couldn't have been more illuminating.

That attack, Shara knew, was the triggering mechanism that had set the rest in motion. The cop dead, she had to flee, and the flight wasn't random. She sensed, just as it had been with her, this woman had a goal in mind. She had a score to settle, something in her past she had to confront.

She didn't know if this Terése had knowingly transmitted the images, but she was certain there were more to come. Like an onion, layer by layer, she would learn more about her prey until she got to the core. She wondered, though, whether this was a two-way street. Was Terése able to access Shara's memories, or would Shara have to willingly open herself to this woman?

Drawn almost against her will, she recalled, yet her decision to visit the old crime scene had been correct. Before her trip was over she knew Terése would willingly lay bare her innermost secrets. But why? To make things interesting, she sensed. She and Terése were adversaries, but this woman wanted to make the hunt interesting. Who was hunting whom, though, remained to be seen.

Shara only wished Terése would be more careful when and where she shared information about herself. Shara had no desire to see another eighteen-wheeler rushing at her like a linebacker at a defenseless quarterback.

Shara arrived in Dismal thirty minutes later. Normally an aggressive driver — pulling around cars going too slow for her and constantly changing lanes — she saw visions of the truck that she had narrowly missed, and kept to the speed limit.

The police station itself looked . . . well, dismal on the outside, Shara thought, and her spirits sagged. Once inside, though she was dumbfounded by computers and other high-tech law enforcement equipment that lay before her.

An old — no, she corrected herself — an *ancient* man worked a counter that separated the entrance from several desks, only one of which was occupied.

She identified herself, telling him FBI Agent Cleary had called the sheriff to ask for his cooperation. The officer listened without comment, then literally shuffled to an office in the back. He almost seemed unable to lift his legs. Shara hoped his mind was sharper than his body. A minute later she saw the other officer in the room pick up his phone, listen, say something she couldn't hear, hang up, then walk over to her.

"I'm Deputy Clay Fluery, Miss Farris," he said with a pleasant enough smile. "The sheriff asked me to help you out."

"I was hoping *he'd* take me out—"

"You're interested in the McIntyre killing," he said, interrupting her. "In big city parlance, I was the primary on the case. Actually, I found the late Kenny McIntyre and *was* in charge until the FBI pushed us aside. So it's *me* you want to speak to," he said, again with that easy smile of his. "Of course, I can get the sheriff, if you insist."

"You're making fun of me, Deputy," Shara said with a smile of her own. "Look, I made a fool of myself; a big-city know-it-all wanting to speak to the big cheese himself. It's not my usual style, but . . . I'm not quite myself today. How about we start over? I need your help, Deputy. Do I get a second chance?"

"Let me check my schedule," he said, pulling out a notepad, and glancing at it. "Looks like you're in luck," he said with a grin. "Just give me a minute or two and I'll take you out to the crime scene. I take it—"

"Yes," Shara interrupted him this time, "I'd like to see the crime scene."

He suggested his car, and they drove for several minutes in silence.

"Look, Deputy—"

"Clay," he said. "I'm not big on formalities."

"Shara," she said in response. "Pardon my curiosity, but it's been on my mind since I decided to come down here. Just how did this . . . town or whatever, get the name Dismal?"

"It's a town. Far smaller than Virginia Beach, but a good sight larger than Isle of Wight, which has a main street and little else. We've even got a motel here, I'm proud to say."

"You're mocking me again."

"Well, you've already drawn your own conclusions. And sorry, but there's no good yarn to spin about how the town got its name. We border Dismal Swamp, which was surveyed by Colonel William Byrd in 1728. Why he called it Dismal Swamp remains a mystery. About the only thing it's known for is being a refuge for runaway slaves. The town itself took its name from the swamp. End of story. Sorry to disappoint you."

"I've got a good case of foot-in-mouth disease, it appears, today —"

"And you want to start over again," he chimed in.

Shara laughed.

"What's your interest in the McIntyre killing, Miss Far — I mean, Shara?" he said, taking her off the hook.

"I'm a bounty hunter," she replied, waiting for a distasteful retort, surprised when there was none.

"There's no fugitive to capture," he said after a moment of silence.

"Actually my partner — he's in Atlanta — and I are independent contractors, but whenever I tell that to a local law enforcement officer, they say, 'Oh, you're a bounty hunter,' so I've tossed away the euphemisms. We *normally* hunt fugitives, but sometimes we take a case where a private reward is offered. A cold case the police have given up on. Thirty thousand dollars is plenty of incentive."

"But the FBI is still working the case," he persisted.

"And they've come up empty. Not only that, but the killer's gone to ground for close to three months now. I'd say the trail is cold."

"You don't look like any bounty hunter I've seen."

"Because I'm a woman?"

"Don't be getting all PC on me. I've seen my share of female bounty hunters. You just don't fit the image. I guess I mean that as a compliment," he said, sounding a bit flustered.

"I'm successful because I *don't* fit the image. I don't look like a bounty hunter and it's to my advantage. I kind of sneak up on those I'm after. They're cuffed before they know they've been had."

Clay Fluery reminded Shara of a small-town athletic hero — the high school can't-miss-quarterback with all the girls. Only he couldn't quite cut it in college. A backup who had returned home still a conquering hero. And what was someone to do with more brawn than brains? A deputy at a police department in a town where a barroom altercation was the month's major crime would suit him fine.

He was good-looking enough; about her age, wiry, but muscular from working out, with a thick shock of brown hair and a choirboy face. Still, she felt, there was something she was missing about him.

"You don't think too much of us down here, do you?" he asked.

"Why would you say that? I haven't formed any opinions . . . yet."

"You come in and the first thing to greet you is old Thatch. Doesn't make for a good first impression."

"You mean that old geezer—"

"*That* old geezer," he interrupted, "was the sheriff for fifteen years. He had a stroke eight years ago. He's not the man he was, to be sure.

Then his wife passed three years ago. He could be sitting at a nursing home, watching game shows and soap operas, but we have more respect for our own than they do where you come from," he said with an edge to his voice.

"Thatch — a nickname he got when he had this thatch of hair on top of his otherwise balding scalp — is no charity case. He moves slow, but his mind's still sharp. We don't give a damn the impression he makes. He gets the job accomplished, kind of like you do. What do they say where you come from about perception not being reality?"

"Got me again," Shara said, "but if you're so damned efficient, how do you explain your official report on the McIntyre killing? The one the FBI was kind enough to provide us," she said, holding out a piece of paper.

For the first time he seemed genuinely angry, but not at her.

"Damned FBI. A dozen agents flooded us and took the case over like we were a bunch of hayseeds," he said bitterly. "Fat lot of good it did them. When they left, this woman — the agent in charge — Cleary, handed me a report they *suggested* as the official police report. That's what they gave you."

"Why?"

"'Cause they don't want the media or someone like you putting two and two together and causing a panic . . . or so she said. There have been four killings now. Three highway attacks. Look at the *official* reports and you'll see no connection. Here," he said, handing her a file, "This is *my* official report."

He stopped the car as he gave her the folder.

"We're at the crime scene," he said.

She heard, but ignored him and focused on the detailed report he'd written.

"I hate to repeat myself," she said when she was finished, "but can we start over *again*. You're right, I prejudged you based on the report I had, then was greeted by . . . Thatch, and . . . I'm an asshole. What do you say we end this sparring and cooperate? I *do* need your help."

"I don't know," he said, stroking his chin with his hand, a smile playing at his lips. "I kind of enjoyed sparring with you."

It was then that Shara knew what had been bothering her. Hidden under his small-town-cop visage was a mind as keen as hers. He, too, wasn't what he seemed. His laid-back persona was a weapon to keep you off guard. He was like her. He snuck up on you unsuspecting. Perception and reality — he'd had her going.

She laughed. "You enjoyed having the upper hand, but you no longer have me at a disadvantage. I'm wise to you, Clay Fluery. I won't underestimate you again. That I promise you."

He shrugged. "You caught on quicker than most. Hell of a lot quicker than that fool FBI agent, Cleary," he said, with a genuine smile. "So what can I do for you?"

"You were first on the scene. Want to give me your impression?"

Now he looked at her quizzically.

"Look, Clay, I'm not here simply to look at a three-month-old crime scene," she said, deciding to level with him. "I want to worm my way inside the killer's head. For that, I need to know what you saw; not just the details of your report. I need your take on the killing."

He closed his eyes, as if reliving the scene, then looked at her, a bit ashen.

"The amount of blood was what hit me first," he said, in not much more than a whisper. "I thought she had slit his throat with a knife, but later found out she'd done it with a chain," he said, shaking his head. "Had to be a powerful woman to do *that* kind of damage with a chain."

"Anything else unusual?"

"His pants were unzipped," he said, reddening.

"And?"

"His . . . ," he seemed to be searching for the right word.

"His cock, pecker, Johnson was hanging out," she said to help him out.

He looked at her sharply, then grinned again. "No mincing words with you, is there? Yeah, his . . . pecker was hanging out of his pants."

"Had he raped her?"

"There was no semen. It may have been his intention, but no, he hadn't raped her."

"In your opinion, did she play him? You know, make a pass at him, and when he wanted more, decided she didn't?"

He seemed to ignore her question when he answered.

"In high school there was this beautiful girl. Face, body — everything. Every guy salivated after her. Only, she had the worst case of B.O. you could imagine. It was glandular. She tried to cover it up with perfume, but it only made her smell worse. Beautiful as she was, she never got a date."

"There's a point to this, I take it," Shara said.

"I must have arrived twenty minutes after she'd killed McIntyre," he said. "The odor in the car — not from his body; *her* stench made this girl in high school pale in comparison."

"Then why did he try to rape her?"

"'Cause Kenny McIntyre was one sick fuck, pardon my language," he said, no longer grinning. "He had an extensive rap sheet, mostly for abusing women. He beat up the woman he was living with regularly, but she always dropped the charges. When he bought a woman a few drinks at a bar, he considered it down payment on a night of sex — *rough sex.* A few women complained. He even went to trial, but he was never convicted because nice girls down here don't go to bars and get drunk unless they want it. Giving this woman a lift was like buying her some drinks. He expected to get paid . . . to get laid."

"And the FBI dismissed all of this?" Shara asked.

"I wasn't asked to share my expertise with them. Maybe that's why I was so hostile and suspicious of you. You know, a Southern country-boy. What could I offer? It's my turn to apologize. I had you pegged wrong. You *do* care what I think."

"Let's forget about the apologizing," she said. "Tell me about your witness."

"Russ Phelps," Fluery said and laughed. "He wasn't much of a witness. He saw this woman coming out of the woods a good two miles back. He would have stopped to give her a lift, except he was turning off for home half a mile from where he saw her."

"Why did he give her a second look?"

"He's a man," Fluery said, and laughed. "We see a woman, we make sure we get a look at her. He didn't get *much* of a look, actually. What struck him was how disheveled she appeared. Hair a fright and dirty as sin were his exact words. But she didn't signal for help, so he didn't stop."

"Did he ID the FBI sketch?"

"Didn't get a good enough look. Could have been her," he said. "Look, Russ don't have too much upstairs," he said, pointing to his head. "A real sweet guy, but tying his shoes is a task."

"Putting down a local. I'm aghast," she said and laughed.

"Just telling it like it is. He saw the woman, but there's not much he can offer."

"You know where he saw her?"

"Of course," he said crossly. "That's my job."

"FBI check it out?" Shara asked, ignoring his tone.

"No, all they cared about was the crime scene."

"Can we?"

"After—"

"Now, *before* the crime scene," she interrupted.

"Why?"

"My gut tells me there's something there that's been overlooked."

Fluery started the car and turned around.

"Who am I to argue with your gut? Want to talk to Russ Phelps?" he asked.

But Shara hadn't heard. Another set of images was being down-loaded, and Clay Fluery and everything else became simply background noise.

Terése was in the woods, blood on her jeans. Then she was naked, blood streaming down her leg. Her period, Shara understood. Terése, still naked, eating an animal, raw. Then sleeping, covered by a quilt of leaves. Terése looking at herself in a stream; filthy, grimy, legs-unshaven, gamey. Shara could smell her — urine, feces, the blood from her period — and it made her wince.

" . . . all right? Shara, are you—"

She looked at him and saw he'd pulled over. Concern was etched on his face. She gave him a weak smile.

"What happened?" he asked. "You spaced out on me. I thought you'd had a seizure."

"I'm fine," she said, trying in vain to put some life into her voice. "I just felt nauseous for a moment. Must have been that greasy spoon of a diner I stopped at just before I got here."

She offered him another smile, hoping to convince him there was nothing wrong.

"We can do this later," he said. "You need—"

"I *need* to see where your Russ Phelps saw her come out of the forest," she said, having recovered from her latest . . . *vision*, she guessed she'd call it. Still, the smell remained. Not as pungent as before, but there nevertheless. She now knew what Clay had experienced; what he'd smelled in the car she had been in. Like he'd said, it put the worst case of B.O. to shame.

He shrugged and handed her a flashlight. "Point it at the trees to the left. Shoulder high. You're looking for an orange arrow . . . any minute now."

He drove slowly, and Shara saw a series of arrows and told Clay to stop. Turned the flashlight off and the arrows were gone. Looked at the flashlight, then at Clay, who smiled at her.

"I wanted to know where Russ Phelps saw her come out of the woods, just in case, but I didn't want the whole world to know."

She looked at him without understanding.

"I figured if she kept killing, no way the FBI could hush it up forever. When word got out, I didn't want a horde of media traipsing around looking for God knows what. The arrows are only visible under the UV light."

"I *did* underestimate you," Shara said with a smile. "You know your stuff."

"Why shucks, ma'am, you gonna make me blush," he said with an exaggerated southern drawl.

"Stop mocking me," Shara said, with a pout.

They crossed the road and Shara stood, sniffing. Her sense of smell would hopefully direct her to the lair where Terése had stayed during her period, if she'd accurately interpreted the images she now replayed.

"So what are we looking for?" Clay asked.

"You'll know it when we find it."

"That's a help."

"Look, don't ask me *how* I know, but I think she . . . camped around here for a few days before leaving the woods." *Camped* seemed to be the best way to put it to Clay. He wouldn't believe what she thought was the truth until she could prove it. "We find where she stayed, we might learn something about her. Is there a creek or a stream nearby?"

He pointed. "Dismal Swamp itself, about half a mile."

"She would have stayed closer to water than the road."

"It would take a dozen men—"

"We'll find it, if she was here. Trust me."

He shook his head in resignation. "It's your show. Lead on."

They split off after a short distance. He told her to keep talking, as he would, so they wouldn't get separated. Shara let her nose guide her. She had developed an acute sense of smell when she'd been on her killing spree; had retained it ever since. She could smell the woman's scent, even after three months.

Clay was talking. "Look, it'll be dark in an hour. We can come—"

"I've found something," Shara interrupted. "Follow my voice."

Shara had found Terése's lair. The smell around the perimeter was still pungent. She had marked off her territory by urinating. And there was a fallen tree covered by a blanket of branches and leaves. It was just like the image in her mind. This is where she stayed during her period.

Clay soon joined her, but looked bewildered at what he saw.

"*This* is it? I don't see any campfire."

She didn't make one, Shara would have told him. She had roughed it here, like a wild animal. She had been cold at night. Shara had felt the chill when she'd seen the image of the woman sleeping. She said nothing, though, but walked over to the fallen tree and pulled off the blanket of branches.

"Son of a bitch," Clay said at what he saw.

There were the remains of small animals under the tree and what looked to be dried blood in a shallow body-length furrow dug in the ground. Unlike on the periphery, the branches acted as a protective covering and the blood was clearly visible.

"Do you know what kind of animals they are?" Shara asked.

"Rabbit," he said, lifting one with a stick. "Lots of blood for such small animals, though," he said. "Maybe she was injured."

"It's her blood, but she wasn't hurt," Shara said. "She was on her period."

He stared at her.

"I've gone along with your . . . hunches, but there's more to it, isn't there. Mind sharing with me how you knew *where* to find her camp, and how you know she was on her period?"

"You wouldn't believe me."

"Try me," he said, sounding irritated, then he softened. "What's it to you if I *don't* believe you?"

Shara shrugged. "Remember when I got sick back in the car?"

He nodded.

"I was getting images of a scene like this."

"You're telling me you're psychic."

Now she looked at him. He didn't say it with the skepticism of Briggs. He stated it as fact.

"No. I'm not psychic. That's the thing. I've got some sort of connection with *this* woman and she alone. I had dreams about her months before I took the case. The same dream, actually, and it still makes little sense. Then today, I've had two flashes of images; scenes so vivid, it's like I was there. One was when she killed that cop in Atlanta. He'd raped her, I think. She killed him in self-defense. Then, back on the road, I had images of a lair like this."

"Does she talk to you?"

Again, Shara was surprised that there was no scorn in his voice.

"I get pictures, but no sound. I can smell, taste, even feel what she's gone through as if I were there, but it's a silent film, open to my interpretation. I guess that sounds crazy. I know—"

"Unless you're the killer, it's the only explanation that makes sense," he interrupted. "I'm not saying I buy all of this hook, line and sinker, but I'm not dismissing it either." He paused in thought for a moment. "Why would she camp here, though, during her period?"

Shara wasn't sure, but thought it might have something to do with the wolf she saw in her dreams. *That* she wasn't ready to share with Clay.

"I don't know yet, but it's another piece of the puzzle."

"And knowing about this lair helps you how?"

"Helps me to get into her head. Like I said, it's a puzzle. Individual pieces may have little relevance. But they help you see the whole. At least that's my hope."

He took out two small evidence bags. He put a sample of the blood in one, and the bone of one of the animals in another. Then he took out a small can and sprayed the surrounding tree trunks.

"My magic paint," he said, with a grin. "Without it I'd have trouble finding this spot again. I'll come back tomorrow and cordon off the area. Preserve the scene," he added, with a wink.

"Can we go to where she killed McIntyre now?" Shara asked.

"We've only got about forty minutes of daylight left." When she said nothing, he shrugged. "Why not? What surprises you got in store for me there?" he asked.

"Damned if I know," she said, wondering just who *was* in control — she or this Terése. "Probably nothing, but . . ." she shrugged, and let the thought hang.

At the crime scene, Shara walked into the woods. She suddenly felt lightheaded, as she had when Terése had flooded her with images. But this time it was as though the woman herself was in her head. Without knowing why, she began to run, just as she knew Terése had after the kill. She heard Clay behind her, calling out, but he sounded like he was behind a closed door, and she couldn't make out the words. *She* was definitely not in control. Without looking where she was going, she didn't trip or stumble over fallen tree trunks, and she deftly avoided branches without really seeing them.

She came to the swamp and entered it, making her way upstream; again without knowing her purpose. After about five minutes, she tried to cross to the other side, the water rising as she neared the middle. Shara didn't know how to swim and soon found herself struggling to run, after her feet could no longer touch the bottom. As she went under, she realized Terése was gone, and panic swelled within her. She clawed for the surface, but something held from below. She looked down and saw Terése grabbing her leg to keep her from surfacing. It was Terése, but it wasn't *her* hand. It was that of a man.

Terése was shaking her head. Suddenly the hand released her and she reached the surface, lightheaded and choking, swallowing water.

She started to go down again, when something grabbed her and pulled her out of the current towards the shore.

Still coughing, she looked up and saw Clay, his face ashen, dragging her from the water.

While in the water, she hadn't felt its chill. Terése had kept her warm, and when she'd left Shara underwater, survival had been her only thought. Now, she began shivering and couldn't answer Clay's non-stop questions.

Finally he understood.

"It's hypothermia," he said. "I'll take you to the hospital."

Shara shook her head. "M-m-m-motel," she finally said. "H-h-hot shower."

Clay said nothing, but carried her back to his car. He had a blanket in the trunk, which he wrapped around her. Five minutes later they were at a motel. Shara was curled in a fetal position, doing all she could to keep from blacking out.

"I'll get a room." He opened the door, then looked back. "Don't go away, now."

Despite herself, Shara laughed. "S-s-some comedian," she said, unable to finish the thought.

Clay had her in a room within minutes. He wrapped several other blankets around her. When the feeling began to return to her extremities she knew the worst was over.

"Let me get you into the shower," he said, looking as shaken as she felt. He was also soaking wet, and the cold must have been biting into him, too.

"Thanks," she mumbled, "but it's only our first date. I think I can handle it alone."

"You sure?"

"Dry clothes," she said, still only able to talk in sentence fragments.

"There's a store—"

"No, no," she interrupted. "Carryall in my car. Keys in my pocket."

"I don't want to leave you alone."

"Go. I'll be fine."

He went, reluctantly.

Shara didn't *know* if she'd be fine. She had put on a good face for

Clay, but she didn't feel well at all. She didn't know if she even had the strength to get to the bathroom to the shower. What she did know was Clay couldn't see her naked. The tattooed eyes on her breasts would be staring at him. There would be too many questions, and she wasn't up to manufacturing answers.

With difficulty, her toes and the soles of her feet still numb, she managed to get into the shower. The hot water caressing her like a lover, she slowly recovered feeling in her body and mind.

Getting out of the shower, she looked into the full-length mirror that hung on the inside of the door. Her body was still pale, but the color was returning.

The image staring back at her changed suddenly, and she was staring at Terése. She looked gaunt like an injured wolf who hadn't had a meal in days, sadness radiating from her.

"What the fuck do you think you were doing?" Shara said to the image.

Silence.

"Why feed me your story, then try to kill me?"

No response from the figure in the mirror, but she began to hear a dim voice in her head.

"Not me. A *part* of me, but not me. I fought him. Made him let go."

Shara remembered the hand that had held onto her leg and tried to keep her from surfacing. It had come from Terése, but it had been a *man's* hand. And, in her dream, there had been the face of a man trying to emerge from Terése to stop her pursuit.

"Tell me about him," Shara said, but the voice in her head was gone.

She reached out to touch the figure in the mirror. A wolf's paw slapped her hand away. She looked at her arm and saw a wide gash oozing blood. She grabbed a towel to stem the flow. Initially there had been a sharp pain, then a dull throb and now the pain was all but gone. She removed the towel and saw the gash healing. Before it closed, she licked her arm and tasted the blood. It was real. It hadn't been her imagination. But as in her dreams, within minutes her wound was healed and the blood gone.

Shara looked into the mirror and saw only herself staring back.

Terése, she knew intuitively, had no intention of harming her, but could she control that part of her that for some reason *did* want to wound her? The thought made her shiver anew.

She heard a knock on the motel door. Shit, it's Clay, she thought. She quickly wrapped a towel around her top and another around her waist.

She opened the door and Clay entered, his face reddening when he saw her.

"Get a hold of yourself," she told him. "You see a hell of a lot more skin on the beach."

She took the bag he held out, and shaking her head in dismay, went to the bathroom and came out wearing jeans and a sweatshirt.

"Better?" she asked. He didn't respond. "How did you get dry?"

"I've got an extra uniform at the station," he said, still looking uncomfortable.

She sat on the bed, and he in a chair. They were both silent for a few minutes, then he seemed to recover.

"You want to tell me what that was all about in the swamp?"

"That's the route she took after she killed McIntyre. Only the stream wasn't so deep. She crossed there."

"She told you this?"

"I felt her within me."

"Did she want you to drown?"

He sounded angry, she thought, not at her, but at Terése, who he thought tried to kill her.

She wasn't yet prepared to tell him about the old man or the wolf. He must have had trouble enough accepting what she'd already told him, and what he'd seen.

"Maybe she wanted you to save me — save *her*," she said, knowing her answer explained nothing.

"You're not in this for the money, are you?" he said, abruptly changing subjects. "You're hunting her down because you get off on it."

He'd been looking away when he spoke. Now he looked at her, and Shara was staring at an old man with long white hair and a tanned, weathered face and wrinkles upon wrinkles. A formidable opponent with little compassion, if he resided within Terése.

Shara looked at Clay's hands and they were that of an old man. Gnarled, but strong.

"You best be careful. You don't want me. Don't want me. *Don't want me*," he repeated.

"Are you okay?"

Shara blinked and saw Clay looking at her.

"Maybe you *should* see a doctor," he said when she didn't immediately answer.

"No, I'm fine. I'm just exhausted. I was going to go back to Philly tonight, but all I want to do is sleep."

"Want me to tuck you in?" he asked, with a smile but she saw concern etched in his face.

She threw a pillow at him. He caught it with one hand and threw it back — but not too hard.

"Catch me when I'm feeling up to it and you'll have a pillow fight on your hands," she said, smiling.

"Your color's returning," he said. "I guess you don't need me here babysitting you."

"You can stop by tomorrow morning around eight with coffee and a bagel and cream cheese," she said. "They do have bagels here?"

"You're asking for it," he answered. He got up and came over. "Coffee and a bagel with cream cheese. Eight tomorrow." He paused for a moment. "You gave me a scare," he said and turned for the door.

"Clay—" she said and paused. "Thanks for saving my life . . . and not thinking me deranged with my story about the visions and all."

Shara thought he seemed about to say something, but thought better of it.

"See you in the morning. Now get to sleep. Doctor's orders."

Alone, she lay in bed for a while thinking of Clay, Terése, the old man, the wolf and . . . Clay.

Briggs had scoffed at her dreams. Shara knew a bullshitter when she saw one, and Clay hadn't been putting her on. He had wanted to believe her when she found Terése's lair. He'd become a believer after her trek through the woods and swamp. She *could* tell him about the old man and the wolf and he would believe. Someone to confide in without having to divulge *all* her secrets.

She knew she could trust Clay Fluery. Suddenly, she no longer felt so alone.

TWENTY-ONE

Shara awoke with a start at 2 a.m. She had gone to bed a little after eight and now all her strength had returned. Not dreaming had helped her to heal. But now she was restless. She had to go back to the lair. *Go now.* She wasn't sure why, but she followed her instinct.

She dressed and walked the half mile through the woods, a three-quarter moon the only light to guide her. But she needed no guide. She could see the den in her mind's eye and was there in twenty-five minutes.

Intuition told her she had to experience what Terése had. She removed her clothes, marked the periphery with her urine, as Terése had, then lay under the fallen tree — away from the blood — covering herself with the quilt Terése had fashioned. The ground was coarse, hard and uncomfortable, and the leaves offered little protection from the cold of the night. But this was how Terése had felt.

Soon she slept, her defense against the cold.

She was awakened by a presence, yet saw nothing. She looked at her clothing, but felt no urge to dress. The presence was Terése.

"You're here," Shara said aloud. "I know. Why won't you show yourself?"

A figure popped into view. It didn't materialize, but just seemed to walk through an invisible doorway. It was Terése, but she wasn't really there, Shara knew. It was a projected image, like a hologram. Nevertheless her essence was there.

"I'm getting to know you," Shara said.

"Only because I'm feeding you information." Her voice was slightly muffled.

"Why help me catch you?"

"You're a worthy adversary, but you got in the game late, so I'm leveling the playing field."

"Look, Terése—" Shara began, then stopped. "That's not your real name, is it?"

"That's good," the image replied. "*That*, I didn't tell you."

"What's your name, then?"

The figure looked at Shara for a moment and finally shrugged.

"Mica."

"Wouldn't care to tell me your last name, would you — you know, a proper introduction?"

"You *are* good," she said, with a wary smile. "There are too many Micas to check them all out. Tell you my last name, and I might as well draw you a road map. I don't think so."

"Can't blame me for trying."

"You *can't* catch me, you know. You're good, but the woods are my turf. I have you at a disadvantage."

Shara shook her head. "You've been on the prowl for what . . . seven months?" Shara said. "I've been dogging others far longer. I *will* bring you down."

"I could hurt you, you know — here and now."

"Maybe, but you won't."

"How can you be so sure?"

"You're no killer," Shara answered.

"You know better than that."

"You're not a *random* killer," she corrected herself. "You've got an agenda. You kill sexual predators. You won't kill me. Won't harm me."

"I won't, but I *can't* guarantee your safety," Mica said, and Shara felt some tension in Mica's voice.

"The wolf. The old man," Shara said.

"I best not underestimate you," Mica said, nodding.

"You can't control them?"

"I can . . . for now. Why must you bring me down?" she asked, as if not wanting to talk about her control or lack thereof.

"It's in my nature," Shara said. "In a way, I *am* the wolf in you."

"You talk in riddles. You won't open up to me like I have to you."

Shara shook her head. "You told me what you wanted me to know, nothing more. You're as much a secret to me as I am to you." She paused, then went on. "Will we meet again before the end?"

"If I want."

"When you're ready to tell me why you're on this mission of yours, I'll open up to you and tell you why I'll bring you down. Fair enough?"

There was a noise. Someone was approaching. Shara turned to see.

"Until then," she heard Mica say. She turned to see Mica take a step back and then she was gone.

Shara quickly dressed and Clay appeared. He looked worried and relieved at the same time.

"I thought you might be here."

"What time is it?" Shara asked.

"Five in the morning."

"What are you doing here?" she asked.

"Your partner called the station. He was told you were at the motel, but you didn't answer, so he called the station again. They called me."

"Called you? Why would they do that?"

Clay looked at the ground for a moment, and when he spoke, ignored her question. "I checked your motel room. Your carryall was there. Clothes hanging to dry. Your car, well, it's still at the station, so I figured you might come here to . . . what did you say?"

"To get into her head."

"You slept here." It wasn't a question.

Shara was silent.

"Did you learn anything?"

"It's cold. About the same temperature it must have been in October when she was here or in November in Philly; her last two kills."

He shrugged. "What does that tell you?"

"December, January and February would have been colder still. She couldn't take that kind of cold. I think she's holed up in Philly — hibernating, so to speak."

"So it's back to Philly, then," he said, with a trace of disappointment. "On with the hunt."

He began to cordon off the area with yellow police tape. Then he took her back to the motel.

She was packing and saw him following her every move with his eyes. "Are you going to tell the FBI about the lair?" she asked.

He thought for a moment. "Fuck 'em. This is *your* find. Something you can trade with."

"I've got a better idea. Did Cleary give you an e-mail address?"

"She gave me a dozen ways to contact her. Everything but a carrier pigeon."

"I'll be here for another hour or so. Go back to the station and e-mail her, but call me before you send it, and make a hard copy for your files."

"What do you have up your sleeve?"

"I can intercept the e-mail. I'll delete it, but it will be stored as mail sent and read. When I spring it on her, she'll come at you tooth and nail, but you'll have proof you sent her the message."

"You're a sly one," he said, "but I like it." He paused a moment. "Look, if you're ever back . . . well, I could buy you dinner."

She looked up at him, startled.

"You hitting on me?"

He flushed.

"*You are!*"

"I'm sorry—"

"Don't be," she interrupted. "It's just been a long time since some-one flirted with me."

"Get off."

"Since I've *let* anyone flirt with me," she corrected herself. "When I'm on a job I don't allow intrusions. You caught me off guard; sorta penetrated my defenses."

Do I want you? Shara thought, looking at Clay. She'd never wanted *any* man — *anyone*, except the first Shara, who had been more like an older sister.

"You don't want me." It was the old man in Clay again. There for a split second, then gone.

She ignored him. "I'd like dinner," she told him, "when this case is over. Like it a lot. But why me? There's more than enough for you here."

"You're not at all like the women I've met."

"Bedded," Shara said.

"And bedded," he admitted. "They're either shallow or feel threatened. Even liberated women with good jobs. They refuse to let their guards down. They fear it will show weakness and vulnerability. So they've surrounded themselves with a protective shell — a facade — that's swallowed up their sensuality. Others are overbearing. Want to show they're in control."

"And me?" Shara asked.

"You're . . . you're so unlike anyone I've ever met. No pretenses. You wear your strength and vulnerability on your sleeve, without fear. And you're so damned unpredictable."

"And I'd be hell on wheels in bed," Shara said, feeling a bit uncomfortable with his analysis of her. Not offended, but it seemed he knew her a bit *too* well.

"You've got a dirty mind, young lady," he said, but he was smiling. "I'd like to get to know you better. Kind of get into *your* head. Find out why I'm attracted to you. Contrary to public opinion, I don't bed every woman I date."

"I'm sorry," she said. "I get kind of flip when I'm complimented. Like, that *can't* be me you're talking about. Like I said, when this is over, I'd like to have dinner with you. Right now this woman is all consuming. We could go out and I wouldn't be all there. My mind would be on her. Do you understand?"

"That's part of your charm," he answered. "Your honesty. I do understand. Just don't string me along, okay?"

"I wouldn't do that. I meant what I said. You intrigue me, too. There's more to you than meets the eye. I've been so absorbed with this woman, I've been too distracted to get inside *your* head. You're more than just a good cop. I want to know you with no outside diversions. Does that scare you — my worming myself into your head?"

"I don't scare easily," he answered.

"You hear of her arrest," Shara went on, "make reservations. And if she shakes me, you'll hear from me. You can offer me consolation."

"Well, I better get to the station and get that e-mail written," he said, looking a bit uncomfortable. "By the way, I had another deputy drive your car over. It's right outside."

Shara smiled, as he left all flustered. *Damn,* she thought, *he flirted with me and it felt good.*

She took a shower, waiting for his call. Lathering off the dirt from sleeping naked on the ground, she thought of him.

For the first time in her life, something other than death had aroused her. Because of her half-brother, her sexuality had lain dormant for fourteen years. She'd had sex with the first Shara, but not often.

And after, she'd had an identity crisis. At the police academy she showered with women enough to know she wasn't a lesbian. Yet no man had aroused her. She knew it was of her own choosing. She had to maintain her distance. She had too much to hide, and getting close to someone meant either lying or letting it all out.

Her only sexual companion had been her. She could make herself feel good. Yet sometimes, she had to admit, she was bored with only herself and the fantasies she concocted.

With Clay, it had been so natural — his flirting with her when she'd least expected it, and had been unprepared. She felt she was finally awakening from a long slumber.

She felt . . . she felt . . . , she tried to find the right words. She felt *alive*. She was no longer merely sleepwalking through life. All of a sudden it was like all her circuits were functioning. It wasn't just about sex. It was emotions, and a dam was bursting.

Toweling, she knew she *had* to dwell on these self-revelations. She knew this was one of those defining moments in her life.

Clay Fluery had flirted with her and it felt good.

TWENTY-TWO

(DECEMBER 1998-MARCH 1999)

MICA

Mica had *finally* been face to face with Shara, in a manner of speaking, in the woods near Dismal Swamp. Yet she was distraught and horrified that she had almost killed the woman.

She was aware more aware than ever of a battle raging within her for control. The wolf understood his role was solely to protect her. He would fend off an attack, but he would never take the initiative.

Her grandfather, though; why the hostility towards Shara? she wondered. Did he fear Mica wouldn't need him now that she had Shara? Was he like a spurned jealous lover? Or was he protecting Mica from herself, fearing Shara was far more clever than Mica gave her credit for?

What her grandfather didn't understand was how much more alive she now felt with Shara in the hunt. She was confident — even overconfident, she'd be the first to admit — even though Shara had surprised her with her dogged persistence and stubborn insistence that she would take Mica down. Deep down Mica didn't believe it for an instant. Shara was a worthy opponent, but invariably a vanquished one.

At the same time, she felt in Shara someone who had followed a path similar to her own. She wanted — *needed* — the challenge Shara provided. And she wanted to get to know this woman more. To pursue her as she did, Mica knew Shara must have demons of her own to keep at bay. Here was someone with whom she could finally share herself. Someone who would understand.

She was angry with Shara for not opening herself up to her. But a part of her was glad. She wanted a full course, not fast food. *In time*, Shara had promised. *In time*. That time would come, Mica promised herself.

It had taken Shara long enough to begin her pursuit, Mica thought peevishly. When Mica had walked from the airport to Philadelphia, almost three months earlier, Shara hadn't yet gotten wind of her.

Mica had been a wreck when she'd arrived in Philadelphia in December, though she effortlessly blended in with the weird and wonderful eccentrics who populated the east end of South Street.

She'd been weak. She'd been cold. Her face ached from where Steven had punched her. In Steven she had met pure evil, and for the first time since she'd left Atlanta she had feared for her life. Killing the bastard had saved countless women indignities he would have heaped upon them, thinking money could buy their silence.

Mica marveled at South Street. When she was a child, its renaissance had just begun. Now it was both a full-fledged tourist attraction and hangout for the rebels of society. Two men walking down the street, arm in arm, didn't draw a second look. Women embraced one another without embarrassment. She saw clothes and hair styles that reminded her of those futuristic movies where the degenerates of society were consigned to a contained area. Unlike those movies, though, there was a festive mood here. Crammed next to one another were fast food establishments and chic restaurants serving food of every ethnic persuasion. Chain clothing stores and independently-owned boutiques coexisted in harmony. Classy beauty salons and tattoo parlors were side by side. It was a madman's design that somehow was far greater than the sum of its parts.

Mica, funky as she smelled, didn't stand out in the least. With jeans, her jacket and a baseball cap to cover her blond hair, she was almost *too* normal. She stopped at a CVS pharmacy and bought a bar of soap. It was her first purchase since leaving Atlanta.

She found a restaurant that served thick, relatively rare hamburgers and ordered two, along with an order of fries. While they cooked, she went to the bathroom and washed herself clean. She didn't want to draw attention to herself, and while she looked normal enough, her gamey smell would have drawn unwanted stares.

Hungrily devouring her food, she saw a four or five year old girl, a few tables down staring at her. She smiled at the child, but received nothing in return, then looked more closely. The child was looking at Mica with a haunted, vacant stare.

Mica looked at the couple she assumed were her parents. The mother, like the child, was an attractive redhead, but was wearing shades in the evening in a restaurant with little light. Mica instantly knew this was a battered woman. The man who sat across from her had carefully groomed hair and a short cropped beard. He was a business-man where good grooming was a necessity, she assumed. He talked quietly to the woman, but Mica could see he was seething. The woman's hands hung at her side, balled up. She was doing her best to take his verbal abuse without bursting into tears. She removed her sunglasses for a moment, and Mica could see bruises and a solitary tear course down her face.

The woman took her daughter to the women's room. Mica followed. A few minutes later the woman and child emerged from one of the stalls and went to the sink where Mica was washing her hands. The woman still wore her sunglasses and moved listlessly, as did the child.

"You don't have to take it," Mica told the woman, who looked at her startled, as if awakening from a trance. Mica expected a defensive, even antagonistic response. She was a stranger, after all, butting into affairs that had nothing to do with her. But she was surprised when the woman looked at her and, her voice choking back tears, answered.

"That's what my friend says. But what would I do? I have no skills. No money. No place to go. I'm at his mercy and he knows it."

"Think of her," Mica said, looking at the child who now stared at her, but still wouldn't smile. "Has he hit her yet?"

"I'd leave him in a heartbeat if he did," the woman answered, with some life in her voice. But Mica wondered if she really would. *No money. No skills. No place to go.*

"He will, you know."

As a dominatrix, Mica had met men like this woman's husband, though she had never taken them on as clients. They wanted to dominate. They wanted *all* their women to be submissive. They were bullies who had usually advanced to a certain position and could progress no further. They lacked that something to get to the next level. Some had affairs. Others took their frustrations out on their family. First the wife, then the children. In their homes they were top dogs, and they exerted total control over their spouse, so divorce or flight was often fruitless.

"He's already traumatized your daughter by brutalizing you," Mica went on. "Soon she'll spill something or have the television too loud and *she'll* be his target."

The woman looked down, as if she knew Mica spoke the truth.

"Take it one step at a time," Mica said. "Is there some place you could go? A relative, maybe?"

The woman took off her sunglasses and looked Mica in the face.

"My friend says the same things. She suggested a shelter for battered women. There's one just a few blocks from here, but he'd find me."

Mica bent down and squeezed the little girl's hand, then looked up at the mother. "One step at a time."

Mica went back to her table and finished her meal, keeping an eye on the couple. She had been wondering where she'd stay. Not just for a few days, but for the winter. The demands of her body overruled any thoughts her grandfather might have about getting on with her mission. She would end up dead in a ditch if she heeded him now. She couldn't stay on the streets, living as one of the hordes of homeless in the city. Chances were the police would stop her for something, and she couldn't allow that.

She'd stick out like a sore thumb in any hotel or motel, which she assumed the police would be canvassing. Homeless shelters, too, were out of the question. Women were raped all too frequently at the shelters. She wouldn't even entertain the thought. But a shelter for battered women — *one a few blocks from here* — that was different. A safe haven for the winter.

For no reason in particular, Mica followed the family when they left the restaurant. She was surprised they weren't walking to a car.

They walked two blocks east to Fifth Street, then turned north and walked another two blocks to Pine, where they entered a town house built for the upper-middle class when the South Street revitalization was underway.

She stood outside the house for fifteen or twenty minutes.

"You're next," she whispered aloud.

Her other victims had been faceless and nameless; chosen randomly. Even Steven, what did she know of him? But this man — he *deserved* to die.

She would do her grandfather's bidding, but this time *she'd* choose the victim. She wouldn't allow that child to be traumatized further. She had to put an end to the girl's torment. Friends might sympathize, but would turn a deaf ear if the police questioned them about alleged abuse. It wasn't their business, after all. Teachers might wonder, in years to come, at the girl's stoic silence. But, as long as she came to school without visible marks, the schools were too overburdened to intervene. And the mother *might* flee, but not yet. Mica could tell she wasn't near ready. The child needed a guardian angel. An *avenging* angel. With the decision made, Mica went off to find the shelter.

Just south of South Street on Ninth, The Haven was a nondescript building, like many that hadn't been torn down and rebuilt as part of the remaking of South Street. Buildings to the north of South Street had been gutted, with expensive townhouses taking their place. Buildings south had been treated like abandoned stepchildren. They were virtually untouched. Any renovation had been in the interior only. Such was The Haven.

Mica was greeted at the door by what she assumed was a volunteer. She'd prepared a cover story, buttressed by the bruises Steven had inflicted on her face, but she had scarcely gotten out a sentence when the flummoxed greeter excused herself to get Charlie.

Charlie was Charleen Phelan. She came out of what must have been the kitchen, wearing an apron with flour covering it, as well as her hands and face. She greeted Mica with a wide smile; a *genuine* smile, not one of those pasted-on counterfeit varieties. She was Mica's height, stocky without being fat, but carried herself with the dignity of someone who was used to mingling with the rich and powerful.

"I'm Charleen Phelan — Charlie, for short, and I run The Haven."

"Mica Reynolds," Mica said, shaking hands. She had a driver's license and other ID with that name, though until now she had never used them. "You run the kitchen, too?" Mica asked.

"I do a bit of everything," she said with a hearty laugh. "I own the building and run The Haven. I'm the Board of Directors. I'm no absentee landlord, though. For me The Haven is a hands-on operation. Actually, it's my life. I help in the kitchen, counsel, help women get jobs and legal aid, even clean the bathrooms if help is in short supply. I'm making some bread for tomorrow. Come into the kitchen and we can talk."

Without waiting for Mica's response, she turned, expecting Mica to follow. Charleen Phelan was a bundle of energy, Mica thought, but also used to getting her own way. Once in the kitchen, she gave Mica an apron and quickly showed her how to make dough for rolls. For a few minutes both worked in silence.

"From your bruises, I gather you need our services," she said finally. "What did he do that you finally *had* to leave him?"

Mica looked at her. "Cut right to the chase, don't you?"

"I can be subtle when necessary, but we have limited resources. Maybe The Haven's not what you need. And, maybe you're not right for The Haven. I won't throw you out," she added quickly, "but what you need might be better handled by someone else I could refer you to. So why are you here and what do you want from us?"

"I come from a long line of abuse," Mica started. "My mother and I were physically abused and so was my grandmother. It might sound like a cliche, but I seemed to gravitate towards men like my father. I married one and at some point decided the cycle of abuse would stop with me."

"So you left?"

"No. I refused to bear him a child. Three times I became pregnant, and each time I deliberately set him off so he'd hit me. Until today he had never hit me in the face. He had never left a mark that could be seen unless I undressed. I goaded him, pushed all the right buttons and he would hit me in the stomach or my torso. Three times I miscarried."

"My God," Charlie said, seemingly aghast.

"I don't apologize for what I did. At the time I felt there were no alternatives. I was utterly alone. I had no close friends or relatives to confide in. I did what had to be done."

"So why did you finally leave?" Charlie asked, sounding genuinely intrigued.

"We had an awful argument earlier today. I was so angry I told him what I'd done. Told him to hurt him, because more than anything in the world he wanted a son. I told him he'd killed his son three times. That's when he hit me in the face. He left, to go to a bar, I'm certain. In my gut I knew when he returned he would kill me. So I fled. I took nothing. I wanted nothing but my life and my freedom."

"What can we do for you here?" Charlie asked.

"I hadn't planned on leaving. I need a refuge, I guess, to sort things out. Time to decide where to go from here."

"So you might return to him?" Charlie asked.

"No, you misunderstand me. *That* part of my life is over. I can never return to him. I have to move on, but I need time to decide what's best for *me*."

"At The Haven, we let women and their children stay as long as six months. We provide counseling and arrange for job training and placement. We can also help with drug and alcohol dependency."

"Counseling I can use, but I never turned to drugs or alcohol for solace," Mica said.

"Good for you," Charlie said with genuine enthusiasm. "My problem is space. We're filled to the gills, I'm afraid. One of the women will be leaving in a week —"

"You mean go back to him for a week?" Mica asked, trying to sound confused and terrified.

"No, no, you misunderstand me. Like you said, you can *never* go back to him. What I can offer is to put you up in a common area we use for children whose mothers work evenings. I don't know—"

"That would be fine," Mica interrupted, now trying to sound both relieved and desperate.

"All right then. You can take all the time you need to come to grips with what you have to do before we need to discuss job training—"

"I won't take charity," Mica interrupted again, and this time she meant what she said.

"I'm not offering charity."

"I don't need time to be with myself to know what's best for me. I want to work right away. *Here*. I can help cook, clean, answer phones — whatever you need."

"You're a strange one," Charlie said, looking at Mica. "If you insist on working, I'll pay you. Not much—"

"You're giving me room and board," Mica said, again interrupting her host. She sensed Charlie wasn't pleased with her rudeness, that she was used to making decisions for others. Mica was letting Charlie know this would not be the case with her.

"Yes, but how can you make a start for yourself without money?" Charlie asked, sounding exasperated.

"I'm too tired to argue with you. Tell you what. You put aside what you'd pay me. If I need money I'll ask. And when I leave I'll either take the money or give it back as a donation."

Mica wasn't about to tell Charlie she had $5000. It was bad enough she had lied to worm her way in. Worse, that some other woman who was truly battered might be turned away. Taking money as well would be pouring salt on a wound. She would earn her keep to lessen her guilt.

Over the next two weeks Mica stalked her prey in the mornings and spent the rest of the day making herself invaluable.

Establishing Richard Ogden's routine proved easy. He jogged faithfully at five-thirty each morning, then left for work at eight-thirty. He worked at an ad agency at an office building not far from City Hall on Market Street. She followed him discreetly for a week, mostly interested in his jogging routine and what he did after work.

She soon saw he enjoyed flirting with women. After his jog, he'd often stop at one of the trendy cappuccino coffee shops that dotted the area, talking and laughing with a nineteen- or twenty-year-old girl behind the counter. Often Mica would see the girl blush.

A real charmer, she thought. He had to be thirty, maybe even a few years older, but he liked them young — like Danziger.

The fifth day he didn't jog, but met the girl from the cappuccino shop at a park at 6th and Chestnut, and the two of them walked east. Mica was surprised to see the two of them enter a two-story house on 8th, between Spruce and Locust Streets.

Mica thought it might be the girl's apartment. She waited and the girl left alone forty-five minutes later. After another ten minutes, Ogden exited and jogged home. Not her apartment, Mica thought. *His.* Incredible, she said to herself. Battered his wife *and* cheated on her.

Mica also learned his wife's routine. Monday, Wednesday and Friday Deborah Ogden went to a health club, leaving Julie, the sad-faced waif with a neighbor.

Before Mica would purge the world of Richard Ogden, she had to assure herself his wife could make it on her own. Several times Mica walked into the health club amidst several others members to locate Deborah's locker. On one occasion, she took Deborah's house key, had a duplicate made and returned the original.

Two days later she let herself into Ogden's home and found his insurance policy. She saw Deborah had nothing to worry about if her husband died.

Mica continued her surveillance of Ogden, seeing him bed two other women prior to the onset of her period. Her plan formulated, she waited for her period to end.

At The Haven Mica did a little of everything for a week, but for a reason she couldn't fathom she was best with the children.

Mica had never considered marriage or motherhood while in Atlanta. Thinking about it now, she didn't know why there had never been a desire to mother, though she was certain Ralph Danziger was responsible. The rape and subsequent death before she could avenge herself had left a void in her. She wouldn't allow herself to get close enough to anyone for a lasting relationship — not even Jeremy. Something else Danziger had robbed her of.

Sleeping with the children, she quickly earned their trust. She found their honesty refreshing. They were not catty or neurotic like some of their mothers. All had been emotionally abused, some physically and sexually, but she saw a resiliency in them she envied. Yes, they needed help to cope with what life had dealt them, but they weren't yet lost. That would come later to some, maybe most.

They also took to her and confided in her. Maybe it was because she was a good listener, not offering the platitudes they so often heard.

And she never probed. If they had something to get off their chest, fine. If they stopped in mid-sentence, she let them be.

Renee, at sixteen, the oldest, intrigued Mica most. She seemed to grasp Mica wasn't a member of the staff, and didn't shield herself from Mica. Renee's father had taught her how to play backgammon, and Mica had noticed that she would cheat in order to win.

"Why do you cheat, Renee?" Mica asked, without voicing anger or condemnation. "Doesn't it take the fun out of the game?"

"My father never let me win. He would cheat if he had to."

"So you play solely to win."

"Winning's more fun."

The next three games, Mica intentionally allowed Renee to win, making it obvious with ludicrous moves. After the third game, Renee flipped the board over in a tantrum.

"It isn't fun anymore," she yelled at Mica.

"Why not?"

"You're letting me win."

"Don't you want to win?"

"I want to *beat you*, not have you let me win."

"And if I play my best, you're going to cheat, even though I *know* you're cheating. That's fun?"

Renee looked at Mica, gently biting her lip, as she mulled over Mica's words. She was a light-skinned black girl, with long silky hair, which she asked Mica to comb nightly. Mica never asked, but she thought her father was white. She could have passed for white had she wished.

Renee stopped cheating for the most part after their conversation. If she lost two or three games in a row, she reverted back, but often admitted to Mica later that she had cheated.

Once Renee had blurted out, "I wish you were my mother."

"Why's that?"

"I can talk to you. You listen. You don't tell me what to do."

"That's because I'm *not* your mother. As a friend, I have no responsibility. As your mother, I would. I'd still listen, but at times I'd tell you what to do even if you didn't like it. You'll see when you have kids of your own."

"I'll never have children," she answered vehemently.

"Why?"

"They'll get beaten. Just like me."

"Not if you pick the right man." She asked Renee to tell her good things about her father, as well as what she disliked.

"When you're looking at a boy — a man when you get older — avoid those with the bad qualities of your father. It's easier said than done, I know, but you're no fool, Renee. You'll make a wonderful mother. I see how you act with the little ones here. You're patient, understanding, and you care. What more could you ask for in a mother?"

Renee flashed her a smile. Mica thought she had the most infectious smile she'd ever seen and was only sorry Renee didn't show it more often.

Inside of two weeks Charlie asked Mica if she wanted to work solely with the children and Mica agreed.

The week she was on her period she came up with the idea of the playroom. *Shara's Playroom.* How did she know? she wondered. She knew so little of Shara, probably because Shara wasn't yet after her. But she'd somehow peeked into Shara's mind, saw the playroom, and knew instantly a modified version was just what these kids needed.

At times they were so full of anger, hurt and guilt they would fight among themselves. They needed an outlet where no one would get hurt. Someplace where after they vented they might talk, if not to Mica then to one of the trained child psychologists.

Mica went to Charlie.

"That money you've been saving for me. I'll need it."

Charlie opened a drawer and gave her $150.

"It's not what you're worth—"

"It'll do."

"I know you've grown close to Renee," Charlie said, misunderstanding why Mica wanted the money. "But it would be a mistake to buy her a gift without getting something for the other children. They'd resent it. Resent Renee. Resent you."

"Are you telling me that I can't spend this money on Renee if I want to?"

"No, not at all. It's yours. You've earned it. I just—"

"Can I take the kids with me when they return from school? Just to a toy store a few blocks down South Street," she added.

Charlie looked at Mica, and she knew the woman was dying to ask what she planned to do, but was too proud.

"Sure," she said, exasperation in her voice.

"Can I have a piece of The Haven's letterhead?"

Charlie gave Mica a piece without comment.

Mica took eight of the older children to Kay Bee Toys. She told them to browse while she spoke to the manager.

"My name is Reynolds. I work at The Haven," she said when the manager had been paged. She put the money on a counter that separated her from the manager. He was a Hispanic in his thirties whose eyes darted to the kids in his store. "I need some special toys for an anger management class. This won't be enough. I was wondering if you would make an equal donation?"

"I'd have to contact my corporate office—"

"Which will take weeks, even longer," Mica interrupted, then lowered her voice. "Let me put it this way. I can bring these kids here *everyday*. They have nothing. They'd really enjoy playing with the toys here. They can be a bit rambunctious, and if something breaks . . ." she stopped, letting the thought hang.

"That's extortion," he said.

Mica looked at him, but said nothing.

"I need a request on your letterhead," he said, as if seeing a loophole.

Mica pulled out the stationery she had been given. She wrote something and gave it to him.

"You didn't put an amount in," he said.

"You insert the amount. Do we understand one another?"

He shrugged in resignation. "Take what you want," he said sullenly and turned away.

Mica had the kids pick out Nerf toys, water guns and balloons. She had them bring the toys to the counter, where the manager rang up the total. $297.

He looked at the figure, looked at Mica, then looked at the toys she had selected.

"You weren't conning me," he said, his Spanish accent thick.

"Like I said, they're for an anger management class."

"Roger," he called to a youth who worked in the store. "Get me a few dozen Nerf balls and half a dozen bats — no, make it a dozen."

Turning to Mica, he said. "My donation. When you need more just ask."

"Who do I ask for?" Mica said.

He smiled. "Luis. Luis Hernandez."

"Thank you, Luis," she said. She turned to the children. "What do you say to Mr. Hernandez?" There was a chorus of "Thank you, Mr. Hernandez."

Back at The Haven, Mica rearranged a playroom used by the children. Charlie passed by and came in to watch, as did some of the other women. Mica laid down some ground rules for the children and soon Nerf balls were flying and the children were harmlessly pummeling Mica and one another with Nerf bats. Water guns were fired, then reloaded from a sink in the corner.

One of the kids, Sydney, a seven-year-old with tar black skin and large oval brown eyes, went up to one of the women who was standing in the room, observing, and hit her with a Nerf bat.

Charlie, who had stayed in the background, stepped forward and grasped the boy's arm as he turned to flee.

Everything stopped.

"Was that nice?" Charlie asked the boy. "What did she do to you?"

Mica came over.

"Those are the rules, Charlie. Anyone in the room is fair game."

Charlie looked at Mica. Mica knew Charlie was strong-willed and ran a tight ship. She was glad she would only be here temporarily, because the two women would bang heads sooner or later, and Mica would be asked to leave. For now Charlie backed off.

"If those are the rules, so be it."

She left, as did all of the other women except for Jane. Jane Doe was the name given to her at the hospital where she had been dumped. Her husband had apparently thrown acid in her face, then took her to the hospital and drove off. She had been at The Haven for four months. She had total amnesia; no memories whatsoever. The right side of her face was hideously disfigured, as if someone had used her skin for an ashtray. The other women tended to steer clear of her. If Jane cared, she didn't let it show. Now she stood watching the children vent their anger.

The children ignored her, but Renee — wise beyond her years, Mica thought — walked over and gave her a Nerf bat. Jane stood there, the bat at her side. Soon Sydney came over and hit Jane. He hit her again and then a third time, his anger seeming to build with each unanswered swing. Finally Jane hit him back. Not hard, but she had responded to him and he laughed.

Soon other kids were pummeling the woman who responded in kind. She'd been accepted by them, Mica saw, and making eye contact with Renee, Mica nodded almost imperceptibly. Renee blushed and looked away, but Mica could see she was smiling.

*   *   *

Two days before her period ended, when Mica went jogging, she intentionally bumped into Ogden, making it appear as if she hadn't noticed him. She went sprawling, and got up slowly, apologizing for her clumsiness.

"No need to apologize," he said, as Mica saw him giving her the once over. "Are you hurt?"

"Me and the sidewalk are old friends," she said with a laugh. "This isn't the first time we've met. Won't be the last, either."

They jogged together and he did most of the talking — spewing his line. He told the truth about his job. He lied that he was single. He was definitely on the prowl. He didn't care about her as a person, Mica could sense. She was just a slab of meat, a piece of pussy he wanted to sample.

Not wanting to be too forward, and not yet ready to strike, she abruptly told him she had an appointment and had to leave. She gave him a parting wave to show her interest.

She jogged up to him the next day, the last of her period.

"Hi, stranger."

"Not going to bowl me over again, are you?" he asked, with a hearty smile.

"I'm the one who fell on her face," she answered, returning the smile.

Again, he did most of the talking, but finally asked if she were married or seeing anyone.

"I find most men far too possessive," she answered. "I go out with one a couple of times, go to bed, and it's like I'm his. If I have an appointment, he wants the details, like I'm sneaking off behind his back to sleep with another man. Truth be told, I'm not looking for a commitment."

He offered to buy her coffee, but she begged off.

The next day, her grandfather wanting what was rightfully his, she made sure she was ahead of Ogden, but let him catch up. She wore no underwear, and she could see he was fixated on her bouncing breasts.

They jogged in silence for several minutes. Yes, she thought, today he'd hit on her.

He complimented her on her jogging, then challenged her.

"Race you," he said. "If I win, you come over to my place for coffee."

She didn't ask what *she'd* get if she won. As far as he was concerned, his winning was a foregone conclusion. Though she could have outrun him easily, she let him win, and followed him to his bachelor pad.

After he ushered her in, he asked if she wanted to shower. While she couldn't prepare herself as she had done in the woods, she noticed the wolf within, during her period, gave off a smell that to others might offend. She declined his offer of a shower.

"I like the smell of me," she said in explanation.

"It's pungent, I'll say that," but he let it drop.

There was to be no coffee. No sooner were they seated on a plush couch, then he was kissing her and mauling her breasts.

She pushed him off.

"I thought this was just for coffee. You're moving a bit fast for me."

"Please," he said derisively. "You knew perfectly well what was on the menu. Don't play coy with me." He slid his hands under her sweat-shirt.

This time when she pushed him off, he slapped her. This was getting old, she thought. She seemed to be a punching bag for every man who hit on her.

227

"No more playing games," he said harshly. "I don't like it when I'm angry. You'll like it even less."

He pulled off her top, then her jogging pants, surprised both that she wore no panties, and at the thick growth of pubic hair. He ran his fingers through it.

"Can hardly see the forest for the trees," he joked, and laughed.

When he lowered his head towards her genitals, she wrapped the chain around his neck. There would be no more foreplay, she'd decided. She already knew *too much* about Richard Ogden.

This time her grandfather allowed her to determine how he would die. At first Ogden tried to punch, then grab her at the throat, but wolf paws emerging from under her arms parried his blows, and he began to lose consciousness.

"Tell you what, Richard," she said. "I *could* kill you. *Should* kill you, but I'm in a forgiving mood. Answer me truthfully and you live. Lie and you die. Are you married, Richard?"

"Of course not," he said with difficulty when she slightly loosened her grip on the chain. With the lie she tightened it.

"What an asshole," she said. "You *really* don't want to live. One more time. Are you married?"

"Y-y-yes, I'm married."

"And you hit your wife, don't you? Hit her a lot."

He began to say no, but Mica tightened her hold on the chain, and he admitted he was abusive. He admitted it all; his inability to control his temper, his morning and after-work trysts, how he resented his daughter for curbing their social life.

And when he'd confessed, Mica let her grandfather kill him. Let the wolf drink his blood, then showered and left.

Showering, for the first time she noticed her pubic hair was nowhere near as bushy as it had been when Ogden had made his joke. With her other kills, she had been on the run right after, stopping only to quickly wash at a creek or stream. At Ogden's den of lust and degradation, she felt no need to hurry. The other women she had seen enter had stayed a full forty-five minutes.

This was also the first time she had felt good after one of her kills. *All* of the others may have deserved to die, but they had been sacrifices to her grandfather. She had felt neither guilt nor remorse at being his unwitting pawn. She felt nothing. With Ogden, though, she had freed his wife and spared the child the horror she saw at The Haven daily. And *she* had chosen him. Maybe she and her grandfather had reached an accommodation.

＊　　　＊　　　＊

The next month at the shelter flew by. She couldn't recall a time when she was more content.

Oddly enough, there had been no mention in the media over the next several days of Richard Ogden's death. It should have been "the big story" she thought, mimicking the catchphrase of Channel 6's Action News.

She wondered if he'd even been found. A week after his death, though, she saw his obituary. It confused her even more. According to the paper, he had died of a heart attack. Considering he was heartless, she thought it ironic. But, there was no way his death could be attributed to a heart condition. What were the police up to? she wondered.

Actually, she gave it only a few moments of thought then tucked it away. At least he'd been found. Now Deborah and Julie could move forward with their lives.

Working with the children at the shelter was therapeutic for Mica in ways she'd never imagined. Even without training and degrees that testified to her prowess in the field, she knew she was helping them. Once withdrawn, almost totally silent, Evan opened up to her after a session in the playroom. His father had hit his mother, but she in turn had hit Evan. He feared them both.

Mica had no qualms telling Charlie. She wasn't bound by any confidentiality, other than what she promised the children. Evan hadn't asked her to remain silent. Charlie confronted Evan's mother. She was told she could either go into therapy or DHS would be contacted. And Evan wouldn't leave The Haven until Charlie was certain he wouldn't be the target of his mother's frustrations.

Mica also found she was a natural storyteller. At first she had read stories from books at bedtime, but they had already heard most of them, or found them boring. And, with children of so many different ages, it was difficult to find something they could all relate to. So Mica made up her own story, involving all manner of creatures, both real and imagined. It became a neverending story. She never planned what she would say in advance. Her biggest challenge was remembering all the characters she had introduced, but she even made that part of the story-telling. The kids participated by asking for characters she had forgotten or sometimes she'd play dumb and ask, "Who haven't we heard from tonight?"

There was only sadness when a child left. Two had gone since Mica had arrived; their mothers having been trained, found jobs and a place of their own to stay.

Even though her heart ached, she made their departures into a festive occasion with a party, complete with gifts, compliments of Luis Hernandez. He had visited the shelter once and had seen the playroom in all its glory. When he entered, he'd been greeted by a fusillade of Nerf balls, water balloons and eventually hugs from all the kids. The next day additional toys had been delivered. After Mica confided to him how upset she was when a child was leaving — expecting nothing in return — he began providing party supplies and gifts for any youngster departing.

There *were* good people in the world, Mica was becoming aware. People who gave and asked for nothing in return.

And there was Jane. Mica found it appalling that these battered women, who should have been full of compassion, shunned Jane because of her facial scars. Mica had to admit it took time to adjust, looking at the woman without wanting to turn away, but it was time well spent.

Mica didn't approach Jane until she was no longer repulsed by her scars, then she sat down at the table where Jane usually ate alone. Jane immediately looked down, not wanting to make eye contact with her.

"Am I that ugly?" Mica asked.

"I am," Jane said, not raising her voice, but she looked at Mica in confusion.

Jane, Mica saw, tried to become invisible when she had to be around others. She *knew* others looked at her as a freak and talked behind her back. Mica thought she was in her mid-twenties. Her black hair she'd heard others describe as nappy, but only because Jane washed it, then just tied it in small knots with rubberbands. She had a sensuous body which she hid in dresses several sizes too large for her. All she seemed to want to do was be ignored. Now she was telling Mica she was ugly.

Mica stood up and went over to Jane, bending down so they were eye to eye, Mica looking at the scarred mocha-colored side of Jane's face. Jane turned her head to the left and Mica came around the table, bent down and stared again. Right, left, right, left. Every time Jane turned away, Mica moved to face her.

Suddenly Jane began laughing. "You're making me dizzy," she said, but she was no longer averting her gaze.

Mica laughed in return. "You have a beautiful smile when you allow others to see it."

"Don't be teasing me," Jane said, looking to her right.

"Do I have to get up again?" Mica asked.

Jane laughed, then looked at Mica. "Why are you sitting with me?"

"Because I don't care much for them," she said, turning her gaze to six women who sat at another table, eating and talking and gawking. "They all seem to have their little cliques. For women who share so much in common, doesn't it seem odd the black women sit only with other blacks and the white only with their kind? And all they do is gossip. I'm not into that."

"What if I am — into gossip — will you shun me, too?"

"Yeah, but because of what you are, not how you look."

"I've got no war stories to tell," she shrugged. "I still can't remember."

"Like I want to hear about *their* problems; *your* problems. I've got enough of my own. I see a lot of self-pity here. And a lot of can-you-top-this. They wear their battle scars a bit too proudly. One says 'My husband put my head in the toilet until I almost passed out,'" Mica mimicked one of the women. "Another says, '*My* husband put my head in a vice, and made it tighter and tighter.' Then a third says, 'My husband took an ax and cut off my head. *Top that!!*'"

Jane laughed. "She should have quit while she was a head." Both she and Mica laughed.

"I told a joke," Jane said, startled at the revelation.

"A good one at that," Mica answered.

"So what do we talk about?" Jane asked. "I mean I have *no* memories."

"What we're talking about now. Sometimes maybe nothing. You know, just sit and eat. A novel concept."

Even though Jane had taken part in the playroom activities that one time, she was reluctant to return. When Mica got to know her better, she asked why she refused to come back to the playroom.

"They're afraid of me."

"Some, but not all. Look, kids are more resilient than adults and less judgmental. They'll tell you up front you're ugly, but once they get to know you, your looks won't matter." She touched her chest. "It's what's here they care about; your heart. They'll accept or reject you on your own merits."

And they did. Jane became an aide of sorts to Mica, playing with the kids, even allowing them to touch the scar on her face.

A week later Jane opened up to Mica. She was picking at her food. Mica said nothing. If Jane wanted to speak, she would.

"I miss it," she finally said.

"Miss what?"

"Sex."

Mica almost choked on her food, and Jane laughed.

"Sometimes I remember things. Just bits and pieces. I remember the sex," she whispered. "It's odd, I can't recall his name, can't make out his face; but at times I get flashes of having sex with my husband that are vivid. He was rough, but I liked it. I miss it. Miss it terribly. What's worse, I'll never have sex again with another man."

"Why do you say that?" Mica asked.

"Look at me, Mica," she said bitterly. "Who would want to have sex with me? Maybe if I put a bag over my head. I want to have sex with a man. I know I could please him, but it'll never happen."

"Not as you are now."

Jane looked at Mica.

"Not how you *look*, but that self-pity you're so fond of. Look, we play cards together, but you never attempt to play with the others. Sometimes you have to make the first move."

"They don't want me to join them."

"That's their problem, and you're wrong. *Some* don't want you to join them, but others will accept you once you stand up for yourself. And it's the same with men. You can stay here in this shelter your whole life, or you can get on with your life. Find something you want to do, get trained, then go out and get a job. Yes, you'll experience pain and rejection. You'll also find those who will accept you because you're a good person, an intelligent woman with a sharp wit, a good sense of humor, and a body many of those women would kill for. *Then*, you'll find your man."

It took awhile, but one day Jane joined in a card game. Two of the five women excused themselves, but the other three stayed. Jane was good at cards — whatever the game — and routinely beat Mica. But she was no fool. As Mica watched, she saw Jane lose more often than she won, but win enough so the others wouldn't tire of her presence. And every once in a while, she'd wink at Mica; a silent communication that spoke volumes.

*   *   *

In late January, Mica killed her second assailant in Philly. She hadn't targeted anyone this time. She simply walked through Fairmount Park one night, waiting to be attacked. She had no doubt whatsoever some animal would want to take what she refused to offer.

As before, even though she left the body in plain sight bordering the woods, the media was silent, as if no body had been found. As before, she didn't dwell on it, but knew if she outstayed her welcome, the police would set a trap for her.

While it hadn't snowed since she'd arrived, except for some flurries, it had been bitterly cold at times. She had to stay at least one more month and take her chances. The police — and probably the FBI, she thought — may have been stymied by her change of pattern; Ogden in his love nest, and the other in the park. Neither one killed in a car. They would hope a pattern would emerge so they could prepare for her. One more month — *one more kill* — and she would be on her way.

February was mainly a battle of wills between Mica and Charlie.

Even if Mica wanted to abandon her mission, her brutal honesty would have been self-destructive at The Haven. She knew come the first or second week in March she could tolerate the elements, so she refused to hold her tongue. It had never been in her nature, as an adult, to be submissive. Unlike others, she saw Charlie for what she was; a benevolent despot, and Mica refused to submit to her will. The question was would Charlie tolerate *her* for another six weeks?

For all the good she did, Mica knew Charlie had her own personal agenda, whether she was aware of it or not. As she'd said the night Mica had arrived, she was her own Board of Directors. She set policy. Employees who questioned her decisions were soon pounding the pavement for work.

Mica had learned from listening to the other women that Charlie had herself been a battered wife. Her husband had been a successful stock broker who had taken the pressures of a volatile market out on his wife. Yet she had refused to leave him. He'd died at forty-five in a freak auto accident, and with her children grown, she'd had a huge house that had never been a home.

She was unaware that some of her other high society friends also faced abuse until she had spoken of her husband's failings. Like her, they had all suffered in silence.

She had promptly sold the house, then spent a year visiting shelters for abused women, trying to find out the best recipe for a shelter she would run. She had bought the house that was now The Haven eight years earlier, intent on it being more than a halfway house. With contacts from her marriage, she'd been successful both at fundraising and opening doors for job training and opportunities for graduates of The Haven. She *had* given her life to The Haven, and Mica had to grudgingly admit that she had every right to set policy.

Charlie had told her story in dribs and drabs, while counseling others. She was one of them, she wanted other battered women to know, not someone who hadn't experienced their pain. She had no tolerance for those who mouthed the empty platitude "I know how you feel" when they couldn't. They hadn't been there. She had.

But Mica questioned just how alike she and the others were.

There had been a skirmish between the two in mid-February. Mica made it a habit of cooking special desserts for the children after they had gone to bed, several times a week. Once in a while Renee or one or two of the older girls would help. Mica had little idea what she was doing at first, not having been much of a cook herself when in Atlanta. Though she followed directions in cookbooks Charlie gave her, the results were often disastrous. The children poked fun at cakes that sagged in the middle or were over or undercooked. Still, they loved her all the more for the effort.

While stubborn, she was no fool, and allowed Charlie to school her. One evening when the two of them were alone, pies cooking in the oven, Charlie complimented Mica.

"You're wonderful with the children. And your befriending Jane is appreciated."

"Do you think I view Jane as a charity case, as part of my job?" she had asked, her ire rising.

"She's no great conversationalist," Charlie responded. "You two have nothing in common."

"We have a world of hurt in common. You don't have a clue about Jane, do you? She's a basket case to you, so lost all you can do is provide sanctuary. Put yourself in her place. You wake up one morning with no memory of your past. Do you have children? Are you a loving mother? Do you have a job? Maybe a teacher, a doctor or a lawyer. Do you have a damn sense of humor? She doesn't know what the hell she is. She's like a newborn, unaware just what she is, struggling to make an identity for herself. I can't imagine anything more frustrating."

"I hadn't thought of it in those terms," Charlie said.

"Of course not. Neither you nor most of the women here view her as a person. She's got to reinvent herself and that will take time. You gave her sanctuary, but no hope."

"That's not true. We're trying to help her restore her memory."

"That's *not* what she needs right now," Mica said, frustration making it difficult not to raise her voice. "Look at her and you know what I see? A woman living in a convalescent home. You feed her, house her, clothe her, but you don't meet her needs."

"We meet her needs," Charlie said stiffly.

When alone with her, Mica noticed Charlie seldom wore her ingratiating smile. Maybe that too was a facade.

"Would you get her a man she could have sex with?"

"What?"

"Jane wants a man. Not someone to fall in love with, but solely for sex. Would you use some of your precious funds and connections to procure her a male prostitute?"

"There's a limit—"

"*You* set the limits," Mica interrupted. "You set all policy here. Jane's needs offend *your* moral code, so you won't hear of it. But Jane will never be complete without a man. You want to set her on the road to recovery, you find her a man, pay him to have sex with her to make her feel like a woman again."

"I'm sorry Mica, but I have to live with myself each night. I sympathize with Jane's plight, I honestly do, but I won't be bullied into doing something that's morally reprehensible."

Mica was ready to blow. Charlie was a sanctimonious and self-serving do-gooder, and Mica wanted to tell her so. The Haven's moral and ethical standards were those of Charleen Phelan. You toed the line and you were welcome. Mica couldn't leave yet, and she couldn't win this argument with bluster. She decided to settle for less than she wanted.

"How much money is in my account?"

"I won't have you spend it on a prostitute for Jane."

Mica wanted to remind her it was *her* money, but held her tongue.

"I'm going to buy Jane some clothes and get her hair styled, so at least she can feel like a woman. Do you have a problem with that?"

Charlie gave her an exasperated sigh, but didn't object.

When Jane and Mica returned from their shopping spree the next day, there were stares, but it was because the Jane Doe who had left that morning had never returned. In her place was a sensuous woman; a young woman in tight-fitting jeans, a blouse that accentuated large but firm breasts, and hair permed — curls flowing — and styled to partially cover her scarred face.

She was a changed woman within, as well. She moved with confidence, where before she had shuffled along, weighed down by her misery. She looked like a woman on the prowl, but with Mica's help didn't look like a slut. Neither Mica nor Jane knew what she'd worn in her previous life, but she looked good and felt even better in what suited her figure. She would no longer hide within the dreary dresses and housecoats Charlie had provided her.

Charlie looked at Mica sternly, not attempting to hide her disapproval, but said nothing.

There was yet another encounter a few days before Mica's period began. Those days before her period, with the wolf within her denied his freedom, she knew she wasn't easy to be around. Even the children found her irritable, but she had explained her mood swings to their satisfaction.

"I'm one of you," she told them, when she flew off the handle for no good reason. "I'm not here because I want to be. I've suffered just as you have, and I have my good days and bad days. Usually, you kids are enough to make me forget my hurt and pain. Sometimes, though, it catches up with me. So yes, I'm cranky. I'm ornery. I'm—"

"Bitchy," Renee said, and the others laughed.

"Yes, *bitchy*, but it would be wrong for me to hide it from you. I promised myself never to lie or deceive you. You're seeing me on one of my bad days. Deal with it."

They had been in the playroom. After a moment's silence, Sydney walked over to Mica and hit her with a Nerf bat. Soon she was being assaulted from all sides, and she grabbed a bat and defended herself. When she finally raised her hands in surrender, a genuine smile on her face, she knew the playroom wasn't solely for children. She wondered what therapeutic value Shara got out of *her* playroom, then wondered why this woman was on — maybe *in* — her mind so often. In time, she knew. *In time.*

Seated and sweating, Renee sat by her.

"I'm sorry for being so selfish," she told Mica.

"Selfish how?"

"When you're happy, I'm happy — well, *happier*. You were . . . ," her voice trailed off.

"Bitchy," Mica finished for her.

"Yeah, bitchy," she said with a smile. "And it made me mad. I thought you had no right to be bitchy around us. That was pretty stupid of me."

"We're all stupid sometimes. You learned I'm human, Renee. Don't put me on a pedestal. I'm your friend and I can advise you, but I'm no role model. Better still, don't put *anyone* on a pedestal. We all have our warts and shortcomings. Elevate them to where they're more than flesh and blood and you'll only be disappointed."

Baking that night, still feeling bitchy, she touched on a subject that was a sore spot for Charlie. A scab to be picked at before it healed. Mica couldn't help herself.

While most women stayed at The Haven for three to six months, on a number of occasions Mica had seen a woman with one or more children enter in the dead of night and be gone two or three days later, without having shown her face. Mica had an idea what was going on and decided to put Charlie on the spot. It wasn't just her oncoming period that led to the confrontation. Charlie's holier-than-thou attitude with Jane was a constant itch that begged to be scratched. And while Charlie provided an essential service, if Mica was correct she was also a hypocrite. Bringing her down a notch or two from *her* pedestal had its allure.

"What happened to Jodi?" Mica asked nonchalantly while washing off the counter. Jodi had arrived two nights earlier with her young son, had stayed holed up in a room she'd been given and had now left, after it had turned dark. Her meals had been brought to her, and she hadn't left her room or mingled with either the staff or other women while she had been there.

Charlie eyed her suspiciously, as if Mica were going somewhere she didn't belong.

"Jodi decided The Haven wasn't for her," Charlie said, evasively. "Like I told you when you first came, in some cases there are other places better suited for women with certain needs."

"Jodi *never* meant to stay here," Mica said. "Fess up, now Charlie, you were helping her flee."

"It's none of your concern, Mica. Why not drop it?"

"It *is* my concern when you have a double standard; one for the likes of Jodi and another for Jane."

"You'll hound me until I explain, won't you?" It wasn't a question. "It's not a quality of yours I admire."

"You're beating around the bush," Mica said.

Charlie sighed. "There are factions within the battered women's movement. We don't all think alike. With gay rights there are those who want to 'out' all who remain in the closet, while others feel the decision to go public should be made by each individual when and as they see fit."

She had been wiping the counter furiously, though it was clean. Now she stopped and looked at Mica.

"Look at the anti-abortion movement. Radicals preach violence, pass out wanted posters with the names and home addresses of doctors who perform abortions. Their goal is to incite others to violence. Others picket and work to get legislation passed. It's no different with us. Some women defy court orders and, according to the police, kidnap their children to save them from abuse. They disappear, helped by others."

"And harboring them is illegal," Mica said. "So you wouldn't be a participant. The Haven itself could be held culpable if a fugitive was given sanctuary here."

"I agree completely. I look at the big picture," Charlie said. "I want to help as many women as possible to pick up the pieces of their shattered lives. I've chosen one path, yet I don't condemn those who help battered women and children who've been further abused by the courts."

"Yet you *do* provide temporary refuge. I don't understand how you can rationalize doing so, when it violates your principles and endangers the shelter."

Charlie sighed again. "I help on occasion. The underground knows my feelings. But in times of crisis, I'll put up a traveler for a few days. I ask no questions, so I can tell no lies. It's not something I lose sleep over. These women *do* need help. We're just a way station, if you will."

Mica shook her head. "You straddle the fence with your scruples. You violate the law for total strangers, yet you refuse to help Jane."

"That's different, and you know it," Charlie shot back.

"Really? Harboring a fugitive is against the law. Procuring a male companion for Jane is no different. Hell, the police would turn a blind eye if you were caught. Repercussions would be far more severe if you were found harboring Jodi."

"Prostitution is repugnant to me, no matter how benevolent the intentions," Charlie said, raising her voice.

"Listen to yourself, Charlie. *Both* are breaking the law, but only prostitution raises your moral indignation. That's called hypocrisy."

"You have no right to preach to me, Mica. No right to judge. I've helped hundreds of women start new lives."

"On *your* terms. Look, I don't mean to be cruel," Mica said, knowing she did, "but much as you say you're one of us, you've led a privileged life. And when you tell us of your abuse, you're vague. You listen to the horror stories of the women here, but you don't get down and dirty with us. We're terribly complicated people who need more than a sanctuary, counseling and jobs. We can't all meet your lofty standards, yet you thrust your principles down our throats, as if it were gospel."

"You're trivializing all I've tried to do for eight years. I won't have it," Charlie said, her hands shaking with rage.

"No, I applaud what you do. But understand, you're *not* really one of us. You don't want to *be* one of us. You counsel, but I don't see you eating with us or playing cards with us, as we tell one another our most personal secrets: the atrocities that have been committed against us. You don't play with the children. And worst, you ignore Jane, like she's part of the plumbing. You're a wonderful administrator. You have accomplished a hell of a lot more than I'll ever accomplish, but don't delude yourself. You remain above the fray and pass judgment on us daily. If we don't pass muster, we're failures." She paused. "I've said too much. I imagine you've had enough of me and will send me packing."

"I *should*," Charlie said, visibly upset. "No one's ever spoken to me as you have. You've been on my case almost since the day you arrived, pushing the envelope, testing my limits, passing judgment on *me*."

"You're right," Mica said.

Charlie made a sound that was almost a growl. "That's what's so exasperating. It's almost as if you're intentionally baiting me, hoping I'll toss you out."

"That's probably right, too," Mica said. "People like us are self-destructive. We invite scorn and punishment."

"Well I'm far more complicated than you think, young lady," Charlie said. "There are times I abhor you, Mica. And I disapprove of many of your methods." She paused, then lowering her voice, went on. "But they work. I'm not ruled by my emotions. I'd be a fool to let our personal differences determine your fate here. You do try me, but I won't force you out."

She lapsed into silence, spent. Mica had no further fuel to add to the fire. She had met women like Charleen Phelan in Atlanta. They followed the course they set for themselves against all reason, rationalizing the means they used to achieve their ends. Charleen Phelan could never be persuaded or dissuaded from the path she'd chosen. She would stew over Mica's barbs for an hour, but by the time she went to bed, the substance of her ridicule would be forgotten. It was how the woman reconciled harboring a fugitive, yet ignoring Jane's needs.

*   *   *

Three days later, Mica was in South Philly at Roosevelt Park, across the street from what had been the Naval Yard before the government had shut it down. It was within hailing distance of Philly's sports complexes — Veterans Stadium where the Eagles and Phillies played, and two indoor arenas; most notably the new First Union Center that housed the Sixers and Flyers. Mica didn't know what the old arena now held. It stood looking forlorn, reminding her of some of the children at the shelter who weren't abused, but were ignored.

Earlier, she had walked through the teeming streets of Center City. It was far different than the isolation of the woods; almost claustrophobic. Here she felt a thousand eyes on her. She felt as if she were being sized up and raped by each and every one. It was suffocating. She was glad her stay here was near its end.

At Roosevelt Park she walked, was attacked and dispassionately claimed her final Philadelphia victim.

*   *   *

Two weeks, Mica thought, then she would leave. She hadn't been surprised this time when all the *Inquirer* reported — in a capsule article in the "Metropolitan Area News in Brief" column — was that a man had been found murdered in the park. The police were keeping a tight lid on the case. She most definitely had worn out her welcome. They had to know she was ruled by her menstrual cycle, so they would know *when* she would likely strike again. She had the feeling the police would be out in force.

She was an emotional wreck those two weeks. She not only wanted to go, but *had* to go. Yet leaving the children would be no easy task. Telling them would be harder still. She refused to just slip out quietly one night without an explanation. They'd been abandoned too often already, and deserved better.

Charlie made her decision easier by surprising Mica with an offer.

"I'd like to offer you a position here . . . permanently," she'd said, once again in the kitchen where they had clashed so often. "I've come to realize the children need someone to bond with, not just whoever's around to volunteer. I could start you out at $20,000, plus room and board. I'd pay for you to take some psychology classes, to help you better deal with the children's needs. And there would be a budget for materials you'd need. You'd have complete discretion over the funds."

"I appreciate the offer, Charlie." Mica said, knowing how difficult it was for Charlie to swallow her pride for what was in the best interests of the shelter. "I really do. But I was going to tell you soon that I'll be leaving shortly — a week, week-and-a-half at the most."

"Why?" she asked. "I thought you and the child—"

"I love the children," Mica interrupted, "and it saddens me to have to leave them. There are complications you don't want to know about, trust me."

"There's nothing I can say, nothing I can offer to change your mind?" Charlie prodded.

Mica almost laughed. Charlie was so used to getting her way, she wasn't good at all with rejection.

"It wouldn't work out, even if I could stay," Mica told her. "We've come to verbal blows any number of times. No matter what you say now, you're still the boss. I'd still have to answer to you. We're not good for one another. We both know it."

Charlie must have seen the determination in Mica's eyes because she uncharacteristically fell silent. After a few moments, her voice cold, she seemed to have made another decision.

"Then it's best if we slowly wean the children from you."

"You're going to punish *them* because I turned you down," Mica said incredulously. "Showing your true colors, aren't you? Showing who's boss."

"No, I'm merely being practical. Part of my offer was a room for yourself, anyway. You can stay with the children during the day, but you'll no longer sleep with them."

"You have no room for me," Mica said.

"There's Jane. I haven't been able to find anyone to share her room in months. I tried when she first came here, but the other women were . . . uncomfortable."

"Figures," Mica mumbled.

"She's been alone for two months now. The two of you have grown close. It will do her good to have company."

Mica could have tried to argue with Charlie, but saw it would do no good. Actually, forcing her hand was probably for the best. Mica would have to tell the children of her intentions now, rather than continuing to put it off as she had.

"One favor." Mica paused, in thought. "No, a suggestion, actually. Give consideration to offering Jane the same position you extended me. She gets on well with the children, and it will build her self-esteem."

"You *are* exasperating," Charlie said, offering Mica a tight smile. "You reject my offer. Reject *me*, and the next minute you're offering advice. You infuriate me to no end, but you could probably run this place someday, if you wanted. I won't make any promises, but I'll take your recommendation to heart."

It was as near to a concession as Mica would get.

It was time to tell the children, she thought. She had nothing prepared, but it was probably for the best.

On the way to the playroom, Mica felt a chill, as if someone were walking on her grave. She felt someone reaching out to her — no, *for her*.

Shara!

Shara at the beach.

Shara in a forest with bare trees.

Shara and Alexis.

Shara and this Alexis talking about *her*.

Shara was on the prowl, in the hunt, in the game. *After her*.

Soon, Mica thought, they'd meet. Not face to face yet. But with Shara after her, she needn't remain hidden from her any longer. No more standing by her bed, able to touch, but not allowed. For over six months, it had been a big tease. Promises of things to come, yet hollow promises, it seemed. But *finally*, Shara was on her trail. *Soon, Shara*, Mica thought, *we'll see what you're made of*.

In the playroom, Mica gathered the children around and told them she'd be spending days with them, but sleeping with Jane at night.

"Don't you want to be with us?" little Sydney asked.

"Of course I do, but Jane needs me, too."

"We need you more," Ethan, a nine-year-old red-head said with a pout.

"That's selfish."

"That's what I'm told all the time," Syretta, an eleven-year-old with coffee-colored skin, said sullenly. "I don't want to leave my father. I don't want to leave my friends. I don't want to leave my home. 'You're selfish,' my mom said," mimicking her mother. "*She* was being selfish, too, and now so are you. Why can't *we* be selfish?" she said, tears in her eyes.

"The truth is I'll be leaving for good, soon," she said. There was silence in the room. Mica had never had a more captive audience. Had never felt so miserable.

"My grandfather once told me a story. Two men found a treasure chest by the sea, full of golden coins. It was too heavy for either man to lift alone. One man claimed it as his. The other said, no, he had found it first. They argued for hours, until the tide came in and took the chest. They ended up with nothing. My grandfather was talking about cooperation and sharing. If both men had agreed to take half, they could have lifted the chest together before it was claimed by the sea. The same goes with me. You can have half of me or all of nothing, for as long as I'm here."

"Why can't you stay? Don't you like us anymore?" Sydney asked.

"I'm *one* of you, remember," she said, placing a hand on Sydney's shoulder. "I came here for shelter. There's something I must do for *me*. I'm telling you now so you won't think I'm abandoning you when I do leave. I haven't loved anyone in well . . . I don't know how long, but I love you. You're all I have, and I *don't* want to go. When I go, you'll still have one another. It's me who will be alone."

Sydney got up and got the Nerf bat and began hitting Mica. And soon the room was in chaos, as always when anger ruled and had to be vanquished.

Renee was the only one who didn't take part. When their anger was spent, and the children grudgingly acknowledged half of her was better than nothing at all, Mica asked Renee to come outside with her.

Mid-March, and it was warm today, Mica thought. Warm enough to have been on her way, though she knew the nights would chill, and the weather could turn without notice. They walked around the block, Mica saying nothing, waiting for Renee to open up.

"Who do I confide in when you leave?" she finally asked.

"Others. Someone you can trust. There will be others, you know."

"But they'll leave, too. They all do."

"You want things tidy, Renee," Mica said, stopping and making eye contact with the girl. "Life ain't tidy. It's complex. It throws you curves. You get shit on. You bounce back because there *are* people who care. Don't view me as a role model. I've told you that before. Do as I say, not as I did. I shut out the world for eight years, and only now am I seeing what I lost."

She told Renee about her rape by Danziger and Donato.

"In between those two moments that shaped my life, I let no one in. Trusted nobody. I was wrong. A fool. Don't make the same mistake,

Renee. The years fly by and they can never be retrieved. What I'm saying is sometimes it's better to hurt than to feel nothing at all. I hurt now because I don't want to leave you. But letting you in has meant the world to me. I'll think of you often and the pain will lessen, yet the good memories will remain."

Renee fell silent again, but as they walked she moved close to Mica and put her arm around her waist. Mica put hers around the youth's. As they rounded the corner, half-a-block away from the shelter's doors, Mica stopped.

"One more thing, Renee. Someone will come looking for me. Soon. Her name's Shara, and she'll ask about me. Tell her what she wants. Hold nothing back. It's important."

"I don't understand," Renee said. "Is she after you?"

"She . . . and others. She won't harm me, though."

"You want her to find you?" Again, she sounded confused.

"I want her to get close. We're very much alike, I think. I'll tell you a secret, though. She won't catch me. I'm crafty, like a wolf."

"Like a fox," Renee corrected.

Mica looked at her and smiled. There were *some* things she couldn't tell Renee — her killings, her grandfather, the wolf. They were for Shara and for Shara alone.

That night before going to bed, in what had been Jane's room, Mica told Jane she would soon be leaving. Told her about Shara. Told her to answer all of her questions.

Jane turned away and Mica played their game of hide and seek until Jane relented and laughed.

"You're very special to me, Jane. I'm a better . . . happier person for knowing you. You've got a life to live, on your terms. Don't let Charlie or anyone else bully you."

The next morning when Mica got up, Jane was sitting in bed looking at her, smiling.

"What's so damn funny? I know I look a sight—"

"You talk in your sleep," Jane chimed in.

"What did I say?" Mica asked, knowing she could never spend another night at The Haven.

"Words that make no sense. You said her name a lot: Shara."

"Well, we all have our faults," Mica said, trying to pass it off. "Hope I didn't keep you awake too long."

Jane was silent, looking at Mica as if her best friend had died.

"You're leaving today," Jane said finally.

"Not because of you," Mica answered honestly. "But it's time."

Jane nodded knowingly.

Passing the kitchen, Mica saw Charlie there alone, peeked in and said hi. She wanted to thank the woman, but didn't know how. When she left today, she wanted no party, no tears. She had said her good-byes. All except to Charlie.

Despite Charlie's efforts to stifle her, The Haven had proved to be more than a place to cool her heels over the winter. She hadn't been aware of it, but the emotional isolation that had been her protective armor for eight years had taken its toll. Here, she had opened up to Jane and the children. Even her sparring with Charlie had been cathartic. She had never felt more alive. She'd searched for something to say, and all she could think of was, "Hi."

She went upstairs shaking her head.

She knew that after today there was only one person left she could turn to: Shara. But Shara had Alexis, Lysette and Deidre. These were names and images that assaulted Mica's as she tried, with little progress, to glimpse into Shara's world. No, she thought, Shara had *no one*.

"She is me and I am she," Mica mouthed aloud. Sisters. Soulmates. Kindred spirits.

In her room, Mica wrote a note to Shara, for she knew she would come to the shelter in search of her.

You have Alexis.
You have Lysette.
You have Deidre.
Are they enough?

She put the letter in an envelope along with a tape of a song by the Temptations, "Soul To Soul" — a R&B slow jam that expressed her churning thoughts better than anything she could write. She had played the song often, and now sang along with it. It spoke to the loneliness she felt and the need for someone to confide in who would understand her anguish. She knew that person was Shara.

She brought the note and tape to Charlie, giving it to her in an envelope.

"Someone will come by looking for me. Her name is Shara. Tell her whatever she wants. Forget, for once, your vow of confidentiality. I release you."

"Who is this Shara?" Charlie asked.

"I don't know . . . yet. Give her these, too." She gave Charlie the envelope.

Again, she wanted to say something more, but couldn't find the words.

"Gotta go see the kids now," she said, and left.

After dinner, after tucking the kids in one last time, after squeezing Renee's hand — who she was sure knew she was leaving — she left The Haven to resume her quest.

Two days later she had her first encounter with Shara, when Shara had slept in her lair. After replaying the conversation in her head, the words to the song "Soul To Soul" seemed even more appropriate. Like in the song she desperately needed someone to talk with who could understand why she was driven to return to Emory.

"What's your story, Shara?" she said aloud. "Why do you want me so?"

She fell asleep in a small cave, thinking of the children, but mostly of Renee, of Jane, of Charlie, and of Shara. Always Shara.

TWENTY-THREE

SHARA

Shara was waiting at the airport for Briggs. She hadn't spoken to him until she had returned to Philly. She'd been preoccupied by thoughts which troubled her, but only slightly. She was normally so single-mindedly focused when hunting her prey that she had no time for stray thoughts. That's why she had declined Clay's dinner invitation. No, not declined, *put off*, she told herself. She couldn't think about him with Mica preoccupying her every moment. But here *he* was intruding again. She hated to think how she would be if she ever fell in love with Clay. *With anyone*, she countered.

Still, she couldn't banish him entirely and knew it could cost her. If she lost her edge, she would lose Mica. It could even cost her her life. On the other hand, her life had been so barren and Clay had made her feel alive. Caught between a rock and a hard place, like Everett Gaines. Better, she decided, to feel alive and face death than live but be dead within.

When she'd talked to Briggs, he was at the airport, waiting to board a plane back to Philly. He'd been circumspect, like he had had a secret he couldn't or wouldn't share over the phone.

"Cleary wasn't particularly forthcoming," he had told her.

"We expected as much, didn't we?"

"Even more so than usual. Look, they're calling my flight. Just wanted you to know I got a picture of this Terése, sort of."

"What do you mean, *sort of*?" she had asked. She wanted to tell him her name was Mica, but with a plane to catch, it could wait.

"You gotta see it to know what I mean. Gotta run. See ya soon."

As usual the plane was fashionably late, giving her more time to think of Clay.

She and Briggs were silent until they got to Shara's car.

"So show me this picture," Shara said, now impatient.

"At the house," he said, referring to his home, literally a ten-minute drive from the airport.

Shara looked at him crossly.

"I need room," he said, as if that explained it all. "Anyway, the picture is just part of a larger story."

"So begin. How wasn't Cleary forthcoming?"

"First, Terése was no high-priced call girl. She was a dominatrix, which is why she probably never had a police record. She catered to the rich and powerful, which didn't hurt either."

Briggs opened a pack of the peanuts they give you on planes and emptied the entire contents into his mouth. After a moment or two of chewing, he went on.

"Cleary also failed to mention Donato probably raped her. They did have sex—"

"He did rape her," Shara said. "I saw it," she said, then stopped, when Briggs gave her an odd look. "But go on. I'll tell you how later."

"I'll agree she was raped. There were bite marks on Donato's lip and fresh scratches on his face and neck. Her skin was under his nails. Tell you this, she gave as good as she got."

"No, Briggs. She didn't give as good as she got," Shara said tersely, her voice rising. "She got *raped*. You men, you get beat, you get hit by a car, hell, you get shot and you heal. You don't recover from rape. It's the ultimate control mechanism men have over women. It's debasing; the most vile of violations. Tell you something, Briggs, if I wanted information from a man, I wouldn't torture him. I'd get another man to stick it up his ass. Humiliate him; break his spirit. That's how you break a man. Take away his dignity. Once it's lost, it's gone forever. That's what it's like to be raped. You *never* give as good as you get. Of all people, you should know that better than most. It so traumatized Alexis, she's repressed it."

"You're right," Briggs said, scarcely above a whisper. "Look what it did to *me*, and I wasn't the one raped. I'm sorry for trivializing it."

"You're a man. What do you know," Shara said dismissively. "But you're forgiven. Go on, what else did you find out?"

"One odd thing at the crime scene. Donato's gun was out — in his hand actually. There was only one bullet in it, yet the gun hadn't been fired."

"He was playing Russian Roulette to terrify her," Shara said. She pointed her index finger at Briggs' head. "'Click,'" she mimicked the sound of a gun fired, with no bullet. Then at her head. "'Click.'" Then at Briggs again. "'Click.' Then she relented," Shara said, omitting the gun being jammed up Mica's genitals. Briggs wasn't ready to handle that, yet.

He looked at her. "How the hell do you know?"

She gave him an abbreviated and carefully edited account of her time in Dismal.

"When you told me about the gun, well, I thought I saw it in the images she . . . downloaded to me. But it was more than that. I felt her terror and her rage emerge from within. I smelled the breath mint Donato had eaten, then her pussy—"

"I don't need the details," Briggs said, turning away from her.

"You *do*. What he did to her, it opened some door — a doorway to hell, and unleashed something within her I still can't grasp," she lied.

Briggs shook his head. "You're projecting. I told you about the gun. *I* thought it might have been Russian Roulette, too. *You* conjured up specifics, but not through any psychic connection."

"How come I knew about it *yesterday*? And how did I find my way to her lair in the dark? And what about the old man warning me in the face of the deputy? Just my imagination? What about the gash on my arm from the wolf's paw?"

"Pull over," he said. "Which arm?"

She showed him.

"What gash?" he snapped. "Nothing. Look for yourself."

"I told you, it healed before my eyes. But I tasted the blood."

"Are you having a breakdown on me?" he asked, sounding concerned.

"Her name's Mica," she said, ignoring him. "Don't ask me why. Don't ask me how, but we're somehow connected."

"Whatever," he said.

She could tell she'd lost him. She had to regain his confidence in her by bringing him back to reality. "Tell me what else you found out. I promise to keep my mouth shut."

"No more psychic ramblings," he said skeptically.

"Facts. Deductions, based on facts. Promise."

He paused, then relented. "Okay, so where was I?" He thought for a moment. "Oh yeah, Donato was no Boy Scout, something else Cleary glossed over. He'd been in vice nine years, and rejected several promotions."

"Was he a user?"

"In more ways than one. They found cocaine in his system at the autopsy. But he had remained in vice, so I was told, for the sex. He'd had three complaints in his jacket from hookers who said he blackmailed them into having sex with him over protracted periods of time."

"And nothing came of the complaints?"

"They were all withdrawn. I spoke to one woman. Now that he was dead, she opened up. He got her hooked on cocaine, had his way with her for three months, then tired of her. *She* tried to blackmail *him*. She needed money for her habit. If he didn't give it to her, she would drop a dime. He visited her a day after she filed the complaint. Gave her a thousand dollars, but told her no pusher would take a cent of it. He'd passed the word not to provide her with cocaine. Pushers *knew* Donato. *Knew* the consequences of fucking with him. She had the money, but it was worthless. So she caved in. Dropped the complaint and all of a sudden her money was good again."

"Nice guy."

"A prince," Briggs concurred sarcastically. "The way I heard it, there was supposed to be a bust at a S/M dungeon the night he was killed. But someone pulled strings and it was called off. I figure Donato heard about it and was waiting for Terése—"

"Mica," Shara corrected.

"Mica, then. Raped her. Wanted to possess her like the others, but she refused. Somehow she got the best of him," he said, looking at Shara to see if she would interject her version.

Shara held her tongue, though.

They were at his house.

"Give me a few minutes with Vivian and Alexis. Then, I'll run the rest down for you."

She saw him embrace Alexis. Hug her and refuse to let go. Unconditional love, she thought. He could be exasperating, but watching him, she was envious. Seeing his genuine affection for his daughter, she could forgive him almost anything.

Rather than going to a study she knew he now used as his office, he took her upstairs to the bedroom.

"We're going to need the room," he said, as he guided her upstairs.

"So we know Donato initiated the attack," Shara said. Once in the bedroom, he sat on the bed, she on a chair he had pulled up for her. "We know he's a bastard with a history of abuse. Let's assume, for the sake of argument, she killed him in self-defense. Why did she run?"

"Who would believe her?" Briggs answered. "She didn't know of his history of abuse. Dominatrix or whatever you want to call her, to the average cop, she was a whore. She panicked and ran."

"There's more to it than that."

He gave her that look that said "Don't go there."

"Gut instinct, Briggs. Look at the facts. Why has she killed at least three more times? And look at her path," Shara said, taking out a map she carried with her. "It's not random. Northeast. She has a final destination. What did you learn about *her*?"

"Precious little. She was pretty much a loner. There was one exception, a guy named Jeremy. No last name. Jeremy, like Madonna or Roseanne. He was an artist and she was his patron, I guess you'd call it."

"Did you speak to him?"

"He blew town around the time she did. I think they might be together."

Shara *knew* otherwise, but she couldn't tell Briggs she'd seen Mica alone in her den when she had sent Shara the images.

"My gut tells me she's traveling alone," Shara said. "So does the evidence. Only she was seen in Dismal. And the crime scenes show no indication of a second attacker. If he were with her, he would have helped her. It doesn't add up. What did you find out about him?" she asked.

"Here it gets interesting," Briggs said, as if enjoying building the suspense. "He was considered a ladies' man. He painted a lot of women in the nude."

Briggs took out three Polaroids from his satchel and handed them to Shara.

"Are these the same woman?" she asked. They all looked similar but they weren't really portraits at all. They were abstract paintings of the subject's inner self, she assumed. You couldn't tell the women had posed nude. Had posed at all, for that matter, she thought.

"Different women, but the same type. Came from money, with influential husbands. The youngest was thirty-eight, the oldest forty-five. They got the best of both worlds. He painted them in the nude, but their husbands would never know by looking at the paintings. Just lines and dots."

Shara was still eyeing the photos when he paused, and she looked at him.

"Here's the kicker, though," he went on when he had her attention. "*He* spread rumors that he'd slept with each of them. Only they deny it. They *allowed* him to spread the word, as long as it didn't get back to their husbands. Here's this young stud — they said he was about twenty-five — saying he's banging these older women and they're eating it up. When confronted, though, each admitted he had never even made a pass at them. *My* gut tells me they're telling the truth. Maybe he was impotent. Maybe a fag," he added.

Briggs then took out a larger painting from his satchel, and laid the canvas on the bed for Shara.

"That's Mica?" Shara said, disappointed. Just as with the others, there was no face, no body — just an abstract painting. Beautiful, but no help, she thought.

"In the flesh. Actually, in the nude," he corrected himself. "I kinda let myself into Jeremy's loft and he had this satchel," he said, touching the case on his bed, "labeled *Nudes of Terése*."

He then took out six other paintings of Mica.

"What do you make of these?" Briggs asked.

"He's in love with her," Shara said after looking then touching each one.

"Your gut again," he said irritably. "That's quite a leap."

"It's no gut reaction," she said. "Here, look at the Polaroids. He's painting just what he sees. It's as if, in his mind, there's no substance to any of these women. They're all variations on the same theme. All rather bland. He's emotionally detached."

Shara then shifted to one of the paintings of Mica. She traced an outline, telling Briggs what was Mica and what was the background.

"He's caressing her with his brush. See," she pointed at the longer, broader strokes — some dark yet visceral, others vibrantly bright and emotionally charged; not vapid as those of the other women.

"Now compare it to the Polaroids," she said, pointing at one. "A brushmark here. Another there. Altogether you get something . . . something some may find interesting, but they're devoid of passion. With Mica, the strokes are bolder. He's caressing her on canvas, just like he'd want to in bed."

Shara then laid out all seven paintings of Mica. "What do you see?"

"They're all different. Same woman, but each is unique," Briggs said.

"The different sides of Mica," Shara said. "He's painting the woman within. He's not looking for, or can't see, the inner woman with the others. With Mica, he's painted all her many moods. He's in love with her."

"Okay, then, if he's not with her," Briggs said, "where the hell is he and why did he bolt?"

"I haven't the faintest," Shara said. "But these paintings will tell me something about Mica."

"How so?" Again, she saw that look of suspicion he wore when she even intimated the explanation might deal with the supernatural.

"Her many moods. I'm getting into her head, Briggs. Forget the visions I've had of her. I've been where she's been. I've slept where she's slept. The deputy I spoke to gave me his impressions of the crime scene — not at all like what Cleary provided. I'm getting a handle on her, just as you do when conducting a homicide investigation. You want to be in the killer's head, so you can be one step ahead of him. And these," she said, touching one of the paintings, "they'll tell me more about her still."

Briggs said nothing, but nodded.

"The question now is what is Cleary hiding from us?" Shara said. "We need to know what she's holding back, so we can leave her holding an empty bag."

"That she's killed again. Probably three times, in conjunction with her menstrual cycle," Briggs said.

"Not on the highway, though," Shara added. "It's too cold for her. She's . . . hibernating, for want of a better word."

"In Philly, you think?" Briggs asked.

"Where better?" Shara asked. "A big city where someone could get lost, not far from her last known kill. Still, the urge to kill — *the need* — is there."

"Cleary could keep it under wraps," Briggs concurred. "She's good. Look what she handed us compared to reality."

"We've got to find out who she's killed. Any ideas?"

Briggs smiled. "I've still got friends in homicide. Even if the FBI has put a lid on the killings, homicide is involved. The department wouldn't just sit back. Let me call in a few markers," he said.

"Then we go to Cleary with what she's held back, and tell her about Mica's lair," Shara said.

"What are you going to do?" Briggs asked. "Get inside her head through these paintings?"

"Better. I'm going to find out where she stayed for the winter."

"It's a big city."

"You're the detective, Briggs. She needs to get indoors, out from the elements and prying eyes. Where would you look?"

He thought for a moment.

"I'd eliminate hotels and motels," he said. "If she's killed here, the police and FBI would have checked them out. You know she could be holed up in some abandoned house. There are enough of them in Philly. More than enough."

"Hole up with addicts, winos and mental cases?" Shara said, shaking her head. "She's just been raped a few months ago. She wouldn't put herself in such a vulnerable position."

"Where then?" Briggs asked, stumped.

"Possibly a shelter," Shara said, without much conviction. "But not your typical shelter. I've read horror stories about those. Men preying on women where there's little or no security. She wouldn't go to one of those. Mmm," she said, pausing for a moment. "But maybe, just maybe one for women only — abused and battered women, not homeless women. A roof over her head, hot food, a bed, a shower. She could blend in."

"A shot in the dark," Briggs said.

"Beats staring at these paintings while you do your detecting," she said.

"There's a certain logic to that," Briggs said. "I'll make some sandwiches before we leave. You want to spend some time with Alexis?"

"Do bears shit in the woods?" Shara countered.

"I hope you don't talk that way in front of her," Briggs said, only half-kidding. A father protecting his daughter. Shara liked that. Liked it a lot.

Going downstairs with Briggs, she was hit with a new set of images: Mica surrounded by children. Mica with a disfigured black woman. Mica arguing with a woman named Charlie. Mica being hit with Nerf bats. Mica hitting back. Mica smiling. Mica with one teenage girl, in particular. Mica smiling.

When there were no more, Shara found herself standing on the staircase, holding onto Briggs for dear life.

"Are you okay?" he asked. "You blacked out for a minute. Almost took a tumble."

"I'm fine," Shara said weakly. "Didn't have any breakfast," she said hastily, as an excuse. "Haven't eaten much the past day, I've been so into Mica. It must be catching up to me."

Inside she was churning. *Damn you, Mica*, she thought, her mind reaching out to Mica, if she could hear. *That's the second time you put me in danger. I want the images, but you have to work on your presentation.*

She knew from the images she'd been right. Mica *had* been at a shelter. And the image of Mica arguing with a woman — a woman named Charlie? — *that* had been repeated several times. She couldn't hear the argument itself, yet somehow the woman's name was part of the download. This Charlie wasn't just some woman working at the shelter. She *ran* the shelter. That's what Mica had been telling her. Locating the shelter itself wouldn't be difficult, with what she now knew. She'd let her fingers do the walking.

She was pissed, though. Mica seemed to be leading her by the hand, controlling the hunt. There was something at the shelter she wanted Shara to see, even if Shara hadn't been interested in finding where she had stayed over the winter. At some point Shara would have to wrest control from Mica. She wanted to explore those parts of Mica's mind that were kept hidden. For now she'd follow Mica's lead.

With Briggs in and out of the kitchen, there was only so much she could tell Alexis.

"Your father infuriates me, sometimes," she said quietly. "I get these images of Mica — the woman we're after. I even spoke with her. But he won't hear any of it."

Alexis signed "stubborn" to Shara.

"You can say that again," she said, and Alexis did.

Just before Briggs came into the kitchen again, Alexis told Shara to be careful. "You're going to be on her turf," she signed. "Not just the woods, but maybe her hometown."

"True," Shara said. "But she underestimates me."

"Just like you underestimate her," Alexis signed.

"Smartass," Shara whispered. "Lecture heard. Lecture understood."

Shara was going to drive Briggs to the police station in town after he made some calls. Before calling shelters, Shara went upstairs and looked at the paintings of Mica again. This time she thought of the painter.

"Where the hell did you go, Jeremy?" she said, aloud. She had a feeling he was part of the puzzle. She had no clue just where he fit.

TWENTY-FOUR

JEREMY

He felt the soft caress of Shara's fingers, as she touched his paintings. She understood, he knew — as much as she could, at least — that he had painted the Terése no one else was aware existed. He felt Terése's inner turmoil, even if she had refused to tell him what had so traumatized her. He'd painted her peaks and valleys, and everything in between. What neither Shara nor Terése knew was he painted her from the eyes of a wolf. What appeared to be abstract art was how the wolf within him visualized his mate — or more precisely, he corrected himself, his *mate-to-be*.

He had been waiting for someone like Terése for fourteen years. He knew he wasn't alone. He didn't consider himself an aberration. Others like him existed, whether it be a handful or in the hundreds he didn't know, but he was not unique; of that he was certain.

Yet he'd prowled streets, alleyways and forests to no avail. Oddly, he hadn't been discouraged. He knew he wasn't alone, and patience was one of his virtues. The irony was, when he had found her, she had literally snuck up *on him*.

He'd been startled that first day at Piedmont Park, when she had approached him as he was painting the scene by the lake. He immediately knew she had buried within her the same beast that was a part of him. Her scent wasn't as strong as his, and her senses weren't as finely honed. She was drawn to him, but she didn't know why. While she confirmed that there *were* others — that his wait hadn't been in vain — he needed only one mate; his mate for life. She *was* the one, even though she was totally unaware of what they shared.

He'd been Stephon Lassiter, an only child living on a ranch with his parents in Minnesota. His mother had developed an inoperable brain tumor when he was ten. The doctors said she could live a year, maybe two before she succumbed. What they hadn't known — or hadn't told his father — was that she would become delusional — *dangerously so*, soon after.

There were days when she thought her husband was a complete stranger, there to terrorize and harm her. And, there were days when she viewed Stephon as an equal threat.

With the benefit of hindsight, Jeremy now realized, in her mind, she had to purge herself of these threats to her safety. At the time what she did after a visit to her doctor made little sense. She had come into the kitchen with a shotgun. Without saying a word she had fired a shotgun blast that had obliterated his father's head. She shot Stephon, too, but he'd scrambled to the floor and his wounds were superficial.

He had escaped, as his mother reloaded the gun. He ran for the woods that bordered the ranch as his mother fired yet again. He was out of reach of the shotgun, but saw his mother had no intention of allowing him to escape. She followed him as he ran pell-mell through the woods. His mind told him he was making far too much noise with his thrashing, but his body wouldn't respond.

He came to a clearing where a large gray wolf stood staring at him — staring through him, he felt.

Unlike most ranchers his father had wanted to coexist with the wolves that had been reintroduced to the area. Most ranchers perceived wolves as a threat, but in fact they preferred animals in the wild. Cattle were sometimes attacked, but not with the frequency most ranchers suggested. Stephon's father hadn't lost any livestock to a wolf.

His father had taken Stephon camping often. When his son shivered as the wolves began to howl in the evening, he comforted him.

"They won't harm you, son. They're a damned sight more fearful of you than you are of them. Have you seen even one wolf in the wild, Stephon?"

He admitted he hadn't.

"Yet we both know they're here. They stay clear of us, as if knowing we pose a threat. I've seen one. A disperser. He'd left the pack," his father explained. "I can't tell you why. Maybe he lost a battle for dominance and left in disgrace, or possibly he left to find a new pack where he could lead. Or maybe, like some people, he simply shunned the company of others. I've seen him a number of times; stared him in the face, one time. He didn't flee, yet he didn't attack, either. We seemed to come to an understanding in those few moments. You might encounter him one day. He'll know you're mine, and you'll be safe."

Now the wolf stood his ground. Stephon could advance no further, yet his mother still pursued him. He stood frozen, not knowing what to do. Whatever his decision, it seemed death awaited him.

The wolf lunged at him without warning. It entered him, became a part of him, rather than knocking him down. And it had felt right. It was as if his father had prepared him for this moment. He didn't try to rationalize the impossible. He simply accepted it and gave himself over to the wolf.

With its help, Stephon eluded his mother for several hours. Then, as he slept in the woods, he heard a single shot. Walking home, he saw his mother lying next to his father. She must have regained her senses, as she often did, saw what she had done and could no longer live with what she had become. He didn't love her any less. His *mother* hadn't killed his father.

While he grieved for them, he was no longer the same person he'd been earlier that day. The wolf within wouldn't allow his grief to consume him.

There was no longer any reason to stay. Within him now was a yearning to roam and find others like himself. He ventured east, leaving Stephon behind, taking the name Jeremy.

Unlike Terése, he and the wolf within became one. He was Jeremy, but he was much more. And unlike Terése, he willingly gave part of himself over to the wolf. Not only did the two reside in the same body, they were a single entity. Just as the animals his father had told him about, he had become more humane — possibly more *human*, even though the wolf shared his body. He had no desire to accumulate money, nor live extravagantly. He had no need to bully others, though he could defend himself when necessary. He lived for today, making no plans for the future.

When he'd met Terése, he knew he had to possess her. Knew, too, the wolf within her was dormant most of the year. He felt no urgency to claim her as his. He wouldn't mate with her until February, anyway, so there was only the desire to be near her and protect her.

When she looked at his painting of her, she saw how he had captured her many moods. And he had. Yet, what he painted was how he actually visualized her, something he couldn't yet divulge. What she called abstract painting was how a part of him saw her.

He had begun spreading rumors about his sexual prowess when Terése had questioned why he hadn't made advances on her. He couldn't tell her he went into heat but once a year. And he couldn't — *wouldn't* — either mate with another, nor have sex with her when he knew neither was ready.

He invented liaisons and torrid affairs so she would think him a *normal* human being. Yet, the thought of having more than one mate repulsed him. What was *human* about bedding every woman you encountered, just for the momentary pleasure or the need for conquest?

Their February together had been more exhilarating than even he could have imagined. And while Terése thought he was mimicking her out of thoughtfulness, when he sniffed her, it was *his* wolf within acting out a natural ritual. When she urinated on him, a signal she wanted to be mounted, he responded in kind. What she viewed as a game they shared was actually him giving vent to his true nature.

He'd badly wanted an offspring, but something within her wouldn't yet allow it. There was unfinished business she had to attend to, he knew instinctively, before she could give herself to him completely and bear his children.

When she disappeared, he had followed. Even without her letter he knew she had killed the policeman in self-defense. He made sure she wasn't aware of his presence. She was on some mission, and until it was completed, they couldn't begin their life together. Patience, he thought. If not today, maybe tomorrow.

When she camped at a cabin, he stayed in the woods, much as he had the many years he had traveled east to Atlanta. Unlike Terése, the elements didn't bother him in the least. It had been far colder when he had begun his journey.

Then there had been Shara. He had come upon her, as she slept in the lair abandoned by Terése. He'd sniffed her, and found no wolf within. Yet, there was something predatory about her. She was every bit the wolf he and Terése were, without the animal residing in her. He found this terribly intriguing.

As with his kind, he didn't view Shara as a threat, but a competitor of Terése's. The two would battle for dominance; for the right to mate with him and bear his offspring. He had no right to interfere. Females of his species, he knew, often challenged one another for the right to mate with the dominant male. Actually, he thought Shara's hunt for Terése quite grand. Two worthy opponents vying for the right to be his lifetime partner. He had to let nature take its course, and it made his journey so much more interesting. Terése was at home in the woods, he knew, but Shara seemed more than up to the challenge.

At times he had mixed feelings as to whom he wanted to prevail. His human side, he thought, had loved Terése. But how could that be when she had never let him enter her life emotionally? He didn't begrudge her this need for emotional detachment. She didn't know the bond they shared. And their February trysts had been purely physical. The wolf in him didn't want an emotional commitment, then. They were both in heat and the drive to mount and mate was all-consuming.

So Jeremy wasn't surprised at the ambivalence he felt when Terése was challenged. The human part of Jeremy would certainly want to emotionally bond with Shara, if she triumphed. But the animal in him wasn't hung up by such nonsense. The animal was intrigued with the game of cat and mouse, and was waiting for their final confrontation.

The only fly in the ointment had been the man who had brought the paintings of Terése to Shara. He could tip the scales in Shara's favor, which Jeremy couldn't allow. True, Terése had her wolf within, while Shara did not, but he felt Shara every bit Terése's equal. The man was an interloper. For now Jeremy wouldn't intercede. But the final confrontation *had* to be between Terése and Shara. To the victor would go the spoils.

He knew Shara was aware of him. As she touched his paintings he felt a chill down his spine. Maybe, he thought, it was time to allow her to know of his existence; to let her know what awaited her if she was victorious.

TWENTY-FIVE

SHARA

While Briggs made his calls — calling in his markers — Shara went upstairs, as if drawn by the paintings of Mica. She envied Mica. No, she corrected herself, she was *jealous* of the woman. To be so adored . . . it was something she had never experienced. And to allow someone to bore so deeply within symbolized a trust she could only imagine.

Yet oddly, Jeremy wasn't in Mica's thoughts. There had been no mention, so to speak, of Jeremy in any of the images Mica had shared. Shara was getting a real sense of the woman, aside from the images. At times it was if she could crawl into her head and lounge around amidst her thoughts. But Jeremy wasn't among them. If Shara was misinterpreting their relationship, maybe she was off the mark in other more crucial areas.

Shara had the sense that in leaving Atlanta, Mica had left *all* behind. She had abandoned her lover for something more important. Whatever drove Mica had to be so all-consuming, she'd burned all her bridges. Such obsession saddened Shara, because she had been there and it had all but destroyed her.

She didn't know if she would ever find that special someone. If she did, she wondered if she could she leave him without so much as a second thought. A puzzle, she thought. A puzzle.

Something else about Jeremy disturbed her, as well. *Why* had he disappeared? Where had he gone? Caressing the figure of Mica, as Jeremy had in painting her, Shara suddenly felt drained and lay down. A catnap. Half-an-hour. It was all she would need.

She dreamed, but for the first time in seven months, it wasn't a rehashing of the forest chase. This time she and Mica stood naked in a forest clearing. She wasn't staring at herself, but at the Mica who had visited her at her lair.

It was a final confrontation — a fight to the death, with the prize being . . . she had no idea. But she knew they were fighting for something or someone. It appeared Mica had the advantage. Shara saw the hands of an old man — aged, but still powerful — where Mica's should have been. And protruding from her stomach was the wolf's head and two front paws.

Still, Shara felt confident. She had her police training and street fighting skills, which she had learned from Rudy. She sensed that Mica herself was no fighter. If she could withstand the blows from the old man's fists, parry the wolf's paws and avoid its jaws, she could prevail.

Mica lunged at her. Shara went for her eyes, with her fingers. Blinded, Mica would have no advantage.

Mica winced as Shara hit one eye, but Shara's other hand was grabbed by the old man's. At the same time one of the paws ripped at her abdomen, opening a deep gash that sprouted blood. Shara kneed the wolf's mouth as it lunged for her neck. He retreated into Mica's belly for cover.

Her belly. Her neck — her most vulnerable areas. Shara had to protect them at all costs. *Go after Mica,* her instincts shouted. *Take the offensive or you're doomed.*

She grabbed Mica's long hair and pulled her down. At the same time she raised her knee so it would connect with Mica's jaw. If she rendered Mica helpless, the wolf couldn't attack . . . or so Shara hoped.

The blow to the chin dazed Mica. She fell to the ground. Shara picked up a heavy branch and slammed it against the outstretched arm of the old man, and Mica let out a howl of anguish. Shara raised the branch again, intent on clubbing Mica's skull, but the wolf lunged from Mica's back. With its teeth it tore into Shara's arm, refusing to let go until Shara dropped her weapon.

Bleeding and woozy, Shara retreated. A battered and groggy Mica did the same.

Like two armies, they had gone back to lick their wounds and plan fresh strategy. As in a title fight, round one had been a draw. This was to be a battle to the death, though, and neither of them would get much rest before the next encounter. . . .

Shara awoke with a start, her stomach and arm aflame with pain. Blood from her wounds dripped onto the painting of Mica, she'd been caressing. The blood was absorbed by the canvas.

Shara stumbled into the bathroom to view her wounds. She was distressed and near panic when the blood continued to flow and her injuries refused to heal.

Fatigue washed over her and she fell to the floor. . . .

She opened her eyes to see the concerned faces of Briggs and Alexis.

"Alexis found you in the bathroom. She came in because she . . . sensed something was wrong," Briggs said. She knew Briggs was uncomfortable. If Alexis had *sensed* something then she *must* have psychic abilities. Briggs *wouldn't* accept that, yet he had reluctantly uttered what he felt was impossible. Alexis *sensed* danger.

Shara saw she was clothed, and neither her arm nor her abdomen were bleeding. But she wasn't entirely healed. Her stomach ached, as did her arm, and she felt terribly weak . . . as if from loss of blood.

"This is the second time—" Briggs began, but Shara cut him off.

"Look, Briggs, after what I told you about last night, I guess I'm still a bit out of it. If I can rest here a bit, I'm sure I'll be fine." Another wave of nausea hit. "Go," she said, gritting her teeth. "You've got to find out who Mica's killed. Alexis can stay with me."

"I don't know," Briggs said. "Your color's bad. If you're suffering from exposure from your night in the woods, I should take you to the hospital."

"Nonsense. Look, I have no death wish. If I don't feel better, Alexis can dial 911. All I need is a bit of TLC — tender-loving-care from my favorite person," she said, conjuring up the best smile she could.

Briggs stubbornly waited half an hour for Vivian to return from some grocery shopping. He waited outside the bedroom, but like an expectant father poked his head in every five minutes.

Alexis applied a cold compress to Shara's head, signing to her that she had a fever.

"Burning up," Shara said "But it's nothing a doctor can cure."

Briggs finally left, after Vivian returned and the two had consulted on what should be done.

Vivian took Shara's temperature, looked at her with concern and gave Shara two Tylenol.

"If your temperature doesn't go down, young lady, it's to the hospital for you. You can't bully me like you can my husband," she said, clearly distressed.

Shara slept in fits and starts, waking each time to see Alexis gazing at her anxiously.

"Reach out to her with your mind," Alexis signed to her when she seemed fully conscious. "The two of you are one. Together you can make yourself whole."

Shara wasn't about to argue. She still felt like shit, and neither the rest nor the Tylenol had been of any help.

With her mind she reached out, searching for Mica, and found her laying in the woods, looking as ill as Shara felt. No words were exchanged, but they grasped each other's hands and held on.

Shara felt some reserve of strength within her seep into Mica. She felt so tired. Too tired to maintain her bond with Mica, but Mica now refused to release her. As color returned to Mica's face, Shara felt a tingling in her fingers, then *her* strength returned.

The two women looked at one another, each having helped the other recover, and then Shara felt Mica slipping from her grasp.

She opened her eyes and saw Alexis and Vivian.

"Your color's better," Vivian said, then took Shara's temperature. "You're fever's gone," she said looking at the thermometer. "You had me worried for a while, but it looks like you're out of the woods. I'll call Lamar. He's been pestering me all day."

When she had left Shara looked at Alexis. "What did she mean *all day*?"

"It's five o'clock," Alexis signed.

Shara sat up. The pain in her arm and abdomen had subsided to a dull ache, lessening even more as she spoke.

"We healed each other," Shara said excitedly. "We both had the same dream, I'm certain."

She looked at the painting resting on the floor. "It was Jeremy. He's a part of this, somehow. But why would he attack us both?"

Alexis asked her to explain her dream. "Maybe he lost control," she signed, after Shara told her.

Shara got up and stretched. "Imagine what your father would say if I told him what made me sick."

Alexis signed a smile.

"This is more than I bargained for. It's bad enough with Mica sending me these images at . . . inopportune times, but now there's a third player in the game. A wildcard. I don't know what the hell he wants or what he's going to do next."

"He wants you . . . or Mica," Alexis signed, holding the painting. "He wants you two to fight . . . fight to the death for *him*."

"Arrogant bastard," Shara said. "He's in love with Mica, so why would he want us to battle over him?"

Alexis shrugged. "It's his nature, that's all I get," she signed.

"He fucks with us again, he may lose the both of us."

"You must be feeling better," Alexis signed. "You curse when you're angry."

"You know me all too well, Alexis. All too well." She paused. "Thanks for staying with me . . . and telling me to reach out to Mica. For once I'm glad you could read me. It may have saved my life."

"Hers, too," Alexis signed.

"We saved each other," Shara said. "Neither one of us wants an intruder's interference. Eventually it will come down to Mica and I."

Shara went to the bathroom and washed her face with cold water.

"Stay the hell away, Jeremy," she said to the image of herself in the mirror. "Neither Mica nor I want your meddling."

Something was tugging at her mind about the dream she normally had. She wondered if Jeremy were lurking somewhere in that dream, observing. She would be on the lookout the next time she dreamed.

When she returned to the bedroom, Alexis had a phonebook opened to shelters.

"Smartass," Shara said, but gave Alexis a smile.

It took all of three calls before someone recognized Charlie's name, and said she could be found at The Haven. The woman gave her the address.

"It's been fun," Shara said to Alexis, her sense of humor returning, as they embraced. "We'll have to do this again sometime."

Driving towards Center City, Shara was aware that Mica was still calling the shots. Yet it had been Shara who had reached out to Mica at their moment of need. Perhaps she could do so again, and become the aggressor, rather than a docile receptor. Something to think about *after* learning what Mica wanted her to find out at the shelter.

TWENTY-SIX

Mica knew she'd had the same dream as Shara, but had no idea of its source. How someone could intrude upon them baffled her. That someone could at all was even more disquieting. And she had been so weakened by the aftermath of her fight with Shara, she had nearly lost consciousness. It was Shara who had reached out and saved her, just as she then returned the favor.

That Shara could reach out to her was unsettling in itself. The rules of the game were changing without her permission. *She* was supposed to guide Shara to her. She was to reveal what she desired, when she desired. She *had* underestimated Shara, she now knew. She would have to shield her innermost thoughts from this woman. She wanted to confront Shara on her terms. She couldn't allow Shara to interfere with her mission.

She knew Shara had reached out to save herself, but Mica couldn't deny that without Shara she would have probably died. She so wanted this woman to open herself up to her. Shara was almost a total mystery. What drove her? Mica wondered. From where did she derive her strength? Even in this dream, Shara had battled her to a draw when Mica had both her grandfather and the wolf at her side.

271

Soon, she thought. After her next kill there would be only one remaining. Then, they would meet.

Mica had only another day or two to travel before her period began. The evening was warm for late March. She would sleep in the woods tonight envious that Shara was talking right now with Charlie, Jane and Renee. A pang of regret passed through her, but she tossed it aside. She knew what she must do to retain her sanity, avenge herself and move on with her life.

Twenty-seven

Jeremy cursed himself. He'd gone too far and had almost lost those most dear to him; the Mica he knew, and the Shara he was growing to admire.

Just *when* he had lost control, he didn't know. He readily admitted to himself the events he had set in motion had gotten away from him. He'd wanted a bit of sport. But, not only had the two been evenly matched, he hadn't been able to exert his will to put an end to the carnage. He had watched, helpless, as the life had oozed from both.

It was Shara who had somehow known that to live she would have to save Mica. It was Shara who had reached out to Mica. Not that he was keeping score, but Shara had clearly been victorious.

He'd been a fool. He would have to be more vigilant than ever. Mica had no idea he was on her trail. Shara, on the other hand, was very much aware of him.

His arrogance had almost led to disaster. He had to curb his human impulse to intercede. Having learned his lesson, he was now content to merely observe, while keeping an eye on the man with Shara to make certain he didn't give her an unfair advantage.

TWENTY-EIGHT

SHARA

Shara was ushered into The Haven by a volunteer. Rehearsing in her mind the cover story she had concocted, she asked for Charlie. While waiting, she looked into a lounge. A woman who had been one of the images Mica had thrust at her was at a table playing cards with three other women.

Mica certainly hadn't been subtle. She had wanted to make sure Shara was aware of this woman, Jane. The images, Shara now grasped from her mind, were of Jane's disfigured face. Each image was more stark and vivid than the previous one — first Jane's entire face, then the side with the scar, followed by a closeup of the scarred tissue alone. It had been so graphic and unsettling that looking at Jane now, Shara didn't feel the least bit uncomfortable. Except for the disfigurement, the woman was ravishing with simmering sexuality. She wore tight-fitting jeans, and a blouse tied in a knot above her waist, with several buttons at the top undone to expose a good deal of cleavage.

"That's Jane." Shara was startled by a voice from behind. "She tells me she's *becoming*," the woman said disapprovingly. "*Becoming what*, I don't know, but it's your friend's fault."

"Charlie, I take it," Shara said, looking at the woman who was still gazing at Jane.

"Charleen Phelan. But yes, Charlie. You're *the* Shara who Mica told me to expect."

Shara was taken aback. There was no need for a cover story. Mica had already provided an introduction of sorts. Shara had been told on the phone that Charlie ran The Haven. She had assumed Charlie and Mica had been close, but she felt a distinct chill when Charlie referred to Mica.

"Come with me to my office," she said and turned without waiting for Shara to respond.

A woman used to giving orders and having them followed, Shara thought. She didn't think Mica would take to such a person. But that was why she was here, she assumed; to learn more about Mica.

The office turned out to be a kitchen. Charlie gave Shara a knife and told her to cut some carrots for a salad.

"If you're going to disrupt my routine with questions, you'll have to earn your keep," she said, not unkindly.

Shara sensed some hostility in the woman, as if either she or Mica had rubbed her the wrong way.

"Mica said you'd be coming. I assume it has something to do with her husband. Tell me about him."

"I don't know her husband," Shara said evasively. "Someone wants me to find Mica. That's all I can divulge."

"She's not married," Charlie said.

"No, she's not."

"Was she battered or abused?"

Shara assumed Mica had used a cover story of abuse to gain access to the shelter. She hadn't been lying. "If you call being raped seven months ago abuse, she most definitely was."

Charlie visibly relaxed.

"What did Mica do here, and how long was she here?" Shara asked, deciding to take hold of the conversation.

Charlie talked without letup for ten minutes, ending with, "She was a thorn in my side to be sure, but I have to admit she was a positive influence for the most part. The children adored her, and the Jane you see out there is a direct result of Mica's friendship. I don't approve of her new appearance, but I have to admit Jane's more confident, spirited and alive than when she first arrived."

Charlie then handed Shara an envelope.

"Mica said to give this to you."

"I gather you read the letter and listened to the tape," Shara said when she saw the contents.

"Mica didn't say it was confidential," Charlie responded, with a thin smile. "The letter's gibberish, in any event, and the tape is merely a song."

Shara read the letter. She felt Mica's loneliness and anger. How much she knew about Lysette, Deidre and Alexis, Shara didn't know. More than ever, though, she felt she and Mica shared the same churning emotions.

"May I speak with Jane?" Shara asked.

"If I said no?" Charlie responded with a question of her own.

"I was being polite," Shara admitted. "This is a shelter, not a prison or hospital. I really don't need your permission."

"That's what I thought," Charlie said. "There's a lot of Mica in you. You're right, of course, you don't need my permission. I suggest you go to her room . . . for privacy."

Charlie introduced Shara to Jane, and Jane said nothing until they were in her room. Jane sat on her bed, the scarred side of her face away from Shara. Shara joined her on the bed.

"Mica said you'd be coming. She said to hold nothing back. Mica's in trouble, isn't she?"

Shara decided not to lie to the woman. The images she had told of a special bond between the two. "Yes, the police want her. I want her, too, but I won't harm her. That's why she wants you to hold nothing back. Tell me about her, Jane."

"She gave me back my life," she said, making eye contact with Shara. She told Shara what had happened to her, and how miserable she'd been until Mica arrived. She showed Shara a picture of herself in a house dress, with her hair unkempt.

"This was how Mica found me. I was full of self-pity. Mica told me if others turned away, it was their problem. She made me feel human again. Helped me reinvent myself," she said, pointing to her clothes and hair. "She gently pushed me to interact with others, and because of her I'm now in charge of the children."

This was truly a side of Mica of which Shara had been unaware. She now knew why Mica wanted her to visit the shelter. Shara knew something of the demons within Mica, but Mica was far more complex than she had imagined.

"Did she tell you she was going to leave?"

"She said she would be leaving, but she didn't say when. I knew why she left, though."

"Why?"

"She talked in her sleep. The first night we shared this room, she talked in her sleep. I told her in the morning and laughed and thought she'd laugh, too. But she turned white as a ghost. She looked scared. I knew she would leave that day — three days ago. It was my fault."

"It wasn't your fault, Jane," Shara said, taken with the woman, and not wanting her to sink back into despair that might swallow her up. "She *had* to leave before I found her. She would only have stayed another day or two, at the most. There's something she must do. It's like she's driven." Shara paused. "What did she say?"

Jane turned away from Shara, not wanting to answer. Shara got up and faced Jane again. Jane turned and Shara followed. Turned. Followed. Turned. Followed. Shara kept it up until Jane finally laughed. Shara found herself laughing, too.

"You're like her, you know," Jane said. "I'd turn away from her, but she wouldn't let me. She wouldn't let me hide and when I laughed, she did, too. Laughed with me, not at me. Just like you."

"Jane," Shara said, making eye contact with the woman. "Mica told you to tell me *everything*. What did she say in her sleep?"

Jane hesitated, as if in thought. "Mostly words and phrases that made no sense. She said *your* name over and over. And 'Emory.' And 'settle things.' Once it was 'Emory, to settle things.' Then other names — 'Not Lysette. Not Deidre. Not Alexis.' Then your name four or five times."

Emory, Shara thought. A person or a place. *The* key, regardless, and something Mica might not have wanted Shara to know. It was what Shara needed to become the aggressor and gain the upper hand.

She and Jane talked a bit more and Shara got up to leave.

"Mica was particularly close to one of the children—"

"A teenager," Shara said, describing her from the image in her mind.

Jane looked at her oddly. "Yes, that's her. Could you speak to her, tell her you mean Mica no harm? She's been lonely and out of sorts since Mica left."

Mica had sent her the images of the girl for a purpose. Yes, Shara most definitely wanted to meet her. Unlike with Charlie or Jane, Shara didn't know her name. "Of course."

Jane led her downstairs to where the children slept while their parents worked, telling her to be quiet — Charlie would be angry if they were caught.

"So what if Charlie's angry," Shara said. "This isn't a prison and Charlie isn't the warden. Stand up for yourself. Don't let her push your around. From what you tell me, she needs you more than you need her. Mica trusted you. The children trusted Mica. The children trust you."

Jane looked at Shara in surprise. "I'd never thought of it like that."

Jane awakened Renee and pointed to Shara.

"Mica told me about you," Renee said, stifling a yawn.

"Seems she told *everyone* about me. And you're . . ."

"Renee."

Shara blanched, as if hit by a punch in the gut.

"What's wrong?" Renee asked.

"That's my name," Shara answered, still reeling from a name long forgotten.

"But you're Shara. Did you change your name because you didn't like it?"

"That's not it at all," Shara said, keeping her voice low. "I *had* to change my name. It's a long story, but deep down part of me is still Renee."

"Mica won't let you hurt her," Renee said with some hostility.

"I have no intention of harming her, Renee. But others looking for her might, if I don't find her first."

Just as with Jane, when Shara asked Renee to tell her about Mica, she opened up. "She created this special room for us, for when we're in a foul mood or angry at the world. Want to see it?"

"Sure," Shara said.

When they got to the playroom, Shara felt she'd been hit again. It was a children's version of *her* playroom. Somehow Mica *had* gotten into her mind. She wondered just how much she knew.

"First we had just Nerf balls, water guns and balloons. But Mr. Hernandez saw how much more we needed it and he gave us whatever Mica asked for . . . and more."

She pointed to a wall that had a similar mirror coating to the playroom in Shara's basement.

"Mica came up with this last. There's spongy material behind the mirrors. You can hit the mirror — *hit yourself* — and not get hurt," Renee said. She went to the wall and demonstrated. "Mr. Hernandez is going to do it to all the walls. That's what Mica wanted, but he can only do a little at a time."

Renee then picked up a Nerf bat and flipped it to Shara, then picked up another and advanced on her. "Defend yourself," she said with a smile. She hit Shara several times, and Shara looked at Jane.

"Don't just stand there. Hit her back. That's the way it's done in the playroom. You won't hurt her."

Shara defended herself, for the most part landing just a few blows to Renee's body and butt. Renee, for her part, seemed caught up and hit Shara with all her might, tears falling down her face. Finally, she sat down and buried her face in her hands.

"I miss her so," she said between sobs. "I need her so."

Shara sat beside her and let Renee's head rest on her shoulder.

"Mica had to leave. I know she didn't want to."

"Why did she have to go?" Renee asked.

"Didn't Mica tell you?"

"No," Renee, answered sullenly.

Shara was silent for a moment. "We all need our secrets, Renee," Shara said finally. "There are some things best left unsaid. Or it may be that Mica didn't think the time was right. Whatever, if she didn't tell you, she had her reasons. You've got to respect her need to keep some things to herself. I hope you understand."

Renee nodded. "You *promise* not to hurt her?"

"I won't harm her. Promise." It was a promise she hoped she could keep, recalling her dream of their confrontation.

"You won't catch her, you know," Renee said with pride.

"You're not the first to tell me that."

"Will you come back and let me know what happens between the two of you?"

"If you want."

"Promise?"

"Promise," Shara said.

"Don't say something if you don't mean it," Renee said, "just to make me feel good."

Shara looked Renee in the eye. "I know you don't know me, but I do what I promise. I'll come back, but you have to promise to get on with your life, just as Jane has — just as Mica told you."

"You mean forget Mica?"

"No, not at all. Mica will always be a part of you—"

"But I have to learn to trust others," she finished for Shara.

"Yes."

"Even though some of them may leave and hurt me."

"You remember what she told you, see. If she's so important to you, you've got to do what she said. Trust me, it's better than being alone. I envy Mica. She had you and Jane and the other children."

"You don't have anyone?" Renee asked.

"Not as much as Mica. And I've been hurt lately by two of my friends. But I have to go on; let others in. I can't live with only me." Shara knew she was talking to herself, as much as she was to Renee.

"If you stayed, I'd be your friend," Renee said.

Shara smiled. "I'd like that, but I can't stay. You know Mica and I will meet. Or at least I've got to try to catch her. When it's over, I promise I'll come back and tell you all about it. If you want to confide in me then, I'd like that, too. But in the meantime, there's Jane, and I'm sure others you'll find to confide in."

"You *are* like her. Almost sisters."

"I've heard that before, too," Shara said.

Jane had been watching silently.

"It's time to get back to your room, Renee," she now said.

Renee gave Shara a hug. Gave her a kiss on the cheek. "That's for Mica. When you return, I'll have one for you."

"Promise?" Shara asked.

"Promise," Renee said with a broad smile.

Outside the playroom they were confronted by Charlie. Shara saw both Jane and Renee cringe. Again, it made Shara wonder about this woman. Whether she intended to or not, she gave off the aura of a warden — even if she was a benevolent one.

"Jane, who told you—"

"I did," Shara interrupted. "If you've got a problem, blame it on me."

The two made eye contact. Shara refused to back down. Charlie finally turned and went back to the kitchen, mumbling something under her breath Shara couldn't make out. Renee scampered back to the children's room.

"You remind her of Mica," Jane said. "Charlie does what she thinks is in our best interests. She's only human, though, and not always right. Mica reminded her of that often. Too often for Charlie. Now she sees Mica in you. She doesn't like it one bit."

"Fuck her," Shara said, and both she and Jane laughed.

"You're alike, but you're different," Jane said when she'd composed herself. "I never heard Mica curse. You're also more assertive than Mica. You go for the jugular with Charlie. Mica was a bit more subtle."

"You're a good judge of character, Jane. I don't know if I like your observations, but I respect them."

"Can I ask you something?" Jane asked.

"Of course."

"I've been thinking of changing my name. I'm becoming me because of Mica. Part of becoming me is giving myself a name. I thought maybe Mica, but it felt wrong to take her name. Renee is pretty and so is Shara — already taken," Jane said with a smile. "I don't know what suits me."

"What about Terése," Shara said impulsively, then knew why. It was a name Mica had abandoned, readily available.

"Terése," Jane said, letting the name roll off her tongue. "Maybe," she said, with a smile.

They said their goodbyes and Shara returned to the kitchen.

"Another Mica," Charlie said again with a tone of disapproval.

"We've hardly talked, yet you compare me to Mica. Why?"

"You protected Jane, just like Mica would. You're stubborn like her, too."

Shara shrugged. "And those are my good qualities."

Charlie looked at her and shook her head in bewilderment.

"By the way," Shara said. "You won't have Jane for long."

"Where can she go?" Charlie asked, looking at Shara, sounding genuinely surprised.

"I don't mean she'll leave, but now that I think of it, why is the idea so profound?"

"You've seen her face," Charlie said, as if that explained it all.

"So she's consigned here for life?"

"The world beyond these walls is cruel and unforgiving," Charlie said. "Jane wouldn't be accepted."

"She's stronger than you think, Charlie, and she's gaining confidence each day. One day you *will* lose her."

"What *did* you mean, then?"

"She's going to change her name. Jane Doe is the name given to someone with no identity. Jane is becoming a new person. She'll want a name that suits what she's become. Swallow your pride and let *her* choose whatever name she wishes."

"Just like Mica — telling me how to run *my* shelter."

"Maybe that's your problem. You view this as *yours*. It's *theirs*. Could that be what Mica was telling you?"

Charlie didn't answer.

"If a donation was made in the name of a particular individual here, with a specific purpose in mind, would you honor it?" Shara asked, seemingly out of the blue.

"What are you getting at?"

"Did you ever look into plastic surgery for Jane?"

"A plastic surgeon at the hospital was consulted — yes. It's way beyond our means. Besides, Jane isn't the only one with special needs. I don't approve of special treatment for one while denying others. It's bad for morale, and others here would resent Jane."

"I think Jane could handle it," Shara said sarcastically.

"It's not wise—"

"She's lost her memory, for Christ's sake. People find her grotesque. That's more suffering than *anyone* should have to deal with. If a donation were made," Shara repeated, "in Jane's name for plastic surgery, would you honor that request?"

"I'd have to," she said, resignation in her voice, "and I would."

"An anonymous donation."

Charlie shrugged. "There are better uses for such money."

"I'm not wealthy, Charlie. I don't give a fuck what you *could* do with such a donation. I don't care how many others it could help. So don't bother trying to twist my arm. You'll have the money tomorrow. For Jane and Jane only."

Charlie walked Shara to the door.

"Do you live in town?" Charlie asked.

"Nearby, actually."

"We could always use another volunteer," Charlie said.

Shara was taken aback. "We might have problems — like you and Mica."

"To tell you the truth, it's been a little dull since Mica left. I could live with some combativeness," she said with a tight smile.

"You might find me more obstinate than Mica. We're alike, but not mirror images."

"It would be a challenge."

"For a masochist," Shara countered.

"Think on it. We could use the help."

Shara left not knowing what to make of Charleen Phelan. The woman's heart was in the right place, but she dispensed charity like some kind of god. It made Shara uncomfortable.

Then her thoughts turned to Mica. In three months she had won over battered and abused women and children, from whom trust was not given easily. They were fiercely loyal to Mica. And what did Shara have? Alexis — and with Alexis, she could keep no secrets. Maybe it didn't matter, she thought. Maybe it was *her* hang-up. Maybe *she* had to learn to live with some limitations on their relationship. Accept Alexis for what she was; her gift that was a curse.

In her car Shara played the tape Mica had left, while reading the note again. Mica must have felt like Shara had two years earlier. There was no one she could share her secrets with. Shara had shared many of hers with Deidre, Lysette and all with Alexis, and two of them had abandoned her.

As close as Mica had gotten to Jane and Renee, there were things she couldn't tell them. Only to Shara. Shara badly wanted to share with someone who would truly understand. She hoped she wasn't setting herself up for another fall. Once Mica had completed her mission, would she have any use for Shara? She might be another Lysette; just into *becoming*, with Shara reminding her of an unwanted past.

Fuck the self-pity, she chided herself and drove home.

At home, Shara called the plastic surgeon, whose name Charlie had given her. He was the one who had been consulted at the hospital. He told her what could be done and the cost.

"I can't undo all the damage," he said with the hint of a Latino accent. "Please understand, but to answer your question, yes, others could look her in the face without being repulsed."

"No offense, but could another . . . more expensive surgeon do better?"

"No offense taken. To be blunt, you'd be wasting your money. There's just so much that can be done in Jane's case, as I said. You could — *should* — seek a second opinion, but no one could do any better whatever the cost."

Shara intuitively liked the man. She trusted him and that was enough for her to make a decision.

"I like your honesty, doctor. Expect a call from Mrs. Phelan from The Haven within a few days."

She hadn't given her name, so she didn't have to request anonymity.

She would make a withdrawal from the bank the next day. She would easily be able to recoup the money by playing the market. And, she thought, what good was money anyway if it wasn't spent on what you wanted — what you needed. Jane had provided her with an invaluable clue. "Consider it a finder's fee, Jane," she said aloud.

She got out a map of Pennsylvania. She remembered Jane's words.

Emory. To settle things. She only hoped the name was a place. If it were a person . . . she wouldn't face the thought. Not yet.

Mica had been traveling north and slightly east since leaving Atlanta. Shara's finger moved north from Philadelphia, past Allentown and there it was. Emory, Pennsylvania — in the Poconos, about eighty miles north of Allentown.

"Gotcha!" she said aloud. "*Emory. To settle things.* That's where *we'll* meet. *To settle things.*"

Her pager beeped, startling her. It was Briggs. She dialed a number and he answered.

"I've got Cleary's secret. Can you come down to Pat's Steaks? I want you to hear it from the horse's mouth."

Shara agreed. She wasn't about to tell Briggs what she'd found out, yet. She knew it was far more significant than what he had learned. Still, knowing Briggs, it was essential to give him his moment in the sun.

Pat's and Gino's — literally a block apart, were the only places in Philadelphia Shara knew that served *true* Philly cheese steaks. At restaurants all over the city, a Philly cheese steak was chipped beef. At Pat's and Gino's, where Philly cheese steaks originated, the steak was sliced, not chipped, and out of this world. You couldn't consider either place to be restaurants per se. Each had a few tables on the sidewalk, but most people ordered takeout. You wanted *real* Philly cheese steak, you forgot about ambiance.

When she arrived, Shara saw Briggs with Nina Rios, his former partner. Shara felt the anger within her build. Why had he brought her down here? She would only resent Shara.

And as she walked over, she saw she was right. Sitting at one of the few tables, for those who wanted their steaks without going home, Nina looked at her with unveiled hostility. Before she could say anything Briggs spoke.

"We were waiting for you before I ordered. You up to a beer, Shara? Or do you want soda?" he said, rising.

"Beer will be fine," she said coldly.

If Briggs noticed, he didn't respond. He went to the counter, leaving Shara and Nina alone.

Shara sat down. Nina wouldn't meet her eyes. She was Hispanic, in her mid-twenties, a bit on the scrawny side with shoulder-length wavy brown hair.

"I don't know what game he's playing, Nina, but I apologize."

"Apologize for what?" Nina asked. "For my being envious of you? *Jealous* of you? Hell, that's *my* problem."

"There's nothing to be jealous about," Shara said.

"He was *my* partner, dammit. I talk to him, now, he tells me about *you*. I lost a partner and you gained one. So I'm envious and jealous."

"What does he say about me?" Shara asked, genuinely curious.

Nina looked at Shara oddly. "Stuff," she said.

"Personal *stuff* we share about our lives?"

"No. You're a puzzle to him and he can't make the pieces fit. You test him, exasperate him with those visions you say you have. At the same time you get results, and he respects you."

"Nina, when you were his partner, did you open up to him?"

"After we gained one another's confidence."

"You're *still* his partner. I'm his employer. Hell, we don't spend much time together. He was in Atlanta while I was in Virginia. We spoke for half an hour when we returned, and then he was with you, and I was off on my own. He speaks of you all the time. Your rough start together; how you wouldn't let him browbeat you; how you opened up to him while I'm a closed book; how he regrets not calling you *before* he went after Biggie Shaw. If anyone should be jealous, it's me."

Nina looked at her with surprise.

"He talks to you about *me*?"

"All the fucking time. Look, Nina, I don't want a partner. I've been a loner most of my life. I value my privacy . . . maybe too much," she added. "Like with you, Briggs has learned to trust me. Push comes to shove, he knows I'll guard his back. But he bares his soul to you, not me. You'll always be his partner. If you doubt it you're a fool."

Briggs returned before Nina could say anything further.

"You ladies have a nice chat?" he asked.

"You're an asshole, Briggs," Shara said. "What were you expecting — a catfight, bringing us together?"

"What the hell are you talking about?" he asked, looking confused. "I found some answers, but I thought you might have some questions. So I'm the villain here? Give me a break."

"Yes," both Shara and Nina said, in unison. They both laughed.

Briggs shook his head. "Women."

"All right, Briggs," Shara said. "You're forgiven. So tell me."

Briggs looked at the two of them, took a bite out of his steak, then as they ate, he shared what he'd learned.

"Cashing in my markers was easier said than done. Most of my sources pleaded ignorance, and others didn't want to blow the whistle on an FBI operation fearing retribution. I finally called Nina out of desperation. I didn't want to get her in trouble."

He looked at Nina. "You tell the rest."

Nina swallowed a piece of her cheese steak and washed it down with some beer.

"Your lady's killed three times in Philly," she said, looking at Shara. "Following her menstrual cycle." She took out a pad and occasionally flipped pages for specifics. "The first was Richard Ogden. My Sergeant's squad caught the case. I'd taken a few personal days. By the time I'd returned, the FBI was involved and my Sarge was out of the loop."

"You mean the FBI was in charge," Shara said.

"That, and on our end the case was reassigned."

"That's not standard procedure. Any idea why?"

"For some reason my Sarge has been in the doghouse lately. More than lately, actually. Morales was passed over for a promotion several times since The Nightwatcher case. He really didn't seem to mind, but when they reassigned the Ogden case, he went ballistic. Not that it did him any good. Somewhere along the line he's pissed off someone with clout, is all I can figure.

"Anyway, after Briggs called, I went to Morales and laid out what he wanted. He'd been following the case — what he called *their lack of progress*. He made four calls and I had everything you need."

Nina paused and took another bite of her steak.

"We didn't know at the time, but that first killing didn't fit your girl's pattern."

"How so?" Shara asked.

"He was found in an apartment he rented."

"That *doesn't* fit the pattern," Shara said. "You sure he's one of her victims?"

Nina nodded, chewing on her steak.

"Fingerprints, pubic hairs, method of killing — all the same. *That's* when the FBI got interested."

"What do you know about the victim . . . Ogden?" Shara asked.

"He abused his wife and cheated on her. The apartment he was found in was his love nest. His wife knew nothing about it."

"*That* fits her profile," Shara nodded.

"The FBI put a lid on the case," Nina went on, "and wondered where she would strike next. She's killed two more times."

Nina took out a city map, which already had three red circles on it.

"This was the first killing," she said pointing to a residential neighborhood. "The second killing was in Fairmount Park. And the third was at Roosevelt Park."

"Any involve autos?"

"None. The other two were found in wooded areas of the parks. There was no attempt to conceal them."

"Still a break in the pattern," Briggs said. "And she didn't move on as she'd done in the past."

"What do you know of the other two victims?" Shara asked.

"The second was black — Ogden was white, by the way — and had an extensive rap sheet. He had just gotten out of prison for a rape, two months earlier. The third committed only one other rape we know of, but as you know, many rape victims don't report the crime, so there could have been more."

"What was his story?" Shara asked.

"He was married, but his wife was cheating on him . . . with another woman. He had no previous record, but that's what the shrinks feel set him off — his wife finding a woman more suitable than him."

"And what's Cleary got planned now?" Shara asked.

Nina bent closer, as if someone might be listening. "Cleary knows when she'll strike, so both the department and the FBI have mobilized.

A three-day operation. The day before she normally strikes — two days from now — the day she should strike, and the day after. Plainclothes officers spread throughout parks in the city."

"How are they going to keep it from the media?" Shara asked.

"If it leaks, Cleary said they'll offer an exclusive for silence. If she doesn't strike, they have a cover story. If she kills and escapes, the shit hits the fan and they go public."

"Any questions?" Briggs asked.

"You covered it all," Shara said looking at Nina. "I know Briggs has thanked you, but I owe you one," she said with a smile.

"No, we're even," Nina said, glancing at Briggs. "You opened my eyes."

Nina got up. "I know you guys got some talking to do about things I shouldn't hear, so I'd best be off." She looked at Shara. "Take care of him, now. I'm depending on you."

When she was gone, Shara turned on Briggs.

"What got into you, Briggs? Bringing us together? You had to know sparks would fly."

"I was counting on it."

"You *are* an asshole," she said, turning away from him.

"Let me explain, will you?"

Shara looked at Briggs, but said nothing.

"I talk with Nina regularly. I still feel guilty that I didn't call Nina for backup when I went after Biggie Shaw. Partners don't go off half-cocked like I did. And she was so protective after. Lately, she's been . . . I don't know, out of sorts, I guess. Cranky. Irritable. Pissed off."

"I get it, Briggs. She was no happy camper."

"It was because she thought she'd lost a partner, and I'd gained one. You were on the force. You know finding a good partner is no easy task. We had our differences, but we worked them out and worked well together. I took her under my wing, and she made sure I curbed my excesses."

"So why bring us together?"

"Because I knew you would straighten her out. I know why you offered me a job. It wasn't charity. It wasn't because you wanted or needed me. Sure, it's worked out like you said, but you wanted me here in Philly for Alexis. I don't know what it is between you two, but you're good for her, and I gather she's good for you."

Shara looked at Briggs as if seeing him for the first time.

"I underestimated you."

"That's because we're *not* partners. I don't know squat about you and you have no interest in me, other than Alexis. We work together. Work *well* together, but that's as far as it goes. You talk about your crazy visions, and I need an outlet. For me, it's Nina. Only she was so full of self-pity, she wasn't thinking right. I knew you'd straighten her out. Since you two weren't going at it tooth and nail, I assume you did."

"Yeah," Shara said. "We worked it out. You could have given me some warning, though."

"It had to appear natural. Nina's too important to me. If she's pre-occupied thinking she's lost a partner, she could screw up and cost someone else their life. I couldn't let that happen."

Shara pinched Briggs on the cheek. "You're a pussycat, Briggs, behind that gruff facade. I see it with Alexis, but she's your flesh and blood. A fucking pussycat," she said again, and tried to pinch him again, but he gently swatted her hand away.

"So how do we handle Cleary?" he asked, changing the subject.

First Shara told Briggs what she'd learned at the shelter. Then they worked out their strategy, disagreeing on only one point.

"We gotta tell her Mica may not strike in Philly," Briggs told.

"We can't. We could spook her."

"Are you willing to sacrifice someone's life?" Briggs asked. "Because if you're right — and I believe you are — someone *will* die."

"First of all," Shara answered, "it would be no innocent, but that's beside the point. We *know* where she's headed, but she won't have had time to get there before her period. We set a trap and she sniffs it out, all bets are off. She may feel she can't go to Emory to settle things, and if that's the case she'll change her pattern, that I guarantee. We'll have a loose cannon on our hands and you tell me how many more might die before she's caught."

"I agree, but I couldn't live with myself if we said nothing."

"How about this," Shara said in exasperation. "We don't tell Cleary, but what if the area police get an advisory the three days Cleary will be mobilizing here?"

"You can pull that off?" he asked.

"Yeah," she said. "The locals can be on the lookout." She pointed to a map she had taken out, showing Briggs where Emory was. "Look, we know where she's headed, but look at all the ways she can get there. We don't know how far she's gotten. No way the FBI can cover where she might turn up. You'd need the fucking National Guard. The locals know the lay of the land better, anyway. We got a deal?"

He mulled it over for a few moments, looking none too happy, then relented.

TWENTY-NINE

As in their first meeting, Cleary greeted Briggs warmly and all
but dismissed Shara. Just what Shara wanted.

"I'm disappointed in you, Claire," Briggs began.

He was to take the lead, but this time Shara would intercede when
the time was right. Briggs had reluctantly agreed, knowing, he told her,
all hell could break loose.

"You knew a hell of a lot more than you told us, and frankly we
wasted time unnecessarily."

"I don't know what you're talking about, Lamar," Cleary said.

"That Donato raped the woman, for instance."

"We don't know that for a fact," she said calmly.

She still thought she had them, Shara thought. She still thought she
was in control. *Stroke her, Briggs, then let me in for the kill.*

"That he had sex with her, then. That he blackmailed prostitutes,
so he could have them any time he desired. That he was found with a
gun in his hand — unfired, but with just one bullet."

Cleary sighed. "Look, Lamar, my hands were tied. I was told what
I could tell you. You've dealt with asinine supervisors while you were

with the department. I'm sorry, but you *did* get what you wanted because I told the authorities to cooperate with you. And it was a professional courtesy on my part. You have no official standing in this investigation. I could have shut you out and made it much more difficult for you, but you know the respect I have for you. Frankly, you disappoint me, Lamar. You're accusing me of deception after I provided access to anyone you needed to speak to."

The woman did like the sound of her own voice, Shara noted again. *Time to fuck with your mind*, she decided. *Then we'll see what you're made of.*

"You didn't tell us about Richard Ogden," Shara said. "Or the other two rapists found murdered in the last two months."

"They didn't fit the pattern, Miss . . . Farris," Cleary said, as if forgetting Shara's name. She continued looking at Briggs, as if Shara was still inconsequential.

"You knew it was *her*, though," Shara went on, like a pesky gnat.

"Not until—"

"You knew from day one," Shara interrupted. Cleary finally acknowledged her by making eye contact. "Fingerprints, pubic hair, the throat slit with a chain — the same in *every* case. So cut the crap. You intentionally held back so you would have something to barter with if we caught a break and came up with something you'd missed."

"I don't have to explain myself," she said, addressing herself to Shara with unvarnished animosity. "And since you have nothing to put on the table, there's nothing more to discuss," she said, getting up.

"Claire, when we first met, remember what I told you?" Briggs said quietly, trying to defuse the tension. "We find her, we turn her over to you *or* the locals. You misled us. No," he said and paused, as if to compose himself. His voice had been rising. "You *lied* to us, so unless *you* have something to offer all bets are off. You'll look pretty foolish if locals find the woman. The FBI, after all, has had seven months to locate her. That won't help your resume at all."

Shara liked the way Briggs twisted the knife she'd stuck in Cleary's gut. She was glad to see Cleary finally appeared unnerved.

Standing, Cleary rested her palms on her desk, red-faced, and glared at Briggs. "You're an arrogant bastard. You come with nothing, then threaten me? Get out."

"But we didn't come with nothing," Shara said, rising. "Maybe Sergeant Morales will be interested in what *you* missed."

Briggs too had risen, and Shara saw Cleary's hand go to her mouth momentarily, as if to bite a nail that was already bitten to the quick.

"What did you find?" Cleary said, spitting out each word one at a time.

Shara turned around and flipped a Polaroid onto Cleary's desk. Cleary picked it up — a bit too quickly, Shara thought — looked at it, then at Shara.

"What the hell is this?"

"A way to save your ass," Shara said. "If you ask nicely. With this you can show your superiors progress has been made. Keep them off your back for awhile if your mobilization doesn't pan out."

Shara fell silent. She definitely wanted Cleary to squirm. There was a stifling silence, while Cleary debated what to do. Shara loved it.

"I apologize if I was dismissive," Cleary finally said, asking Shara and Briggs to sit down. "We've all been under the gun with this one."

Each word came out as if forced. But Shara saw panic in the woman's eyes. Cleary needed what Shara had to offer. Cleary's job — or at the very least any chance of a promotion — probably hung on solving this case.

"In Dismal, Virginia," Shara said, "you interviewed a witness who gave you a vague description of the killer."

"I remember. What does—"

"He also told you the woman came out of the woods," Shara interrupted. "I went into the woods and came across that." She pointed to the photo in Cleary's hand, then paused. She wanted Cleary to ask — to beg, to grovel — as she could see the woman was still in the dark.

"And this is . . . ?"

"Your killer travels through the forest, which is why she's so difficult to locate. But for some reason, at some point she rests. She makes camp, and only after does she go to the highway for her kill."

Shara wasn't about to go into any detail. She was going to be as forthcoming as Cleary had been with them. "The bones are from a rabbit she ate. The locals get credit for that one." Shara approached Cleary's desk, staring at the woman sitting before her. "Our bone to you is that you'll find a similar camp near the airport kill. Claim it as your own. That will keep your superiors at bay . . . for a bit."

She saw Cleary's hand trembling as she held the Polaroid. Shara knew Cleary badly needed what she had to offer. Even so, she was trying to compose herself, so she could make light of it.

"If it pans out," she said finally, "I'll—"

"Keep playing us," Shara interrupted, again, "because you're a bureaucratic pencil-pusher. This is a contest to you. You owe us — *owe us big time*. You want us to turn this killer over to you when we catch her, you'd better find something to offer us in return. This was a charitable donation. Your last."

With that, Shara turned and walked to the door. Briggs followed.

"You made a powerful enemy," Briggs said, once they had gotten to Shara's car. "She would rather burn in hell than cooperate with us, now."

"You don't get it, Briggs," Shara said. "She had nothing more to offer. *Will* have nothing more to offer. She *can't* open up any more doors for us. She's got squat and she knows it. She fucked us over and there's a price to pay."

"So don't fuck with Shara Farris, is that what you're telling me?"

"It's what I'm telling *her*. But, yes, it applies to anyone. We saved her ass for now, but I know her kind. No way she's going to hand us anything significant. It's her nature. And you're no naive rookie. You know I'm right. So she and I are enemies. I can live with that. On the other hand, if she wants to get back in our good graces . . . ," she let the thought hang.

"She'll come to me," Briggs said, finishing Shara's thought. "Son of a bitch," he said. "You played her. Made yourself the enemy, but left her an out. Son of a bitch."

Shara smiled. "And enjoyed it, too," she said.

THIRTY

Shara had been going non-stop for four days since meeting Estelle Winston. All of a sudden she was no longer a participant, but an observer. The next move was up to Mica. Shara could invent avenues of investigation, but knew she would end up wasting her time.

Waiting — that had always been hardest for her. And, as so often happened, she felt deflated. She wasn't very good at waiting.

She had gone to her playroom both for a workout and to be with herself. She had never minded being alone. For some reason, though, she now found herself poor company. Her mind kept returning to Jane and Renee at the shelter. Mica, who had been as much of a loner as she, had opened herself to others, with no hidden agenda — not needing someone with whom to share her secrets. Shara hated to admit it, but she felt envious of Mica. She knew she had Alexis, but with Briggs home now, Alexis needed him more. Actually, she thought, they needed each other.

She thought about going to the shelter, but decided against the idea until her hunt for Mica ended. Until then the shelter was Mica's territory.

She thought of calling Clay, having that dinner he had suggested, but tossed the idea aside, as well. She was still too preoccupied with Mica to be good company.

Deidre, Lysette — they had cast *her* aside. She only had *herself*, and it depressed her.

After her workout, she walked to the park at Fifth and Chestnut and saw Deborah Ogden. Richard Ogden's *wife*, it dawned on her suddenly. With all that had gone on, somehow the connection had eluded her until just then.

She lived just three houses down from the Ogden's. She didn't know Deborah Ogden well, but they had struck up a conversation a few times before her husband died.

At the time, she didn't know he had been *murdered*. The obituary had said a heart attack. Thinking about it now, she recalled that something hadn't seemed right about his death. Half a dozen policemen had come to the Ogden house, but no body had been removed and no ambulance had arrived to transport a body. There had been a steady stream of police for two days, then others — FBI agents, she now knew, going in and out. She even remembered seeing Cleary. She hadn't gotten a real good look at her, but she remembered thinking how she had tried to blend in with the male agents in attire, walk and demeanor.

It had all occurred well *before* she'd begun her pursuit of Mica, and being none of her business, Shara hadn't dwelled on it.

Watching five-year-old Julie chasing after a puppy, Shara could see a change in the child. When her father was alive, she'd been listless. At the park she would sit with her mother, sometimes throwing pieces of bread to pigeons. Shara had noticed that Deborah Ogden sported the tell-tale sunglasses of a battered wife. Now, though she still wore black, she sat on the bench straighter, laughing at her daughter chasing the dog.

Shara went over to Deborah and sat down, and struck up a conversation.

"How are you holding up?" Shara asked.

"To tell you the truth, the grieving wife doesn't become me," she said, giving Shara a smile. "Richard was abusive, yet I feared leaving him. Now that he's dead and I know I can make it on my own, I wonder why I didn't run long before. The irony is, for all his faults, he provided for us in the event of his death. I never have to work. I never have to worry about pleasing anyone for fear I'll be left destitute. In the end he was good for me. But I want more out of life than just being a mother. Before I married Richard, I'd been training to be a nurse. I enrolled in a program last week. I'm going to complete my training," she said proudly.

Shara hadn't been able to get a word in edgewise, yet she was content to listen.

Deborah Ogden looked around, as if someone might be listening. "I've been dying to tell someone, and seeing as you're sort of in law enforcement, can I tell you something in confidence?"

"Of course."

"Richard didn't die of a heart attack. The bastard was cheating on me. They found him at an apartment I never knew existed," she said, keeping her voice low and leaning close towards Shara, as if afraid of being overheard.

Shara was going to comment, but Deborah went on, her eyes darting to the left and right, like a deer afraid predators were on her heels.

"I had to identify the body. His neck was slit," she said, making the sign of a knife with her hand across her throat. "The police said it was from the autopsy, but I'm a nurse . . . well, *almost* a nurse," she said, with a laugh. "He was murdered," she whispered, her eyes moving left and right, to make sure no one was in earshot. "The police suspected *me* at first. Then the FBI came around and I was cleared."

She went on with a host of details. Shara only half-listened. Frankly, she was bored.

"Tell you the truth, I'm ready to date. I'm horny as hell. At first Richard got off on raping me. He liked violent sex, but it was sex, nevertheless, you know. The last few months he hadn't touched me. *Now* I know why. If it weren't for my vibrator, I wouldn't have had sex at all. Thank God for the man who invented batteries," she said with a laugh. "I've been going through them like water."

Shara was finally able to extricate herself from the woman and walked back to her apartment. Subconsciously, she thought she'd wanted to strike up a friendship with the woman. They had both been victims of violent crime, but Shara had a feeling Deborah was willing to tell everyone she had an acquaintance with all the gory details.

Even though Shara was glad to see the woman had rebounded, and gladder still to see her daughter no longer had a cloud over her head, she knew she could never be friends with such a woman. Shallow and superficial were the words that best described Deborah Ogden. There are some things you keep to yourself, Shara thought. Your vibrator was one of them.

Shara knew that many women — too many for her taste — confided their innermost secrets and fantasies to friends. They told one another about sex with their husbands or lovers in explicit detail, and they vicariously lived through the stories of others. Shara wasn't one of those people. Deidre wasn't. Lysette wasn't. Mica, she knew, wasn't. Deborah Ogden was.

Being with herself suddenly had its appeal.

Shara decided to take a catnap when she got home, and wondered if she could consciously control the dream she'd had for seven months now, while asleep. There was something she had been missing, she knew. Could she make herself look for that detail? She closed her eyes and hoped for the best.

The dream itself was no different than the countless others, but this time when she lunged at Mica, as she crossed the stream, Shara focused on the trees on the other side, rather than on Mica. She and Mica collided and went under. She *did* see something that had been on the edge of her consciousness; what had before been an insignificant detail that she had easily overlooked.

She awoke and watched herself heal, feeling the aches vanish. She lay in bed and smiled. In the trees, possibly waiting for Mica, or even her, had been Jeremy. He was little more than a blur, but with his long black mane of hair and the single earring of a wolf that dangled from his left earlobe, she was positive it was him.

Shara was also certain Mica was unaware of his presence, even in her own dreams. Whatever their relationship, if she knew he was dogging her, she would have confronted him. She would have told him to leave or they would have gone on together, but no way would she have ignored him.

When thinking about him, now, the word that immediately came to mind was, as before, a *wildcard*. He was unpredictable and possibly dangerous. She'd have to keep an eye out for him. Would he intervene on Mica's behalf? she wondered.

"No," she said aloud, though she had no idea why.

THIRTY-ONE

Shara was jogging the next morning when a black sedan pulled ahead of her and two men got out. Looking at them she knew they were FBI agents, and she had a terrible premonition.

"Miss Farris," the taller of the two said, flashing his ID. "Would you come with us." It wasn't a request. "Special Agent Cleary would like to speak with you."

"*After* my jog. *After* my shower," Shara said. She was going to go by them, but the squat heavy-set man blocked her way.

"*Now*, Miss Farris," said the tall red-head. He was the talkative one, his face expressionless.

Shara looked from one to the other, royally pissed.

"Don't shoot the messenger," the taller man said, his voice softening a bit. "We don't make the rules. We just follow them."

Shara raised her hands in a sign of surrender, and ten minutes later was ushered into Cleary's office. Briggs was already there, refusing to meet her stare. Shara knew he'd told Cleary that Mica had left Philly. What Shara didn't know was how much he'd told her. A fucking Judas, she thought. He must have picked up on it somehow, because he sank further into his chair.

"Sit down, Miss Farris," Cleary said, sounding smug.

Shara sat, waiting for clues. She had already decided to admit only what was necessary.

"You left something out yesterday, didn't you?" she said. Shara could almost see her gloating.

"If I remember correctly," Shara said, sitting on the edge of her chair, "you asked us to leave."

Anger welled within her, and she knew she had to control it. Though the night had been nippy, it had been warm out as she had jogged. Her jogging suit was dotted with sweat. She felt clammy and in need of a shower.

"I don't have to tell you squat," she added.

"We can detain you," Cleary said, not breaking eye contact with Shara.

Shara got up and approached Cleary, knowing she smelled rank. "Then do it. See if I give a fuck."

"Let's be civil," Cleary said.

"Did you find the killer's camp near the airport?" Shara asked, ignoring her. She refused to refer to it as Mica's *lair* or *den* in front of Cleary.

"Yes," Cleary said. "And we've sent a team back to the Virginia site."

"Yet you want more? Didn't Briggs give you all you need?"

"He—"

"There wasn't a hell of a lot to tell, Shara," Briggs interrupted, with a belligerence Shara didn't at first grasp. "All you said was she'd left the city. You didn't provide details. Like always, you hid as much as you told."

Shara looked at Briggs for the first time. Pissed as she was at him for his betrayal, she now knew what he'd told Cleary. He was acting out a role for Cleary. He was the team player, while Shara was used to getting her own way, regardless of the cost.

"We'd like details from you," Cleary said.

You want details, I'll give you details, Shara thought.

"She lived off the street during the winter," Shara said.

"Why?" Cleary asked.

"Because it was too damned cold to travel during the winter, if I had to hazard a guess. She didn't call me for an interview. It's a commonsense assumption."

"And just where did she stay?"

"No one particular location for very long. There are abandoned homes all over the city — havens for the homeless."

"And you *know* she's gone."

"I was told she had left."

"By who?"

"Let's say a confidential informant," Shara said with the hint of a smile, "who will remain confidential. Look, Cleary, I know you did a background check on me. Being a bounty hunter I've got a lot of connections in the bowels of the city, so to speak. My source tells me she's gone."

"And you think she went north," Cleary said.

Shara walked over to a map that showed Mica's attacks. "I must be psychic," she said sarcastically, while running her hand along the path Mica had traveled, highlighted in red with pushpins at each of the kill sites. "She's been going north since she left Atlanta."

"So you don't know specifically where she's heading?"

"It ain't Kansas," Shara said. "No, I haven't a clue."

"Anything else you've omitted?"

"What are you going to do with what Briggs told you?" Shara asked, ignoring the question. It was time to be the aggressor.

"*My* gut tells me she's still in the city," Cleary said. "We'll go forward with our plans."

"Whatever," Shara said.

"If you learn anything else—"

Shara had had it with this woman. She walked from the map to where Cleary was standing so she would be face-to-face with the woman.

"I'm not doing your job for you, lady. You've fucked with us from the start, wasted our time and withheld information from *us*. And now you want to tell me what to do if we find something you're too incompetent to unearth? I think not."

"Don't give me attitude, young lady," Cleary said. Shara could see her hands balled up into fists, as she unsuccessfully fought for composure. "I can — *I will* — detain you as a material witness. You can cool your heels for a few days as our guest, or you can cooperate with us."

"One phone call, Cleary," Shara said, not raising her voice, "and you're fucked. A call to Deidre Caffrey and she blows the lid off your incompetence. One call and the entire city knows you've been sitting on three murders. Everyone will know about your lack of progress. Everyone will know you ignored what the Virginia yokels told you about the killer's camp. One call and you can kiss your promotion — hell, maybe your job — goodbye. I'm not Briggs. I don't play with a full deck, and I certainly don't play by your rules. Call my bluff if you've got the balls."

She turned and walked towards the door.

"You coming, Briggs?" she asked, without looking at him, "or joining forces with them?"

Briggs stood and followed Shara out.

Cleary said nothing as they left. Shara knew the woman was dealing from weakness. If any of what she'd threatened became public, Cleary *was* fucked and she knew it.

Shara was too angry to wait for the elevator. She took the stairs down, with Briggs in pursuit. One landing down, he grabbed her arm.

"Please," he said, as she pulled herself from his grasp. "We've got to talk. I'm sorry. I had to tell—"

"Look, Briggs," Shara interrupted. "*You've* got to talk — and yes, *we've* got to talk — but this isn't the time. I say something now, I'll probably regret it. I ask only one thing," Shara said, and fell silent.

"What?" Briggs asked, exasperated.

"I want to — *need to* — take Alexis down to the shore. To think. To sort things out."

Briggs looked taken aback.

"You want to go down to the shore with Alexis, *now*?" he asked incredulously.

"Yes or no?"

"I . . . we . . ." he started, flustered. "All right," he finally said, nodding his head.

"I'll pick her up in forty-five minutes. I need to shower and change," she said, without hiding her irritation, and continued her descent.

Briggs followed, but kept his distance.

THIRTY-TWO

On the drive down to Cape May, Shara said little. With Alexis unable to answer, other than by signing, conversation would have been impossible. She briefly told Alexis what her father had done, then fell silent. But even as she seethed, just having Alexis next to her had a calming effect.

She now knew she had been wrong when she had told Alexis she needed someone closer to her age — someone who had experienced life — to confide in. She'd been wrong, because *she'd* been an emotional cripple for close to ten years. She had more in common with Alexis than with Deidre or Lysette. She knew Alexis could read her thoughts. She *wanted* Alexis to know what she was thinking now. Wanted her to understand, because her father's betrayal had awakened her to what she had been avoiding — *in hunting Mica down, she would learn about herself.*

Alexis looked at Shara and signed a smile.

At the beach, before going into the forest, Shara took Alexis to the ocean. The angry surf fit her mood. Like her, in March, the sea felt abandoned and betrayed.

Once in the woods, as usual, it took Shara a few minutes to get over the transformation in Alexis.

"I guess today I'm here for you," Alexis said, as Shara sat cross-legged on the fine sand, her expression pensive.

"Selfish of me—"

"Don't, Shara," Alexis stopped her. "You know how I love it here. How I need to be here to feel . . . like a person. A whole person. But I'm no spoiled child. You need me today. It's not selfish. It makes me feel needed."

"But look at the position I'm putting you in. I'm asking you to judge your father. I have no right."

"You're asking for my opinion. You know I love my father, but I treasure you, too. You're the only one who accepts me for what I am. I can't help it that I can read your every thought, but at least you haven't avoided me. You haven't shunned me. I know Lysette couldn't deal with it. My father doesn't even want to try to deal with it. If I think you're wrong I'll tell you. What we have can survive a difference of opinion."

Though said in the same listless monotone Shara had grown to accept, Alexis' eyes blazed with emotion. Much like her, Alexis felt alone. She was loved by her parents, but not understood. Alexis *needed* her. When was the last time someone truly needed her? Shara wondered. She thought Lysette had, but only for a short period of time. Other than Lysette . . . there was no one.

"Jesus, Alexis," Shara said "Fifteen going on thirty."

"Part of my gift . . . or my curse, as you sometimes call it," she said and signed a smile. "Now about my father . . ."

"What do I do about your father?" Shara asked. "He betrayed a confidence. He stabbed me in the back."

"He's a cop," Alexis said. "Was one, still is — in his mind, anyway. Didn't he have . . . ," she paused, as if trying to grasp the right words.

"A moral imperative," Shara said sarcastically, finishing Alexis' thought, "to save some fool rapist."

"I was thinking of obligation, but yeah," and she again signed a smile.

"Forget the signing, Alexis. I can read your emotions in your eyes."

"He has a cop's mentality," Alexis went on.

"He couldn't understand someone might have to be sacrificed for the benefit of many? I can't accept that."

"Cops don't always look at the big picture. No way my father could allow one person to die so others could be saved."

"And look what it got him," Shara said. "Not a damn thing. Cleary still thinks Mica's in Philly."

"Isn't that good?" Alexis asked.

Shara looked at the youth, as if reading *her* mind. "You mean he won't trust her again. He risked betraying me and she turned her back on him."

"He would never confide in her again," Alexis concurred.

"And he knows he can't fuck with me anymore," she said, nodding.

"It's like if I told my dad something in privacy and he told my mom. If I forgave him, he wouldn't dare break a confidence again. He'd lose me for good."

"Lose me for good," Shara said aloud, but she was talking to herself. Then to Alexis. "I can live with that."

"Shara," Alexis said and paused. "I think there are some things you can't tell my father. *Shouldn't* tell him. And there's nothing wrong with that. Remember always, he's a cop. Maybe you'll rub off on him in time, for better or worse, but for now be cautious. Don't put him in a position where he has to choose between you and his moral code."

Shara shook her head again in wonder. She knew Alexis was right. Shara had to be careful what she divulged to Briggs.

They sat in silence for awhile. Alexis looked at Shara and waited. Shara felt so comfortable around Alexis. She had been looking for someone to confide in, and Alexis had been there the whole time. Someone who wouldn't be judgmental and wouldn't turn against her for her many failings. Someone you could be silent around without feeling it necessary to fill the void with idle chatter. She'd been searching for Alexis, and Alexis had been there the whole time.

"Remember what you said when I told you about my dream?" Shara said. "How you said in hunting Mica I'd learn about myself?"

Alexis nodded.

"You were right. Until today though, I saw individual branches and leaves without seeing the entire tree. What your father did hurt me. He betrayed a trust—"

"Like you with Deidre," Alexis added.

"Yes, smartass, like me with Deidre," Shara admitted with a tight smile. "But it opened a floodgate and suddenly I see the tree. For as long as I can remember — since after the first Shara died — I've let no one in. Even after I killed my half-brother and the shame and terror were behind me, I was still a fraud. I had to keep *me* hidden, even as I interacted with others.

"But this past year, I've reentered the real world and interacted with others — even made friends. I'm experiencing situations and emotions for the first time. It's like I've been in stasis. Now there's you, Deidre, Lysette, your father — people I'm not hunting or using to get leads for a hunt. I'm dealing with them on a social and professional level, and I'm out of my league. I've made errors in judgment, lied and deceived, hurt others and been hurt in return." Shara paused, searching for the right words.

"So what is the big revelation?" Alexis asked.

"That pain and disappointment are as much a part of relationships as joy. I could withdraw like I did before and become an island unto myself. Or I can face life head-on. You know, take the good with the bad and hope there are more moments of happiness. I can't go back to what I was — a rock with no feelings. I've been there and it's left me emotionally maimed and mutilated . . . and utterly alone. I thought all I needed was myself for companionship, but I was deceiving myself. I was miserable, hanging with only me. I guess what I'm saying is that I've got to take life's blows as they come and do what Jil told me when life rocks me like your father's betrayal. *You go on*. Does that make any sense?"

"All the sense in the world," Alexis said. "It's the only way I've been able to exist. I've lost the friends I had when I was whole. In exchange, I gained my father and you. Not such a bad trade. What about Mica?" she asked.

"I don't think there's much more I can learn from her. She *has* opened my eyes, but I don't need a kindred spirit anymore. I need people like you who will accept me for what I am."

"Does the hunt go on?"

"The chase is part of me, Alexis. You can understand because you know my secret. I'll take Mica down because that's my nature. And she's a challenge. My equal. You know I can't resist a challenge."

"And if she eludes you?"

"She won't."

"Shara," Alexis said, not allowing Shara to avoid the question.

"I'll deal with it," she said, letting a smile escape. "It'll be a blow to my pride. There may never be another one like Mica. I'll kick some holes in some walls, be a bitch to be around for awhile, but I'll handle it. I'll move on."

"I'll be there to help," Alexis said.

"Thanks, girlfriend, but I still intend to bring her down."

They talked for another half an hour — chit-chat between friends, then both fell silent. Shara knew from the murmuring she heard, but couldn't decipher, that something in the woods — maybe the woods itself — was again communicating with Alexis. Knew Alexis had a secret she wasn't yet prepared to share. Oddly, it didn't faze Shara a bit.

As they prepared to return to Philly, Alexis stopped Shara before they left the forest.

"There are times I don't want to leave here," she told Shara. "Times I just want to stay with the two of us talking. Like, talk forever." She paused. "It hurts, Shara . . . being so alive in here, and a vegetable on the outside."

"Alexis—"

Alexis put a finger to Shara's lips.

"I try so hard to be strong, but sometimes . . . I want my life back, Shara. I want to be whole like I was. Sometimes, at home, I feel so alone. I want to stand up and shout. My mind says, 'Do it,' but . . . I can't. I didn't want to burden you . . . but I was wrong. You look at me and marvel at my strength, but inside it's tearing me up. You're the only one I can tell. The only one who can understand. I can't — won't — be like this forever. It's not living. It's . . . just . . . *being*."

She fell silent and walked out of the forest with Shara.

Driving home, possibly for the first time in her life, Shara felt whole. She *did* want to bring Mica down, but she also wanted to talk with her face-to-face; both to thank her and chide her. Whatever her mission, Shara wondered if it was worth leaving people like Jane and Renee. She knew of nothing that was so important that she would be willing to sacrifice Alexis' friendship. And Alexis, finally opening up to her, both saddened her and made her feel needed more than ever before. The two of them needed one another. Shara vowed to always be there for Alexis, as Alexis had been there for her.

THIRTY-THREE

At three the next afternoon Briggs called to tell Shara there had been another killing. This one had been on the Northeast Extension, thirty miles south of Allentown.

While Cleary had been marshaling her forces the night before, Shara had played poker with Shelly Burke, Rudy and Douglas Frazier. She'd played more aggressively than usual and at one point had Frazier flustered and off his game. It was time, Shara thought, to prove her mettle. If they couldn't take a woman winning, then she had underestimated them. She had paid her dues. Now she was going to hold nothing back.

Frazier hadn't recovered his equilibrium until the last three hands. To his credit, unlike Shelly and Rudy, he'd stuck to his game plan and ridden out some rough hands, losing little money. Then in each of the last three hands Shara knew she should have folded, but overconfidence had kept her in to the end. Frazier won each. She had come out even, all the same.

At game's end, there was a customary cigar. Shara had been scrutinized by the three the first time she had been offered one, and while a non-smoker, she knew to gain acceptance she'd have to make sacrifices. The cigar hadn't gone down well, but the post-game camaraderie had been worth it. She had since gotten used to and even enjoyed the aroma, if not the taste of the stogies. As she puffed, Frazier looked at her.

"You had me on the ropes there, Shara. Now that you've wormed your way into our hearts, we're going to have to watch you. Methinks you've been holding back. That, or you're taking lessons," he said with a smile.

As compliments go, they didn't come much better. She'd been accepted and no longer had to worry about bruised male egos if she won. She hadn't gotten home until after 3 a.m.

She spent the day playing the market. Jane's surgery had depleted her cash reserves. Though she had no immediate need for money, she enjoyed the rhythm of the market. On days like today, when she wanted to be totally preoccupied, she took to day trading. She could liken it to a chase. She was playing volatile stocks, where you had to get in at the right time and often sell within minutes to make a profit. Most important, you had to stay focused. Even going to the bathroom could prove disastrous.

She was buying and selling based on research and instinct. She didn't need the money, so there would be no illegal shortcuts. Just after two-thirty when she had put through her last sell order, she'd almost recouped what she had spent on Jane's operation. Sweat covered her body; a healthy sweat, from a hard-fought contest. She had just finished showering when Briggs called.

In his car, he told her what few details he knew. Shara remained silent. She hadn't thought of him since her talk with Alexis. The card game, her concentration on the whims and vagaries of the market — she knew she had deliberately chosen those activities just so she wouldn't dwell on Briggs' duplicity. She understood what had driven him to what he'd done, but the wound was still raw.

"Is it going to be like this from now on?" he asked when he was finished, and she still said nothing. "Because—"

"No, Briggs. I blame myself. I put you in an untenable position without thinking it through. You *had* to warn Cleary. I know that now."

"And I got kicked in the balls," he said morosely.

"Serves you right," she said, although without rancor. "Look, I can't forget, but I can forgive. Spill anything I tell you again, though, and I'll have to kill you."

He looked at her.

"That was a joke, Briggs."

"I want to apologize," Briggs told her. "*Not* for warning Cleary, but I should have told you what I intended to do. I can't say there won't be a next time, but if there is you'll know about it first."

"I can live with that," Shara said.

"At least Cleary won't be able to keep us away from the crime scene. She owes us."

"Oh no? Watch her," Shara said.

"You think you have her pegged, don't you?"

"I have her pegged all right. If there's anything a woman like Cleary hates more than being outmaneuvered by a man, it's being bested by another woman. It's bad enough Cleary has had to fight sexism her entire career. Now one of her own has challenged her. I don't regret one thing I said, but we need some insurance."

"What are you getting at?" he asked uneasily.

Shara smiled, ignored him and dialed a number on her cell phone. "Clay," she said, "It's Shara."

"I was just thinking about you. You made my day today, actually," he told her.

"How so?"

"Our good friend from the FBI called earlier, fit to be tied. Pissing bullets because I hadn't told her about the lair you'd found. When I told her I'd e-mailed her, she as much as called me a liar. I faxed her the hard copy with her e-mail address at the top, and the date at the bottom, and I could feel her seething over the phone. She didn't apologize. Didn't acknowledge her error. A conspiracy, she must have thought," he said and laughed. "Anyway, she sent a crime scene unit down. They've been here all day. First they scoured the lair. Then, on Cleary's orders, they started searching the entire woods trying to find something you missed."

Shara, who had been smiling as she listened to his story burst out laughing. Every time she stopped, Clay would add something to set her off again.

"They're still out there, so help me God. One of them got lost and you should have heard him."

"Please, Clay, I can't take much more," Shara finally said, wiping a tear from her eye.

"They're coming back tomorrow . . . with dogs."

"Clay, stop it!" Shara said after another bout of hysteria.

"Did you send out that advisory yesterday afternoon?" he finally asked. "It had your subtle touch."

"Guilty as charged," she answered. "I promised my partner," she said, looking at Briggs. "And I keep my word. Look, Clay, I need a favor," she said, finally getting down to business. "There's been another killing—"

"Right on schedule," he said. "Sorry. On schedule, but three months late."

"I'll tell you about it, but—"

"How can I help?"

"Do you know a . . ." she looked at Briggs, who gave her a slip of paper. "Sheriff Roger McCandless from Epiphany Falls?"

"We've been to a couple of conventions in Atlantic City. Good man, but lousy at Twenty-One."

"Could you call him — *now* — and put in a good word for me? Cleary will be at the crime scene, and I kinda pissed her off royally."

"Now *that* you'll have to tell me about," he said. "Consider it done. As I said, you've made my day."

There was a moment of awkward silence, which Shara finally broke. "You scoped out a restaurant, yet?"

"You weren't just being polite?"

"Polite doesn't become me, Clay. Neither does stringing someone along. One way or the other, this will be over in twenty-eight days. Make a reservation for thirty days from now."

She disconnected and looked at Briggs, who was staring at her. "What are you gawking at?"

"You. Dinner with the deputy," he said, "What *did* you do down in Virginia?"

"None of your damn business," Shara said, blushing.

"I've never heard you laugh," he said after a few moments. "You know, that uncontrolled—"

"I know what you're talking about."

"You've always been so serious. You'd get a real kick when we brought a fugitive to ground, but there was never any . . . joy, I guess, in the capture. Now you're here planning a date and laughing your fool head off."

Shara knew he was right. The last — and possibly only — time she'd had a laughing fit was with Deidre, when they were talking about Spike, one of the strippers at the club where Lysette had danced, before her surrender.

"Maybe I haven't had much to laugh about recently," she said with a shrug.

"We square?" he asked.

"I'm pissed at you, Briggs, but yeah, we're square."

Just over an hour later they were at the crime scene. Briggs was identifying himself to a deputy when Cleary spotted them and came over. In a trenchcoat with hair tied tight in a bun, Shara thought she looked like one of the guys. She again ignored Shara, this time out of peevish acrimony, Shara thought.

"Here to gloat, Lamar?" she said coldly. "Looks like you were right, after all."

Shara was content to be a non-participant.

"Gloating's not my style and you know it."

"What about her?" Cleary said, glancing briefly at Shara, but talking to Briggs.

"I don't speak for her, Claire. All we want to do is check out the crime scene."

"I wish I could let you, Lamar. I *do* owe you. The problem is this is a joint investigation and the locals—"

"Ask the locals," Shara cut in. "We'll abide by their decision."

Cleary looked directly at Shara for the first time. There was a hint of a malevolent smile. "I'll check with the sheriff," she said and left.

"Bitch," Briggs said.

"You read my mind," Shara said, looking at him.

"She never had any intention of sharing information," Briggs said, shaking his head in disappointment. "She's changed. It must be this case or pent-up bitterness. She used to be one of the better ones . . ."

"Well, she's in for a surprise," Shara said. "She thinks she has the sheriff in her pocket. Of course, he'll do as she suggests. Watch. Enjoy."

Cleary went over to speak to a tall, broad shouldered man who Shara assumed was McCandless. He had a black handlebar mustache, and wavy charcoal black hair, tinged with gray. His face was weathered from time spent outside. He could have been forty or he could have been fifty. Shara couldn't tell.

The scene that unfolded almost made Shara burst out in laughter again. Cleary wasn't much taller than she, a full foot shorter than McCandless, so she literally had to look up to him. At first she calmly did all the talking. McCandless responded with a few words, then Cleary was gesturing with her hands and moving closer to him, so she could register her displeasure without being overheard. McCandless shook his head and Cleary stomped off, away from Shara and Briggs.

McCandless approached, stroking his mustache, and Shara could see a twinkle in his eye. He'd enjoyed whatever had transpired. Good for him, Shara thought.

"Roger McCandless," he said, extending his hand. "You must be the infamous Miss Farris." He shook hands with Briggs. "And *you*, I know all about. You're a hero around here, Detective Briggs."

"I'm not—"

"Once a detective, always a detective. I'd ask you if you really killed that bastard Shaw, and got someone else to cop to it, but it makes no nevermind to me or my men. Beating the fucker up . . . . There's scum, Briggs, that don't deserve the rights the Constitution accords them. We talk the talk, but actions speak louder than words. It's good to meet you."

Shara knew Briggs had heard this before. Wherever they went, many of the locals echoed similar sentiments. It's what made his mere presence invaluable. Briggs had long ago learned not to argue, protest his innocence, or tell of the anguish his losing control had caused him.

McCandless turned back to Shara.

"And you," he said with that twinkle in his eyes. "*You*, I've also heard about. Clay Fluery called me about an hour ago. Seems his story and FBI Agent Cleary's don't exactly jibe. *She* says her people found a site where the killer camped before a ride in Virginia. Clay says you found it — a good three months after the kill. I'll take Clay's word over that pistol any day," he said glancing at Cleary. "Clay also suggested you may have something to do with that advisory we received," he said, his fingers playing with the tip of his moustache.

"I don't know anything about an advisory, Sheriff, but I do have the utmost respect for Deputy Fluery," Shara said with a smile.

"The advisory may not have prevented the attack, but we increased our patrols and checked any cars that had pulled over. We missed the killer by no more than twenty minutes, thanks to . . ." he let the thought hang. "Can you help us with this mess?" he asked.

"I can allay your fears," Shara said. "The killer's long gone. Her M.O. is to hit and run."

"Not in Philly, according to Cleary," McCandless said.

"She lives in the woods, Sheriff. She couldn't in the winter. Let's say she hibernated the past three months. Her kills there were to fulfill some primal need, but now that she's on the move again, like I said, she's long gone."

"That's a load off my mind. I'd hate to think of the folks around here a month from now — all armed to the teeth, shooting at any shadows that moved."

"Did you try to follow her trail?" Shara asked.

"That's what we spent the last hour doing." He pointed to the woods near where the victim's car was parked. "She went straight back into the woods. Left a trail easy to follow until—"

"She came to a body of water," Shara said.

"You know your prey. She's slippery. Crossed the stream any number of times, then went upstream, we figure. No way to track her."

"And her camp?" Shara asked.

"Agent Cleary and I were discussing that when you arrived. She says it could be ten miles north or ten miles south. An awful lot of ground to cover. Care to weigh in?"

"Why would she camp north, then travel south, then cross over and hitch a ride north?" Shara said.

"Why indeed?" McCandless said. "So we focus south of here."

"Closer to five miles than ten, to narrow it down a bit. And she would be close to a body of water. No more than a quarter to half a mile into the woods."

"Want to tag along?" he asked.

"I don't think Cleary would appreciate that. Why not let her think she's leading you? If you don't mind, we'd like to check out the car."

"The body's been taken to the morgue," McCandless said. "But you're welcome to look around." He gave Briggs a Walkie Talkie. "I'll call you when we find the campsite."

He looked up at an officer, standing by the car. "Bruce, whatever they want."

The man nodded.

"Do you know anything about the victim?" Shara asked McCandless, as he turned to leave.

"He was no saint, that I'll tell you. Salesman from Pittsburgh. Rap sheet indicates arrests for indecent exposure, spousal abuse and rape. Never went to trial on the rape charge. I won't know why until tomorrow."

"Did he try to rape the killer?"

"His pecker was out, Miss Farris. I'd say yes. Whether he succeeded or not will take our lab . . . or the FBI a few days."

Shara saw Cleary eyeing them, and told McCandless anything else she needed could wait. He gave her a wink, then walked over to Cleary.

Shara wondered if Mica would send her images as she looked in the car. She didn't — *didn't have to*. When the deputy opened the passenger side of the door Shara and Briggs were assaulted by a stench that made them both wince.

Shara recovered and for the first time smelled Mica, who apparently hadn't bathed in a week. She must have been so rank only someone with the sick mind of a rapist would have picked her up and made a move on her. She smelled the blood from Mica's period, her urine, her sweat and something she couldn't identify. There was also the victim's blood and feces.

Shara could see Briggs was badly shaken.

"I've investigated a lot of homicides, but *never* smelled anything like that," he said.

"Yet this Good Samaritan gave her a ride and hit on her, despite her stench. Damn shame he had to die," Shara said sarcastically.

Briggs looked at her and was going to say something when the Walkie Talkie barked.

"We've found the campsite." It was McCandless. "About four miles from you," he said. Shara could picture the twinkle in his eye. Shara had outfoxed Cleary again, she imagined him thinking. She was scoring points with McCandless. She would need them since she knew Cleary would block her path every step of the way.

"Drive south. A deputy will flag you down and lead you to the site."

Fifteen minutes later, they were at Mica's lair, which was not much different from the one in Virginia. A fallen tree had been her shelter. There was a blanket of branches and leaves and the bones of several small animals.

"I'd like to get a feel for the site," Shara told McCandless. "I won't disturb anything."

"Cleary's dead set against it," he answered. "Threatened to call the Mayor if I told you where the site was. Problem is the Mayor's my former brother-in-law," he said with a smile. But it was his expressive eyes that spoke volumes. "We grew up together, best buds. Still are. Let me go speak to Her Majesty."

"A piece of work," Briggs said.

"Who?" Shara asked.

"Cleary. Who else?" Briggs said.

"McCandless," she said. "He's enjoying her discomfort — hell, her humiliation. She comes out thinking she can bully him and he won't have it. He's a piece of work — in the positive sense."

Again they saw McCandless and Cleary in an animated discussion, and again it appeared McCandless prevailed.

"Be my guest," he told Shara. "Cleary threatened to call Congressman Mathis, who just so happens to play cards with the Mayor and I whenever he's not in Washington. I told her she could call the damn President if she wanted. When she attacked my manhood, I told her to back off or I'd deputize the both of you. Then she could call anyone she damned well pleased and it wouldn't do her a bit of good."

Both Shara and Briggs had to turn away to keep from laughing.

Shara finally composed herself.

"We appreciate your help," she said.

McCandless gave her a smile. "Except that a man's been killed, I'm having the time of my life. I don't take kindly to bullying. She's got a real bug up her ass, that one," he said, looking briefly at Cleary. "It's not just disdain for me and my men. I sense panic. Someone who hasn't gotten results and she's taking it out on everyone. She reads people like she's blind. I'll cooperate with anyone, but cop an attitude and try to belittle me — well, it brings out the beast in me. Anyway, Miss Farris, it's yours," he said, gesturing towards Mica's lair.

Shara first walked around the periphery. She saw and smelled the blood that was mixed with urine Mica had excreted to mark her territory. Just as in the car, so soon after her departure, everything was so much more vivid than in Virginia. She felt like a woman who'd had cataracts removed. Dim images were now seen in full detail. She smelled, felt, could almost see Mica's presence . . . and more. The smell that had gnawed at her in the car she now identified as that of the wolf within Mica. With darkness having crept in, half an hour before, Shara began to feel the cold seep in. She wondered how Mica had withstood the elements.

While the nights in Philly were still nippy it was downright frigid here. Before the night was over it would be bitter.

Flashlight in hand, she went over to the tree, under which Mica had slept and ate. She saw the pool of blood from her period.

Suddenly Shara felt an icy breeze, though looking at the trees, the branches appeared not to be affected. The air in front of her face shimmered as if something were pushing its way through. Without warning Shara saw a dismembered hand appear. It reached for her throat.

It wasn't Mica, but the old man. At first he held her without squeezing. She heard a voice in her head utter, then repeat, the same tired phrase — *stay away*. The voice was raspy. She was able to conjure up the image of an old man with a weathered face and long white hair. Was he an Indian? she wondered. Without thinking, her mind answered, "No." Then she felt his hand tighten its grasp, and she was unable to breathe. She wondered where Mica was. Had the old man finally wrested control from her?

Rather than fight back, some instinct within her told her not to struggle. Physically, she was no match for him. Instead, she tried to penetrate the man's mind. Maybe he wasn't as guarded or cautious as Mica.

Concentrating, trying to ignore her difficulty breathing, she began to see images. Mica and the old man camping. The old man hitting a younger man, then tipping what appeared to be a farm tractor over onto the man. Numerous other images of the old man and Mica at different ages. The old man and a young wolf, side by side. Then she heard names, some that were attached to the images. The one most often mentioned was Augustus — *his name*. Each time she saw him with Mica she heard the name Grandfather. When she saw Augustus killing the other man she heard the name Danziger.

She was close to blacking out, now. Possibly close to death. In her mind she shouted to Mica, *Why is Augustus killing Danziger?*

For a brief moment, she felt Mica awaken. The hand appeared to be yanked back into the portal through which it had come. Just as suddenly, she saw the wolf's paw. It raked her across her face, slicing completely through her cheek, so that she tasted blood. Just as quickly, that paw was sucked back into the rupture that allowed the attack to take place.

Mica must have finally prevailed.

Falling to the ground, as if in slow motion, she saw the reactions of the others. Briggs and McCandless, who had seemed paralyzed, moved towards her. Cleary, who had appeared drained of all color, recovered. She showed Shara a tight bitter grin, then turned and began to walk away.

A rage Shara hadn't felt since she had killed her half-brother engulfed her. The tattooed eyes on her breasts began to itch, as they had when she'd stalked her victims. She wanted nothing less than to choke the life out of that bitch.

She tried to rise and found Briggs holding her down. Trying to wriggle free, kicking with her feet and thrashing with her hands, she heard herself yelling, "I'll kill you, bitch."

McCandless spoke to Briggs. "She's having a seizure."

Shara stopped struggling.

She had thought the urge to kill had been forever quelled, but now knew it had only been dormant. Without Briggs and McCandless she *would* have killed Cleary, without regret, without remorse. Shivering inside at what she'd almost done — what she had wanted to do — Shara began to breathe deeply. She heard McCandless calling for an ambulance. She tried to speak, was unable, and instead shook her head. She still tasted blood and wondered if the wounds would heal this time. With Augustus in control, maybe he could inflict actual injury through Mica. If Mica hadn't interceded he could have choked her to death.

Just as she was ready to panic, she felt the wound closing. She had been able to stick her tongue through her cheek, as if she'd had a second mouth, but now she felt resistance when she tried.

"Are you—"

"Don't ask, Briggs," she said, choking the words out. She knew he was going to ask if she were okay. "No . . . but I will be," she answered. It was incredible to her how people often reacted. You cut your hand slicing a bagel, drawing blood and the first words uttered — "Are you okay?" You trip, falling down several stairs and you hear — "Be careful." A little late for something so inane.

"Her color's returning," McCandless said.

"Your handkerchief . . . ," Briggs said, then seemed at a loss for words.

Shara knew though. She was getting her wits about her. McCandless was staring at the handkerchief he had used to stem the flow of blood; only it was no longer bloody — something Briggs couldn't grasp. And her cheek had healed before his eyes — something else he couldn't comprehend. *Welcome to my world*, she thought.

"Now . . . you . . . can ask," Shara said, looking at Briggs, her voice getting a bit stronger with each word.

"What?"

"Am I okay?"

"Are you?"

"Better," she said, and with Briggs' and McCandless' help she sat up. The world spun before her. "Briggs, I need . . . water."

Briggs looked flustered, as if he didn't comprehend.

"I'll get—"

"No," Shara said, shaking her head, when McCandless volunteered. "Briggs."

McCandless told Briggs to go to one of the deputies who had been too far away to see anything.

When Briggs had left, Shara looked at McCandless. "What did you see?"

"A disembodied hand choking you, then a wolf's paw slash your face. Same as Briggs."

"You don't seem . . . surprised," she said, her throat parched.

"I don't let it show."

"Bullshit," Shara said, without the intended force.

McCandless shrugged. "In this neck of the woods you hear stories. Hell, I grew up on Indian myths and legends, like kids in the city grow up on stories of ghosts, vampires and the bogeyman. I'd never seen anything like what happened to you, but I have seen things that defy logical explanation. So I'm just more accepting that what happened to you *could* happen."

"But you've never seen it before."

"No, and hope to never see it again."

Shara saw Briggs returning.

"You won't tell anyone," she said, grasping his arm.

"What's to tell? I wouldn't be believed."

Shara smiled at him.

"You watch out for yourself, young lady. Someone besides agent Cleary is mighty pissed at you."

"Help me up," Shara said.

She was standing when Briggs brought a canteen back. They heard a siren.

"The ambulance," McCandless said.

"No need for it," Shara said, her voice returning, but the words still a painful struggle to get out.

"You're going to the hospital," Briggs said, trying to sound forceful, but not quite pulling it off.

Shara shook her head. "Compromise. I'll stay the night at a motel."

McCandless looked at Briggs. "It's an argument you won't win," McCandless said. "There's a motel not far from the hospital. If she has a relapse hit 911 and you'll get door to door service.

Briggs still looked shaken, but agreed.

They had adjoining rooms at the motel. Shara showered, then knocked on Briggs' door and asked him to come in. She knew she would have a captive audience. He wouldn't be resistant to her visions after what he'd seen. What disturbed her, though, was Mica's seeming loss of control. It was time to reach out *to her*.

When Briggs entered he looked worse than she did.

"Never saw a black man turn white as a ghost before," Shara said to break the tension.

He gave her a tight grin as he sat on a chair he had dragged to the bed.

"I'd dismissed your talk of visions," he started. "I'd been guided — *hell, driven* — by facts, logic and deduction all my life. Sure, I go with my gut or play a hunch, but I'd dismissed your visions even though I couldn't explain how you knew some of what you did. Then tonight . . ." he trailed off.

"You saw the impossible."

He nodded.

"Want to hear some of what I've learned, or will you find some way to explain away what you saw? It was dark. Or, the flashlight—"

"I saw what I saw. Even if I can discount what I saw, I can't dismiss the gash to your face that healed by itself, or the blood that disappeared. You didn't have to go to such extremes, but you made a convert," he said with a tired grin.

He was ready to believe what she had told him about Mica, but she wondered if he was ready to accept the idea that his daughter had psychic abilities. Or that in a forest by the shore she could speak, even dance. Don't get ahead of yourself, she thought.

Thinking of Alexis made her recall what she'd said just two days before. There was only so much she could tell Briggs. *Right, Alexis,* she thought now. She had told him only what was essential: Mica's downloading of images, her recurring dream where she had first encountered the old man and the wolf and Jeremy's attack, which had endangered both her and Mica. She left out the end of her nightly dream where in confronting Mica she faced herself.

"That day, when I appeared sick," she said, "that was Jeremy. He's lurking about. He's a voyeur, kind of a Peeping Tom, primarily interested in which of us prevails. Still, we've got to keep an eye out for him."

As she finished Briggs shook his head. "It's an awful lot to digest, and I take it you've given me the edited PG version," he said, smiling wanly.

"There's something I gotta do, Briggs," she told him. "I've got to reach out to Mica to find out if she's still in control."

"Is that wise after what almost happened to you?"

"It's got to be done," she said evasively. "Mica's been predictable, so far, but that was when she controlled the old man and the wolf. If the balance of power has shifted, all bets are off. I've got to know."

"I can't stop you, I know that. But I want to stay—"

"You can't," she interrupted. "It's got to be me and her. Look, I'll leave the adjoining door unlocked. You think I'm in danger, you come running."

Briggs nodded. "I don't like this one bit, but how can I argue with something I can't understand — argue with something that's so utterly impossible."

"Go to your room, Briggs, and come to grips with it. Then together we'll prevail."

Briggs went to his room. Shara waited a few moments then quietly locked the adjoining door. No way would Briggs intervene, she'd decided.

First, before she and Mica met, Shara had some unfinished business. She took out her laptop computer, which she'd brought with her from Philly. She closed her eyes and recalled Cleary's reaction to her attack. Thinking Shara was seriously injured, possibly dying, she'd been glad. Shara also recalled her own rage. She *would* have killed Cleary if Briggs and McCandless hadn't been there. Something else she had learned about herself. She wondered if she would have to wrestle with that uncontrollable urge to kill for the rest of her life.

She wasn't about to kill Cleary, now — only destroy her.

Shara hacked into Cleary's e-mails, and quickly found the message Clay had sent. She first responded to his e-mail with a message of dismissal, using words and phrases Cleary continually used in her e-mails.

She forwarded Clay and Cleary's messages to Cleary's supervisor.

Then she checked Cleary's daily progress reports. She breathed a sigh of relief when she saw the report from the previous day had gone unread. She called it up and saw no mention of Briggs' telling her Mica might no longer be in Philly. She inserted a paragraph detailing her conversation with Briggs, dismissing him as a meddlesome amateur. She forwarded it to Cleary's supervisor, then sat back satisfied.

When her supervisor read the three e-mails, Cleary was fucked. It was clear that her arrogance may have led to an additional death. At the very least, she should have brought Briggs' information to her supervisor's attention. Some decisions you don't make alone. There was no way her insolence could be overlooked. With another victim and mounting pressure, Shara had handed Cleary's supervisor the perfect scapegoat.

Not done yet, Shara thought, a mischievous smile spreading across her face. She forwarded Cleary's daily reports for the last few weeks to Deidre. The reports summarized the attempt to mislead the media and mentioned the three Philadelphia killings in enough detail that Deidre could easily fill in the blanks.

If Cleary's supervisor *didn't* act, Deidre would force his hand. And, having been manipulated by the FBI, Deidre might run with the story regardless. Then Cleary would be exposed publicly. The Bureau would bury her to save face.

Satisfied, she knew it was time to confront Mica. She had a plan she hadn't told Briggs. To make it work she was going to give Mica what she wanted most; something Shara definitely couldn't let Briggs know.

She had reached out to Mica before, in a moment of need, and knew she could do so again. She lay down and focused on a painting on the wall, to her left. It was a painting of a barn, surrounded by a pasture filled with cows. Soon, though, she saw the forest through which she so often chased Mica, then the stream. She crossed the stream and headed north. Like bursting through a bubble, she suddenly saw herself face-to-face with Mica.

Mica was curled into a fetal position, shivering in a small cave. The fire she had lit had gone out.

Mica turned to Shara, her eyes filled with terror.

"How—"

"I'm not here to hurt you," Shara interrupted. She didn't know if she was speaking to Mica, Augustus or the wolf, so she had to make her intentions known quickly. "I'm here to give you what you want."

"I'm sorry," Mica said weakly, "for what happened before."

"Are you in control?" Shara asked.

"Yes. No," she said, then shook her head. "I'm not sure. After I fled I must have passed out. The water was so cold and the night had been so bitter. They were protecting me."

"You didn't need protection."

"I've made that clear. It won't happen again."

"Are you sure?" Shara asked.

"No, but if you give up the chase now—"

"No way," Shara said.

"As long as I'm in control, you're safe."

"That will have to do."

Shara approached Mica. "You wanted to know why I'm so confident I'll bring you down. It's time I opened up to you. It isn't pretty."

Mica nodded her understanding and reached out. As their hands touched, Shara opened a portion of her mind to Mica — a past she could never outrun. She let Mica see Bobby taking pictures of her in the shower. Let Mica see her caged in the basement, naked, with her half-brother photographing her as he forced her to masturbate with foreign objects within her that destroyed any dignity she possessed. Let Mica see him use a cattle prod when she refused to do his bidding.

While she was opening up to Mica, a part of her stole into Mica's mind. With Mica preoccupied, just maybe she could find Mica's final victim. She came to two open doors — images Mica had already downloaded. Then there was just another door — closed. Shara moved toward it, but the image of Mica's grandfather materialized blocking her entry. A smile of triumph crossed his weathered face. Shara retreated.

Shara let Mica see each of her kills, culminating with her half-brother's. Let Mica see each tattoo of a pair of eyes applied to her breasts symbolizing the eyes that would no longer torment her.

Finally she spoke to Mica. "Why did your grandfather kill Danziger?"

As she spoke, that part of her within Mica's mind scampered towards the closed door. She heard a primal scream erupt within Mica's head — Mica's grandfather. Its reverberations were like aftershocks of an earthquake. This was Shara's chance. But as she touched the knob she was bowled over. She got up to see Mica's grandfather again standing guard. But this time a look of rage had replaced the condescending smile.

Shara couldn't maintain the link she'd established with Mica. She felt herself being sucked back. It happened so quickly she didn't have a chance for parting words. She had no chance to gauge Mica's reaction to her revelations.

She woke up in bed, drained, cursing her failure. She had learned nothing. Mica, it appeared, might be losing control, which would make her both less predictable and more dangerous. And Shara still had no clue to her last victim. Worst of all, she had made an enemy far more powerful than Cleary. The one sentence she'd uttered to divert Mica's grandfather's attention had distracted him, but he'd quickly recovered. She recalled the look on his face and shivered. She wondered if she had awakened a monster and feared that Mica would be consumed by the rage of her grandfather. If that were true Mica would no longer be a kindred spirit when they next met.

She was brought back to reality by a groan from next door. It was Briggs.

THIRTY-FOUR

MICA

Having discovered what drove Shara, Mica for the first time
wondered if she would prevail. Her torment paled in comparison to
Shara's. And Shara had already avenged herself without being caught.
Mica's one advantage was that their final confrontation would take
place on her home court.

For the moment, though, Mica had other concerns. She now knew
she'd been a fool to leave Philly when she had. Yes, it had been warmer,
but she should have realized how different the climate was here in the
mountains, especially at night.

North of Philadelphia, she'd found cabins to hole up in prior to her
period, but she had foolishly deferred to the wolf within when her period
began. Five days naked in the biting cold had weakened her terribly.
Then after her grandfather's kill there had been the trek through
the frigid water. At some point her body had rebelled, and she had
collapsed — feverish and ill. She had awakened to see her grandfather
choking the life from Shara.

She'd rationalized that both her grandfather and the wolf had
merely been protecting her, but she couldn't be certain.

Then Shara had appeared for the second time. She had opened herself up to her, *then* tormented her with the revelation about her grandfather. *Why did your grandfather kill Danziger?* Why indeed, she wondered.

She could only converse with her grandfather when she slept. Weakened as she was, she was asleep within minutes.

Confronting her grandfather from within, she saw that he had aged with the disclosure he had killed Danziger.

"You killed the bastard who raped me. Why?"

"You sought vengeance," he told her. "Your parents and the police wouldn't intercede. I loved you so. I thought if Danziger was dead you could move on. So yes, I killed him and made it appear to be an accident."

"Why didn't you tell me?" Mica asked.

"Instead of feeling vindicated, you were *worse* after his death. I thought I'd helped you, but you needed your own revenge. I'd forgotten about the need for closure. How could I tell you I'd ruined any chance you had to exact retribution?"

"And then you left me when you let me kill you," she went on, her anger mounting. "How dare you continue to make decisions about what was best for me. I needed you *alive*. I needed your comfort, your wisdom . . . needed *you*. And you took that from me, too."

"I was wrong," he said, looking tired and worn. "But what I did was out of love. Hate me for what I did, if you must, but never doubt my love for you."

"And now you're doing it again," she went on, ignoring his plea, knowing she must get him to acquiesce now or he would interfere again. "I want to — no, I *must* meet Shara on my own terms without your meddling."

"She's your equal . . . and then some. I can't—"

"Then so be it, Grandfather," Mica cut him off. "I'm not a child anymore. I know what's best for me. I will have my revenge. I'll rid myself of *my* demons, like Shara did. But neither you nor the wolf you control will interfere. If you won't allow me to finish this on my own terms, leave now."

"I never meant to harm you . . ." he said, defeated. "It all went so horribly wrong."

"I don't love you any less for your failings, Grandfather. And I know what you did was out of love, but it's time to allow me to determine my fate. Will you?"

"If that's what you want . . . I won't interfere. I won't disappoint you again."

When Mica awoke, though weakened and still feverish, relief washed over her. She had feared that she had lost control. She had even feared her grandfather had malevolent intentions. Or worse, that he was using her; destroying her essence from within, so he could live another lifetime.

But she had been wrong. He'd always had her best interests at heart. She knew he would keep his word. They truly had reached an accommodation.

With her mind at ease, Mica knew she had to find shelter. Food and rest was what she needed. It would only take a few days to get to her final destination. She would need all her strength when she met Shara. It would be just the two of them. She smiled. Shara *didn't* know her plan, and the home court was hers. Her confidence was returning.

THIRTY-FIVE

BRIGGS

After leaving Shara, Briggs went to his room and lay on the bed, staring at the ceiling. A part of him loathed Shara. In the span of a minute his whole belief system had been shattered. A disembodied hand. A wolf's paw with no body. A bloody wound that healed on its own. Blood disappearing as if it never existed.

As a cop, when his shift had allowed he'd watched *The X-Files*, *Star Trek* spinoffs and horror movies with supernatural creatures. Yet he had bolted from the theater when he'd gone to see *Silence Of The Lambs*. He could enjoy escapist horror, because he knew it wasn't real. But *Silence Of The Lambs* — *that* was horror he knew. It was part of the sewers he traveled daily. Now he had faced the impossible, which he finally knew to exist, and he didn't like it one bit.

Worse, he could no longer look at Alexis and dismiss Shara's talk of her psychic abilities and a healing forest.

He had always known, deep within, Shara hadn't been lying about Alexis. But what she said had been easy to dispel. As a cop he had been forced to deal with clairvoyants and psychics. Most were quacks. Those who had actual insight into a case, he dismissed as lucky hunches. One psychic had, in fact, been the killer. But if Alexis could read his mind, he could never go with her into that healing forest of hers. Seeing his daughter healthy, even for a few hours, would later conjure up thoughts that she could read. He wouldn't be able to hide his frustration that Alexis might never fully recover and she would know. She might misinterpret his disappointment.

Sure, he wanted her whole. What parent wouldn't? But he loved her no less when she could only sign to him and shuffled when she walked, as if her feet were rooted to the floor. Now he feared hurting her with his idle thoughts, that could too easily be misunderstood.

All these churning thoughts were giving him a headache. He thirsted for a beer, but he couldn't leave Shara to drive to a bar. He took the room's ice bucket and went to get some soda. He'd seen a vending machine just a few doors down. He bought two cans of Diet Pepsi and two Milky Way bars, then filled his bucket with ice.

He remembered just a few years ago when he would polish off half a dozen of the candy bars a day. He'd been fat and lumbering. After the attack on Alexis, he'd given up candy and other foods he craved and exercised obsessively. It was all in preparation for the day when he would meet Biggie Shaw. No one would ever escape him because he lacked stamina. Biggie Shaw sure hadn't, he reminded himself. Every once in a while, though, he indulged himself. He made a mental note to jog an extra mile in the morning to alleviate his guilt.

His hands full, he dropped one of the cans of soda and bent down to retrieve it.

Before he was aware of a presence behind him, he felt a knife at his throat.

"Let's go to your room, Detective," a man behind him with a deep guttural voice commanded.

As Briggs got up, he turned slightly, and immediately recognized the man from a description he had been given in Atlanta. The shoulder-length black hair, the tawny complexion and the earring with a wolf dangling.

"What do you want, Jeremy?" Briggs asked, trying to keep the fear out of his voice. He said nothing about *not* being a detective any longer. That Jeremy thought he was a cop might work to his advantage.

"To your room, Detective. Now!"

Once in his room, Briggs looked for an opportunity to surprise his attacker, but Jeremy gave him no chance. He was told to put the ice, soda and candy on a bureau, then lay on the bed, on his stomach, with his hands behind his back. Only when Jeremy cuffed his hands behind his back with Briggs' own handcuffs did he remove the knife from his neck.

"Shara told you about me, then," Jeremy said, sitting in a chair, far enough away so Briggs couldn't use his feet as a weapon. Briggs noted that he lounged more than sat. Jeremy appeared to be someone very comfortable with himself.

"No, I told *her* about you," Briggs countered. "I went to Atlanta. You left in a rush. You also left a lot behind. A ladies' man who never bedded the ladies he bragged about. Why's that, Jeremy? You got some kind of problem?"

"I misjudged you," Jeremy said, "but we're not here to talk about me."

"Why not? You're going to kill me. What's the harm in satisfying my curiosity?"

"Kill you," Jeremy said with a laugh. "Why that wouldn't be . . . wouldn't be *human*." He laughed again. "I'm not going to kill you, but I am here to warn you. No, make that I'm going to try to reason with you."

Briggs looked at the young man. There was absolutely no tension in him. It was as if two friends were just shooting the breeze with one another. He sat with his feet spread, his hands behind his head. *The little prick is fucking enjoying himself*, Briggs thought.

"You're not to help Shara anymore," he said without rancor.

"But you can help—"

"But I'm not," he interrupted. "I haven't assisted Terése. I'm merely observing. You, on the other hand, are tipping the scales in Shara's favor. It ceases now."

Briggs wondered why he referred to Mica as Terése, but decided to play along.

"Your Terése has more than enough help without you."

"Still, your Shara has been her equal. The two will meet, without either of us interceding. The two of them matching wits with one other. It makes no difference who prevails."

"You're one sick fuck, Jeremy, you know that?" Briggs said, hoping to goad the man so he'd come within striking distance. "I value Shara. I won't stand by and see her harmed."

"Noble sentiments, but you have no choice. Nature will take its course," Jeremy said with a shrug.

"Then you'd better kill me, because I won't stand idly by."

"A pity. I'd hoped you'd understand."

Jeremy got up, planted a knee in the small of Briggs' back and placed the knife at his throat. He undid the handcuff on Briggs' right hand.

"Place your hand on the table . . . and don't try to be heroic. I'm not going to kill you. I'm a man of my word. And, you're in no position to overpower me, so don't be foolish."

Briggs reluctantly did as he was told, reaching out for the table just to the right of the bed.

"I sincerely apologize," Jeremy said, "but you leave me with no choice."

Jeremy raised his free hand and brought it down like a sledge-hammer against Briggs' extended arm, just above the wrist. Briggs felt the bones shatter. Needles of pain shot through his body. He felt a scream escape from his mouth, then his head was thrust into the bedding to silence him.

"You'll thank me later," Jeremy said. Briggs felt a second blow to the back of his skull.

THIRTY-SIX

SHARA

Hearing Briggs groan, Shara knew something was wrong. Briggs' door was slightly ajar. She entered his room, gun in hand, ignoring Briggs momentarily as she checked to make sure they were alone.

Briggs was lying on the bed on his stomach. The phrase "Are you okay?" almost escaped from her mouth, but she pulled it back. Of course he wasn't okay. "What's wrong?" which she did utter, sounded almost as foolish, but she needn't have asked. Briggs right arm dangled off the bed. Shara could tell by its s-shaped curve it was broken. With his left hand, Briggs was holding the back of his head.

Shara thought to call 911, but decided to take Briggs to the hospital herself.

"Can you get up?" she asked.

He gritted his teeth, said nothing, but nodded, then groaned. Shara tore strips of material from one of the sheets and made a makeshift sling, which she gently wrapped around Briggs' neck. As she placed his shattered arm in the sling, he let out a howl.

"Sorry," Shara said, then laughed.

Briggs looked at her.

"I *am* sorry, but I don't know what to say. Anything I do say sounds so foolish, it's almost comic."

Briggs said nothing, but nodded, as if he understood. Shara thought this was how he must have felt when he'd seen her attacked. Utterly useless. And whatever you said came out sounding cliched or just plain wrong.

Allowing Briggs to lean his weight on her, they made their way to his car. She grabbed the keys and Milky Way bars from the bureau by the door as they left.

In the car, she fed him one of the Milky Way bars.

"For the pain," she said. "Imagine it's a bullet."

He again looked at her oddly.

"Hell, it's the best I can do. You *don't* want to bite on a bullet, do you?"

He shook his head.

Shara drove to the office, where a sleepy-headed old man told her how to get to the hospital.

"Five minutes, Briggs, that's all it'll take," she said, gunning the engine.

"It . . . was . . . Jeremy," he said, gritting his teeth.

She was going to say, "Don't talk now," but that, too, made little sense. He wasn't bleeding. Talking wouldn't hurt. It might actually take his mind off his arm.

"You two have a disagreement?" she asked.

"Shut up, Farris . . . and let me talk."

Good, Shara thought. He's angry. Maybe that will free his mind from the pain.

"Snuck up on me, fool that I am."

Shara remained silent.

"Told me not to meddle. Said he wasn't. It was between the two of you."

"And you told him to fuck off," Shara said, knowing that's precisely how he would respond to such a demand.

"That's . . . the gist of it." He paused, then went on. "He's not psychic like you and Mica."

Shara was going to say she *wasn't* psychic, but again decided this wasn't the time to debate semantics. She understood what he meant.

"He thought you told me about him. Didn't know I'd been to Atlanta. And he called her Terése."

It confirmed what Shara had thought. Mica had made no mention of Jeremy, and she'd had no sense of him at all while she'd been wandering in Mica's mind trying to get behind door number three.

"Looks like he got what he wanted," Shara said. "You're out of the game."

"No way," he said and groaned as Shara made a right hand turn. "Why don't you hit a few potholes . . . while you're at it?" he said.

"You want to get out and walk?"

"Don't make me laugh. It . . . hurts too much."

"Look, Briggs, with the cast you'll be wearing you'll be a liability. I'll be hunting Mica and protecting you at the same time."

"He caught me unawares. It won't happen again. I can still help, and . . . you won't need to protect me."

"And what do I tell Alexis if something happens to you?"

"What do *I* say to Alexis . . . if something happens to *you*?"

"Smartass."

They were at the hospital. Shara had called ahead on her cell phone. Briggs was rushed to an emergency room, and Shara had to cool her heels in the waiting room, alone with her thoughts.

She wasn't aware how long she'd been there, but she must have dozed. When she opened her eyes she looked up and saw McCandless.

"Hanging in there, Miss Farris?" he asked, concern etched in his face.

She looked at her watch. Two hours had passed.

"It's been a while," she said, not trying to hide the worry she felt.

"He's got a double compound fracture, and part of his wrist's been shattered. They'll put him together, but he's out for the season," he said with a tight grin. "Want to tell me what happened?"

"Fell, clumsy oaf," Shara said.

"Our friend didn't return to help him with his fall, did she?"

"No, Sheriff," Shara said, looking at him and seeing that twinkle in his eye. Hell, she thought, the truth wouldn't hurt. "She's long gone, but a friend of hers has been dogging her since she left Atlanta. Not helping her, but just keeping pace. I don't even think she's aware of him."

"Why the attack on Briggs?"

"Briggs gave me an unfair advantage — at least in his mind. So he leveled the playing field, so to speak."

"Would a search be of any use?"

Shara shook her head. "He's made his point. He's long gone."

"I don't suppose you'll be abandoning your hunt, even with your partner out of the picture."

"No . . . and Briggs insists he's still in the hunt."

"He's a good man."

"A pigheaded man," Shara said.

"It's going to be a while, yet. Want me to hang around?"

"Don't you have a family that needs you?"

"I'm a nineties man. Married and divorced three times. In between relationships now."

He stayed with her, though they said little. Shara was plotting what to do next and looking at McCandless. He seemed content to just be there to comfort her.

A doctor finally came out and repeated for Shara what McCandless had said.

Shara thought the doctor would be older, but he looked to be about twenty-five and he bore an uncanny resemblance to the sheriff.

"He'll be off his feet for a few days, and in a cast up to his shoulder for at least twelve weeks. He'll need therapy to get the strength and motion back in his wrist. The long and short of it is he'll be none the worse for wear, assuming he puts in the effort. He'll be sleeping for another three or four hours. Why don't you let my father buy you a good breakfast?" he said, with a wink at McCandless.

Shara agreed, and they went to a diner — one of those old-fashioned diners that looked like a railroad car.

Shara was ravenous.

"So your son's a doctor," Shara said.

"Damn proud of him."

"And a matchmaker," Shara said between bites of pancakes that were dripping with butter and syrup.

"He knows a good woman when he sees one," he said, with that twinkle in his eye. "You're too much woman for me, though . . . especially at my age."

He drove Shara back to the hospital. As she was about to get out he gently touched her arm. "You take care now. I know there's something between you and this woman you're after, but Clay Fluery's counting on that dinner. You don't want to disappoint him."

Shara looked at McCandless. "That's why you didn't hit on me. Professional courtesy."

"I've never stolen another man's woman, and don't mean to start now."

"But you would, if I weren't spoken for."

"I'd sure think about it . . . , but no man's gonna domesticate you. Like I said, you're too much woman for me. But I'd sure think on it."

Shara went into the hospital smiling. Hit on by two men in a week. Next thing they'd be fighting over her.

THIRTY-SEVEN

Twenty-eight days can be a fleeting moment or an eternity. It all had to do with one's perspective. With twenty-eight days before Mica struck again, Shara learned to empathize with Cleary's frustration, though it didn't change her perception of the woman in the least.

The wait was interminable at times. Shara wished she could go to sleep and when she awoke, the final scene could be played out.

Against Dr. McCandless' orders, Briggs had signed himself out the day after the attack. Shara had driven him home to recuperate. He'd gone on about people going to hospitals to die and tempting fate just by being there. Shara was slightly amused. Even Briggs had his fears — demons of his own.

Briggs slept the entire ride home and from what Alexis told her later, slept most of the following three days. With his arm shaped like the letter L, the bulky cast extending from his fingers past his elbow, she thought sleep would have been difficult. The good doctor must have given him strong pain killers. Maybe he'd be lucky, she thought, and wouldn't awake for twenty days.

Actually, Shara hoped he would reconsider going to Emory with her. He was in no shape to take on Jeremy, who wouldn't take kindly to Briggs' obstinacy. She would have to babysit him, which was a distraction she didn't need.

Shara, for her part, was on a guilt trip of her own. No matter how many times she told herself she wasn't responsible for Briggs' injury, when she looked in the mirror she had only herself to blame.

While Briggs slept, she worked out her frustrations by cleaning. When busy, she often let her home to go to hell. Laundry would pile up, dishes sat in the dishwasher, and dust gathered everywhere. Only when she was wearing her last clean pair of panties would she trudge down the street to the public washing machines. At times she postponed the inevitable by handwashing her underwear.

But when life dealt her a cruel blow, as when Deidre and Lysette had dumped on her, she would obsessively attack every nook and cranny. She would root out every speck of dust, scrub the kitchen floor until one could eat off of it, and scour the bathtub of water marks. She was most thorough in the room that housed her computers. She would clean every air vent and disassemble the computers and other equipment until the room could pass for an operating theater in a hospital.

She couldn't control Jeremy. She couldn't protect Briggs. She had no clue who in Emory Mica would attack. But her home, she *could* control.

She only stopped after she had received a call from FBI Special Agent Walker Cooper. He *requested* a meeting. Cleary had been re-assigned, she was told. After seven months it was felt a fresh perspective was necessary. He'd been polite — almost to a fault — willing, he said, to share information, and truly listen to any theories she or Briggs might have. Looking at him, all she could see was Cleary with a cock. Use her, then abuse her. A smile to her face, a knife in her back. She gave him nothing.

She'd been home for ten minutes after her meeting, deciding what to attack next, when Briggs called, asking her to stop by.

"You've been avoiding me," he said when she entered his study. He was working out on a stationary bike.

"No, I've been letting you heal. The doctor said three days in bed—"

"He didn't mention solitary confinement," he cut in.

"So, I've been feeling sorry for myself; guilty. I know," she said as he was about to interrupt, "it's without cause, but I had to work things out my own way. We both had to heal."

"Isn't it time we went up to Emory and narrowed our list of potential targets?" he asked.

"You're in no shape—"

He extended his good hand, and she was staring down the barrel of a gun.

"I'll be ready for him next time," he said with a malevolent grin.

"You're not going to shoot him," Shara said. "That would be overkill, and against everything you stand for."

"I won't kill the fucker," Briggs concurred, "but a bullet to the knee would even things out a bit. Anyway, you need me to get in the good graces with the sheriff there. And there's no way you can keep an eye on all of Mica's targets. I can—"

"All right, you've made your point," she said in surrender. She realized he had been rehearsing what he would say, expecting a pitched battle. She knew when a battle was lost. He was intent on accompanying her. "Just remember, *I'll* be doing the driving," she said with a wicked smile.

The next morning they left early. Briggs had spoken to Emory's Sheriff Dan Fallon. Briggs had been vague, but at least they would be expected.

Shara, for her part, kept the gas pedal planted to the floor, making Briggs pay for his obstinacy. They discussed a cover story, then Briggs napped to maintain his sanity as Shara drove maniacally.

Emory, a dot on the map, was not much more in reality. They passed a smattering of farms, a lumber mill and came to Main Street — literally the *only* street in the town. There was the police station, a diner, hardware store, barber shop, general store, a bar and little else.

Sheriff Fallon, in his fifties with a rapidly receding hairline and a paunch from either too much beer and good eating or sitting on his ass each day with little to do, greeted them warmly. His cheeks were chubby, his face clean-shaven, and his uniform newly cleaned, pressed and starched. There was the obligatory "What happened to your arm?"

question and Briggs' equally evasive "Took a tumble" answer. Then, in Fallon's office, they quickly got down to business.

"So what can I do for you?" Fallon asked.

"We're looking for someone who lived here about eight years ago, Sheriff," Briggs began. "Name was Mica. Had a grandfather—"

"Augustus Swann," Fallon ended. "Mica Swann. A troubled child. What has she done?"

"She's wanted in a homicide investigation," Briggs answered without elaborating.

"And why would she return here?"

"She was sexually attacked in Atlanta, Sheriff," Shara interjected. "We think something happened here in her youth and she's out for revenge."

"Let's not beat around the bush, shall we folks?" Fallon said with a grin. "You're talking about this Terése Richards." He showed Shara a FBI wanted poster. "Wanted in a homicide investigation. A bit more than that, isn't it?"

"We apologize—" Briggs started, but Fallon lifted a hand to stop him.

"No apology needed. You're not with the FBI or the police. You told me what you wanted to tell me. Now that we're on the same page we don't have to pussyfoot around. I'm more than willing to cooperate. As I said, Mica was a troubled child. She's no longer one of ours, and it's my job to protect the people of this town who are."

"Does that picture resemble the Mica you knew?" Shara asked.

"It's her. I wouldn't have given it a second thought, though, if you hadn't called."

"In what way was Mica troubled?" Shara asked.

"She claimed she was raped by a neighbor, Ralph Danziger."

"Was she?"

"He denied it. Her parents didn't want to pursue it. And, there was no physical evidence. As I recall, she showered after the alleged attack. It was his word against hers. You've got to understand this is a small town. If Mica was viewed as damaged goods, it would have been difficult for her. Or she might have been seen as easy, which would have been just as bad. I'm not condoning the way people think around here, please understand," he said, looking at Shara, "only giving you the facts of small town life."

"So you didn't investigate?" Shara said.

"As I said I talked to Danziger. Mica withdrew her complaint. Danziger died a week later in a freak tractor accident. He was a bit of a drinker, if you get my drift, so it didn't come as any great shock."

"I must have missed something," Shara said. "You said she was troubled, but if she was raped—"

"Her problems started *after* Danziger died. She got into arguments and fights at school. She was suspended for one fight. She broke a boy's nose with a bottle, I recall. Then she went camping with her grandfather and he had a heart attack at the campsite. He died in his sleep. We found her sitting by his body two or three days later. As I recall, within two weeks she ran away. She hasn't been heard from since."

"For the sake of argument, Sheriff," Shara said, "if she is returning with revenge on her mind, who would be her likely target?"

Fallon mulled it over for a few moments, straightening his tie, which didn't need straightening.

"Hard to say what resentment's been building up after all these years. Her parents are obvious targets. She might feel betrayed by them. Then there's Danziger's son, Ralph Junior. If she can't have the father, maybe she wants the son. And there's Josh Farrell, the boy she had the fight with at school. She humiliated him, and he tried to turn the other students against her. That would seem to be it."

"There's always you," Shara said. "An authority figure who she felt didn't believe her."

"Agreed, but then you'd have to add the school's principal. He *did* suspend her. He passed on a year ago. Stroke. But if she doesn't know . . . ," he let the thought hang.

"We'd like to talk to people around town," Briggs said. "How would you suggest we handle it?"

"I don't want the town spooked," Fallon said, looking troubled. "Most everyone up here hunts. Fact is everyone has any number of guns and rifles. The only murder we've got on record is over a hundred years old, and that was a poisoning. Still, trigger-happy folk fearing for their lives, shooting first and asking questions later isn't a pleasant thought. It could happen if word spread."

Fallon got up and walked to the window and looked out. He said nothing for several minutes, then turned back to them. He brushed a speck of dust off his pants, then shook his head as if he'd made a decision.

"Mica had two brothers. Mitchell, the younger of the two, died a year ago when terrorists bombed one of our embassies in some third world country. Both he and Michael had joined the army. Michael's stationed in Kentucky, I believe." He paused, then looked at Shara. "Miss Farris could be a reporter doing a story on how a small town copes with the death of one of its own, killed overseas and all. You could be helping her out, Mr. Briggs. You wouldn't arouse any undue suspicions, handled properly."

"Sounds good." Briggs said. "And we will be discreet. One other concern . . . The FBI. They think she's followed her pattern and will be out of the state by the time she strikes next."

"Don't worry about me contacting the FBI," Fallon said with contempt. "I've heard what happens. We'll have more agents up here than townsfolk. If Mica is after someone here, she'll wait until they're gone then strike. As far as I'm concerned I want to maintain a low profile."

With Fallon's cooperation secured, Shara and Briggs spent the day talking with potential targets and others who knew Mica, first getting impressions of Mitchell Swann for their article. They stayed at a nearby motel and were back the next day to finish up.

With nothing more to be accomplished, they returned to Philly and spent days debating who might be the likely target. Then there was the interminable wait Shara dreaded.

Two days before Mica was to strike, Shara and Briggs drove to Emory.

They'd intentionally stayed away from one another the last four days. They'd agreed each needed space to analyze what they'd learned without the other's interpretation. Maybe one of them would come at the four possible suspects from a fresh angle. Maybe, Shara thought,

Mica would give her a clue from door number three of her mind. It was nothing more than wishful thinking as it turned out.

Driving to Emory, they discussed each of the possible victims. Briggs still thought Mica harbored deep-seated resentment against her parents.

"She was raped and they passed it off as something you live with — almost a rite of passage. It led to everything else; her problems at school, her grandfather's death, her feelings of isolation," he argued passionately. "Since the Atlanta rape triggered her vendetta, I'd put my money on them."

Shara had given his oft-repeated argument a good deal of thought the past four days. She couldn't tell Briggs about her mother, but if anything, Shara was treated far more shabbily by *her* mother than Mica was by her parents.

Shara's mother had neglected and ignored her. Loretta Barrows never wanted Shara and she blamed her for all the weight she had put on and could never lose. That she spent a good portion of each day eating, after Shara was born, was irrelevant. It was Shara's fault. Later she blamed her weight gain — hence Shara — for not being able to keep a man. But Shara knew the only men who would have a fat cow like Loretta Barrows were desperate souls out for a quick fuck.

Her mother also was aware Shara's half-brother snuck into the bathroom when she showered and took photos of her. Yet she had never once reprimanded him. Her mother had given her *no* love, and treated her as a maid, not a member of the family. Shara knew, only too well, how it felt to be betrayed by family.

Would she kill her mother if she could? She loathed the woman. But *kill* her? *The thought had never crossed her mind*.

On the other hand, Shara wasn't Mica. Shara didn't have to search for a target. Her personal hell began and ended with her half-brother. Unlike Ralph Danziger, he hadn't died — not until Shara had ended his pitiful existence. So with no one else at whom to direct her wrath, maybe the resentment Mica harbored against her parents for abandoning her when she most needed them had festered. Still, it didn't feel right.

Shara brought up Ralph Danziger, Junior, not that she passionately felt he would be Mica's target. It had to be considered, though.

"Both Mica and her grandfather believed in an eye for an eye," Shara said.

"And she may have thought like father like son," Briggs added with a chuckle.

"Yeah, and the apple doesn't fall far from the tree," Shara said, laughing.

"Keep your eye on the road," Briggs said, putting his good hand on the dashboard as Shara veered around a RV.

"She could blame the son for the sins of the father," Shara added and Briggs groaned.

"Enough of the cliches, already. Is he a viable candidate?"

"He's a surrogate for her rage," Shara said. "And as she doesn't know anything about him, she might feel he had taken up where his old man left off."

"A waste of rage, as Junior despised his father," Briggs said, shaking his head.

They had learned Ralph Danziger spent a hell of a lot more time drinking and womanizing than working his farm. Most of the chores were left to Danziger's son. And Ralph Junior saw his mother crumble before his eyes, as Ralph Senior sought out new and younger conquests. She felt she was the laughingstock of the town. Three years after her husband died, when Ralph Junior was nineteen, she'd left to go down south to live with a relative. She'd never remarried and died two years after — and Ralph Junior blamed it *all* on his father. Still, Shara thought, Mica knew none of this.

"And there's Fallon," Briggs said. "He could have done more. Even he admits he was dismissive — it was Danziger's word against Mica's."

"But just like her parents, wasn't Fallon protecting Mica?" Shara said, playing Devil's advocate. "There was no proof of an attack. In a small town, Mica's accusation would announce she was no virgin. And even if they believed he raped her, there would be many who would have thought she at the very least had led him on. She had no visible injuries, so they'd say she hadn't put up a fight, because deep down she consented. Later, guilt-ridden, she rationalized to herself she'd been raped."

"You would have made a great defense attorney for Danziger, if he had gone to trial," Briggs said.

Shara shrugged. "Even in Philly a woman attacked is considered partially culpable if she dresses seductively or frequents singles bars. Emory is a century behind. I'm not saying what Fallon did was right, but his advice was prudent, given the circumstances."

"But does Mica think like you?" Briggs countered.

"That's why he's still on our list," Shara sighed. "And Josh Farrell," Shara said, giving the argument for the fourth culprit. "Now he's a piece of work."

They had found out that Farrell's confrontation with Mica had been a defining moment of his life. He'd been a prankster, but after Mica humiliated him, he'd turned mean. He had bad-mouthed Mica to anyone and everyone when his suspension ended. Mica, meanwhile, didn't return to school until after her grandfather's funeral. When she did, she was vilified by Farrell's friends. When she left Emory, soon after, many blamed it on Farrell, and he'd become something of an outcast himself. He'd been divorced three times — something almost unheard of in Emory — because he used his wives as punching bags. He'd even spent three months in jail for beating up a woman he had picked up at a bar.

"If anyone deserves killing—" Shara started, but stopped when she saw the look on Briggs' face. "I'm not saying I'd condone his death, but with all he's done since, he hasn't exactly been held accountable. A slap on the wrist was all he received."

"Only, as with Ralph Junior, Mica doesn't know what he's become," Briggs said. "The question is just how great is her resentment towards him?"

"Round and round we go," Shara said.

They were off the Northeast Extension now, traveling along a two-lane road with twists and turns. Shara was still doing fifty and Briggs was holding on for dear life.

Shara came around a S-curve and a deer emerged from the forest, ramming the passenger side of the car, even as Shara veered to avoid it. She lost control for a moment, and the car went off the road and slammed into a tree.

Shara was more stunned than hurt. She looked at Briggs and saw he had a gash on his head and was holding his shoulder.

"Are you—" she started, then bit back the words. No, he *wasn't okay* — anyone could see that. And she was to blame, driving like a bat out of hell on a roadway populated with "Deer Crossing" signs.

She helped him out of the car, and ministered to his head wound from a first aid kit they carried. It was superficial, which didn't mean it didn't hurt.

"How's your arm?" she asked, her voice unsteady.

"Still broken, but the cast did its job. My shoulder's bruised, though."

"Look, I'm sorry. I—"

"For once, it wasn't your driving, so don't fault yourself," he stopped her. "Though it would serve you right if I did put you on a guilt trip. Your driving *will* be the death of me yet."

"What do you mean it wasn't my driving?"

"I've done some hunting. The look in that deer's eyes. It was almost a Kamikaze attack. It was spooked by something in the woods. It was running for its life *before* it was on the road."

"You're saying it was intentional?"

Briggs nodded, and groaned. "Mica."

"No. Jeremy," Shara said. "Wait here a minute, and keep your gun handy in case he tries to finish the job."

Shara went into the woods where the deer had first appeared. She smelled for any sign of Mica. There was none. Mica would be at her lair, this being the final day of her period. They were twenty miles from Emory. Shara knew it wasn't Mica, but she had to be sure. She *was* aware of someone's presence, but it wasn't Mica's. She sensed Jeremy. But if she tried to track him, he might double back and attack Briggs. She gave it up and returned to the car.

"Jeremy was definitely here. May still be, but he won't attack the two of us."

"That deer made a beeline for the passenger door," Briggs said. "It was like Jeremy had a slingshot and launched it. He's pissed I'm still around."

"He's also a damn fool," Shara said, loud enough so Jeremy could hear if he was still in the vicinity. "We both could have been killed or seriously injured. If I'm out of commission, there's no confrontation. That's the second time he's lost control."

They both went to take a look at the deer, whose forward motion had taken him into the woods not far from the car. It was a buck.

"He looks almost relieved," Briggs said.

"Bullshit, Briggs," Shara answered. "You can't tell that from his eyes."

"Call it a hunch," he said with a weak smile.

The car was damaged, but operable. Half an hour later — Shara adhering to the posted limit for the most part — they limped into Emory.

They told Fallon the edited truth. They had swerved to avoid a deer.

"Not an auspicious start," he said, looking concerned.

Fallon had no problem, though, with Briggs' plans for protecting those who might be in danger. While Shara and Briggs had formulated their plans together, Shara deferred to Briggs as he presented their suggestions to the sheriff. He and Fallon spoke the same language, were cut from the same cloth, and both were men. It was what Briggs brought to the table. He was convincing and authoritative without being pushy and condescending.

"Shara will keep an eye on the Swanns and I'll focus on Ralph Junior. You have three deputies, right?"

"Not usually on duty at the same time, but yes."

"One keeps on eye on Josh Farrell. A second is assigned to you. The last stays with Mrs. Swann until her husband gets home, then he'll give each of us a breather. That sound like a plan to you?" Shara knew Briggs wasn't soliciting Fallon's advice, but massaging the man's ego.

"Except for wasting a deputy on me," he said.

"We've gone over it, Sheriff," Briggs said. "Face it, she may have it in for you. I know," he began, when Fallon was about to protest, "you can take care of yourself, but we *do* have the manpower. At least you'll have company."

They'd already discussed and dismissed the idea of searching the woods. Fallon had been dead set against it.

"Two reasons," he'd said. "First, folks in town would get wind of it, and the last thing we need is panic and unsubstantiated rumors. My deputies and I would end up spending our time calming their fears, rather than protecting those in danger. Plus, Mica knows the woods as well as any of us. You two would be no help, no offense. If she caught wind of us, there's plenty of woods and she'd make herself scarce."

Both Briggs and Shara had agreed.

After dinner had been brought to them at the police station, Shara and Briggs agreed to sleep in their car for the night. They didn't want to draw attention to themselves, and the only alternative was a jail cell. Briggs was particularly skittish, having literally spent a month in prison. Shara had no desire to be boxed in either — even with the cell unlocked. It reminded her too much of the cage where her half-brother had kept her imprisoned. She didn't want to revisit *those* memories.

"I can feel her," Shara said, after a twenty-minute argument over who would get the back seat. Briggs wanted to be chivalrous. Shara was practical. She knew he needed the room. Both his head and shoulder still ached. He had reluctantly agreed.

"I can smell her. I can almost touch her. As we've gotten physically closer to her, it's like blinders being taken off."

"Any new insights?"

"She's shielding her thoughts from me. I thought she might offer a bone, but she's playing it close to the vest. This is, after all, what the past eight months have all been about."

Shara wasn't particularly tired, but eventually fell asleep, despite Briggs' snoring. She didn't dream of Mica — at least not at first — but she found herself in her playroom. Briggs was there. He *knew* she was The Vigilante he had hunted fruitlessly, and he was furious.

"You humiliated me. Then to make matters worse, you worm your way into my family — make Alexis dependent on you."

Without warning he hit her. He kept pummeling her and nearly beat her to a pulp while she offered no resistance. And each time he struck her she heard her half-brother laugh — egging him on.

She awoke sweating, and saw Briggs staring at her.

"Who's Bobby?" he asked.

"What?" she asked, playing for time to compose herself.

"You talk in your sleep."

"You snore, so we're even," she said, hoping he would drop it, but he wouldn't.

"You called out his name."

"An old boyfriend. He was abusive," Shara said, thinking on the fly.

"You're not the type to get into an abusive relationship."

"I did — once. Maybe it was because I felt guilty. I deserved the abuse. Or . . ." she trailed off.

"Or?"

"Pain is pleasure," she said, remembering what Alexis had said to her.

"What the hell is that supposed to mean?" he asked.

"Mica would understand. Those into S/M enjoy pain — the submissives. They get off on being beaten and humiliated."

"That's not you."

"You don't know me," Shara said, suddenly angry. "You don't know who or what turns me on."

"Who is your type?" he asked.

She could hear he was genuinely curious. "Not you," she snapped.

He looked hurt.

"Don't take it personally," she said, finally regaining her equilibrium. "I know your wife — your daughter. Even if you were my type, I could never make a play for you. Alexis, in particular, would be peering over my shoulder. Alexis would know and damn the two of us."

Briggs shook his head.

"You have a way of saying a lot, yet revealing nothing. I ask your type of man, and you tell me why *I'm* not your type."

"Maybe you're losing your touch," she said, not at all comfortable where the discussion was heading.

"No, I've worked with you almost four months now and you're still a mystery to me. It's almost as if you're hiding something."

"No, Briggs — it's like I told Nina — I'm *not* your partner. We work together. I'll watch your back, but that's as far as it goes. I value my privacy, and I have no desire to pour out my heart to you. No offense. It's not you. It's me."

"You've got no one?"

"I've got Alexis."

"Because she can read your mind, so you say."

"I thought so, but it's become more than that."

"What, then?" he asked.

"You look at her as a cripple, Briggs, but she and I are equals. She's wise beyond her years, and she's literally the only person I know who wouldn't stab another in the back."

Briggs was silent a moment. "I love her to death, you know that, but before she was attacked she was a normal kid. She'd get into arguments all the time with her friends, then make up a few days later. That's not the Alexis you're describing."

"You're right. She has her faults, don't we all? But she's not the person she was before her rape. She's got precious little to do but think; about her plight, life passing her by, you, me."

She paused and stretched, feeling the onset of a cramp in her legs.

"You know, sometimes you're a fool," she went on. "Your moral code, which forced you to betray me to Cleary. Well, Alexis lives by that code of yours. The only difference is she would have told me *before* she went to Cleary. You brought her up well. She's taken the best of you and Vivian. It's all that allows her to maintain her sanity. Inside she's thirsting — *lusting* — for life, yet she's a prisoner of her own body. Try to imagine it. I couldn't deal with it. She can because you and Vivian provided a foundation. She's one special kid. You shouldn't underestimate her. Think about it, Briggs, I'm going to sleep."

"Still didn't tell me anything about yourself," he mumbled, then fell silent.

It took awhile, but when Shara fell asleep again, she was back in familiar terrain; chasing Mica in the forest.

For once she was glad.

THIRTY-EIGHT

MICA

In the woods just outside his house Mica wondered what she would do when she faced him. It was her grandfather who killed. Could *she* kill him? Did she want to kill him? If not, why the hell had she come back?

She had seen Shara the evening before, sleeping in her car with her partner in the back seat. She'd been tempted to tap on the window. It seemed like they'd shared an eternity. But the time wasn't yet right. "Tomorrow," she whispered, and snuck back to her lair.

The week of her period she'd stayed where she and her grandfather had spent their last night. She had been particularly vigilant, since this was the one place the police might think to look. She could easily escape, if need be.

And now here she was waiting. She wore no watch, but sensed it was close to midnight. It had been raining steadily most of the day, but now a fine mist fell. Though soaked to the bone, tonight Mica was oblivious to the elements.

A car drove up and *he* got out. He said something to the driver, then moved hurriedly towards the front door of the house.

Mica moved stealthily towards the car. She placed a water pistol she'd bought on the way to Emory at the driver's head as he smoked a cigarette.

"Not a sound and you won't get hurt."

He had no intention, she realized, of playing the hero. With his handcuffs, she cuffed his hands behind his back, and made him get in the backseat. She made sure the police radio was on. He could listen, but he wouldn't be able to transmit.

She had already been in the house earlier in the evening and knew its layout. She went upstairs to his bedroom. A freshly pressed uniform was on the bed. The bathroom door was closed. She could smell him taking a shit. Smells almost as bad as I do, she thought. He flushed the toilet, then she heard water running as he washed his hands. When he emerged — clad only in an undershirt and his boxers — she was aiming her gun at him.

He turned ashen when he saw her. His knees almost buckled.

"Why me?" he asked, his voice shaking.

"It all started with you."

"*No*, it started with Danziger. *He raped you.*"

"But you could have ended it right then and there. All the dominoes that toppled were the direct result of your inaction. Danziger wouldn't have died if he were in jail where he belonged. The problems I had at school. My grandfather's death. My running away. And eight years lost because I was dead inside — *all your doing*. It's time justice was served. Take off your clothes," she commanded.

He hesitated and Mica almost laughed. She might kill him if he defied her, yet he was too proud or ashamed to be seen naked in front of her.

She stood up, extending her arm with the gun. "Don't make me repeat myself. You know you wouldn't be the first."

He took off undershirt and drawers.

She could see why he'd been reluctant to undress. He wasn't at all pleasant to look at. He was hairless, except for his pubic hair. Some women would envy him his breasts, and his paunch, she was sure, made him unable to see his own cock. Not that he was missing much. A little dick for a chubby man.

"On the bed. On your back."

He did as she commanded.

"Arms behind your head."

She took his uniform and derived a perverse sense of pleasure ripping it apart to tie him. She recalled how important his appearance was to him. She tied him as she had so many of her submissives: arms and legs spread, but not too tight.

She sat on his chest, her legs spread apart, so he could smell her crotch. He winced as he caught a whiff. She had her chain in one hand, his Walkie Talkie in another, which she now placed on his chest. She had brought a mini-cassette recorder with her, and placed that on a night table next to his bed.

"We're gonna chat, Sheriff. Remember back eight years? Back to the day I walked into your office and told you Ralph Danziger raped me? To that day you called Danziger, and had a chat with *him*? I heard what the two of you said. You *do* remember, don't you?"

"I made a mistake, but he died a week later, for Christ's sake," Fallon said, his eyes pleading for mercy. At the moment, she knew, he was still too proud to verbally beg for her forgiveness.

"You made a mistake . . . *and ruined my life*. You made a mistake and Danziger died. My grandfather died. And I couldn't live with myself here. You're going to admit your mistake. Confess your sins," she said, holding up the Walkie Talkie, but not depressing the button.

"You'll only have a minute, so let's rehearse," she said.

She held the Walkie Talkie up to him.

"What did Danziger tell you when you asked if he'd raped me?

Fallon said nothing.

"What did you tell him when he admitted he'd raped me?"

Fallon remained silent, but she could see sweat breaking out from his forehead. Thirty seconds had passed.

"I'll have to convince you how serious I am, then. Like I said, when I press this button, you'll only have a minute. Any longer and the cavalry will have arrived."

She removed her top, exposing her breasts, and held out her arms for Fallon to see. Slowly her arms became those of a man's — tanned with the white hair and shriveled skin of age. She saw Fallon's eyes widen. Saw them bulge even further when he looked at her chest and saw the face of Augustus Swann emerge.

Still, it was Mica doing the talking. Her grandfather was doing *her* bidding. Mica would decide Fallon's fate. She turned her head and looked at Fallon's penis. He had an erection.

"Your soldier's saluting, Sheriff," Mica said. "Didn't think you had it in you to get a hard-on."

She rose off him and stood by the bed, wrapping the chain her grandfather's hand held around the base of his penis.

"You've got fifteen seconds. What did Danziger tell you?"

Silence.

"Think I'm bluffing. Maybe *I* don't have the balls to do it, but Augustus Swann wouldn't give it a second thought. What did you tell Danziger?"

Fallon was still silent, but she saw his lips quivering.

"Four, three, two, one," she counted. Then her grandfather's hands yanked the chain, cutting off Fallon's penis. It rose in the air like a missile, and Mica caught it as it descended.

Blood gushed from the wound. Fallon let out a blood-curdling scream, muffled only when Mica placed a remnant from his uniform in his mouth.

She looked at the dismembered organ and put it in her jeans pocket. Now she wrapped the chain around Fallon's neck. His face was ashen and gleaming with perspiration.

"You've got one chance to live, Sheriff," Mica said calmly. "I'm not really myself, you know," she said with a smile, showing Fallon her gnarled male hands. "My grandfather gave his life because of you. He was a religious man, you know — an eye for an eye. Now, let's go over this one *last* time. I'm going to turn on the Walkie Talkie. You'll have one minute, before the troops arrive. Tell the truth, you save your sorry ass. Lie or remain silent and it's your neck — *literally*. With *these* hands. You remain silent, I give you over to Augustus."

She took the cloth out of Fallon's mouth. "So, which will it be?" she asked.

"I'm bleeding to death," Fallon said, grimacing.

"Not to worry. A little pecker, a little blood. Tell the truth, help will be here in a minute. Act the fool and they'll find you dead."

She depressed the record button on the tape recorder, and placed it on his chest, then depressed the button on the Walkie Talkie.

"One minute, starting now. What did Ralph Danziger tell you when you asked him if he'd raped Mica Swann?"

Fallon looked at her wide-eyed. She put some tension on the chain, which she held with her free hand, and showed him the watch she'd taken from Fallon's bureau and that now rested on her wrist. Ten seconds had passed.

"He admitted he raped you," Fallon said hoarsely, the words rushing out. Self-preservation had won out.

"What did you tell him you'd do?"

"Take care of things. Make it go away."

"What did you tell Mica that Danziger said?"

"That he'd denied it. It was his word against yours."

"So you lied?"

"Yes, but—"

"You let a rapist walk?"

"Yes," Fallon said with resignation.

"I'm done with you."

She put the chain around her neck and put on her top. Her grandfather's hands were again within her. She left Fallon's bedroom, without looking back, as he began bellowing for help.

Downstairs, she had placed lighter fluid on rags at the two entrances to Fallon's house — not enough to start a conflagration, but just enough to get the attention of whoever was first on the scene, to help cover her escape. She lit them, then dashed for the woods.

At the edge of the woods she crouched and waited. She saw Shara drive up. She opened her mind and let Shara into door number three.

THIRTY-NINE

SHARA

As soon as Shara heard Mica on the police radio, she knew Fallon was the target.

"Briggs, I'm going to Fallon's. Stay with Ralph Junior. Mica may come for him next."

She told the other two deputies to go to Fallon's as well.

Driving, she ignored Briggs, who was trying to reach her on the police radio. He wanted to join her. *This is between the two of us*, she would have told him.

As she came to the front of Fallon's house, Mica downloaded the last of her secrets. This time, though, amidst the images there was audio, and it was mind-numbingly loud. She heard two men talking, though the images that flashed through Shara's mind were of a man raping a young Mica. Heard them laughing; good buds having a chat.

"You gotta curb your appetite for young pussy." Shara recognized the voice as Fallon's.

"You know I like the young ones." Must be Danziger, she thought, as she saw the images of the rape. "What you gonna do, Dan?" Danziger pleading.

"Make it go away," Fallon again.

Like a tape loop the whole thing was repeated over and over. With Mica so close, it was deafening, the sound reverberating in her head, rendering Shara helpless. With her last reserve of strength, she reached out to Mica and found herself once again in her adversary's mind. She went to the third door. Standing by it, but not blocking her path was Augustus. Smiling. Not a malevolent grin, but one of triumph and vindication. Shara closed the door and was pulled back into herself. Opening her eyes, she wiped the tears that had erupted from the raging noise in her mind. She dimly saw Mica look at her a moment, then bolt for the woods.

Two police cars arrived seconds later.

"She may be in there," Shara said. "Search the entire house. Be careful. She may be armed."

As they put out the smoldering fire, Shara heard her Walkie Talkie. It was Briggs, again.

"Stay put, Briggs. We're searching Fallon's house. As soon as I know anything, I'll get back to you."

She tossed the Walkie Talkie onto the car seat and dashed into the woods after Mica.

*　　　*　　　*

Briggs flung his Walkie Talkie onto the car's floor. What the hell was Shara up to? he wondered. He knew, deep within, she would go after Mica alone.

Driving with one hand had been no easy task, but Briggs had started practicing two weeks earlier. He had also used a knife to weaken the cast at the elbow. He didn't know what it would do to his healing bones, but he'd worry about that later. With his good hand, he now separated the cast at his elbow, so he'd have freedom of motion. Only his arm wouldn't respond. His muscles were like lead, refusing to budge, as he tried to extend his arm.

He knew he was wasting valuable time. With his good hand he started the car, put it in gear, then floored the gas pedal.

After a quarter of a mile, he dimly saw a figure in the road. There was a man blocking his path. Jeremy. "You want to play chicken!" he yelled to himself. "Fine!" he answered, and floored the car.

Jeremy refused to move.

"C'mon motherfucker!" Briggs bellowed. "Get the hell out of the way!"

Jeremy held his ground.

At the last second, Briggs jerked the wheel to his right, leaving the road, and coming to a halt just before hitting a tree. He could get around Jeremy now, he thought and gunned the engine, but the car refused to move. The back wheels spun uselessly in the mud.

Briggs got out of the car and looked at Jeremy.

Jeremy smiled at him. "Neither of us will intercede."

Briggs released the gun from the handmade device he had fashioned on his good arm. He pointed it at Jeremy.

"I'm unarmed, Detective," he said, holding his hands out. "And, I'm done with you. Shoot me in the back if you want or go to the aid of your friend."

Jeremy turned and walked into the woods.

"Bastard," Briggs said aloud, to himself. He placed the gun in his pocket. Light rain dripped from his shaved head down his face. He wondered how long a run it was to Fallon's house. As he began to run, helping Shara was his only concern.

*   *   *

It was just like her dream, Shara thought. She was clothed, but Mica was naked, and she could see both the wolf and Mica's grandfather emerge from Mica's back, only to be yanked back from within.

Shara ran, oblivious to the branches that threatened to gouge her eyes out. Only this chase was real. Any injuries she incurred wouldn't heal because she was awake.

No matter how fast she ran she could make up no ground. She saw water ahead. Not a mere stream, but a river. Saw Mica wade into the water. Followed her. And just as in her dream, she lunged at Mica. But, as she lunged, Mica disappeared and Shara found herself in water above her head.

The previous month had seemed an eternity. She had done all she could to make the time fly by. The one thing she'd forgotten to do was to take swimming lessons. Cursing herself she went down, swallowing water. She struggled to the surface and saw a figure on the other side of the river.

Jeremy.

He stood, looking forlorn, his arms at his side, his palms extended, facing towards Shara, communicating to her that she was on her own.

Shara went down again, swallowing more water.

She felt something grab onto her jacket, felt herself being pulled to the surface, then towards the shore.

Then nothing.

F ORTY

Shara opened her eyes and thought she was looking in a mirror. The same gaunt face. But as her eyes adjusted, she saw the features weren't hers. Slowly her head cleared. It was Mica, squatting in front of her.

Shara was sitting. She tried to rise, but couldn't.

"Sorry about that," Mica said. "I had to handcuff you to a tree. I didn't know what to expect when you recovered."

"How long has it been?"

"Just a few minutes. I wanted to meet you face to face before I left. Your partner's not here yet, but he will be soon."

"What happened?"

"I was going to ask you the same thing," Mica said. "I'd set this wonderful trap for you." She pointed to a tree not far away. "I stayed here the last day. Made it into a lair. I even brought bones from where I stayed until yesterday. I was up in the tree. You'd come by, see — or sense — my presence, check out the lair and I'd jump you. Only you kept running like you were chasing—"

"Chasing *you*." Shara said. "I saw *you*, just as I have for eight months in my dream. Only when I got to the river and lunged at you, you weren't there. You . . . you saved me!"

"With some help."

Shara looked at her in bewilderment.

"My grandfather. I didn't ask him. I reached out for you, but the current was taking you down. Then I felt my grandfather's hand grab you. His feet were anchoring me. He was making amends, I think, for mistakes he'd made in the past."

"Thank him for me," Shara said, then paused. "I gotcha," she said with a weak smile.

Now Mica looked puzzled. "I'd say it was the other way around," Mica said.

"No. I *found* you. Catching you would have been icing on the cake. But without your help, I knew you would come here and knew where that would be."

"Kind of in the right church, but the wrong pew," Mica said.

"Had I known what Fallon did to you . . . ," she shrugged, and let the thought hang.

"My final secret."

"Your final kill," Shara said. "Or is it?"

"I didn't kill him." Mica removed the penis from her pocket. "I had to cut off his pecker to show him I meant business, but otherwise he's safe and sound." She looked at it with distaste, then put it back in her jeans.

"I don't understand."

"The other kills were my grandfather's. He had demons of his own to purge. After you reached out to me the last time — that's when I first found out he'd killed Danziger. That was when I regained control. I didn't know what I would do to Fallon. Killing him would have been too easy — *for him*. He put me through eight years of hell. With his confession, he'll live out the rest of his sorry life in humiliation."

Shara had a thought, and it brought a fit of laughter.

"You find what I'm telling you funny?" Mica said in irritation.

Shara shook her head, and composed herself.

"I'm sorry. I was thinking of our *confrontation*," she said, and started giggling anew. "Look, I've been told a half a dozen times we'd have some kind of apocalyptic encounter."

"Like our dream?" Mica asked.

"Yes, a catfight to the death."

"It turned out to be a one-round knockout," Mica said with a smile.

"A one-punch knockout," Shara said. "A bit of a downer. A disappointment to our many fans."

"You talk in riddles," Mica said, but she was still smiling.

"Because of our connection, I've come into contact with others who knew us both. There were expectations from some that you'd make quick work of me. They would probably feel cheated. Like they'd plunked down big bucks to see this catfight of major proportions, turned to buy a hotdog, and I'm being counted out."

"Do you care?"

"No. I just see the humor in it. You've had the weight of your quest on your mind — not to mention the elements and the fight for control within you. I don't suspect you've seen much humor in anything lately. I, on the other hand, can look at it from a different perspective."

"I'm glad we met," Mica said.

"More glad it's over," Shara said, and paused. "It is over, isn't it?"

"That's up to you," Mica said.

"No, actually, it's up to you."

Mica looked at Shara.

"Are you done killing?" Shara asked.

"Yes."

"Then it's over. Even if I were still consumed, I couldn't find you if you didn't kill again. Anyway, I've done what I set out to do."

"But I eluded you," Mica said, still seeming confused.

"It was never about bringing you back for me. The reward meant nothing to me. You, of all people, should know that. You've peered into my hell. I need the chase. That's what drives me," she said, then paused. "What about your companions — your grandfather and the wolf?"

"I no longer need them. You'll see," she said with a mischievous look. "It's too bad I've got to go. We could have been friends. I know it sounds odd—"

"Not at all," Shara cut in. "I looked upon you as my salvation when this started. In many ways we are alike. But along the way I learned I don't need a mirror image of myself. After ten years, I'm finally alive again. Living has its ups and downs, but it sure beats being dead inside. It's like going through adolescence at twenty-five. I'm experiencing emotions that are completely foreign to me. That's what you've given me."

"We *are* alike," Mica said. "I've been dead since I ran away from here."

"What about Jeremy?"

"What about Jeremy?" Mica asked.

"He's been dogging you. From a distance. He's in love with you, but there's more."

"Go on," Mica said when Shara paused.

"He's been a voyeur, since I entered the picture. He's one of those who relished our final confrontation. You know, two women fighting over *their* man. He loves you, but — no offense — I don't think he would have been disappointed had I prevailed. Not that I would have wanted him, but that's his problem," Shara said, and laughed.

"Why would Jeremy follow me?" Mica asked, but it was as much to herself as to Shara.

They heard voices in the distance.

"Gotta be going," Mica said.

"Keep in touch," Shara said with a smile. "You think we'll still be able to reach out and touch — that connection we have?"

"I haven't the foggiest," Mica said. "It would be nice, though. To have someone to share with, that is."

Mica rose.

"A piece of advice," Shara said before Mica could leave. "Open your eyes, Mica. Your quest's over; that need for revenge that drove you. Next time you meet a Jane or Renee, don't let go. They miss you terribly. You touched their lives, and I'm sure they touched yours."

"That what you mean by living?"

"It's a big part of it."

"I'll keep it in mind," Mica said, then looked at Shara. "I do miss them — especially Renee. She's so fragile. I'd almost forgotten, but now I guess I *can* dwell on it." She dug in her other pocket and took out a tape and put it in Shara's jeans. "If Fallon somehow tries to cover up—"

"I know what to do," Shara said.

Mica picked up her knapsack, walked a few steps, then returned. She took a key out of her jeans and was going to unlock the handcuffs, but Shara stopped her.

"I'll be fine. I need to be locked up or my partner will have questions I'd rather not answer."

Mica nodded in understanding, tossed the key a few feet from Shara so she couldn't reach it, kissed her on the forehead, then began walking away.

Before she was out of sight, she stopped. Through the mist Shara saw the wolf within Mica emerge. This time Mica didn't pull it back. Without turning Mica left.

The wolf lay down in front of Shara.

Shara sensed it would cause her no harm. It was there to protect her until she was found. Shara had read whatever she could get her hands on about wolves, once she learned one was a part of Mica. Its eyes should have been yellow, but they were gray. It suddenly dawned on Shara that Mica had not only rid herself of the wolf, but her grandfather, as well.

The wolf must have sensed Briggs, after another ten minutes had passed, for it raised its head, sniffed the air, then loped off into the forest.

For a moment Shara felt terribly alone and vulnerable. She saw a flashlight, then heard Briggs cursing. He finally spotted her. He came up to her, concern etched in his face.

"Are you okay?" he asked.

Shara burst out laughing.

FORTY-ONE

MICA

After leaving Shara, Mica headed for the river, crossed over, made her way north, then doubled back and went south. She knew Shara wouldn't follow her, but Fallon's deputies might. She had *always* ventured north, but with her mission completed, proceeding south was prudent. *But where*, she thought. Her quest had been so all-consuming, she had never given thought to what she would do once it was accomplished. She literally had no idea.

She was still wanted by the FBI, who had both her fingerprints and a rough sketch of her likeness. She had to maintain a low profile — literally disappear. But where? She came up with no answers, but continued walking aimlessly until it was dawn.

At times, she thought to leave the riverbank and find a cabin so she could rest and formulate plans, but she seemed driven to maintain her course.

Shortly after the sun came up, she rounded a bend and came upon Jeremy. He was seated in front of a huge slab of rock, painting upon it.

He seemed to sense her without turning around.

"So you prevailed," he said.

"How did you know which direction I'd head?" she asked.

"I followed you, discreetly, and when you doubled back, your intent was clear."

"I'm told you've been following me from the beginning," Mica said.

Jeremy turned to face her. "Shara told you that."

"And more."

Jeremy smiled. "She was a feisty one."

"Why Jeremy? Why follow me? Why stay hidden?"

"You don't sense something about me that's familiar?" he asked.

Mica shook her head.

"The wolf within you. Are you so arrogant to think you're the only one?" he asked.

"I hadn't given it any thought."

"If there were one like you, couldn't there be more? Dozens? Maybe hundreds?" He told her what had happened to him as a youth.

"The wolf and I are now one and the same," he concluded. "What I'm trying to say is that we've become one. That first day at the lake, I sensed the wolf within you. We're two of a kind. I couldn't lose you."

"I had no idea. Why didn't I feel anything?"

"You've never given yourself over to the wolf. He lay dormant in you. I didn't know why at the time, but after you had to kill that cop in Atlanta, then left, I knew it had been awakened. Knew you had some unfinished business and until it was completed I'd have to bide my time. But I was intent not to lose you, so I followed, without making you aware."

"The wolf's no longer a part of me," she said.

"That's not entirely accurate. You lived with him for eight years — before you got to Atlanta. His essence remains with you, even though he's departed. You don't live with something for so long and not take on some of its characteristics. And, truth be told, my *human* self fell in love with Terése."

"Mica," she said. "There never was a Terése. That's not quite true," Mica corrected herself. "Terése was a persona I created. What you see now is Mica. What are you painting?"

As usual, when looking at Jeremy's art, Mica saw nothing discernible.

"Shara in the river," he said, pointing to a blotch of paint. "You saving her."

"You thought we'd battle, and it didn't matter who won. That's what Shara said. I don't understand. If you loved me, if we're two of a kind, why wouldn't you intercede on my behalf?"

"Shara's an incredible woman," Jeremy said, avoiding a direct answer. "She's the first I've met with the instincts of the wolf without actually having one within her. It's not our nature — or at least mine — to interfere between two competitors. You see, I didn't view her as a threat to you, but as competition. Just as female wolves vie for the honor to mate with the dominant male, you two had to battle for me. Much as I love you — and I do — I had to let nature take its course. It's what I am."

"What Shara and I shared wasn't about you," Mica said, with some hostility. "And it's pretty damn presumptuous of you to think either one of us would want you."

"Agreed, but I would have pursued the victor, regardless."

"And now you consider me yours?"

"I am what I am, Mica. I can't change that. But I'm human, too. I want to make you mine. I offer you a lifelong commitment, but I know I have to win you over. All I ask is the chance."

Mica took several steps back.

"I don't know. The entire time we were together, you were living a lie."

"Not in February. Not when the wolf within you surfaced. That month together each year, it provided a glimpse of what we share."

"I don't know if I can be what you want. I can never be submissive to anyone. That's part of *my* nature. Yet, you want me to submit to your will."

Jeremy glanced at his painting for a moment, then turned back to Mica. "Where will you go? What will you do?"

"I honestly don't know," she answered and sat down on the ground. "I've spent the past eight months making decisions, and I don't have it in me to decide what to do next. I'm just drained."

"Then come with me. Let me take some of the burden from you. You know what I want, but I know it's not in you to give yourself over to me. Life is about compromises. I won't try to remake you in my image. Yet, there's much we share. Let me help you now, no strings attached."

"Where would we go?"

"Home — my home in Minnesota, to be more precise. When I left, I thought it was for good, but for a reason I couldn't fathom, each year I paid taxes on what had been my home. We can go there and disappear. For a while or forever. We can stay until you're whole again, then travel if you wish. And you know I'd never stray. If you wanted, I'd be yours for life.

"It's your nature," Mica said with a faint smile.

"We take it one day at a time. We don't look far into the future—"

"It's our nature. It's who we are," she concluded for him.

"What do you have to lose? What is your alternative?"

Mica smiled. "You're pretty sure of yourself. Stay with you for just a while and you're sure you'll win me over." She paused, a moment, then shrugged. "What the hell. Let's do it. I genuinely liked the Jeremy I knew in Atlanta. And I'm tired of making decisions. Actually, I'm just plain tired."

Jeremy packed his paints and brushes.

"There's a cabin not too far from here. We can stay a few days until you've regained your strength. Come," he said, beckoning.

"Just one more thing I have to do," she said. She got up, and reached into her jeans pocket for Fallon's dismembered penis. She threw it as far as she could into the river and watched it sink. "You fucked with the wrong person, Sheriff," she said aloud. "Sapped the life out of me for too long. It's time to start living again."

She picked up her knapsack and followed Jeremy. She had nothing to lose. She had her life back. And she wasn't alone. Maybe she had prevailed, after all. She thought fleetingly of Shara and hoped she would find someone, too. Maybe it was the wolf within her, but being alone had lost its allure.

FORTY-TWO

SHARA

Sitting across from Clay in her new red dress, Shara wondered if she had ever been more nervous. She had called Clay as soon as she had returned to Philly, with only her pride in need of some massaging. Clay suggested they have dinner at his house, which conjured up all kinds of images Shara wasn't sure if she was willing to deal with.

"Whoa," she said, trying to sound lighthearted. "This is our first . . . date, after all," she said, feeling foolish for having called dinner with him a *date*. Dates were for teens, not twenty-five-year-olds. "Do you think it's wise?"

"I didn't mean to sound presumptuous; you know, inviting you into my *love nest*," he told her, sounding contrite. "I was just being practical. Truth be told, we'd have to drive a good forty-five minutes for a decent meal, and I'm a damn fine cook. I'm eager to hear all about your exploits with Mica, and I didn't think you'd want to talk about it in public. Really, I had no ulterior motives."

Shara found herself agreeing with him. She did want to get to know the man, and she knew a restaurant could be stifling.

"Okay, but I'm bringing my can of mace," she said, aware a bit of anxiety remained in her voice.

He laughed. "What would you like? I could slave over something like seafood, only to find you were allergic or had no stomach for the meal."

"You're right. Seafood's not my bag," she said. "I'm a meat and potatoes person, myself. A nice Porterhouse — *really* rare, almost blue — and fries, crisp and well done."

He laughed again. "You're making it easy on me. But . . . it's *you* — a predator; meat and not cooked much at all. Mind if I choose dessert?"

"As long as it's not pie — apple, apricot, cherry or anything else fruity. Put it this way, you won't impress me with anything that takes you hours to prepare. But, yes, surprise me."

Shopping for a dress had been a trial, as well. Shara knew she wasn't the typical female shopper. She *didn't* enjoy shopping for clothes and abhorred window shopping. *Isn't this nice? Wouldn't that look wonderful on me?* Get a life, she wanted to tell those who dwelled on what they couldn't afford.

At home, she often wandered around butt naked. On the job, jeans and a comfortable top were practical. She had *costumes* for the many roles she played, but she bought those with a particular purpose in mind. She had never shopped to impress a man before, and she felt lost.

Worse, she had no one to help her. Deidre or Lysette would have gladly helped, but they were lost to her now. Alexis, whose opinion she did value, couldn't get around unless she was in the forest.

She'd gone down South Street and without thinking picked a store. She saw a red dress that looked right, tried it on and looked to a teenage sales girl for guidance.

"It's you," she said. "It goes wonderfully with your skin. And while it accentuates your attributes, it's understated — classy. Is that the look you're aiming for?"

Shara looked in the mirror, again. It did go well with her tawny complexion.

Understated. Classy. Accentuates your attributes. What more could she want?

Her stomach did flip flops the entire trip to Dismal. She had to stop to pee four times. It better be worth it, she thought to herself, with all I'm putting myself through.

When he had answered her knock, she had thrust a bottle of red wine and a box of chocolates at him, knowing it sealed her commitment to see the evening through.

Looking at the candy, Clay laughed.

"Did I do wrong?" Shara asked, the desire to flee very real.

"No, not at all. You'll see."

He gave her a tour of "Chez Fluery" as he called it. It was a big house for one man and without a hell of a lot of furniture — natural wooded floors and walls, a cozy fireplace, TV, stereo, couch and a small table devoid of magazines and not much else filled a more than spacious living room.

"Did you build it yourself?" Shara asked.

"All of us Southerners build our own log cabins," he answered with a wink, in an exaggerated Southern drawl.

"My bad," she said, blushing. "I only meant it *looked* like it was built for you. It's not something that's been lived in for generations."

"It was actually . . . built for me. My brother-in-law owns a construction company. I told him my version of my dream home, and this is what I wanted. So, yeah, maybe I *did* build it," he said with a laugh. "I do use my hands, though," he added, and took Shara into a room with a refrigerated case. In the case were sculptures — crafted out of chocolate.

"So that's why you laughed when I gave you the candy."

He nodded. "I used to sculpt wood. A few years back at a county fair, I had to volunteer for something. So I sculpted figures using chocolate. The kids would get something pretty to look at and something they could sink their teeth into later. I haven't touched wood since."

Shara was drawn to two of the half-dozen pieces in the case. One was a figure of Mica, as Shara had described her to Clay, with a wolf emerging as a second head. The detail was extraordinary. Mica's face looked troubled, even forlorn, yet purposeful — like Mica.

"You've captured her true essence," Shara said.

The second was more disturbing — Clay's face with that of Mica's grandfather emerging from one side. The old man's face was the image she had seen whenever she and Mica's grandfather had crossed paths, but she couldn't recall telling Clay what he looked like. Not in such detail.

"It's him, but how—"

"I told you about the myths and legends I'd heard. I envisioned him as an American Indian. If her grandfather actually resembles my creation, it's purely coincidental."

Shara looked at him and wondered. Clay Fluery played at the good old country boy image, but Shara felt he was far more complex. It only strengthened her resolve to get to know the man behind the facade.

Over dinner — cooked to perfection, with the steak marinated and so tender she barely needed a knife — she opened up to him about Mica.

"I kinda felt cheated at the end," she finished. "I didn't want to fight her, don't get me wrong, but a part of me wanted to capture her."

"And thumb your nose at the FBI when you turned her over to the locals?" Clay asked.

"I don't know if I *would* have turned her over to anyone. Her grandfather did the killings. Yes," she said, as she saw Clay about to protest, "with her blessing, I know. But she didn't kill Fallon, and she won't kill again. Not being a cop, I had no obligation whatsoever. Finding her, capturing her would have been reward enough. I could have done with her as I pleased. I guess what I'm saying is I don't know what I would have done, and a part of me remains curious."

She told him that Fallon had been relieved of his duties.

"I spoke to the new sheriff. The cover story is Fallon had a stroke, but enough people at the hospital saw him without his pecker, so it would be embarrassing if he didn't resign. Another deputy, Mica's age, had gone to school with her. He was incensed by what Fallon had done. He's finished."

Clearing the dishes off the table, Shara looked at Clay.

"You know, you got me doing *all* the talking. I haven't learned word one about you, except you sculpt chocolate and you cook one mean steak."

"There's not all that much to me. What you see is what you get—"

"Bullshit," Shara interrupted. "That line may work with the bimbos you usually date, but not me."

"I *did* want to hear about Mica," he said, "and your chase. I'm a good listener, and I don't open myself up much to anyone."

"*You*. For as long as I can remember I've been living in a shell to protect the inner me," Shara said.

"And I've only scratched the surface. But that's your charm. Getting to know you is like exploring a complex maze. Navigating the many corridors of Shara Farris is a true joy. I don't know if I ever want to get to the end. Whatever the reward, it's not half as much fun as the trip itself."

Shara shook her head. "I ask about *you*, and you change the focus to me. Briggs would like you. I do the same to him. He says I say a lot but reveal nothing. With you though . . . , I don't know. I guess it goes back to not dismissing me out of hand when what I told you couldn't be rationally explained. You know, had to be accepted or be the rantings of someone mad."

Glass of wine in hand, he took her into the cavernous living room.

"Would you like to dance?" he asked her.

"Not to country/western tunes," she said.

"Now you're stereotyping me. I've got far-ranging tastes. Come, look for yourself."

She did, and he was right. There was a lot of jazz and surprisingly, a lot of R&B, along with a sprinkling of rock, classical and the dreaded country/western.

"You've got something for every woman's taste," she said teasingly.

"That hurts," he said.

"You didn't say it's not true," she countered. "It's just an observation, not a condemnation."

She choose "Soul To Soul" from his copy of the Temptations Anthology, a slow jam good for dancing and a tribute to Mica. Without her, Shara knew, she wouldn't be on her first date. He held her close and three-quarters through kissed her. Tentatively, at first, but when she didn't pull away, with more passion.

"You going to seduce me, Clay Fluery?" she asked.

"Do you want me to?"

"I honestly don't know. Tell you what — I'll holler when I want you to stop," and she let him kiss her again. They kissed long after the song was over. Finally she broke away. *Her first kiss*, she thought. She felt the need to back off for a moment, to decide just how far she'd go.

"I was a stripper when I was sixteen," she told him, to see if he'd pull away. He didn't, but seemed even more curious.

"Get out," he said.

"It was the only way I could keep off the streets. But I learned to enjoy it, and I had my first taste of power over others when I danced."

"Your parents—"

"I was a runaway."

"Wasn't it degrading?" he asked.

"Only to those hung up with sex and the human body. No one complains about a musician whose hands allow him to maximize his talents, or singers blessed with glorious voices. And what about athletes whose bodies allow them to do incredible feats? But a woman using her body, that's frowned upon. Fuck 'em, I say. It was wonderfully empowering for me. I gained self-confidence when I needed it most, and enjoyed it to boot. Watch."

She had noticed he had her song — Tina Turner's "Private Dancer." She put it on, told him to sit on a stool, and she began to dance for him, talking as she danced.

"When I danced everyone lived their own fantasy. Mind-fucking. Safe sex. No commitment. No regrets after."

She unzipped the back of her dress and let it fall, exposing her breasts and the twelve pair of eyes she *couldn't* tell him about. Clad only in her panties, she circled around him, came within inches of him. She saw him about to reach out and touch her.

"No, no — touching's against house rules. Let your mind explore."

She slipped out of her panties and saw him take a tentative peak at what they'd covered. A part of her mind couldn't believe *she* was seducing *him*. She'd had some wine — maybe more than some — but she knew what she was doing. She enjoyed performing for him.

When the song was over she felt naked and vulnerable. *You are naked, fool*, her mind answered, *and if you're vulnerable, it's your own doing*. Before she felt totally embarrassed, Clay got up and told her to follow him. He picked up her dress and panties, so she *couldn't* cover herself.

"Time for dessert," he said.

He led her to the room with the refrigerated case of chocolate sculptures, and told her to kneel on a rubber mat and close her eyes.

"Trust me?" he asked.

"I don't know." she said.

"I wouldn't do anything to humiliate you. Trust me, and if you feel uncomfortable, say the word and I'll stop. Promise."

She felt him pour something over her, starting from her shoulders. It smelled sweet.

"Chocolate!" she said.

"What better for dessert," he answered.

She felt the chocolate drip down her breasts, over her stomach, her genitals and legs.

"Open your eyes," he said softly.

He had a can of whipped cream, which he sprayed on her breasts. He'd also taken off his clothes. Then he began licking her clean.

"You want to tell me where you're most sensitive . . . those erogenous zones that drive you wild, or should I just explore?"

She didn't *know* her erogenous zones. She had never been touched by a man — touched by anyone but herself in over a dozen years, much less licked.

"Exploring sounds good," she said, laying down on her back. She moaned softly as he flicked his tongue over the eyes on her breasts.

"Why don't you ask me about the tattoos?" she asked, as he licked the chocolate off each eye. They were incredibly sensitive to his touch.

"You'll tell me when you want," he said, without stopping. "I don't need to learn all your secrets at once."

He continued south, lingering just below her navel. He seemed to know just where those erogenous zones of hers were that she hadn't been aware of. When his tongue reach her genitals, she climaxed.

He reached for a jar of maraschino cherries.

"You're not," she said, with a laugh.

"Tell me to stop."

She wouldn't.

He slipped a cherry into her vagina, and with his tongue searched for it, driving her into a frenzy. He finally fished it out, swallowed it, swallowing her with it.

She pulled him on top of her.

"I want you now," she said to him.

"You're the boss," he said.

He entered her, kissing and licking as he did, and took his time matching her rhythm. They became one, and he was patient, bringing her to another orgasm, without climaxing himself. His hands were all over her. His tongued flicked at her nipples, then he bit gently on one then the other, and this time they came simultaneously.

They lay together silently for several minutes when they were done.

"It was my first time," she told him, not knowing why she was divulging so much to someone who was still a virtual stranger. Yet, she now told him about making love with the first Shara, and how, after she died she'd kept her emotions at bay for over ten years.

"When you hit on me at the motel, it was the first time a man had ever aroused me. First time anyone had, except for her. It was like coming out of a long hibernation."

Her hand reached for his penis. She stroked it, finding herself wanting to lick away the chocolate that had gotten on him. She searched for areas of his greatest sensitivity — behind his knees and just above the crack in his ass — before taking him in her mouth. This time he entered her while he lay prone on his back, his hand kneading her breasts, as if knowing it drove her to heights she couldn't imagine. Again, they came as one.

She didn't want to stop. He'd opened a door within her and it refused to close.

"Do the cherry thing for me again," she asked him. He complied, and this time when he entered her he made her match his frenetic rhythm.

When they were done they lay on their sides, looking at one another.

"I love what you do to me," she said, stroking a slim scar on his chin.

"I thought you were going to say 'I love you,'" he whispered.

"After one date!" she said. "Please," she said, stretching out the word.

"Never heard of love at first sight?"

"*Lust* at first sight," she said, gently biting his lip.

"I can't tell you how much you intrigue me," he said. "You're like an archeological dig. With each layer, more of you is exposed, but so much more remains. So many mysteries."

"Do you have any mysteries?" she asked.

"Me? An open book. Not much beneath the surface."

"I think not, but I'm in no rush to find out."

"That mean you'll see me again?" he asked.

"Not right away. I want to think about you. Think of you. Hunger and lust for you. *Then* see and touch you."

"Not the settling down type, then," he said.

"Are you?"

He didn't answer directly. "I have a friend who was separated from his wife — *still is*, and it's been going on ten years now. He makes excuses that he can't afford a lawyer, but he doesn't *want* to get divorced. He goes from one woman to the next. Not one night stands, but four, five or six month liaisons. Still, he's married, so the relationships can go only so far, then they must end. A month later, he has someone else. His greatest fear is being alone. Me, I'm not looking for a commitment — leastways not yet. I like living with me. You intrigue me intellectually, emotionally and physically. At the same time I have my uncomplicated life here, and you have your responsibilities in Philly. I don't see as either of us wants to give up what we have. I'm satisfied with what we've got. Are you?"

"I just told you I'm a virgin and I've never had an emotional attachment in my adult life. Whatever I might feel for you I have to process. I'm not looking for a commitment either. I want to experience life. I *do* lust over you," she said, with a smile. "And, yes, I'm satisfied with what we have."

They made love once more and fell asleep in one another's arms.

When she left the next morning they said nothing of future plans. He'd call her or she'd call him. They had a silent understanding. They both needed their own space. Each needed the other. Whatever they had wouldn't be stifling to the other.

*　　　*　　　*

Driving back to Philly, Shara couldn't believe she'd laid herself so bare with someone she hardly knew. Her stripping, telling him about being a virgin, her being with the first Shara — some things not even Deidre or Lysette knew. And she wanted to tell him more. Not all at once, but over time — lots of time. For some reason she knew he'd even accept her darkest secret; the significance of her tattoos.

And she thought of the sex. *Thought about it a lot.* It had far exceeded her expectations. She'd expected vanilla sex — a quick in and out, with groans and grunts thrown in until *he'd* felt sufficed. Instead she'd gotten chocolate — *literally*; a hot fudge sundae with all the toppings. It had been both physically and emotionally satisfying, and best of all it had left her wanting more.

And Clay the man. She still didn't have a handle on what made him tick. That only added to his allure. She was a good judge of people; a quick study, who could get others to open up to her. He remained an enigma, though. There was something mysterious about him that made her attraction to him even stronger. She would learn his secrets, just as she'd divulge hers; of that she was sure.

Her last thought before hitting traffic on I-95 just south of Philly — *she couldn't believe she'd gotten laid.*

*　　　*　　　*

Clay watched Shara drive off, munching on the chocolate figure of Mica with the wolf's head.

Shara had been everything he'd expected and more. At some time he would have to level with her, but that was far down the line, especially with what she had told him about Alexis.

What he liked most about Shara was the lack of pretense. What you saw was what you got, and it had been terribly refreshing. She was a woman of many secrets, and they would one day all be his. But he smiled at the thought it would take a long time to plumb them. She would offer them without his having to probe. She very much wanted someone to open up to, and he was nothing if not patient.

Sexually, he couldn't remember when he'd been more satisfied. He knew she'd expected straight missionary-position sex. He'd surprised her with the unexpected, and it *had* been what she'd wanted. For her first time he'd given her something truly memorable. Sexually, she offered him a whole smorgasbord of opportunities. He smiled at the thought; lusting for her, as she said she did for him.

FORTY-THREE

Before Shara went to The Haven she'd taken a short nap — and as had been the case since her meeting with Mica, it had been dreamless. She had slept four hours in Clay's arms the night before and he'd had to prod her to awaken her at seven. And still, she felt tired when she arrived home. She often felt drained after a chase. There was the adrenaline rush and then her tank was empty. And after a chase, she'd have no dreams for a number of nights as the battery in her mind recharged.

Part of it was physical but there was also the expected letdown. The chase was over. While usually satisfied, a part of her wanted the hunt to continue. She often wondered how she would embrace an endless pursuit. Would her circuits overload with no end in sight, or would she be forever jazzed?

She napped thinking of Clay and awoke with him still on her mind. He and all he'd done to her — and *for her* — the night before. For while he had seemed satisfied, some part of her knew, more than his own gratification, he wanted to pleasure her. And what he'd done to her had been good. More than good, she thought, as she replayed their lovemaking. And the stunt with the cherry . . .

She got up and got dressed. Just thinking of him was driving her up the wall, and she had things to do. She wished she had someone to talk to. She didn't think her reactions were abnormal, but what did she know? Deidre and Lysette lost to her. And Mica — she'd tried to reach out to her, but whatever psychic link they'd shared had been severed.

She also had to caution herself not to get too euphoric. Just six weeks ago, she'd hit rock bottom. If she had been suicidal, she might have ended it that night in the car after being abandoned by Lysette. Jil had said *you just go on*, and look at her now.

She had come to grips with the wasted years of her life. She'd finally embraced life. And she'd met Clay. Her first date, first kiss and first, second, third and fourth roll in the hay with a man. Shit happens, she knew, and she didn't want to get so high that the fall would be back-breaking. It was the cynic in her but she couldn't help herself. Things had a way of balancing out, she warned herself. Shit happens.

Where before, when she'd had down time, she'd welcomed just being with herself, she was now eager to mix with others. Even the inevitable sparring with Charlie at the shelter had its appeal.

Entering The Haven, Shara was directed to the kitchen.

"You really must hire a chef," she said. "This is no way to spend your life."

Charlie shot her a glance.

"None of my business," Shara quickly added, before Charlie went off on a tirade.

"You asked if I'd be interested in volunteering," she said instead. "I'd like to, but my lifestyle — being out of town for weeks at a time — doesn't lend itself to any set schedule. I'd hate to disappoint anyone because of a sudden commitment. So, I thought I might be a sort of big sister to one of the kids."

"Renee," Charlie said.

"Yeah, Renee."

"She's gone."

"Her mother got a job?" Shara asked, feeling far greater disappointment than she would have imagined.

"No, her mother's dead." Charlie paused to let it sink in. "Her husband found out she was here. He came by and the two of them had an argument. He shot her, then sat down and waited to take Renee home with him. He put up no resistance when the police arrived. It was as if he hadn't known what he'd done.

"And Renee?"

"She's in a group home," Charlie said, without elaborating.

"Can I see Jane?"

"She's not here, either."

Shara looked at Charlie with concern.

"Someone else works with the children — Terése."

Shara smiled.

"I thought so. *You* were the inspiration."

"Hold on a minute," Shara said, not able to stifle a grin. "Yeah, I suggested the name Terése as a possibility, but she told me she was going to change her name. She now has an identity, so Jane didn't fit. It could have been much worse. One name she was considering was Mica. Would you like another like her in your hair?"

"She's in the playroom," Charlie said, seeming at a loss for words.

Before entering the playroom, Shara looked through a narrow window on the door. Terése was playing with a little boy. When she turned, Shara held her breath, then smiled. The plastic surgeon had done all he'd promised, and then some. Shara entered.

"I'm looking for Terése," she said.

Terése turned around and her eyes widened. She came over and gave Shara a hug.

"Something's different about you . . ." Shara said. Terése looked her squarely in the face. There was none of the bowed head or the turning away that was so prevalent when they'd first met. "Your hair maybe . . . or did you lose some weight?"

Terése laughed.

"What do you think?" she asked. "It's still a little swollen," she said, looking into the mirror on the wall and touching the scar. The doctor says in a week with some makeup . . ." She couldn't finish.

"What do *you* think?" Shara asked.

"I couldn't be happier. I'm no raving beauty—"

"Says who?" Shara asked. "Like you said, with some makeup . . . men will be fighting over you. How'd it happen?"

Terése shrugged. "A doctor walks in one day — one I remember from the hospital — looks at my face and says he'd like to try to help me. Gratis."

"I'm happy for you," she said, seeing Terése beaming.

"Mica?" Terése said with trepidation.

"Mica's fine. We met, she got the best of me — like all of you said — and she's slain her demons."

Terése looked at her. "I know there's a lot more to it than that, but I won't pry. As long as she's all right."

"Tell me about Renee?" Shara asked, turning serious. "Charlie told me what happened. How did she take it?" Shara shook her head. "That's a stupid question. What I mean is what was her reaction? Which way did she go?"

"Into herself," Terése said, nodding and understanding what Shara meant. "She's had to deal with an awful lot the past few months. She withdrew. But she's a survivor. She'll hurt, but she won't let it consume her."

"Do you know where she is?"

"Charlie pulled some strings so Renee could stay here until they placed her. For all her faults, Charlie wants what's best, and she flexes her muscles when push comes to shove. Renee needed familiar surroundings instead of being shunted from one place to another. When it came time to leave, to a group home, Renee wouldn't go unless I went along with her. Sort of give it my blessing."

"I promised I'd come back after I'd met Mica. I'd like to keep my word," Shara said.

Terése smiled, told her where the home was, and they chatted for another fifteen minutes.

Shara left, promising to return — a promise she meant to keep. Terése was *becoming*. She had so much more self-confidence than the first time they'd met. Shara was interested in seeing what was to come.

FORTY-FOUR

Shara was outside of the school in West Philly when Renee exited with a friend, a white girl. Watching the two laugh, Shara was reminded of what Terése had said — *Renee was a survivor*. She would have to be, Shara thought. Aside from her other problems, she knew sooner or later Renee would encounter both whites and blacks who didn't agree with her choice of friends. Light-skinned as she was, she was deemed black by society. She would have to be strong to resist society's pressures.

A few blocks from school, Renee and her friend parted. Renee walked on with her head down. With no companion, Shara *knew* the thoughts that were bubbling to the surface.

Shara crossed the street.

"Hi, stranger," Shara said.

"Shara!" Renee shouted, instantly recognizing her. She gave Shara both a wide smile and a hug. "What are you doing here?"

"I promised, didn't I?"

Renee again flashed her smile. It was so genuine and infectious, Shara thought. Beautiful as she was, it was that smile that set her apart from others who were blessed with stunning looks. Shara also noted she no longer sported the nose ring or four rings in her eyebrows she'd seen her with at the shelter. Something to talk about later.

"I'm sorry about your mother," Shara said.

"Thank you."

Shara shook her head. "You know, I've been mulling over in my mind all day what to say to express my feelings, and that was the best I could come up with. It sounds hollow, but—"

"Your thinking about what to say is more important than the words," Renee interrupted. "It shows you care. I used to try to come up with ways to answer people who offered their condolences, then decided to hell with it. *I'm* the one hurting, and I don't need something else to dwell on. The ones who said, 'I know how you feel' got to me, though."

"No one knows how you feel, right?"

"How many have had their father shoot their mother? They *can't* know."

"I *know* how you feel. Terése knows. Even Charlie knows. We've all faced horrors of our own. Different from yours, granted, but we know how it feels to lose someone or something precious to us. We know the hurt."

"You've been hurt?" Renee asked.

"I more than most. I saw my stepfather shot by the police when I was five. The police barged into the wrong house. And my mother despised me. There's more, but I *know* how you hurt."

"How do you deal with it?"

"The pain never leaves, Renee. I'm sorry, but it's a part of you. It even defines you. But you build up scar tissue. And like a friend told me *you just go on.*"

They walked in silence down the street, the sun bright in a cloudless sky, for a change.

"What are you thinking, Renee?"

"I'm so confused, Shara. I still love my father, though I should hate him. He was vile to my mother, but he never touched me and I loved him so. And I resented my mother. I was mad when she took his abuse. Madder still when she left without consulting me. At the shelter, we would go for walks before school and have terrible arguments. Everything was about *her*. How *she* was going to start a new life. How *she* was going to move down south. *She* this. *She* that. Never *we*. And she didn't want to hear about *my* needs. That last day, I told her I wanted to see my father. We both said horrible things to each other. And now that she's gone, I can never take back what I said. I feel so guilty. I was being selfish when she needed my support."

Tears streaming down her face, she hugged Shara. Shara cried too, possibly the first time she'd cried for anyone but herself.

"And I have no one to talk to. My friends don't want to hear about my problems. They've got their own."

Shara remained silent, but thought Renee's friends might not want to hear what Renee had to say because it hit too close to home. Listen to Renee and the next time *their* parents argued, they'd recall what Renee's father did to her mother.

"I could talk to Terése, but my problems pale compared to hers. Mica's gone. I've got no one. So I live with it inside of me, waiting to explode. I—" she started, then stopped and looked at Shara as if she'd had a revelation.

"You've let me go on and on. I'm bitching I've got no one to talk to and *you're* listening," she said and laughed.

"That's what you needed," Shara said. "An ear, not advice."

She hugged Shara again.

"Tell me about Mica. You promised. Did you meet?" she asked excitedly.

Shara could hear Renee's excitement build with each word. This was becoming old real fast, Shara thought as she gave Renee a recap of their *confrontation*.

"Will she come back?"

Shara paused to find the right words.

"A part of her did some pretty horrible things, Renee. She's still wanted by the police. I'm sorry, but she can't return. There's just too much of a risk for her here. You, Terése, Charlie and all the kids opened her eyes to what she'd been missing. Opened my eyes, too. I'll tell you all the sordid details later. Promise."

Two more blocks and they were at the group home.

"How are things here?" Shara asked.

Renee shrugged. "The other kids are all way younger. And the Warfields are nice, but they're *old*, and they don't want to hear about my problems."

"Would you like to spend the night at my house?"

"I'd love to," she said, flashing that smile again, but it quickly faded. "It's a school night, though. No way the Warfields would allow me."

"I've taken care of that already."

Renee gave her a questioning look.

"I didn't want to disappoint you if you said yes, so I made sure you had permission."

"But you're a stranger to them. I don't understand."

"I called in a favor. A friend who knew someone at DHS who . . . Well, the long and the short of it is they won't object. Go in and get what you need."

Renee came bounding out of the house with a suitcase. Like Alexis, she was old beyond her years because of the tragedy she'd faced, but at times Shara saw the exuberance of youth in her — something of which both she and Alexis had been robbed.

When they got to Shara's house, she let Renee take it in.

"There are no pictures," Renee said, standing in the living room.

"I've got my own reasons for not wanting my picture taken," Shara said, thinking of the many degrading photos her half-brother had taken of her.

"But there are no pictures at all — *of anyone*."

"I was very much into myself for a long time. I didn't start making friends until this past year or so. It's something to think about, though."

Renee walked up to a painting Shara recently had mounted. It was one of Jeremy's of Mica.

"Different," Renee said, tentatively touching the canvas, looking at Shara who told her it was okay.

"That's a painting of Mica," Shara said. Renee looked at her wide-eyed.

Shara came over and undid a hook. "There's actually seven."

Renee went through them quickly at first, then looked at each closely. Shara wanted to see if she could puzzle it out.

"They're the same, but different. This one," she said, stopping at one of the paintings, "reminds me of Mica arguing with Charlie. And this," she pointed to another, "is like she was in the playroom, enjoying herself with us."

"So what are they?" Shara asked.

Renee bit her lip, as if seeming to search for the right word for a few moments.

"Emotions of Mica," she said tentatively.

"You got it. The many moods of Mica," Shara said.

"The artist must have known her well, you know, to be able to paint all that was inside of her."

"He was in love with her."

"She never spoke of him," Renee said.

"She had other things on her mind. And he never spoke of his love for her. Sometimes you can be too subtle. Come, let me show you the room where I spend most of my time."

Shara took Renee to her room filled with computers and electronic instruments.

"Holy shit," Renee said, then covered her mouth. "I'm sorry."

"For what? You heard worse at home, I'm sure, and in the school-yard," she said with a smile.

"What is all of that for?"

"Most is for my job." She told Renee about her bounty hunting and the role gathering information played in its success.

"And I like to play the stock market."

Renee made a face.

"Boring, huh?" Shara said.

"We had a unit on it at school, last year. We were all given an imaginary one-thousand dollars and told to choose stocks. I picked stocks for products I liked. I didn't do any research. I ended up with a hundred dollars. Good thing it wasn't real money."

"What did you learn?"

"The choices I made were foolish. No, the *reasons* for my choices were foolish, actually."

"And what did your teacher say?"

Renee sighed. "I got what I deserved. I didn't put in a full effort, blah, blah, blah."

"Your teacher's the fool, then. You did learn something. If you had to do it over again, you'd go about it different, right?"

"Yeah, but I'm not sure how."

"That's what school should be about. Not whether you earned or lost, but learning from your successes *and* failures."

Shara sat down and pulled up a screen; an account for Jane. Shara made a mental note to change the name to Terése.

"I put a thousand dollars in for Terése a month ago," Shara said.

"There's over seven-thousand now," Renee said and looked at Shara. "*You* gave the money for her operation. I thought it might have been Mica, but it was you."

Shara said nothing, but her expression must have betrayed her.

"Why? You hardly knew her."

"Call it a reward," Shara said. "Mica told Terése to hold nothing back, just like she told you. Terése gave me what I needed to find Mica. That calls for a reward. Anyway, what's the sense of accumulating money just to have it?"

"Why the account for her now?"

"At some point, she might want to leave The Haven and go off on her own. Charlie's not paying her much, so she's still a prisoner in a way. So I put a thousand in and it's grown."

Shara did some more typing, asking Renee some questions, then showed her the screen.

"You set up an account for me," Renee said, touching the screen that read Renee LeShay.

"One thousand dollars, just like in school. Only this time I'll teach you how to invest wisely. As it grows, I'll take my thousand out, and the rest is yours. Only if you want, though."

"What if I lose it all again?"

"You'll still have learned something. The trick is not to play scared. You work at it, and you don't panic. And there are shortcuts — but that's for when you've mastered the basics."

Shara looked at her watch. "Time for dinner. I had no idea what you'd want, so I filled a refrigerator full of choices. We can make homemade pizza, burgers, steak. You have a favorite?"

"Spaghetti and meat balls," Renee said. "When I did well in school or helped around the house that was my reward."

"We'll make it together, then."

While Shara was seasoning the hamburger, she would put one meatball in a pan, then roll up a smaller one and eat it raw.

"Shara!" Renee said, horrified. "That can kill you. Raw meat can have e-coli."

"And one day there is a report eggs are good for you, then another that eggs are harmful. Same with milk and salt. I don't smoke and don't drink much, now, so I'm entitled to my vices. Anyway, I buy the most expensive meat and cook it the same day I buy it. It's time for me to enjoy life. If I get the trots, it's a small price to pay."

Renee said nothing, but when there was just a little meat left, she tried some.

"It does taste good," she said in surprise.

As dinner cooked, Shara asked Renee about her nose and eyebrow rings.

"The Warfields wouldn't allow it. I did it to anger my mother, anyway."

"To get her attention?"

"Yeah," she said and laughed. "I'd never tell her who did it or where I got it done. She was as pissed at them as she was with me."

"What would have been next — tongue piercing? Nipple rings? One for your navel? How about one for your clitoris?"

"Yech!" Renee said.

"Tattoos?"

"Yeah," Renee said. "I thought about that, but passed. Chickened out, actually."

"Why stop there? You'd learn to take the pain. Branding's in vogue now. There are even some who get off on cutting themselves and others, you know. The pain, it's so bad, it's good. But you've got to live with it forever. No turning back."

"Forever is a long time," Renee said, as if thinking over what Shara had said.

"Look, it's your body, but you're too pretty to be mutilating yourself just to anger someone or get their attention, if you ask me." She stroked Renee's face with her finger. "I don't know if I've ever seen anyone more beautiful."

Renee flushed, but Shara could see she was pleased.

They talked well into the night, though Renee had school the next day. They talked about matters of great import to each of them, and other matters so inconsequential they were forgotten soon after the words were uttered. Talking for both of them was therapeutic. Shara went to sleep more contented than as long as she could remember.

She had something to broach to Renee, but now wasn't the time. She had to think it through rather than act in haste. She was struck by the irony. The last time she had shared a home with another *she* was Renee, and another Shara was caring for her. Strange as it felt sharing her home with another, it felt right. And she . . . she felt complete.

EPILOGUE

Driving down to the shore, they were virtually silent. It wasn't the comfortable silence Shara normally felt in the presence of Alexis. She felt claustrophobic — unsettled.

She had seen a side of Alexis that was all too human earlier that day. The Alexis who seemed always above the fray had been a figment of Shara's imagination. She carefully cloaked churning emotions within her; her fears, her loneliness and frustrations. Shara had been so into herself, she took it for granted that Alexis could deal with *her* demons.

She had arrived to take Alexis to the shore and had told her about having Renee over for the night.

"I've been alone for so long I awoke last night when Renee went to the bathroom, thinking there was a burglar in the house," she said with a laugh.

Alexis had signed nothing. She had in fact turned away, and Shara suddenly understood.

"You're jealous!" she said, astonished.

"And if I am?" Alexis signed, looking at Shara, her eyes ablaze.

"You needn't be."

"You had Deidre and lost her. You had Lysette and lost her," Alexis signed rapidly. "You went after the Holy Grail that was Mica, but she wasn't what you needed. You told me you needed *me*. Said you'd learned that pursuing Mica."

"I do need you, but I need more."

"Why?"

"Because I've spent my life in isolation. *That's* what I learned. I've got to get a life and it includes you, but not you alone."

"But I'm here on the rebound when your life falls apart."

"That's not fair, and it's not how I view our relationship."

"I'm just tired of playing second fiddle to the flavor of the month," Alexis signed, but the anger had left both her eyes and her hands.

Shara was glad, though, Alexis hadn't said she was sorry. She, more than most, had every right to be in a foul mood, to be angry, depressed, and even self-pitying.

"I'm worried about today," she signed, as if that explained her mood.

She had every right to be anxious, Shara had thought.

Shara parked and watched Alexis and her father go into the forest.

She went to the beach and was unable to gauge the mood of the surf. It too seemed uncertain.

All Shara knew was that things would never be quite the same again. Shit happens, but you go on. You just go on.

AUTHOR'S

AFTERWORD

Up front I must admit that there's more of *me* in **Judas Eyes** than I might care to admit — at least the *me* writing the book at the time (summer 1998). Shara is generally a loner. So am I. I have few close friends, and those I have I treasure, as well as my brother and three children (as of this writing now 25, 22 and 19 years of age). And, like Shara, I view loyalty as something sacrosanct. I can be loyal to a fault. I stayed with a dentist for over twenty years, because he was *always* able to fit me in when I had an emergency (like a root canal). Little did I know he had auditioned for the part of the Marquis de Sade (or Lawrence Olivier in the movie *The Marathon Man*) until he became ill and I had to go to another dentist two years ago. Root canals with Novocaine? Something I'd never experienced. Hell, *my* dentist dispensed Novocaine like it was a precious metal. So, I changed dentists, but only to *literally* avoid a painful experience. I had been loyal for twenty years.

Loyalty cuts both ways, though. This past year, someone I've been loyal to for over a decade hasn't exactly stabbed me in the back, but had distanced himself from me, and as with Shara, it hurts. Hurts bad.

Shara is self-educated, and in many ways, so am I. I taught *myself* photography, playwriting, directing and producing plays. And, I'm a self-taught writer. I've learned how to write by reading others and having others constructively critique my work. Reading books on writing — something I can't do. Classes on writing — forget about it.

And while my rage isn't equal to Shara's or Mica's, I've dealt with so much incompetence that the rage I commit to paper isn't purely a figment of my imagination. Then there's Shara's disdain for delegating authority. Yep, that's me. Not that I don't *want* to delegate authority, but too often when I've done so I've been bitten in the ass. Chances are if *I* do it, it will be done right. And if I screw up (and I have), I have only myself to blame.

So, is Shara a female version of me? Not really (I don't have Shara's streak of deceit in me, and I'm not searching for a soulmate, for starters), but there's enough of me in her to make me squirm just a bit, just as (for you trivia buffs), there was a lot of me in Tommy Rosati, a minor character in *Eyes Of Prey*. The obvious question is can a man and a woman share the same feelings? Or am I merely projecting male traits onto a female character? I don't think you have to be a female to create a female character (no one complained about my portrayal of Shara in *Hungry Eyes*). I am well aware of difference between men and women (as well as kids, as I taught for 28 years). There isn't just one kind of woman. Variety, after all, is the spice of life. You're the ultimate judge, but I think Shara, Deidre and Mica, and the women in the shelter in this book are feminine.